SECRET DESIRE

Gwynne Forster

ARABESQUE

BET
BOOKS

BET Publications, LLC
www.bet.com
www.arabesquebooks.com

ARABESQUE BOOKS are published by

BET Publications, LLC
c/o BET BOOKS
One BET Plaza
1900 W Place NE
Washington, D.C. 20018-1211

First Printing: November, 2000
10 9 8 7 6 5 4 3 2 1

Printed in the United States of America

ACKNOWLEDGMENTS

To Walter Zacharius for his wisdom and courage in disregarding the notion then current that African-Americans would not write romance novels with African-American heroes and heroines worthy of publication and that the African-American public would not buy and read them. Thanks to his foresight, sagacity and conviction, we African-American romance writers now need only produce work of high quality and publication is assured.

To Monica Harris who brought Arabesque to life; to my editor, Karen Thomas, whose graciousness and counsel make deadlines less ominous; and to my husband who loves me and supports me in all that I do.

Chapter One

"Thank you kindly for nothing."

"You got more than you deserved."

"I didn't seek what I deserve. No amount of money can compensate for the ten years of emotional hell I endured with Nathan Middleton." Kate Middleton waved the check. "This is for my son's future."

She stared at Joshua Johnson's thin pinched lips, hollow cheeks, and cold pigeon eyes, then swung around and headed for the door. With her hand on the knob, she let her gaze sweep the staid office of Johnson and Jackson with its ancient markings of respectability, including the graying old man—attorney for her late husband's estate and a friend of the Middleton family—who didn't raise his head to look at her. She took it all in, opened the door, walked out and closed it gently. Then she turned around, wiped her feet on the doormat, headed down the hall, and didn't look back.

Nathan Middleton hadn't intended to set her free, but that was what her husband of ten years had done when he mocked fate by test driving a new-line sports car. While he'd lived, he'd done his best to rule and control her, pampered her, and tried to stash her away in their elegant home. Her rebellion had been a source of increasing friction between them. For ten years, she'd fluttered around with clipped wings, but now she'd show them all, including her in-laws, who'd told their son that he married beneath his status. The world would know that she could manage her life and take care of her child.

Two hundred and ninety thousand dollars, a pittance of an inheritance for her and her child from the only son of a rich family—but it was more than she needed to get her life in order. She stepped out into the street, tightened her jacket against the sting of the brisk April breeze, inhaled the Grosse Point, Michigan, air, and smelled its familiarity. She had to get out of that town, away from that house with its memories of what Nathan had told her about her in-laws and their unfair estimation of her. She walked rapidly, her mind bursting with visions of her future. For many of her thirty-eight years, life had shortchanged her, but she meant to correct that—beginning right then.

Four months later, having returned with her son, Randy, to Portsmouth, Virginia, where she'd had her only teaching job, the only place she knew besides Charleston, South Carolina, and Grosse Point, Kate embarked on her new life—managing the bookstore that she'd purchased with a portion of the money from Nathan's estate.

"You don't need that sitter. You can leave your boy here with me while you're at your store," Madge Robinson, her building superintendent, said. "I take care of the kids that live in this apartment building while their mothers and fathers are off to business."

Kate looked from the gnarled fingers and wrinkled and heavily veined hands to the lined, weathered face and the hair that hadn't grayed or ever been dyed, and she wondered how many of life's barbed wire fences and spiked gates the poor woman had scaled. She jumped at every opportunity to baby-sit, and Kate suspected that the occasions gave her a chance to talk with her neighbors. Lonely hardly described her. She exhibited the energy of a fifty year old, but the appearance of an octogenarian.

"I'll take you up on that, Madge," Kate said, though she didn't want to be beholden to Madge or anyone else. "And I do thank you," she added, "but I want him to love books so, for now, he can sit in my store after school and read. When you do keep him, I'll pay you the going rate for sitters." She knew Randy would rather not be under her watchful eye, but she had to repair the damage that his father's overindulgence had caused, and that meant keeping a tight rein on him.

Luke Stuart Hickson hugged Amanda and Amy, his sister-in-law and niece, and walked with Marcus to his car. "It's time you got to work on settling down, Luke," Marcus said to his older brother. "We'd be happier if your life was what you want it to be, and we know it isn't."

Luke inserted the key into the lock, opened the door of his blue Buick Le Sabre, and looked off into the distance. "Yeah, but it isn't something I can manufacture. You know that. Don't forget that you backed into paradise kicking and screaming." He let a grin crease his mouth at the memory of it. "And look what you found. If I had a woman like Amanda, I wouldn't be here with you right now. See you next weekend."

An hour and forty minutes later, Luke turned off Route 17 onto Greenwood Drive in Portsmouth and headed home. He thought about what he'd do the rest of the day, his coveted Sunday off, and decided to get a bag of hamburgers and fries, pick up some Sunday papers, and spend the day lolling around. He drove up Deep Creek Boulevard, stopped at Burgundy for the red light, and did a double take. Making certain that his eyes hadn't fooled him, he backed up, stopped, and got out. No, it wasn't a mirage.

His steps quickened as he neared Kate's Friendly Bookstore.

A woman and small boy peered at him from behind the door, handcuffed together, their faces pressed to the glass. It didn't take him a second to figure out that they were prisoners. He tried the door. Locked, as he'd guessed. Too bad he wasn't wearing his uniform. He reached into the inside pocket of his jacket, pulled out his badge, and held it so the woman could see it. If she recognized it as a policeman's identification, she didn't show it.

"Can you hear me?" he asked, but the woman didn't respond. Instead, her eyes grew larger, and tears began to trickle down the boy's face. He tried sign language, but got no response. *There goes my Sunday.* He tried to signal that he'd be back, then went to his car, got a knife and screwdriver, and picked the lock.

"I'm Detective Captain Luke Hickson," he told them when he got the door open. "What happened?"

She didn't appear to believe him, so he showed her his badge again. He gave her points for her caution; she had good reason. "I was locking up last night, and a man pushed us into the store, took the money from the cash register, and said he was going to shoot us. I begged for mercy for my son, and he handcuffed us, took the store keys, and locked us in. We've been here since nine last night. I'm ... I'm so glad you came. My son, Randy, is starving."

He looked at her more closely. She had to be tired and miserable, but you'd never guess it from her bearing. She had an aura of dignity, strength, and soft femininity, and she earned his respect when she didn't apologize for inconveniencing him. That would have smacked of dishonesty.

A half smile settled on her face as she glanced at her son. "You've been a great little trooper, Randy. I hope the captain can get these handcuffs off us soon, so we can get you something to eat." She looked at Luke for confirmation that their hands would soon be free.

"I'll do my best, ma'am, but it may take a while, so maybe you two want to go to the washroom before I start on these handcuffs."

He got the bunch of keys that he kept in the glove compartment of his car and examined them. "Let's get busy," he said when they returned. If none of the keys fit, he'd have to use a cutter.

"Suppose you can't find a key," Randy said, apparently anxious to end his ordeal.

"We'll get them off, with or without a key. It's just easier with a key." *Another ten minutes is all I'm giving it,* he told himself as one key after another failed to fit.

"That does it. We have to go to the station, but I'll stop along the way and get you some food. What do you want to eat, ma'am?"

He didn't imagine the relief that spread over her countenance. "Burgers, fries, and milk for Randy. Buffalo wings, fries, and coffee for me."

"I'm not drinking any milk," Randy said.

Luke let the boy have a steely gray-eyed stare. "Your mother said you're drinking milk, and if you want those handcuffs off, young man, you will drink milk. You got that?"

He'd have sworn that her look was one of thanks. The boy was probably a problem, but his uncouth behavior didn't so much as put a frown on her face, and he wondered about that. His olfactory sense triggered a masculine response. Her perfume again filled his head with ideas that had nothing to do with the work of a police detective,

and he tried to shut it down. When he took her arm to
help them into the back of his car, she turned to him,
smiling, apparently to thank him, and the bottom dropped
out of his belly. He stared into her greenish-brown eyes,
unable to shift his glance until Randy, in another display
of bad manners, jerked his mother's arm. *Get your act
together, man,* he cautioned himself.

He left them in the car and bought their food. Then
he drove with them to his precinct on Crawford Parkway,
"As soon as you finish eating, we'll start on those handcuffs," he said, and with a look at Randy added, "and that
includes drinking all of your milk."

While they ate, he sent a clerk to get the details of their
ordeal. "What's your name, ma'am?" Luke asked her as
he began trying more keys in the handcuffs.

"Kate Middleton."

The sooner he freed their hands, the better; he did not
relish standing that close to Kate Middleton for any length
of time, touching her hands and . . . He shook himself out
of it.

"Where're you from, Mrs. Middleton?" he asked,
though he knew he'd find out as soon as he read the clerk's
report. When she told him, he resisted asking her how
she happened to make the jump from Grosse Point to
Portsmouth, because that was personal, but he wanted to
know all about her. With the fingers of her free left hand,
she wiped perspiration from her brow. He'd already known
she was getting warm, because her spicy perfume got
stronger and stronger—teasing him, daring him to enjoy
her nearness and to prolong the whole torturous experience. He'd recognize that perfume again if he smelled it
in Timbuktu.

"Do you think it'll take much longer?" she asked.

"Can't say. I've got another fifty or so keys that I can
try. Failing that, we'll cut them off, but that won't be fun."
She glanced up and caught his gaze, and embarrassment

reddened her flawless tan complexion. So she was attracted to him! He'd as soon not have that piece of information—she was tempting enough as it was.

"Would you like to walk, or just stand?" he asked. "I know this is tiring for both of you."

That soft sweet smile again. "I'll stand for a couple of minutes, if you don't mind."

"I don't want to stand," Randy put in. "I was standing all night, and I wanna go to bed."

Luke loved children and had always wanted some of his own, but he loved nice kids, not brats. "If she wants to stand, you stand," he said to Randy. "You may not realize this, but it's a man's pleasure to please the women in his life, and you're old enough to practice that. On your feet."

"All right," Randy said, his tone less than friendly.

Luke felt a twinge of sympathy for the boy, but Randy Middleton was going to respect his mother, at least until those handcuffs were removed. She stood slowly, and he wasn't sure whether that was because she was tired or because she was standing so close to him. He moved back to give her some space, and made the mistake of looking into her eyes. He was forty-two, he knew when a woman's interest in him was more than casual. Her warm intense gaze told him plenty. It had been a long time since he'd last wanted a particular woman, but he wanted this one. Not that it mattered. He didn't know a thing about her, and he refused to let himself be sucked into her orbit just because his testosterone had gotten unruly.

Enough was enough! He called a junior detective. "Set up that cutter, will you?"

"I don't know how to thank you, Captain. You've been so kind to us," Kate said, rubbing the wrist that had borne the metal cuff.

"My pleasure. You may go in a couple of minutes. " He handed her a notepad. "Jot down the address of your store and the hours and telephone number, and your home

address and phone number, in case I need to reach you."
He knew his young colleague had taken that information
from her, but he didn't want to raise eyebrows by copying
from the record in the presence of his officers. He gave
her his card. "If you have a problem of any kind, call me."

She did as he asked and thanked him again. "Could I
phone for a taxi, please?"

He looked at the address she'd given. "I'll drop you off
on my way home."

By the time he'd taken them home, the Hamburger
House had closed, so he stopped at the River Café and
bought enough Cajun-fried catfish, French fries, and cole-
slaw for two meals, got the Sunday papers, and headed for
his co-op town house.

For the life of him, he couldn't figure out why Kate
Middleton wouldn't get out of his head. He put on a CD
and listened to his favorite music—a Max Bruch violin
concerto—while he savored his lunch.

Relaxed, he thought back to the time when the woman
he loved, his wife, had needed him and called for help.
But he'd been busy saving someone else's life, and he'd
lost her, a victim of mistaken identity. He was not going
to get involved with a woman he might have to protect.
The fact that the robber had selected Kate's store from
among those nearby, which even the most inexperienced
criminal should have known would yield more cash, made
the crime suspicious. To his mind, it wasn't an ordinary
stickup. It occurred to him that he ought to have someone
put a new lock on her store and get the keys to her. An
expletive slipped through his lips.

Kate crawled into bed and replayed the day in her mind.
Luke Hickson wasn't an ordinary man whom you met on
an ordinary day. The personification of gentleness, but oh,
boy, you would not want to cross him. Power. He exuded

it. Even seven-year-old Randy noticed it, because he hadn't tried any of his usual antics on the captain. She couldn't let her thoughts dwell on him, though, because such a man had to be married. And even if he wasn't, she'd served her years of martyrdom in her marriage, and she wasn't going that route again.

Thank God the robber hadn't come ten minutes earlier. No one would ever know how glad she was that she'd taken all but a few dollars from the cash register and put her day's take in the safe in the back room. She couldn't afford to lose money. Buying a little summer home on the Albermarle Sound, moving Randy and herself into an apartment, and setting up her bookstore had taken over half of her capital. Still, she was thankful. The robber had spared their lives. Tremors shook her at the thought that he might return to finish what he'd started. She hoped Luke Hickson would catch him.

She didn't let herself dwell on the career she'd given up when Nathan moved them to Grosse Pointe, because she couldn't resume teaching music education and advanced piano in the Portsmouth schools unless she took refresher courses or got another degree. Even then, she'd have to pass board exams again. With Randy to care for, she couldn't spare the time or the money. Her career was a thing of the past.

She stretched out on the satin sheets—that her late husband had insisted they use and let her bare skin enjoy the silky softness. Now that she wasn't married, she'd taken to sleeping nude and loving it; that was part of her statement of independence.

She reached for the phone on its second ring.

"Ms. Middleton, please. Luke Hickson speaking."

Currents of dizziness attacked her, and it seemed as though her head had lost most of its weight. "This is Kate, Captain Hickson. Is . . . is something the matter?" She hated the unsteadiness of her voice. The man must be used to having women roll over for him. Not this one.

"I hate to disturb your rest, but it's occurred to me that you need a new lock and key for your store, and you need it now. With the simple padlock I put on it, a criminal wouldn't need much imagination if he wanted to open it."

"What do you suggest?"

"We can take care of it, but you have to be present. I can pick you up in half an hour."

"Thanks. I'll be ready."

What next? She wanted to stay as far away from that man as she could get, but fate seemed to have other plans. She phoned Madge Robinson, the building superintendent.

"Madge, I have to go out for . . . I don't know . . . an hour or two. Could you please keep an eye on Randy for me? He's asleep."

"In that case, I'll go down to your place. It ain't smart to leave a child his age alone. Be right there."

She met Luke in the lobby and knew she'd never hear the end of it, because Madge was standing in the garden, though she should have been inside with Randy.

"Who's with your boy?" Luke asked after handing her the new keys to her store.

She told him and waited, since it was clear he had something else to say.

"He needs a strong male hand. Where's his father, if you don't mind my asking?"

She hated talking about herself. Although he'd asked without seeming to probe, that didn't make her more comfortable. "I've been a widow for fourteen months. Randy is showing the results of his father's pampering and overindulgence. Sometimes he's very unruly."

"I can see that."

He had a way of looking at her intently, of focusing on her as if she were the only other living creature on the planet. Suddenly, he smiled, and her heart flipped over like a jackknifed eighteen-wheeler. She took a deep breath to steady herself.

"You didn't get any rest, but . . . well, since we're out here, do you feel like having a decent meal with me?"

Stunned at the unexpected invitation, she gazed up at him, judging his intent.

His smile widened. "I'm harmless. Besides, everybody in town knows me, so I can't possibly abduct you and get away with it. What do you say?"

An infectious grin, his sparkling white teeth against his dark brown skin, gave her a warm feeling, and the twinkling mischievous challenge in his beautiful gray eyes provoked in her an oddball sense of devilment, a wickedness she hadn't felt in over ten years.

In a reckless moment, she said, "Harmless? Luke Hickson, you're about as harmless as a hungry lion among a herd of antelope."

With his jacket open and his hands in his pants pockets emphasizing his six-foot-four-inch height and his imposing maleness, he gave his left shoulder a quick shrug. "I expect I've been likened to less admirable things, but when a charming woman tells me to my face that she thinks I'm dangerous, there's no telling what will pop into my head." He grinned again. "You willing to risk it?"

Primed for the game, she looked him up and down. "Oh, I don't know. What kind of ideas get into your head?"

His eyes flashed fire, daring her. "You might be surprised."

If he thought she'd back off, *he* was in for a surprise. "Good. I love surprises."

His left eyebrow shot up. "And challenges, too, no doubt."

She pulled on the long strand of hair that hung beside her right ear. "Oh, I thrive on those."

"Ever pushed your luck too far?" he asked, his voice low and dark.

She couldn't remember when she had last enjoyed flirting with a man, giving him back as good as she got. And a sharp-looking brother, at that. She pulled a curtain of innocence over her face and smiled. "Maybe. I don't think so, though I've been told I have got an angel on my shoulder. So who knows? Where's this place that serves a good meal?"

When he stepped closer and touched her elbow with a single finger, she looked around and then glanced up at him. He wasn't smiling, and she knew she'd given herself away.

"If you're checking to see who's around in case you want to play, we're alone in front of your store, four feet from a streetlight."

The thought of playing with him, as he put it, sent a riot of sensation through her body, but she steeled herself against his intoxicating virility. "I don't make a spectacle of myself, Captain. I just like to—"

"Tease?" His grin lacked its previous playfulness. "I like to tease, too, but I know when to draw the line. You'd better watch it. Your kind of funny stuff can get out of hand. Oh, yes. Let's cut the formality, Kate. We're way past that now. There's a nice restaurant about six blocks away. I'll drive us."

"Sure you want to have a meal with this child?"

A frown marred his otherwise perfect features. "Child? What do you mean, *child*?"

She lifted her nose just enough to let him sense a mild reprimand. "I don't suppose you make a habit of lecturing to adults."

She couldn't manage more than a wide-eyed stare as he ran his hand over his hair, gave her a sheepish grin, and finally shrugged his left shoulder. "Come on. Let's go."

His hand on her arm was not impersonal as it had been

when he took her and Randy to the police station. His grasp now bore an intimacy, a possessiveness, and it had a tenderness that made her want to feel his hands skimming her arm. Sensing danger, she told herself to remember to ask him about his wife and children, and to stay out of his company.

Luke had a premonition that dismissing her from his mind and his feelings wouldn't be as easy as he'd thought, that handling his reaction to her would prove as tough a test as any he could remember. Her dignity, charm, and impish ways fascinated him, and something in her eyes seemed to hide the wisdom of the ages and to promise him anything he would ever want.

He watched her read the menu, and wondered what was taking her so long. There wasn't that much to read.

Very soon, it became clear that she hadn't been reading. She didn't take her gaze from the menu, which hid half of her face. "Luke, why aren't you having dinner with your wife and children?"

That set him back a bit, but the question told him much about her. He closed his eyes briefly. "Kate, I'm a widower, and have been for six years. My wife and I weren't fortunate enough to have children."

She folded the menu, laid it on the table beside her plate and looked at him. "I'm sorry. Did you want children?"

Getting into that would drag him down as sure as his name was Luke Stuart Hickson. "Yes, I did. More than anything. What happened to your husband?"

So he didn't like talking about it. Well, that was a kind of pain she could understand. She told him of Nathan's death, and why she'd resettled in Portsmouth. "I was teaching here when I met Nathan. So it was Portsmouth or Charleston, where I grew up, and I didn't think I could raise Randy and make a living for us in South Carolina. I want him to have every opportunity."

He tapped the three middle fingers of his left hand on

the table. "If he doesn't get strong discipline, the opportunities you provide him with won't mean one thing."

She knew she had her hands full undoing the damage caused by Nathan's pampering. He'd mistaken that for love, but she had recognized it as a substitute for the guidance their child needed.

"I know I've got my hands full with Randy, and I'm trying. But he threatens to call his paternal grandparents and tell them he's being abused, the way he tattled to his father whenever I made him stay in his room. He's smart beyond his years, Luke. I haven't told them where we are yet, and with his attitude and a few other problems, I'm not sure I want to."

He seemed to meditate for a few minutes before he said, "Enroll him in our Police Athletic Club. Most of those boys aren't with their fathers, so we give them the discipline they need."

She wasn't sure she wanted to turn Randy loose with a group of underprivileged boys. Medicine that cured one ailment could cause another that killed. "We'll see. I—"

"Some of those boys are from homes just like Randy's, and all of them have learned to respect their mothers, so don't be huffy about it. It may be just the help you need."

One more indication that this man should not be taken for granted. And he said what he thought. "I may give it a try," she said, mostly to change the subject.

"The sooner, the better."

The waiter arrived to take their orders, and she breathed a long breath of relief. "I'll have the leek soup and roast beef," she said to the waiter, then glanced at Luke. "What are you wrinkling your nose for?"

He spread out his hands in a gesture of innocence. "With all this good food—stuffed crabs, crab cakes, Cajun-fried Catfish, rolled veal in wine sauce with wild mushrooms, if you want to get fancy—why would anybody ask for roast beef and mashed potatoes?"

Why, indeed? If he thought she'd tell him that she hadn't read the entire menu because he disconcerted her, he could think again. She caught the waiter's sardonic expression.

"If you'd like to change . . . Captain Hickson eats here regularly. He may suggest something."

She looked from one to the other and controlled her tongue. "I ordered roast beef because I like it. I'd also like a glass of *Chateau neuf du pap*. You *do* carry French wines, don't you?"

She'd known Luke Hickson exactly ten hours, but she would have bet her life that if she looked at him she'd see a grin on his face. He didn't disappoint her.

"Yes, ma'am," the waiter replied. Then he took Luke's order of broiled mushrooms and crown roast of pork and moved away as quickly as possible.

"Aren't you having wine?" she asked Luke.

His grin turned into a full laugh—and what a laugh. If she had any sense, she'd get out of there. The man was like a time-release drug.

He sobered up and answered her question. "I'm driving, so I don't drink. I'm a cop, remember? By the way, do you drive?"

She told him she had a Ford Taurus, but that she drove because she had to and not because she enjoyed it. They finished the meal, and he leaned back and watched her. She folded her hands in her lap, unfolded them, smoothed her hair, and then pushed aside the clump that hung over her right ear. Finally, discombobulated beyond measure, she told herself to relax and went on the attack. "Luke, would you please stop staring at me? You're making me uncomfortable."

Horrified, she could see that his look of innocence was not feigned. He leaned forward, appeared to reach for her, then pulled back his hand. "I'm sorry if I made you uncomfortable. I was enjoying being here with you. I don't often have the company of a woman who wants nothing from me except time and good conversation."

She believed in being honest. "I'm sorry, too. I've got a ten-year layer of social rust, plus I've had a lot more of my own company than was good for me. I'm out of practice, so I hope you'll forgive me. Shall we go?"

"You're wonderful company, rust or no rust," he said, his grin hard at work. "I do want to ask if you have any idea who that man was who robbed you. If a criminal intends to shoot after committing a crime, he doesn't usually let himself be talked out of it."

"He seemed young, not more than twenty-five. I didn't see his face, though, because he wore a hood. I'm wondering if my in-laws didn't find out where we are and put someone up to it. They don't want me to succeed. I'm sure of it."

He sat forward, his posture rigid, as if he sensed approaching danger. "*Your in-laws?* If they're wealthy upstanding citizens, would they hire a hit man? Somehow, I doubt it."

"Then why would he have put the gun away when I told him he was frightening Randy and begged him to spare us?"

Luke drummed his fingers on the table. "Beats me, but I'll get to the bottom of it. Be sure of that."

He stood, looked down at her, and extended his hand to assist her from the booth. She took his hand, but released it as soon as she was safely on her feet. Inwardly, she laughed at herself. Why would a thirty-eight-year-old woman let a man make her jittery? She'd been married and was the mother of an eight-year-old boy, for heaven's sake. She stood straighter and held her shoulders back.

"This has been wonderful. Actually, it's my first night out since I've been here. And what do you know? I think I stepped out with the king of the hill."

He had the grace to be embarrassed. "Come on now, Kate. You're exaggerating."

The waiter didn't bring a bill, and she decided not to ask for one. Since he ate there regularly, he probably had an account with the restaurant or someone had slipped him the check. In any case, he didn't seem the type who'd split the bill with a woman the first time they ate dinner together. A few April sprinkles dampened them as they strolled half a block to Luke's car, but he didn't hurry. She'd already noticed that Portsmouth inhabitants, like the Charlestonians among whom she grew up, took their time about most things. He walked with her to her apartment door, and her nerves started a wild battle with one another. She didn't think he'd ask to come in, but . . .

"I've enjoyed this evening with you, Kate. I enjoyed it a lot. I hope we'll get better acquainted." Before she could say a word, he winked, turned around, and headed down the hallway.

"Luke," she called. "The dinner was wonderful, and so were you."

He waved, opened the building's front door, and disappeared into the night. She stared at the hall that led to the building's lobby and shook her head. She knew herself as a conservative woman, one whom Nathan Middleton in his perverted gentility had taught to wait for the man to make the first move. In a flash, she realized that Nathan had discouraged, even rejected, her advances early in their marriage until she'd stopped making them. Ultimately, he had set the tone of their relationship and called all the shots. Ultimately, she hadn't cared.

Maybe she was about to find out who she was, or to rediscover herself. She couldn't figure out what had gotten into her. She'd dared Luke, flirted with him, and challenged him, and she wasn't even ashamed. Ashamed? She'd enjoyed every second of it. But he'd kept his counsel, and she suspected he'd just let her know that he didn't go in for casual good night kisses, not even pecks on the cheek. It was just as well. If he'd kissed her, she'd probably have landed on the clouds. She had always wanted to fly with a man, and the woman in her knew instinctively that Luke Hickson could take her with him on wings of ecstasy. However, she'd been certain of that once before, and in ten years of groping for fulfillment, she'd gotten nothing but emptiness, a painful kind of loneliness—a thousand disappointments, like a field of scentless roses or an orchard of flowering cherry trees that bore no fruit. She didn't feel like retracing those steps.

Luke propped his left foot on the stepstool he kept in his walk-in closet and pondered his sudden urge to look at his family album. Why, after a dozen years or more, did he need to see pictures of his late parents and of him and Marcus as growing boys? He put the photo album back in its place without opening it, clicked off the light, and wandered into the den. It wasn't a time for nostalgia. He'd loved and cherished Eunice, and until her horrifying demise they'd had a wonderful marriage—a happy marriage, comforting and companionable. But, he realized all of a sudden, it had been unexciting. Kate Middleton exhilarated him. And she had a streak of wickedness that brought out something strange in him, a kind of wildness with which he was unfamiliar. He'd controlled it, but he'd give anything to know what would happen if he felt it again and let himself give in to it.

He knew the danger of taking up a woman's challenge, and she'd practically dared him to show her the man that he was. Not that he was gullible; he'd walked away from more glittering pitfalls. What got to him was the thin layer of sadness beneath her jocular manner. That, along with her wit and charm, made him vulnerable to her, piqued his curiosity, and made him want to know everything about her. He went to the refrigerator, got a can of beer, and took a few swallows. An inner urging told him to bide his time, and he knew he'd better listen.

He snapped his finger as he remembered her fear that her in-laws might be trying to prevent her from succeeding with the bookstore. It didn't quite wash, but to be on the safe side, he'd assign a detective to watch that block first thing Monday morning.

When Kate walked into her living room, she found Madge Robinson snoring in front of the television and Bugs Bunny savoring a carrot while he plotted mischief. She awakened the woman by turning off the TV.

Madge jumped up. "I didn't expect you'd be back in no two hours. If I went anywhere with Captain Hickson, I'd keep him half the night, too."

She didn't have much patience with busybodies. Madge Robinson had known she'd been with Luke because she'd walked to the edge of the garden and peered through the hedge, snooping. "Mrs. Robinson, it's only nine-fifteen, and I'd hardly consider that half the night. Did Randy give you any trouble?"

Madge sat down and flicked the television back on. "I didn't see the rest of Bugs. No, Randy didn't give me a speck of trouble. I went to my place and got him some ice cream, and he went to bed peacefully as a lamb, just like he promised."

Just what Randy needed, someone else to pamper him and cajole him into doing what he knew he should do. "You mean you bribed Randy to go to sleep?"

Madge glued her gaze to the television. "That tiger's gonna catch Bugs if he ain't careful. What? Oh. It was better for him to sleep than give me a hard time. Besides, he was tired, anyway. Poor kid said he hadn't slept all last night."

"How much do I owe you, Mrs. Robinson?"

"What? Fifteen. That's my regular price, and call me Madge, like everybody else does. I'd rather not charge for keeping the tenants' children, but everybody wants to pay. It's a pleasure for me, 'cause I'm always by myself 'less someone wants me to keep the kids. I never had any, so I enjoys it. I 'spec you want to turn in, so I'll go on home soon as Bugs is finished."

Kate inhaled a long breath and sat down to watch Bugs Bunny. Within minutes she had closed her eyes and begun to relive the evening.

She opened her store the next morning at nine o'clock, the usual hour. Beside the doorknob, she noticed a buzzer that hadn't been there before the robbery. She'd ask Luke about that. Half an hour later, she answered the buzzer and opened the door for a policeman.

" 'Morning, Miss Kate," he said, tipping his hat. "I'm Officer Cowan, and I've been assigned to patrol your area. I just wanted to give you my page number, in case you have a problem. I won't be more that eight or ten blocks from you at any time, so feel safe. You can turn this buzzer off till near dark. I doubt anybody's gonna bother you in broad daylight."

The air that whistled through his teeth with each word he uttered and the large patch of black hair beneath his left ear guaranteed that she wouldn't forget him. She thanked him, and he left, but she wanted to ask somebody if Luke Hickson took such good care of every citizen in his precinct. The protection gave her a sense of security, but she didn't want special favors. One way or another, you paid for them. She'd rather spend her precious funds on a store guard and keep her independence.

She rang up a sale, handed the change to the buyer. Then, as her gaze caught Luke heading toward her, she jammed her finger in the drawer of the cash register. She'd thought him handsome, but as she stared at him in his captain's uniform she nearly swallowed her tongue. He glided toward her, his stride purposeful and powerful and his gaze fixed on her.

He stopped beside her customer and touched his cap. "Glad to see you're up and out, Miss Fanny. You had a long siege."

"Oh, Captain," the woman exclaimed, "I don't know what I'd have done if you and your men hadn't kept a close check on me." She turned to Kate. "They're my family. Brought me food and the paper every single day. Good hot food, too, 'cause, honey, I wasn't able to get up and cook. I'm going to bake them some gingerbread soon as I feel up to it." She pointed a finger toward Luke. "He loves gingerbread, gingersnaps, and whatever else I can put ginger in." Kate wrapped the woman's purchases—a volume of poems and a copy of *Fools Rush In*—and handed them to her.

"I'll be back soon as I finish *Fools Rush In*," Miss Fanny called over her shoulder as she left.

"Did you sleep well?" Luke asked.

She nodded. "Wonderfully. Thanks." Then she remembered the buzzer. "Luke, did you have that buzzer put on my door?"

He flipped back his cap and closed his eyes for a split second. "Yeah. Of course I did. It's dark long before you leave, and most of the stores in this block close a couple of hours before you do. You're vulnerable. What's the matter? You don't want it there?"

What could she say? Of course she needed that, and any other protection that would prevent her from losing her store. "Please don't think I'm not grateful. I am—"

He frowned and barely narrowed his left eye. "But what, Kate? Tell me you're going to do this all on your own, that you don't need anybody's help. Fine. Give me a screwdriver, and I'll remove the buzzer.''

Now, she'd done it. What was it about men that made them see things in black-and-white? "I appreciate your kindness, but in ten years of marriage, I wasn't allowed to make a single meaningful decision. I was spoon-fed, managed, and manipulated. You'll forgive me, I hope, if I'm supersensitive about my independence.''

He stepped closer and burned her with his all-knowing gaze. "If your marriage wasn't a happy one, why did you stay?''

"I have a son, and I took a vow.''

She'd said more than she wanted him to know. But then, she'd already accepted that she wasn't normal around him.

Something akin to recognition—or could it be approval?—gleamed in his intense gaze. "You're an admirable woman. I just dropped by to make certain everything's all right. Did Cowan introduce himself to you this morning?''

She nodded, perplexed. The man whose company she'd enjoyed the previous evening had been swallowed by that captain's uniform. She didn't know what to think. "Officer Cowan said he'd be checking on me. Luke, do you think it's necessary to go to so much trouble?''

His gaze didn't waver. "For a simple robbery, I wouldn't take such steps, but you've implied that you're in jeopardy, and until that robbery case is solved it's my job to protect you—whether you like that or not. What time will Randy be here this afternoon?''

She tried to imagine what was behind the question. "Three-thirty. Why? What did you have in mind?''

"I'd like him to come over to PAL." He gave her the address. "You can't begin too early. He has the profile of a kid who needs help, and you have to straighten him out now.''

She knew he didn't exaggerate. "All right. I'll . . . I'll send him."

Her nerves shimmered when his hand covered hers in a gentle gesture of comfort. "One of the counsellors or officers will pick him up at three-thirty and bring him back before you close. Relax, now. He couldn't be in better hands."

She let herself luxuriate in the warmth that leaped out from him. She knew she should move her hand, but why couldn't she enjoy his caring gesture for just a minute? He looked at her the way he had when they sat in that booth without speaking after their dinner—not searching or examining, just communicating in a most primal way. She wanted to ask him if he was telling her he liked her, but she didn't.

She smiled and squeezed his hand. "Be my friend, Luke, but please don't spoil me. I've had too much of that. Do you understand?"

He clasped her hand more tightly, but he didn't smile, and she wondered what had happened to the grin with which he'd mesmerized her Sunday evening.

"I understand," he told her, "but you can't assume that I'd treat you as your husband did. I believe in giving a person breathing space, and I like women who're capable of standing on their own two feet." He touched the brim of his cap. "I'll drop by again to see how you're getting on."

He moved his hand, leaving her with a sense of loss. "Thanks, Luke, for . . . for everything."

As he turned to go she amazed herself by saying, "I make great gingerbread. Randy's crazy about it."

His stare made her want to disappear, for he had to know that her remark had been an attempt to detain him. Then a grin began around his mouth and quickly covered his face in a smile that lit up everything around them. "You may never get rid of me. If you don't make some soon, I'll put in a request. Bet on that. Just thinking about gingerbread gives me a high."

She joined in his merriment, more comfortable with him in the lightened mood. "Ever the officer. Imagine getting high on gingerbread. Well, if that's what revs your engine."

He grinned again and his left eye flicked in a deliberate wink. "That, and one or two other things. See you later."

He strode toward the door with a seductive swing, as though his rhythmic gait had been choreographed by a master choreographer. *My Lord,* she thought, *walking toward me or striding off, the man oozes sex appeal.* She'd have her hands full trying not to become attached to him. He was used to giving orders, to controlling people, and she'd had enough of that. Her one priority was to establish her store in order to take care of Randy and herself. Falling for a man, even a handsome catch like Luke Hickson, didn't fit into her plans. But oh, how tempting he was!

Chapter Two

No sooner had Luke gotten back to the precinct and settled down to work than Axel Strange strolled into his office without knocking and took a seat. Ten years on the force, nine of them at that precinct, and he still couldn't warm up to the man.

"What can I do for you, Lieutenant?"

Axel leaned back in the chair and crossed his right leg over his left knee, as comfortable as if he were in his own office. "I'm told you know where the cutter is."

Luke lay his pen beside his writing pad and prepared for some of Axel's sleuthing. Something about Axel Strange reminded him of grease, always had. He never meant precisely what he said, leaving himself an out. His words had to be decoded. And just when you had to depend on him, he wasn't there. The man never talked about himself, but he always had the goods on his fellow officers and didn't mind talking about *them*. He didn't exactly dislike Axel, but he was more comfortable when the man wasn't around.

Luke let his gaze roam over Axel, cataloging the things

that irked him. "Unless someone used that cutter after I did, it's in its place. Why are you asking me, anyway? Speak to the sergeant in charge of storage."

Axel shifted his demeanor from amiable to harsh, checked himself, and produced another smile. "I just thought you'd know. By the way, who was the woman? I tell you, I couldn't believe you spent most of your day off looking after some dame. Must be some dish, huh?"

Luke stiffened. A little of Axel could last him a long time. "Read the log, man. I'm sure it contains everything you need to know. Cowan's on that beat, and he can handle anything that comes up. I'd better get busy."

It surprised him that Axel didn't move, and he wondered if he'd finally have to pull rank on the man.

"Rick—you know, the waiter at River Café—said you had a sharp-looking gal there with you last night that he didn't recognize. Couldn't have been the same woman, could it?"

Luke strummed his fingers on his desk, his patience waning. "I'm surprised you consider that your business. It isn't."

Axel's smile was about what he expected, given that the man could back away from a position with the swiftness of an Indianapolis 500 racer. "Everybody's curious about you, man. We're all waiting for the boss to be had."

Luke picked up his pen, signaling the conversation's end. "Fortunately, I am not gullible enough to believe the men in this precinct have nothing better to think about than my private business. Since we've both got work to do, I suggest we get to it."

The ugliness that glazed Axel Strange's face so quickly that it was hardly discernible sent a shot of adrenalin streaking through Luke—pure animosity, and he knew he hadn't imagined it. He'd never regarded the man as an enemy, and maybe he wasn't, but he'd bear watching.

Luke missed his camaraderie with Jack McCarthy, whom

he'd replaced as detective captain when the man retired, and he enjoyed an occasional lunch with him.

He sat at his favorite table in the River Café, facing the door, when the old man walked in, tall, straight, and still striding with the regal bearing of a five-star general.

"Great to see you, Luke. How's it going? Chopped any heads off yet?"

That brought a laugh from Luke because he'd come to expect that question whenever they met. "How are you, Jack? I haven't, but my fingers are getting itchy."

McCarthy ordered two beers for himself. "One of the rewards of retirement," he explained. "How are you and Strange getting along?"

Luke cocked an eyebrow. "Fried Norfolk spots today," he told the waiter before turning his attention to his friend. "Do you expect Axel to be a problem?"

Jack enjoyed his first swallow of beer, shook his head and laughed. "Luke, that man *is* a problem. Don't you know he submitted a written application for every promotion you got? Of course, he lost to you every time. I told him it wasn't even a contest. By the time I retired, he'd become obsessed with you. Wanted to know about your assignments, expense accounts, semiannual evaluations, and I don't know what all. I told him the way to beat you was to do a better job."

"Well, I'll be doggoned. I just thought maybe he'd dragged himself up by his bootstraps, and that accounted for his grabbing at everything he saw. It wouldn't hurt him to try hard work."

"Not a chance. I gave him that choice many times, but if he took it, I saw no evidence of it. He takes the easy way every time, and that's unusual for a man with his background. He comes from a topflight family of self-made men, but he doesn't like work, and he's devious. I'd watch him closely."

Luke sniffed the aroma of sizzling spots and hush puppies as the waiter set the plates on the table. " Yeah." He bit into one of the deep-fried balls of spicy cornbread and let himself enjoy it. "I'm glad you told me about Strange, because I've been planning to reassign him. I think I'd better wait on that."

After saying good-bye Luke headed back to the precinct, pondering Jack's admonition about Axel as he drove. He'd rather not have to deal harshly with any of his staff, but if Axel challenged him, he'd teach the man a lesson.

Several days later, Randy raced into the bookstore from his one-hour sojourn at PAL. With a pout that Kate recognized, he flung his book bag on the counter near where she stood waiting on a customer. She stared hard at him until he greeted her and the woman, moved his books, and went into her office. A week earlier, he would have ignored her silent reprimand.

"What's the problem?" she asked him after the customer had left.

"That place is like the army," he grumbled. Even in that short time, his manners had improved, for he answered her without hesitation.

"You agreed to go, Randy, and you're going. You have to keep your word. Why are you complaining?"

"Keep my word. Keep my word," he mimicked. "I heard that fifty times every day I've been there. Next week is my week to deliver stuff to some old people. A guy drives the truck, and I get out and take the stuff in."

She thought for a minute, wanting to shame him. "Can these senior citizens get the food themselves, and do they have the money?"

She knew she'd gotten to him when he hung his head. "Captain Luke says they'll starve if we don't help them out."

"I see. You wouldn't like that, would you?"

It pleased her that his bottom lip no longer protruded and that his frown had vanished. "No, I guess. But Captain Luke said that after next week, I have to teach the other four guys in my group how to do it. But I wanna take tennis lessons."

She'd locked the store before going into the office. When the buzzer rang, she rushed toward the door, saw Luke Hickson in his navy blue uniform, a stunning figure, and tried to settle her nerves. If he didn't turn her heart into a runaway train, he'd calm her just by being there. Looking at him, she thought he could handle anything and anybody.

Luke stepped into the store and gazed down at her. She'd had no cause to doubt her sanity, but when his pupils went from gray to a near-black, with fiery twinkles all around them, she wondered if she'd imagined it.

He grinned. "Hi."

Quickly, she shifted her gaze. If he told her he didn't know the effect of that grin, she wouldn't believe him.

"Hi, yourself. Randy was just complaining about the assignments you gave him," she said, her voice climbing as she strove to reduce the tension between them.

Luke lifted his shoulder in a quick dismissive shrug, and she knew she hadn't taken his mind off them by opening the subject of Randy. "Let him complain. He doesn't fool me, because I know he's enjoying himself. And he's proud he was singled out as group leader."

She stared at Luke. "He was?"

"Yeah. Didn't he tell you? He's doing great."

She let out a long breath. "What a relief. He says he wants to spend his time learning to play tennis."

Luke stuffed his hands in his trouser pockets, his slight frown suggesting that Randy wasn't his priority right then. "I'll teach him how to play tennis, but not till he learns to enjoy helping people who need his help. Where is he?"

She nodded toward her office. "In there."

Luke looked into the distance, seemingly debating with himself. Then he fixed a penetrating gaze on her. "How about dinner? Randy's welcome to come along."

She hadn't expected that, and she knew her demeanor betrayed her eagerness to accept. "I . . . I'd like to, but I don't allow Randy to be out at night if he has school the next day. I'm sorry."

She would learn that Luke was resourceful, and not easily stymied. "Tell you what," he said. "Suppose I go in there and work with him on his lessons, and you get Madge to look after him while we go to dinner? We can get a take-out for him, and he can eat at home. What about it?"

Eagerness be hanged! She wanted to go with him, and she didn't see the sense in pretending she didn't. "Okay."

Madge would probably agree, but how would Randy react to having Luke go over his lessons with him? Well, she figured Luke could handle it. Besides, a good dose of Luke was what Randy needed.

"You want to go back to the River Café?" Luke asked later as he pulled away from the curb in front of the apartment building in which she lived.

She'd liked the place, and readily agreed. "It's very attractive, and I enjoyed the food."

He spared her a side glance, mischief dancing in his gray eyes. "The food, huh? What about the company?"

She sank into the soft leather seat and got comfortable, eager to match wits. "I've had worse. Lots worse. Why do you ask?"

He paused at the stop sign, looked from left to right, turned into Elm Avenue, and headed for Effington Street and the River Café. "Since you ask, I'm wondering the same thing. *Why did I ask?* If you'd said I was a washout, you'd have crushed this poor heart."

Laughter bubbled up in her. "How'd you fix your mouth to say that? If I've ever seen a man with a star on his forehead, it's you. So I'm not going for that humble stuff."

"You mean you're not willing to find out who I am? You think I'm a six-foot, four-inch Samson in a monkey suit? Just like every other tough cop in blue? That it?"

She sat up straight. This man had his vulnerable spots, and she'd better remember it. "Since that remark had a ring of seriousness, I won't joke about it. I also won't back away from what my instincts tell me. If I needed a defender, I'd send for you."

His failure to comment told her more than she was comfortable knowing. They entered the restaurant through a side door, and the aroma of buttermilk biscuits, garlic, sage sausage, and frying fish teased her nostrils as they passed the kitchen on their way to the dining room.

Kate licked her lips in anticipation of the meal. "Is this your regular table?" she asked him as the waiter led them to the one they'd shared on her previous visit.

"I usually sit here," he answered in an offhand manner, as though he didn't merit special treatment. "You eating roast beef and mashed potatoes again tonight?" His gray eyes glittered with devilment, and she braced herself for a blast of his charm.

"I'm having Cajun-fried catfish and hush puppies."

"Glad to hear it. That's what I had for lunch."

He winked at her over the top of the largest menu she'd ever seen, and she couldn't help staring at him, at those eyes that commanded her to get lost in them. Maybe being with a husband who'd paid her little attention for most of their marriage had weakened her resistance to men.

"How'd you and Randy get along with his lessons?"

He waited until the waiter finished serving their food, leaned back in his chair, and looked at her. "Hard to tell. He did his homework. Effortlessly, I'd say. But I'm not sure he likes me. I know he doesn't like being told what to do." He cut off a piece of steak and savored it. "He respects me, or maybe it's my uniform, but I'll take that for now."

"Why did you make him group leader?"

"I didn't. The boys in his group elected him. Now he's responsible for his behavior, and for theirs, as well. It's good for him."

She hoped so. "You said you'd give him tennis lessons."

He finished the last piece of steak. "I will. I'm a pretty fair player, and if he's interested in learning I'll be glad to teach him."

"Well, this *is* a surprise."

When Luke's head snapped up she followed his gaze, and they stared into the mocking eyes of Axel Strange.

"You wouldn't be Kate Middleton, would you?" Axel asked as he cloaked his face in a seductive smile.

"Yes, I am," she said, and would have extended her hand had she not glimpsed Luke's icy regard of the man.

"Ms. Middleton, this is Lieutenant Strange, a detective in my precinct."

Couldn't get much colder than that, she figured. "Good evening, Lieutenant," she said, taking a cue from Luke and sounding as formal as she could.

Her cold greeting made no evident impact on the lieutenant, since he replied, "I've wanted to meet you, but, as usual, the boss jumped in before me."

"Enjoy your meal, Strange," Luke said, dismissing the man. *And rather testily, at that,* she thought.

Abruptly, the lieutenant's smile faded. Then he beamed at her. "Be seeing you, Ms. Middleton."

Luke continued his meal as if they hadn't been interrupted. He didn't comment on the incident, and, since she wasn't in the habit of sticking her nose into hornets' nests, she figured she ought to forget it.

"What happened to that gingerbread you're supposed to be so good at making? Miss Fanny can't bend over the stove yet, and I haven't had any gingerbread in six weeks."

She controlled an impulse to laugh at the childlike petulance in his voice, which belied the tensile strength no one

would doubt he possessed. She presented a face as serious
as his.

"You said you'd put in a request. Is this a request?"

Long elegant fingers grasped the handle of his coffee
cup, and she imagined those strong, masculine hands on
her skin, testing her response to him. His shimmering gaze
told her he had discerned her thoughts and had similar
ones of his own.

His left hand covered her unsteady fingers. "Am I plead-
ing for gingerbread? Does night follow day? You don't
understand, Kate. *I love gingerbread.*"

Laughter poured out of her, then, releasing some of the
tension that took hold of her whenever she saw him and
intensified when she was near him. "Oh, I understand
that, all right, but if you had said *chocolate* . . ."

His gaze, so intense and studied, unsettled her. If he
was trying to find a place for himself in her head, he was
doing a good job. "I know men are supposed to love
chocolate," he said, "but not me. I go by my own educated
taste buds, and do my own thinking. And that goes for
everything." He leaned forward. "I said everything."

She wished he'd leave her nerves alone. What a blessing
he couldn't *see* them. At best, they must look like hair
teased to a frazzle by some foolhardy hairdresser. She told
herself she'd feel better if she knew she had the same
effect on him. He smiled, and she dared to open herself
to him for just one moment and squeezed his fingers,
knowing that her alarm at her behavior had to be mirrored
on her face.

"Don't move so fast, Luke. I'm not there yet."

He smiled a slow smile, his eyes brimming with the
secrets of the ages. "If I ever moved slower, I don't remember it. Trust me, I'm taking my time, and it's as clear as
spring water that you're doing the same."

She diverted her gaze from the eyes that seemed to
invade her soul and focused on the pink dogwood blossoms

that adorned their table. "I wish I had your self-assurance, Luke. You know where you're going, and exactly how to get there."

The long fingers of his left hand stroked his chin in a slow graceful movement, and he perused her as though searching for some truth in her. An expression of hopefulness flashed across his face—or so she thought, because the man concealed his emotions. She couldn't help squirming under his scrutiny.

"Luke, you have to stop doing this to me. I know it's not your intention to make me uncomfortable, but I feel as if you have me under a 4000x-lens microscope."

"Sorry. I . . . try not to second-guess me, Kate. I know how to be rude, if I care to, but I can't imagine myself being discourteous to you."

"Then what—"

"I was trying to figure out what you see in me that makes you think I know exactly what I want and how to get it. There aren't many men I'd say that about."

She didn't believe he'd use that ruse to get his ego stoked, so she told him truthfully. "It's the impression you give me. You're a man in complete command. I'd trust you with my life anytime and anywhere."

Could it have been pain that flashed so briefly in his eyes? A frown darkened his countenance. "Don't ever put complete trust in any mortal. Save that for God. I'm human, Kate, and I have mortal frailties."

"But you seem un . . . unflappable."

Again, a shadow crossed his face, and when he hooded his eyes she knew that if he had an Achilles' heel, she'd come close to it. A long pregnant silence held a tension of its own. She waited, certain that his response would give her a clue as to who he was.

"I learned a few years ago not to let anything stress me out," he said in a voice that had a ring of finality. "I do what I can, and let the rest go."

Kate didn't want their evening to end, though her mind told her she shouldn't spend so much time with him. But he was like a flame seducing a moth, both tonic and irritant. Being with him soothed her, yet fired her nerves, relaxed, yet energized her. She loved being with him, though a rawness seeped in when he left her. At times, like right then, he made her feel like a piece of a jigsaw puzzle placed in its proper niche, like cold fingers greeting the comfort of fur-lined gloves.

"I'd like some more coffee, please," she told the waiter, prolonging their time together.

"So would I," Luke said.

When Luke stared straight ahead, his left eyelid narrowed in a squint. She turned around and saw the lieutenant approaching their table.

"Just wanted to say good night, Ms. Middleton. Hope to see you again soon," he said as if Luke were not there.

She hated rudeness, but she didn't see how she could respond without being discourteous to Luke, so she said nothing. The man plastered a smile on his face and walked on.

This time, she couldn't dismiss the incident. "What's going on between you two, Luke?"

He shrugged nonchalantly, but the way his jaw worked told her he wasn't as unfazed as he'd have her think. "Until tonight, I'd have said nothing was going on between us. Now I'm not so sure. Are you interested in him?"

She glared at him. "I don't know the man."

He motioned for their waiter. "Something tells me you will. Shall we go?"

His deep vibrant voice and his apparent certainty reminded her of her father, and she fought to hide the pain that thinking of him caused her, pain that plowed through her at the thought of him—a proud exemplary citizen brought to his knees. She forced a smile for Luke's benefit.

* * *

Luke braced his right elbow against the wall beside Kate's front door and supported his head with his right hand. Kate seemed flustered looking up at him, and he wished she'd get used to him.

"Kate, I like being with you. If you'll tell me what I do that makes you uncomfortable, I'll stop it."

Her eyes widened, but he didn't care if he'd startled her. She ought to expect a man to enjoy looking at her. At the inquiring expression on her face, he added, "I'm a protector, Kate. It's my nature. Don't be afraid of me."

Slowly, she lowered her long lashes, hiding her feelings from him. He knew what she felt, though, because the rising temperature of her body heat warmed up her perfume and released it to enthrall his senses. Her captivating aura swirled around him. She opened her oval eyes, warm brown orbs that promised heaven to a man, and he swallowed his breath. He'd better get out of there before he did something he'd regret.

He'd taken an oath that if he was ever again personally responsible for a woman's safety, he wouldn't let that woman care for him and place her trust in him. Never again. The burden of responsibility for another person's life was a heavy one, and if that person loved a man and believed in him above all other men, the load was that much more onerous. His head told him to keep a lot of space between them, but she had a way about her that made a man want to explore her very essence.

He straightened up and flicked back his hat. "When can I expect my gingerbread?" That ought to purge the atmosphere of tension.

She tossed her head in what he recognized as an affirmation of her dignity. "I'll . . . uh . . . I'll let you know."

How it happened, he couldn't say, but his left hand

suddenly rested on her shoulder, and he didn't move it. "I want a definite answer."

Without moving a muscle or blinking her eyes, as alert as a sentry on duty, she stared at him a full minute. "Impatience has buried a lot of men."

Well, she wasn't going to disconcert him, and he refused to let her know how she affected him, so he forced an ambiguous smile. "You bet. And I don't expect to join them."

He let his thumb graze softly over her bottom lip. "Thanks for your company. I'll be around if you need me."

The key in his hand caught his gaze, and—careful to avoid looking at the flickering heat in her eyes—he opened her door, handed her the key, and walked off while he had the strength.

"Luke!"

He stopped, swung around, and waited. He did not need temptation right then. "What is it, Kate?"

She seemed to hesitate, as though uncertain of her next move. "I was . . . uh . . . thinking I could make the gingerbread Friday night, and maybe we could—"

He interrupted her, not allowing her a chance to say something they'd have to deal with. "And could I come over Friday night and get it? I'd planned to spend the weekend with my brother and sister-in-law down in North Carolina, but if you're going to give me gingerbread, I'll stop by on my way out of town."

Her demeanor said she'd meant for them to make an evening of it, as he'd suspected, but if she was disappointed she didn't let him see it.

She held up both hands, palms out. "Please don't let me disturb your plans. I just thought . . ."

He walked back to her. "Like me, you want one thing, but you've been there and you don't think you want to go that route again. You've signalled to me more than once that you don't want to get involved with me. Whatever your reason, you're very wise, because it isn't a good idea."

"I know we can't have it both ways," she said. "Just . . . just come by the store on Friday, and I'll have it there for you."

She was so close, so alluring. He stared down at her, accepting his punishment. Then he shook his head, wondering where his attraction to her would take him. Frustration seeped into him, tugging at his insides, and he kissed her cheek and walked away.

I'm going to stay away from that brother, Kate promised herself as she watched the door of the lobby swing shut behind him. *All I need is to fall for a guy who has everything a woman wants and is dead set on keeping it to himself. Once is enough for me. From now on, it's cool Kate.*

The next afternoon, as she shelved a new shipment of books, the door of her store opened and Lieutenant Strange strutted through it. Kate was sure she'd lost her bottom lip.

"Hi," he greeted like a friend of long standing. "How're things? Thought I'd drop by and see how you're doing."

She told herself to smile and be gracious, that as a businesswoman, she didn't need enemies. Somehow she managed it, though it was difficult with Luke's frown mirrored in her mind's eye.

"Good afternoon, Lieutenant," she said, uncomfortable with the cool tenor of her greeting, which was at odds with her natural warmth and friendliness. She wondered if his smile was as practiced as it seemed, whether she looked at the man with Luke's eyes. *Some charmer,* she decided, as he treated her to a strong dose of male charisma. A tall polished man with reasonably good looks and a daunting uniform to cover up whatever flaws he had, he should have presented a more commanding picture. Still, she'd seen worse.

His nasal tone got her attention. "I said, let me give you a hand with that."

A refusal sat on the tip of her tongue, but falling rows of books took care of the matter. She couldn't move unless he helped, and she watched, exasperated, as Axel Strange wormed his way into her life, putting her firmly in his debt.

"Let me take care of it," he said again, removing his jacket and rubbing his hands together as if he were about to get a mouthwatering bite of thick juicy steak. *You'd think he was glad the books almost knocked me over,* she thought with not a little annoyance. He piled the books on the floor, releasing her from the burden of bracing the shelves with her back, and had started shelving them when Luke walked into the store.

Chapter Three

Kate glanced toward the door when she heard it open, and a wave of apprehension swept through her. What a time for Luke to walk in! She hoped he'd realize she hadn't encouraged Axel. She wanted to meet him as he headed toward her, but if she did, he or Axel might consider that a statement of sorts, and it wouldn't have been. It didn't surprise her that Luke stopped short when he saw Axel, his face bearing all the warmth of an iceberg, and that his entire body took on a predatory hostile posture. She waited, wondering what would happen when Axel realized Luke was standing little more that a yard from him.

"I assume you signed out for half a day's vacation leave, Lieutenant," Luke said, his voice dark and overlaid with disgust.

Axel's head snapped up, and the stack of books he'd picked up fell back to the floor. The careless smile he struggled to paste on his face didn't quite make it. He reminded her of a bad actor trying to play Macbeth.

"Well?" This time there was no mistaking Luke's asser-

tion of authority. "I don't recall seeing your report on that arson case that you should have put on my desk no later than five o'clock yesterday."

"Aw, give a guy a break, boss. The lady needed a hand." Axel put his hands in his pockets and let his gaze sweep the store. Then he moved his head to one side and backed away several feet. "I don't see your desk around here anywhere."

Luke narrowed his left eye. "If what I did was any of your business, you'd be the captain. I want to see you in my office in twenty minutes." He turned to leave, seemed to remember her presence, and walked back to her.

"I'm sorry, Kate, but I can't permit the willful disregard of precinct rules. I'll be in touch."

She couldn't fault him, but if he and Axel had to play one-upmanship she wished they'd leave her out of it. Axel resumed the shelving the minute the door closed behind Luke, obviously attempting to impress her with his indifference to his superior's command, and she wouldn't tolerate it.

"Lieutenant, don't continue that, please. I appreciate your wanting to help, but I'll shelve the remainder myself."

"He's just jealous. He can't do a thing to me."

Annoyed at the man's impertinence, she took the books from his hand. "That may be, but if you're going to disrespect your own rank please do it someplace else. One expects more from a lieutenant."

He covered his icy stare so quickly that she doubted having seen it. "Just trying to be of service, ma'am," he said, spreading his hands in affected humility. "I'll call you, and we can get together."

"Good-bye, Lieutenant Strange." He didn't seem all bad, though she had a suspicion that he would go to great limits to irritate Luke and get the better of him. She didn't want to be caught between them, but until the man gave her concrete reasons to avoid him she had at least to be civil. It didn't escape her that he left the store with less of a swagger than when he entered. Nobody had to tell her she hadn't heard the end of it.

Luke leaned back in his desk chair and waited. He had to control the urge to pace the floor, because Axel Strange could misconstrue that as nervousness if he walked in and saw it. Axel had a way of showing his disdain for authority by walking past Luke's secretary and entering his office door without knocking for permission. Anyway, he wasn't nervous, just so mad he could barely wait to let the man know how close he was to endangering his job.

Nineteen minutes. One more, and he'd give him a week's walking leave. The door opened and he stared at Axel Strange, his hands up as though in surrender and his face wreathed in smiles.

"You believe in living on the edge, don't you? You know what happens to detectives caught loafing when they're on duty, and you know the penalty is even stiffer for officers. You're entitled to three warnings in the course of your career."

Axel's sharp intake of breath betrayed his fear that he might have gone too far. "You . . . you're not serious, are you?"

Luke swung his fountain pen in rhythmic taps on his desk. "You're the one who's not serious. Tell me why you shouldn't have an official warning? Suppose other officers ignored the rules. What would you recommend for them?"

"Look, man, I was just passing by, and—"

"Can that. You were on your knees shelving books."

He knew the minute Axel decided to go on the attack. "What I did was nothing. Let's get to the real problem. You're afraid I'll muscle in on your turf. If she wants me, I'm going for her, and your threats won't deter me for a second."

"You're bordering on insubordination."

Axel raised his head slightly and narrowed his eyes. "It's your word against mine."

Luke allowed himself a hard cold smile. "Right. How many warnings have you had?"

"None." The pride in his voice was unmistakable.

"I wonder how that happened," Luke said under his breath. Aloud he said, "Be careful you don't get three more."

Axel lunged toward the desk, and then caught himself, his breathing accelerated and fear glistening in his eyes. "You wouldn't!"

Luke continued tapping his Mont Blanc pen. "I just did. Next time you get out of line, be sure it isn't with me. You're dismissed, Lieutenant." If he'd let him get away with it, he'd be impossible to control.

He hadn't expected Axel's brazen pursuit of Kate. The man usually fought more deviously. Not that he planned to engage him. If Kate's suspicions proved valid that her in-laws had hired a man, perhaps more than one, to ruin her business or to frighten her into closing it, she'd need his protection. And he couldn't stay on his toes if burdened with an overactive libido.

The next day he parked in front of Kate's bookstore and left the motor running to make certain he got out of there in a hurry. He wanted to get to Caution Point in time for dinner, and it was already five-thirty. He also didn't want too much of Kate's company. She had a way of easing herself into him, revving up his engine, and messing around in his head, and she did it with the smoothness of a falcon winging toward the clouds.

"Did you remember my gingerbread?" he asked when she greeted him. He tried not to see the warmth in her flawless complexion, or the temptation of her large, oval, brown eyes and sensuous lips. Everything about her promised him the moon, if he'd just take it. Her smile, so warm and natural, sent fire skittering through him, and he feared she'd hear his pounding heart.

"I hope it's as good as Miss Fanny's," she said. "I've been making it since I was little."

"Not to worry. If it's gingerbread, I eat it. I'll be out of town over the weekend, so here's my cell phone number in case you need me." *Or, in case you'd like to talk with me,* his conscience jeered. He thought for a minute. "Try to close up earlier tomorrow night—say, seven-thirty, along with the other merchants on this block. Trick the criminals."

She promised she would, and he left, though it cost him more willpower than he would have imagined needing. As he drove away, he glanced at the store and saw her standing at the door. He'd noticed on other occasions that she always watched him leave her, and he wondered what it meant.

Kate knew she watched him because she loved the rhythm of his long strides, seemingly carefree and careless. Taking that at face value could get her into difficulty, she knew, because Luke Hickson was not a happy-go-lucky man. She'd learned, too, that his eyes had a crinkle and a glint that could fool her into thinking he was about to break into a smile. But she knew she'd better wait until he actually laughed. That crinkle and glint could get a person into trouble.

She set the buzzer and went into her office. Business was slow, and she had to create some excitement. She wanted the store to become a place where people hung out, a kind of cultural center. She'd thought of putting two round marble-top tables in the front and serving coffee, but discarded the idea. With one cup of coffee and a magazine, a person could occupy a table for hours. *A reading group.* She'd sponsor one, and give the members a fifteen percent discount on books.

She bit into a piece of gingerbread. If Luke said he'd

tasted better, she wouldn't believe him. She posted a sign-up sheet on the wall to enroll customers in the reading group and answered the door.

"How may I help you?" she asked the woman, a stranger.

The woman produced a business card. "My first romance novel is just out, and I was wondering if you'd like me to sign your stock."

Her stock! She had three copies of *Duckie's Love Gone Wild*, and if she sold one of them, autographed or not, she'd be lucky. With its hideous cover, customers didn't even turn it over to read the blurb. She sympathized with the woman, who had to feel terrible about that cover, so she gave her a chair and brought her a bottle of lemonade. If only the woman would drink it, so she wouldn't see her getting the books from the bottom shelf in the section next to Horror and Different Strokes, a euphemism for same sex.

"You only have three?" the author asked. "This is fabulous. You've sold all the rest. I suppose you'll order some more?"

Kate made it a policy not to lie except to save somebody from excruciating pain, and she nearly shouted for joy when the buzzer rang and she didn't have to answer. That joy was short-lived, however, when she saw Axel Strange.

She introduced him to the author, hoping to divert his attention from her, but he had charm enough for both women. And, to her chagrin, he was the first person to sign up for the reading group, and she immediately lost interest in the idea.

"This is a gas," he said. "I love reading and discussing books."

Was that so? Well, he could prove it. "In that case, you'd value a book signed especially for you by the author herself. Ms. Gray is signing books."

As she'd expected, he made a show of getting the book, engaging the woman in a long conversation about his own writing plans, and questioning her about writing—how she got started, and how long it took to write a book. When Ms. Gray showed signs of exasperation, she called him off.

"She's only here for a short while, so maybe you'd like to drop her a note." The woman blew out a long tired breath, quickly signed the remaining two books, thanked Kate, and left. Ms. Gray had evidently had as much of Axel as she could take. Unfortunately for Kate, she was stuck with him.

"How about dinner? The River Café's the best place around here, but I don't walk in other men's footprints, so we'll go somewhere else."

Presumptuous, wasn't he? "Lieutenant, I'm going home to relieve the woman who's taking care of my son. I've had a long day, and I just want to relax."

He half frowned and half smiled in a chiding way. "Aw, Kate . . . I can call you Kate, can't I? You're not giving me half a chance. Don't pay any attention to what old Hickson says about me, I'm—"

She cut him off. "Lieutenant, let me tell you that Captain Hickson has never said a word to me about you. Any impression I have of you is one you've given me."

He ignored that barb. "Oh, be a sport. I'm enchanted with you, and you know it." His face lit up with a smile. "I give a great massage."

She raised an eyebrow. "You mean you work two jobs? Does the police department know you moonlight as a masseuse?" His wounded look could only have been feigned, she decided.

She was not going out with Axel Strange. Might as well be straightforward. "Lieutenant Strange, I'm sorry, but I'm not going out with you."

A smile quickly erased his suddenly cold expression, causing her to wonder whether he lacked substance. "At least you didn't say never. Next time, okay?"

"Good night." She almost asked him to wait until she locked up, but thought better of it. If you gave Axel Strange an inch, he'd take a mile.

Since there hadn't been a customer in the last half hour, she figured she might as well close the store. She put the day's receipts in the safe, flicked off the lights, stepped out of the front door, and locked it.

"Give me your keys, lady."

Oh, Lord. Not again. Fear streaked through her, but she steadied her nerves. She knew her life might depend on her staying calm. "There aren't any keys to this store," she lied. "My security contractor has to open it from his computer."

"I'm talking about your house keys, and hurry up."

"I'm sorry," she said in a voice too strong to be hers, "but I don't have the house keys with me. I leave them with the superintendent, because she takes care of my . . . my place." She looked him in the eye, hoping to convince him.

"Don't give me all that crap. I mean the keys to your house in Biddle, and I want them this minute." He brandished something in his coat pocket that bore the shape of a handgun.

She glimpsed the squad car as it turned the corner, its high beam headlights piercing the twilight, and dashed toward the middle of the street. The car screeched to a halt, and Officer Cowan jumped out. The man raced off down the street.

"What's the matter?" Cowan yelled loudly. He had a hand on each of her arms.

She explained. "I don't have to tell you how glad I am to see your car. The man had just started to get rough."

Cowan yanked off his hat and scratched his head. "He's blocks from here now. I'll drop you home, but I want a description. Come by the precinct tomorrow before you open the store and give me the details."

As Cowan drove her home, she described the man as best she could, but she didn't mention her fear that the man knew Luke's moves and considered her vulnerable in Luke's absence.

At that moment, Luke was assuring himself that he could keep Kate at arm's length, enjoy her friendship, and leave it at that. He stopped at Dillards in Elizabeth City and bought a CD of Burl Ives songs for Amy, who had just discovered the late folksinger, and a toy rabbit for Marc. Amy didn't like sharing her own rabbit with Marc, but she loved the child so much that she didn't want to deny him anything. He bought a colorful set of Bambi and His Friends for Todd. The boy reminded him of Marcus as a small child, exacting a price for his cooperation. If Todd had to take a bath, he wanted as many animals in the tub with him as possible.

His mood shifted as he drove toward Caution Point. He'd been an uncle, first to his wife's nieces and nephews, and now to Amy, Marc, and Todd. He loved all of them, but he was forty-two years old and didn't have children of his own. He parked in front of his brother and sister-in-law's home—the one place where his cares always seemed to take wings, as though trouble was unwelcome there— but this time a cold loneliness seeped into him. He sat in the car for some minutes after parking, willing himself to put on a cheerful visage. Finally, he got out of the car, breathed deeply, and energized himself with the clean fresh smell of ocean air. He looked across Ocean Avenue at the dogwood trees adorned in pink and white blossoms, giving their trunks and limbs up to the will of the soft spring breeze. Birds chirped from the branches of the crab apple tree beside his car, and he felt his loneliness roll off him. Amanda and the children greeted him at the door.

With Amy holding one of his hands and Marc tugging on the other one, he followed Amanda to the back porch.

"Where's Marcus?"

"In Portsmouth. He should be getting home any minute. You didn't see him today?"

He stared at her. "Good grief. I told him I'd have lunch with him. I completely forgot it."

She looked at him as though he'd changed faces. "*You* forgot an appointment?" He understood her surprise. He had a reputation for having a memory like an elephant. She sat down, seemingly oblivious to having Todd examine her face and ears and yank on her hair and clothing. "Luke, you're either working too hard or something or someone has your undivided attention."

He couldn't help laughing. Amanda knew him better than the men who worked with him eight hours a day. "It'll soon be time to open up my place on the Sound, and that guarantees me some lazy weekends for the next four months." He reached for Todd. "Come here, fellow. It's time you and I got to be good friends."

The doorbell rang three times in rapid succession, and pain shot through him as Marc and Amy ran squealing to the door and Amanda broke off her sentence in the middle and followed them. He shook it off. After years of a lean life, his brother deserved all the happiness he'd found with Amanda and their children.

"I didn't realize you expected to have lunch here ... this evening," Marcus said to Luke after they embraced each other.

"Sorry about that, but I got into a set-to with Axel again, and had to straighten him out. I forgot about eating."

"That guy knows how to ring your bell."

Luke shrugged. "One day, he'll take it too far. How's it going at the factory?"

Marcus glanced at his wife, his eyes afire with love for her. "Things couldn't be better. How long you staying?"

Luke stretched out his long legs as Amy joined him in the swing, put his arms around his niece, and gently rocked. "I'm going straight from here to work Monday morning, unless—"

"Great. Maybe we can get in some fishing while you're here."

After dinner, his cell phone rang as he and Marcus cleaned the kitchen. "Captain Hickson."

He hadn't expected that Cowan would have to call him about Kate, but he'd told the sergeant to keep him posted. As a detective, he'd learned to avoid the pitfalls of *It might have been*. He listened to Cowan's report and wondered whether he ought to go back to Portsmouth.

"Nothing you can do, Luke. The man ran away when he saw the squad car, and we couldn't find him, but I turned that corner just in time."

"Continue to patrol that store. Good job, Sergeant."

"What was that about?" Marcus asked him. "Sounds like she's more to you than a professional responsibility," he added after hearing Luke's story. "If she is, I'm happy for you. It's time you got some joy in your life. Who is she?"

Luke stuffed his hands into his trouser pockets and looked toward the garden. "If she wasn't somebody's target—at least that's what she thinks—I'd go for her, but I can't let myself in for that again. I keep thinking of Eunice. She thought nothing could happen to her, that I'd keep her safe, but when she needed me I couldn't be there. Because she'd called me rather than nine one one, I lost her. I can't live through that again. A woman loves me and believes I'm larger than life, bigger than anything that can happen to her, and calls for me because she trusts me more than any other man—more than those who could have saved her."

Marcus stared at him, his eyes wide in astonishment. "You care for her."

"Could be. I'm not sure. It's happened so fast I can't figure out where the heck it came from." He eyed Marcus, who'd begun to laugh. "What's so funny, man?"

"You are. Have you forgotten? This thing gets you right away, and when it grabs you you might as well quit running."

"If anybody can attest to that, it's you," Luke said dryly. "I never saw a man run so hard from pure heaven as you did."

He'd never been able to figure out how Marcus could look so innocent when he was about to wade into a person. He waited for the blow, and Marcus let him have it. "Having witnessed that, brother, it seems to me you wouldn't waste your time running. Trust me, it's useless, anyway. You are not responsible for Eunice's death, so quit using that as an excuse to persecute yourself. And mark my word, if this woman gets into you, either get out of her way or enjoy it." He winked." I suggest the latter."

"You're loaded with wisdom tonight. Excuse me while I make a phone call."

"Sure thing. What's her name?"

"Kate," he called over his shoulder and strode down the hall to his room.

He dialed Kate's home phone number and paced back and forth in his room, waiting for her to answer. Where the heck was she? Strung out with anxiety, he redialed to be sure he'd used the right number.

"Hello."

"Randy. This is Captain Luke. Where's your mother?"

"She's out back. Captain Luke, I have to make my first deliveries Monday."

He was anxious to speak with Kate, and he hoped his impatience didn't show, because getting the boy's confidence was proving more difficult than he'd expected. "You've done well, Randy. I'm proud of you."

"You are?"

"You bet I am," he said truthfully. "And you'll be a fine role model for the boys in your group."

The small voice appeared uncertain. "I guess I have to try. They seem to like me."

So that was it. All the blustering, preening, and bad manners were a cover for insecurity. Maybe he'd have to spend more time with the child.

"Randy, of course the boys like you, and so do all of us officers."

"You too?"

He stared at the phone. "Son, the reason I insist you obey is because I want you to grow into a fine man, one people will admire and respect."

"Like you?"

He hesitated, but only for a second. "I'd be pleased if you wanted to be like me."

A long silence ensued, but he waited. "Gee. Okay. I'll get my mom."

"Luke. What a surprise. I wasn't expecting you to call."

"Cowan told me what happened. Did you get a good look at the man?"

She described the man who accosted her and added, "He wore glasses, but they might have been a disguise. Also, he wasn't the man who locked Randy and me in the store. This one was older and rougher. Robbing my store wasn't his priority. He was after my house keys."

None of it made sense to him, and its strangeness increased his concern. "I want you to put alarms on your door and windows, but we'll talk about that when I get back. Is your garden fenced?"

She told him it was, and eagerness laced her voice when she added, "When are you coming back?"

Was she telling him she wanted to see him? Oh hell, he had to stop thinking about her in that way. "I'm debating that right now. I have a feeling that hood knows me, and that he's seen us together, because he gave me forty-five minutes to get way out of town. And he didn't wait till dark to make his move. Did it occur to you that even though you closed more than an hour early, he was there waiting for you?"

He hadn't reasoned it out before, and now a pain scissored his belly. Simple robbery wasn't the man's motive, and until he knew what the guy wanted he'd be handicapped in his efforts to catch him.

"Be careful, Kate. I . . . Look, I don't want anything to happen to you and Randy. Keep him close to you this weekend. Kate—"

Her voice, soft and sweet, could tempt him to do things he didn't want to do. "What is it, Luke?"

"I'll call you when I get back there. Take good care." A strange undefinable emptiness suffused him, but he hung up without telling her he wanted to see her right then, that he feared for her well-being, and would go to any lengths to protect her.

"Is she okay?" Marcus asked when Luke joined him in the family room. It had been Amanda's living room before Marcus renovated the house and added a wing.

"Yeah. She's fine. I wish I could get a handle on this thing. She's vulnerable, and it occurs to me that I'd better put a man on Randy."

"Who's Randy?"

"Her eight-year-old son. He's wayward, and there's no telling what he'll get into."

"Send him down here when school's out. We'll soften him up."

"Thanks. We'll see about that. Look, I think I'd better head out of here tomorrow morning. I don't like anything about the report Kate and Cowan gave me. I'd better check on her."

"Sure," Marcus said, a grin easing over his face. "And give her a kiss for me while you're at it."

Luke rubbed the back of his neck, anxiety for Kate fighting for supremacy over his desire for her. "You're getting rather fanciful."

Marcus laughed. "Telling you like you told me, just like it is, brother. Get it together. Tell her you need her, and if she's reluctant, drag out the famous LSH charisma and change her mind. Man, you're supposed to be knock 'em dead irresistible. You're ruining your reputation."

Luke's left eyebrow arched. "I wouldn't mind if you kept thoughts like that to yourself. I don't need to hear this from you. I get enough of it from that gang I work with. Axel Strange is preoccupied with the subject of me and women."

Marcus shrugged. "Forget about Axel. A loser. The guy reminds me of a bullfrog on a rainy night croaking for the hell of it."

Worried as he was, Luke laughed. "Well said. See you in the morning."

Now who could that be at eight o'clock Saturday morning, and where was Tex, the doorman? Remembering Luke's words of caution the previous night, Kate opened the peephole. Anxiety, joy, fear, and eagerness battled for possession of her nerves, set her belly to churning, and her heart thumping. She slipped the lock and threw open the door.

"Luke . . . who . . . where? I thought you were in North Carolina." She sought to calm herself in the face of his nonchalance and in the absence of any obvious emotion on his part. From the expression in his eyes, she could have been a broom standing there.

"I asked you to call me if you needed me, but you didn't. I had to see that you're all right. It's my job."

Her joy at seeing him unexpectedly, at knowing he'd wrecked his weekend to see her, withered like wild dandelions beneath a shower of weed killer.

Her gaze caught the fist of his left hand, opening and closing in rapid succession as if he were keeping time or pumping air, and she looked back into his eyes, still casual and indifferent. If she had the nerve, she'd . . .

"I'll bet you haven't had breakfast, so why don't you come on in and have some coffee?"

When his lips parted, she knew he intended to refuse. She hadn't planned it, but then something in her reached out to him. She took his hand and tugged at it, displaying an aggressiveness that she knew surprised him.

"Come on. It's Saturday, and you have the day off. You can afford to waste half an hour with me, and I make great Columbian coffee."

He let her hold his hand as he followed her to the kitchen, and she doubted he would have gone so docilely if she hadn't staggered him with her forwardness. The feel of his big hand in hers filled her head with intimate ideas about him, and fired her body like torched gasoline. He didn't caress her fingers, merely let her hold his hand, so she had to release it.

He sipped the coffee without taking his gaze from her eyes. "I'm not in the habit of doing what I don't want to do."

Uh-oh. Here it comes, she thought. "I don't understand," she said, though she knew he hadn't wanted to enter her apartment.

"I think you do. I had my reasons for speaking with you at your door. For both our sakes, don't test my attraction to you. You may catch me when it's at fever pitch, and the temptation to howl outweighs everything else." He set the cup on the kitchen counter. "I'll be in touch."

She caught herself twisting her hands and stuck them behind her, praying he hadn't noticed. *Best to brazen it out.* She laid back her shoulders, tossed her head, and smiled.

"As far as I'm concerned, Luke, you'd have to do a lot

to unravel your character. Besides, you can't turn a Town Car into a Jeep.''

She couldn't figure out the message in those fiery gray eyes, but his words settled it. "No, but you can trash it. Thanks for the coffee. I'll find my way out."

He strode toward the short hallway, stopped, and turned. "Where's Randy?"

She stood straighter, intent on his knowing that nothing and no one got the better of her. "Randy's painting. It's one thing I don't have to urge him to do."

"Take care." He walked swiftly, almost as though he scented a prize.

She hated seeing women stand akimbo with their hands on their hips, but she did it then, frustration gripping every muscle of her body. Disgusted with herself, she threw up her hands and headed out back to her garden.

She paused on the porch. Why was she so riled up? She didn't want to become involved with him or any other man, did she? Her knees nearly buckled as the truth pierced her thoughts. She wanted him. She'd made a play for him because she'd recognized the vulnerability in him. He saw what she'd done, and let her know he didn't like it. Maybe she was reaching for a thin reed, but she was thirty-eight years old, already past her prime, and had never been in the arms of a man who put her interests, her fulfillment, and her well-being above his own. Luke Hickson would do that, and she wanted him. Deflated and saddened when she recalled his disinterested behavior minutes earlier, she reminded herself of the times when he'd behaved otherwise.

"Why can't I have him, if he wants me?" she asked. She looked at herself in the hall mirror, at the tiny lines at the edges of her still beautiful eyes and the slight creases across her forehead. *I'll take the consequences.*

Chapter Four

Luke got in his car, drove around the block, and stopped. He had to get a grip on his emotions. He rolled down the window and let the crisp bracing wind bruise his face. Memories of the peace he'd known with Eunice flooded his thoughts. Their tranquil moments, easy communication, and quiet loving came back to him, strong, vision-like, as if it had happened the day before. But was that what a man needed—contentment, a sameness that neither exercised the mind or the emotions? Yet, it had been good in its way. Eunice hadn't been imaginative about life, loving, or much else, but she'd always been there for him. And he'd loved her. How different his feelings for Kate! She challenged him, excited and galvanized him. Sometimes he had an urge to bend her to his will and, at others— like this morning—he wanted to open himself to her, let her have her way with him and watch her fly.

He turned the key in the ignition and eased away from the curb. A whole day on his hands. His heart told him he should be spending it with her, but for as long as she was under his protection he meant to stick to his guns and stay away from her.

He hadn't done it on purpose, but he found himself driving in the direction of her store.

He Glanced to the right as he neared it, and slammed on the brakes. Yellow and black chalk marks defaced the door and window of her store. He got out and examined them, searching for a symbol, because he was becoming increasingly more certain that Kate's in-laws had no part in the crimes against her.

He couldn't let her face that ugliness, so he drove to the housing projects just off Frederick Boulevard, got out, and knocked on Rude Hopper's door. He could depend on Rude for just about anything, including the man's vast knowledge of "the street" and what went on there. He'd gotten Rude's younger son away from a gang and into the Police Athletic League, where he exhibited leadership abilities, and he was now college bound. Rude couldn't do enough for him.

"I'll take a couple of friends over there, and it'll be good as new before noon," Rude told him after hearing about the vandalism. "You putting somebody there to watch the place?"

"I'll have a guard on duty from now on. Thanks, brother, I owe you one."

Rude shook his head. "Not me. I'm the one who's in your debt, and I always will be. We'll get right to it. And if I pick up on anything, I'll let you know."

Luke thanked him. Kate opened at twelve on Saturdays, so perhaps he'd saved her the shock of seeing the ugliness. He used his cell phone to call a junior detective and assign him to watch the store. That done, he drove out to Eunice's grave, placed some dogwood blossoms at the headstone, said a prayer, and walked back to his car. For reasons he couldn't understand, he felt lighter than he had in years, and he didn't question it. He picked up a stone and sent it twirling through the air as a sense of release washed over him. Amanda had begged him to try to bury the past, but he'd punished himself with guilt, and had never attempted to forget. He wondered if he could, and if Eunice had forgiven him for not being there when she needed him. For once, remembering didn't hurt so much.

When he went to bed that night, he gave himself points for refraining from calling Kate, but he could still smell her perfume, that spicy floral scent that stayed with him for hours after he'd been near her. Fit to bite nails, he swore at himself when images of her heated his loins, but then a strange peace flooded his being and, with a little effort, he put desire behind him.

He phoned her the next morning, told her about the vandalism and that he'd had the evidence of it cleaned off. She thanked him, and he asked himself why she didn't protest his protectiveness, as she usually did. That was something he had to watch.

Kate got to her store shortly before twelve and let out a deep breath when she saw nothing untoward, but as she unlocked the door she noticed the squad car sitting across the street and walked over to it.

"Are you stationed here, or just resting?" she asked the officer.

"Ma'am, Second Precinct detectives don't rest during working hours unless they want another job. I'm posted here."

"Well . . . thank you," was all she could manage. She went in her office and made coffee. Then she took a cup to the officer, who accepted it gratefully.

"Does everybody get this kind of service?" she asked him.

He took a few sips of coffee, and she could see how much he enjoyed it. "This is good stuff, and I was dying for some. Thanks a lot. Oh, yes," he said, remembering her question. "We do this whenever it's necessary. Just ignore me and go on about your business."

She didn't know what to make of Luke, protective yet distant. She wasn't a lamb born the day before, so he couldn't tell her that every citizen in Portsmouth could count on that level of protection. She was grateful that she hadn't seen her store defaced and that she didn't have to look over her shoulder every minute, but she hated that when men got interested in her they insisted on enclosing her in some kind of shell, as though she were a fragile embryo. She thought she'd left that behind when she buried Nathan. Still, she wouldn't dare complain because Randy needed her safe and healthy. It hung in the mirror of her mind like a brilliant Picasso painting that she was all her son had.

By the end of the day, three more people had signed up for the reading club, among them two sexy young women. If providence was kind to her, Axel would flip over one of them. The likelihood of that seemed remote, however, when Axel arrived at closing time bringing an embarrassingly large bouquet of red and yellow long-stemmed roses. She loved roses of all colors, and she didn't have the heart to scold him.

"You like them?" he asked, more pleased with himself than he had a right to be.

She tried to sound moderately disinterested. "I love roses. Is there a woman anywhere who doesn't?"

Self-satisfaction radiated from every part of him, and she knew he thought he'd scored big with her. "If I know anything," he boasted, "it's how to treat a woman, and especially one like you."

The door opened and Randy bounded in, followed by an off-duty policeman. She didn't think she'd ever been happier to see her son or anybody else.

"I made my rounds, Mom, and delivered the stuff to all

my clients." He turned to the officer who'd arrived with him. "I did real good, didn't I? Mom, this is my partner, Officer Jenkins."

She greeted the officer and shook hands with him, but she couldn't hide her embarrassment as Jenkins stared with all-knowing eyes from Axel to the oversize bouquet in her hand.

A frown eclipsed Randy's face as he stared at the flowers. "Where'd you get those, Mom?"

"Officer Strange just gave them to me."

Randy looked at the man. And looked and looked, while Jenkins watched. She couldn't help wondering how early in life the male of the species adopted territorial prerogatives. Randy had just served notice that he did not like Axel Strange and didn't want him around.

"Captain Luke helps me with my lessons," Randy said. "He's my friend."

She would have banished Randy to her office for that piece of one-upmanship, had not Jenkins begun laughing. And the more he laughed, the more he laughed. She squelched a giggle when she noticed that Randy had gone to stand beside Jenkins, and that Axel's face had become bloated from his ripening anger. Unable to think of a way out of it, she laid the flowers on a table and started toward the office for a vase. "I'd planned to tail you and Randy home, ma'am," Jenkins said, "but—"

She cut in quickly. "Thanks so much, officer. I'll be ready as soon as I get a container for these flowers."

She didn't know what the three of them said to each other in her absence, and she hardly cared, but she'd forever be grateful to Jenkins. Not that she disliked Axel—she didn't. But the man didn't seem capable of modest behavior. She brought out a plastic Chinese-style vase that she'd filled with water, arranged the roses in it, put the vase on the table, and left it there.

"Now the store will have a nice feminine touch," she

said in a gesture to Axel, and thanked him for the roses.
But a bunch of flowers, however beautiful and expensive,
didn't purchase her company, and he'd have to learn that.

She'd thought that had ended it until later that evening
when Randy leaned both elbows on her lap, looked up at
her, and said, "I don't like him. Don't let him come in
the store anymore."

She put an arm around him, loosely because he hated
to be petted. "Randy, my store is a public place, and unless
people misbehave, I can't prevent their entering it. That's
the law. Besides, he'd not a bad person."

"He's not like Captain Luke and Officer Jenkins, and
he doesn't like for us kids to go to the precinct. I don't
want him to give you any flowers."

As much as she loved Randy, she couldn't let him run her
life, but he needed assurance that Axel wasn't important to
her. "Don't worry about him, Randy. He isn't special to
me in any way."

"He isn't?"

"No, darling. Not at all."

"Gee." Evidently satisfied, he skipped out of the room.

Luke didn't care much for parties, not even fund-raisers
for PAL, but as a principal supporter of the organization
he knew that Mrs. Joshua Armstrong, as she liked to be
known, would be insulted if he didn't attend. He dressed
in a business suit, arrived around eight-thirty, and made
certain that his hostess and all of her guests saw him. Then,
he went out on the back porch and sat there in the darkness
away from the fawning women, small talk, and the scent
of liquor. Kate filled his thoughts, and he was glad she
hadn't come. If he didn't see her, he couldn't break his
promise to himself. He closed his eyes and let the night
air blow over him, invigorating him.

Kate hadn't wanted to be the last person to arrive, but

she didn't relish being the first at a party, either. She greeted Mrs. Joshua Armstrong, resplendent in a long red hostess gown—a throwback to the thirties, Kate thought—and took a look around her. She wished she'd stayed home. Axel Strange was the only person she knew in that huge room filled with Portsmouth's moneyed class. Having found her way to an opposite corner of the room, she refused the smoked oysters, wines, and liquors that the waiter offered her and opted for a glass of club soda; after all, she didn't have a designated driver.

"I looked all over for him," an attractive fortyish woman who stood nearby said to her female companion.

"I asked Mrs. Armstrong if he'd showed up, and she said he was out on the back porch, probably asleep, since he hates parties," the woman replied.

"*Asleep?* In that case I wasted my time coming here. I've been dying to meet that man. Girl, if I ever get my hands on that hunk, he can look out."

The snicker that followed would have discouraged most women. "Honey, what have you got that the rest of us *don't* have? Luke Hickson is as elusive as quicksilver. Getting that man is about as easy as grabbing a handful of air."

Kate didn't wait to hear more.

Suddenly alert, Luke cocked his ear at the sound of footsteps, though he didn't open his eyes. And then, tongues of fire leaped through him like a roaring furnace, and he braced himself. Waiting. Delicate fingers covered his eyes, barely touching his flesh. He didn't breathe, couldn't breathe, as he awaited the next move. His breath nearly exploded from his lungs as soft half-parted lips caressed his own, twin butterflies sipping nectar. When he flicked his tongue against them, asking entrance, he heard a quick gasp, then rapid steps—heaven flying from his grasp. The screen door slammed, and he sprang out of the chair and went after her. She could lie if she wanted to, but he knew the wearer of that perfume. Gone was his reticence, his resolve to leave her alone. She'd whetted his appetite and kicked his libido into high gear, and he knew he wouldn't rest until he'd caressed every centimeter of her naked flesh, and lost himself in her.

He found her in conversation with Axel Strange. "Hello, Kate. Imagine finding you *in here.*" He nodded to Axel. "Evening, Lieutenant."

Her smile shone with innocence, but that meant little to him. "You wouldn't have been a track star at some earlier time, would you?" he asked her.

"What does that mean?" Axel asked, his face clouded with unfriendliness. "Haven't you noticed the lady and I are in a conversation?"

Luke lifted his shoulder in a careless shrug and pinned Kate with a stare that he didn't intend her to decipher. "You've been deep in this conversation for every bit of twenty seconds." He winked at her. "Right, Kate? By the way, madame, that's great perfume you're wearing. I'd recognize it anywhere."

He had the pleasure of seeing her blanch and lower her eyes. "What's the matter, Kate? Having trouble getting your tongue to work?" A grin formed on his mouth, and, to his surprise, he enjoyed her discomfort.

"You're in a creative mood tonight, Captain. Very imaginative," she said, though he could tell from the lack of strength in her voice that her heart wasn't in her little act.

He folded his arms across his chest. "Indeed, I am. Thanks to you." Then, to emphasize his point, he rimmed his top lip with his tongue and watched her eyes take on a smoldering haze that betrayed her awareness of him. An answering passion slammed into him. He had to get out of there. "Watch yourself, Kate, and stay out of mischief. Good night."

At home later that night, he sat at his desk shuffling through his mail. Frustrated and piqued that Kate had used Axel as cover for her daring act, he crushed a sheet of paper in his fist and tossed it into the wastebasket. He itched to get his hands on her—even talking to her would be better than nothing—but damned if he'd call her after that cute trick she pulled, kissing him so sweetly and then running away and staging that scene with Strange. All right, so she'd kissed him on an impulse. Why couldn't she admit it?

An airmail letter with a French stamp. Now what could that be? He read it a second time—an invitation to speak at the INTERPOL conference in Nairobi on ways of identifying drug couriers. His interception of a courier had effectively busted a drug ring, and he'd known the operation had gained international attention, *but an invitation from INTERPOL!* A detective thought twice before he turned his back on that august international crime-fighting organization. He replied, accepting the invitation, and was about to seal the envelope when he stopped, leaned back in his chair, and gazed at the ceiling. *What would happen to Kate and Randy if he was out of the country for ten days?* And why did he care so much? All of a sudden, he could feel her lips on him, his mouth tasted of her, and the scent of her perfume came back to him fresh and strong, dancing around his nostrils and heating his blood. He let out an expletive and reached for the phone.

She should have known Axel would be a problem, though if he realized she'd used him to mislead Luke, he didn't voice the sentiment.

"I'll see you home," he announced when she told him she had to leave.

Not if I can avoid it, she told herself. "Thanks, Lieutenant, but I'm driving. Good night."

He let her know he had the tenacity of a Brahman bull— not that it surprised her. She didn't consider him naive or insensitive, but he behaved as if he were, and she'd like to know what he was up to.

"Then I'll tail you. You're in my care, and I'll see you home."

Like a petulant child's, his voice began to rise. Rather than let herself be enmeshed in a scene, she said nothing, thanked her hostess, and left. Besides, she didn't enjoy hurting anyone, and Axel didn't deserve unkindness even though he had a penchant for annoying her.

He followed her as she'd known he would, but he wasn't going into her house. When she reached home, she got out of her car and walked back to him.

"Thanks, Axel. I'm going in through the garage. Good night."

The muscles of his jaw worked, and his face took on a harsh veneer. She started back to her car, but he grabbed her arm.

"Be careful, Axel. I don't like to be touched."

His nostrils flared. "Do you tell Hickson that?"

She knocked his hand off her arm and looked him in the eye. "Captain Hickson has never grabbed my arm."

"Have you let him touch you?"

It was none of his business, but she couldn't resist needling him. "He hasn't tried to *touch me,* as you put it."

His face contorted, and she stepped back, not sure she could trust his self-control. "You want me to believe that? The guy's the biggest womanizer in Portsmouth."

If Luke was, she hadn't seen any evidence of it. She took several steps toward her car. "That's probably all in your imagination. You can believe what you like."

"When can I see you again?"

Better get it straight right now, she thought. "You and I are just friends, Lieutenant, and that's all we can ever be."

All she could think of as she looked at his teeth, bared in a snarl, was the eternally angry bulldog owned by the next door neighbor when she was a small child. She'd been scared of that dog, but Axel Strange didn't perturb her in the least.

"Don't be too sure of that," he said. "Lover Boy doesn't stick with one woman for long. You'll soon see where you stand."

She walked back to him, fists clenched and the print of her nails scoring her palms. "Why do you think I'm limited to a choice of you or him? You need to downsize your ego. Good night." Of all the arrogance! She got in her car, slammed the door, and drove into the garage. The guy needed a reality check.

She gave silent thanks when Madge announced that Randy was asleep, pleaded a headache, and left without her usual small talk. Kate went to the refrigerator for a glass of ginger ale, but as she leaned against the kitchen counter sipping the drink, she hardly tasted it. What had gotten into her? She hadn't meant to do more than greet Luke and spend a few minutes with the one person at the party whose company she would enjoy. But she'd looked at him, his head back, eyes closed, and his face peaceful and sweet. She'd glanced at his long legs stretched out in front of him and at the silky lashes that hid his gray eyes. It had taken less than a second, but she'd seen him there asleep and open to her whims, and her mouth found his. First came a flash of heat, and then alarm shot through her when his lips moved beneath hers, and his tongue asked for entrance into her mouth. Unused to being aggressive with men, she'd fled.

The phone rang and she raced to prevent it from waking Randy, hoping she wouldn't hear Axel Strange's voice on the other end.

"Yes?"

"I assume you knew I'd call."

She sat down and breathed deeply, steadying her nerves. "Why would I know that?"

"Hang it all, Kate," he said in obvious exasperation,

"you wore that perfume the first time I saw you, and you've had it on every time I've seen you since then. Why did you kiss me?"

The sudden acceleration of her heartbeat frightened her. "Wh . . . what do . . . Luke, do you think I'm the only woman who wears that perfume?"

"You were the only one wearing it at Martha Armstrong's house tonight. Unless you want me at your front door minutes from now, answer me. Why'd you do it?"

"Luke, I'm . . . I'm tired. Please say good night."

"If you're tired, it's because you had to tussle with Axel. You'll learn not to play with him. But that's what you did. You used him, and he'll make you pay. Why did you kiss me?"

She wasn't a child that he could back into a corner. "You were there, and I . . . I wanted to."

She could hear his breathing accelerate. "Next time, warn me."

Flustered because she hadn't thought he'd find her out, she rubbed her left side with her free hand. "There won't be a next time."

His laugh came through the wire harsh and knowing. "Oh yes, there will. You started it because you know how much I want you, and you're going to find out how I act when a woman I want wants *me*, and what it's like to kiss me. Count on it."

"Luke, please. I apologize. Let's—"

He interrupted. "You *what*? Don't hand me any apology, lady. You want me as much as I want you, and from now on you'll be the one who puts up the off limits sign. I hadn't planned it, I didn't think it wise, and I fought it—"

"There's no reason for us to get involved. We can just be friends."

His laugh had the sound of an angry growl. "I tasted

you. I want more, and I'm going to have more, with your full and joyful cooperation. I finish what I start."

"You didn't start it."

"That's because you ran. But you can slow down. I'm through punishing myself."

Her fingers rubbed her sides, and she paced back and forth. "Luke, I've walked that road and, except for Randy, most of what I got was unhappiness. Before we married, my husband said I was the flower of his life, but as soon as he had to tend that flower he let it wither to nothing. He promised everything wonderful and delivered ten years of misery. What I want is irrelevant. All I need now is peace for Randy and me."

"That was some other man, not this one. You ought to know that if you kiss a man the way you kissed me, he's going after you unless he's got dead nerves and two peg legs."

She pulled the front bodice of her dress away from her dampened flesh, picked up a magazine that lay on the bed, and fanned rapidly. "Luke, I . . . You were out there alone with your eyes closed, quiet. In the dark, you seemed so vulnerable, and . . . and helpless. I—"

"That was in your mind, baby. I heard your footsteps coming toward me and smelled that perfume before you opened the screen door. I knew who was kissing me, and I wanted it. Otherwise, it never would have happened."

Abruptly he changed the subject. "I'm going to Africa in a couple of weeks, and I'm concerned about leaving you and Randy here alone, at the mercy of whoever's pestering you. I'll work out a plan, and I want you to follow it and see that Randy does."

"Luke, I don't want any more pampering. I've had my fill of it."

"I know you're capable of taking care of yourself, but we're dealing with real crime here, and a determined criminal. If you're not going to do as I say, tell me right now and I'll cancel the trip."

"You wouldn't do that!"

"It's my duty. Look . . . I . . . Have lunch or dinner with me tomorrow. If you're busy then, let's make it breakfast. I want to see you."

He moved like a cyclone, and she could see herself getting caught in the whirling cone of his determination. "You put a twenty-four-hour watch on the store, and Officer Cowan patrols the store regularly, so I don't see what else I need."

"We'll discuss whatever else you need when we're together tomorrow. Suppose we make a day of it. I'll be over for breakfast. What time?"

"Should I have a notebook handy?"

"For what?"

"I wouldn't want to forget what you have to say about what you think I need."

"Trust me, sweetheart, I'll see that you don't."

She knew she should end it right there. He excited her as no man ever had, and she knew she'd find all that she longed for with him, but she had a premonition that getting involved with him could bring her more pain than Nathan Middleton had ever caused her.

She ignored her inner voice. "By nine o'clock Randy's starving," she said, feeling spineless.

"Then I'll be there at nine . . . if it's all right with you, that is."

He had a quality of grace, a gentlemanly demeanor, even when, like now, he was overbearing. But she didn't care that he'd pushed her a little hard; she wanted to see him every bit as much as he wanted to see her.

She swallowed, and had to clear her throat. "It's fine with me."

"You sure?"

"If you're asking if I'm sorry I caved in, I won't know the answer until after tomorrow, and maybe not even then."

"That's right—leave no row unhoed. Nothing like a straightforward answer to keep the record clear. We'll make a day of it?"

"If Randy doesn't have a program."

"Come off it, woman. What kind of program can Randy have that you didn't arrange? You don't need an excuse, Kate. If you don't want to see me, just say no."

She bristled. "How is it that you're such a genius at vexing me? If I wanted to say no, I would. I never do anything I don't want to do. We're that much alike. And you stop trying to bamboozle me. See you in the morning."

She could feel the warmth and the enticement of his laughter through the wires, masculine and suggestive—an invitation to madness, a lure that she didn't want to resist.

"Way to go. I like your tinsel. With you, a man has to stay on his toes, eat his Wheaties, and keep his engine fine-tuned. Till tomorrow."

"Tomorrow." She stared at the phone until the operator told her to hang up. Gone was her bravery of hours earlier, when she'd parted her lips and kissed him. Shivers plowed through her as she let her mind tease her with visions of the ways in which he'd make her pay.

Luke gazed at the food spread out on Kate's dining room table—Plenty of everything the Yankees crammed into their stomachs, but not a biscuit in sight.

"Kate, do you know how to make biscuits?"

"Of course I do."

"And grits and sage sausage, and scrambled eggs?"

"Sure."

"Then—"

"When I start eating that stuff, especially biscuits, I can't stop, and all of it's fattening. And don't tell me I don't have to start, because I can't pass up a biscuit. I'll make some at your place and leave while they're baking, but not here."

Her lashes flew up and a soft gasp escaped her when he pulled her nose and winked at her. "I'll buy that."

"Where're we going, Captain Luke?" Randy asked when they'd finished breakfast.

"Wherever your mother wants to go. Hop in the kitchen and help. If she cooks, you help her clean. I'd help, too, but she asked me to repair this table lamp."

"You're always telling me what to do."

Luke put a hand on the boy's shoulder. "If you behave the way you're supposed to, the only words you'll hear from me will be praise. Now, into the kitchen."

Randy dashed toward the kitchen, and he put his attention on the lamp. Not a second alone with her, and how he itched and ached to get his hands on her. Twenty minutes later she reappeared in a red blazer, navy blue miniskirt, and a pair of sandals laced to midcalf. Her hair fell loose and sexily around her shoulders. He crossed his thighs. She had to know what she did to him. He took a pad and pen from his jacket. "What's the name of that perfume?"

"Fendi."

He wrote it down. "It's worth whatever it costs. Ready?" She nodded. "Could we go look at the boats?"

"You bet. Ever been to the naval base? It's the biggest in the country."

He loved to see her smile, her face sparkling, and the eyes that reminded him of a lover's moon in spring. "I haven't been there yet, but I'd been planning to take Randy."

"Can we get on a boat, Captain Luke?"

It surprised him that Randy took his hand as they boarded *The Carrie B*, a paddlewheel riverboat, for a harbor tour. He pointed out the gray ladies of the United States

Atlantic Fleet—nuclear-powered submarines, destroyers, and aircraft carriers, great hulking figures that seemed out of place against the bright modern buildings that graced the shoreline.

"What's on your mind, Kate?" he whispered while Randy gaped at a mammoth aircraft carrier, lost in the wonder of it.

When she didn't respond, he realized that she, too, was caught up in the magic of the setting as the sun's rays bounced off the green, gray, and black-shaded skyscraper windows and danced in rainbow like colors against the fleet of ships.

He took her hand and relaxed when she let him hold it, but he didn't consider that cause for overconfidence. This wasn't a woman who allowed her libido to dictate the terms of her life; she was as capable as he of turning her back on something she wanted. With gentle pressure, he squeezed her fingers until she looked into his eyes and smiled, and he thought he'd die from the furious pounding of his runaway heart. Her unsuccessful attempt to shift her gaze from his fueled his need, and when she parted her lips and her breathing accelerated, frissons of heat shot through him. She must have seen the signs of his rising passion, for she dropped his hand, rushed to Randy, and put an arm around the boy's shoulders.

"Look, Captain Luke, a submarine's coming up out of the water."

He joined them at the railing as the huge gray vessel broke through the water. Again, Randy took his hand, and he wondered at the child's impulse. Kate wouldn't look at him, and the scene gave him an uneasy feeling, a portent of things to come. *The Carrie B* eased back to shore, but Randy didn't want to get off.

"You must learn to obey your mother and stop giving her a hard time," Luke told him. "She's trying to take care of you, so you cooperate with her."

Randy whirled around and glared at him. "My daddy never talked to me like that. I don't like for you to tell me what to do."

"Mind your manners, Randy," Kate said.

If she wants to raise that boy to be a respectable man, Luke thought, *she wouldn't do it that way.*

He looked at Kate. "I'd wanted us to spend the day together. But I'm not taking another ride on this boat, and I don't allow children to sass me with impunity, so I'll see you another time."

"We're getting off this boat now," she said through clenched teeth, "and Randy is going to apologize to you."

"Aw, Mom."

"This minute, Randy, or my hand is going to your behind."

"I'm s . . . sorry, Captain Luke."

He could hardly believe it when Randy's hand grasped his again. "Apology accepted, Randy." He'd like to know Randy's method of controlling his father, because that was what he'd done. Well, it wouldn't work with him.

Kate sat across from Randy and Luke in a booth at Seaman's Little Nook in Olde Towne, chosen because the management advertised its friendliness to families with children. She thought it peculiar that Randy had elected to sit with Luke rather than her, but didn't say so.

"How long will you be away, Luke?"

His gray-eyed gaze, warm and sensuous, sent her blood flying through her veins. "Ten days, at best. Lieutenant Strange will be in charge in my absence."

Randy grabbed Luke's arm. "No. You can't. I don't like him, and I'm not going to make rounds for him."

"The seniors are counting on you, Randy. As for Strange, he knows how to run the shop. He's done it before."

"But he doesn't like for us kids to go to the precinct,

and besides, he brought my mom a whole lot of smelly flowers. I don't like him."

For a second, Luke focused his gaze on her eyes. Then he shrugged and turned his attention to Randy. "Remember, you're leader of your group and responsible for its members. I expect a good report."

Ten days under the microscopic protection of Axel Strange. If she could afford it, she'd take an out-of-town vacation.

As if answering her unarticulated prayers, Luke asked her, "Want to go to Caution Point with me next weekend?"

Before she could answer, Randy asked, "Me, too?"

"Captain Luke and I will have to discuss that, Randy." She prepared herself for his usual pouting, but he surprised her.

"I guess I could stay with Miss Madge, except I'm starting to hate Bugs Bunny. He's all she ever wants to watch."

Randy raced to his room to play computer games, and she sat with Luke in her living room, her nerves as steady as a leaf in a hurricane. His warm thigh touched her leg, the rough cotton of his trousers brushing the flesh that her miniskirt exposed. She stopped herself from rubbing her arms and placed her hands in her lap. A glance told her that if he looked he could see the hardened tips of her breasts, and she started to get up, but he restrained her.

"You're bold and brazen when you think you can get away with it, but now that I'm touching you, you're hardly breathing. If I didn't know better, I'd think you were a novice where men are concerned." Still holding her hand, he stood. "Did you give Strange a reason to bring you flowers?"

She'd wondered why he hadn't mentioned it. "You know

that man well enough to understand that he doesn't need anybody's reason but his own."

"I take it that was a no."

She nodded. "He surprised me."

"Yeah. I'll just bet he did. He'll spring one on you again, too." He stared into her eyes. "I'm not going to compete with one of my men, and that's all I have to say about this."

Still holding her hand, he started toward the door, and she prayed her rubber legs wouldn't betray the wildness that had suddenly caught her as she wondered if he'd kiss her, and prayed that he wouldn't. Heat gathered in her like a mass of smelting ore, increasing in temperature as they got closer to her foyer.

There, in the dim light with barely inches between them, he turned to her. "Whatever you wanted to do to me last night, you can do now with my permission and full cooperation."

"It's ... it's not sporting to ... to embarrass me like this."

"Is it sporting to kiss a man when you have him at a disadvantage?"

"I ... Luke, please. What do you want from me?"

Every atom of her body plunged into a frenzy when the smoldering fire of desire suddenly blazed to life in his eyes. "You know what I want. I want you in my arms. If you don't want to be there, tell me this minute before this thing roars out of control."

"It's not a matter of what I want. I have to fend for myself and Randy, and that means not being involved with a man."

"The two are unrelated," he growled. "You knew when you kissed me that this minute would come. Put your arms around me, Kate."

She wanted to. Oh, how she wanted to hold him. But she couldn't make herself move. "I ... Luke, for heaven's sake!'' His hands. The feel of his strong fingers on her body. Stroking, caressing. Her hands went to his shoulders, and he pulled her to him. If he'd only . . . she thought she'd explode if he didn't. And then with one hand around her hips and the other across her shoulders, he brought her up to him.

"Kate, kiss me. *Open your mouth and kiss me.*"

Her lips quivered, and a sweet weakness stole over her as she gave in to him. Tension gathered in her, but she fought for possession of herself. Finally, she knew the touch of his lips, and tremors streaked through her. She thought she'd been kissed, but she'd hardly parted her lips when his velvet tongue slid into her mouth as he held her head still. Hot needles of desire shot to her love tunnel, and still she tried to hold back, to prevent his knowing how he affected her. Then he set her on her feet, spread his legs and locked her to him. She couldn't stand it any longer. Her hand went to his buttocks, straining him to her while his tongue frolicked in her mouth, learning her, finding its home and staking its claim. She felt the perspiration that beaded her forehead and knew she should stop him, but his tongue stroked in and out of her mouth, telling her how he wanted to make her feel, and a heavy ache began in her breasts, sensations she'd never known. She grabbed his hand and placed it on her right breast, and had to muffle a cry when his fingers began to pinch, stroke, and tease. Her whimpers must have told him that she needed more, for he fumbled at the buttons of her blouse. And, like a shameless wanton, she helped him. Seconds later she moaned in relief and frustration as his lips closed over one aureole and sucked until she moved against him.

She had to stop him—but the feeling, oh, the blessed feeling! She wanted it to last, and . . . a strange throbbing took hold of her body, and she gasped. Stunned, he brought his head up and looked at her.

"What happened. Did I . . . I didn't hurt you, did I?"

It was the moment she needed. "No. I . . . It wasn't you. It was—"

She couldn't look at him, and she wouldn't; if he knew what had just happened to her, there was no telling what he'd think. She wished she wouldn't tremble, and she wished he'd leave, though she didn't want him to go.

He tilted her chin up, let her see the hot need in his eyes, and clarified the matter. "Do you want me to stay, or would you rather I left?"

His knowing look, full of fire and unbridled desire yet compassionate, nearly undid her. "Tell me what you want, Kate. Nothing that happened between us just now is cause for shame. You're just as I thought you'd be, as I wanted you to be." His voice softened. "Was it too much for you?"

She let herself look at him, trying with all her might to understand what he meant to convey. "Some day you'll understand. You . . . You're a wonderful man."

His half smile, wan and rueful, made her want to hug him. "Thanks. I think. Maybe I'd better leave. Will you be okay?"

Pretense was out of place, so she opted for honesty. "I don't know. I haven't had any experience with . . . with this level of . . . well, you know."

He gathered her into his arms and held her. "Thank you for sharing that with me. When you leave this house, be careful getting in and out of your car, and . . . oh, for Pete's sake. We're going to have to do something about this one way or the other, and we've known that from the beginning."

"I know. You go on home now. Okay?"

His lips seared hers as he squeezed her to him. "Remember what I said. I won't compete with one of my men. All right?"

She nodded, opened the door, and watched him stride down the corridor and out of the building.

"Where's Captain Luke? I wanted him to come see my room. I even straightened it up."

Her hand flew to her mouth. She'd forgotten Randy was in the apartment. "You were supposed to be going to bed, so he didn't disturb you." At his crestfallen expression, she added, "You may show it to him the next time he comes."

"Gee. I'll have to clean up again." His face brightened as though a light beamed on him. "Did he say he was coming back to see us?"

Now, how did she answer that? "I'm sure he'll be back. Now give a hug and go to sleep."

She dropped on the edge of her bed, leaned forward, covered her face with her hands, and tried to work her way out of the haze in which Luke had left her. She hadn't wanted him to go. He had to know that, just as he'd known what happened to her. For a second, she toyed with the notion of calling him, but resisted it. For the first time in her life, she knew physical desire, the feeling that nothing else mattered but relief. In ten years of marriage, she hadn't come close to it. She sat up and shook her head. She had to make a success of her bookstore, and she had to prove to herself and her in-laws that she could raise and support her child. *Luke! Luke!* He filled her head, and she could still taste him, feel his hands on her flesh, and smell his special masculine scent. Attentive and loving—he was that and more. But hadn't Nathan been the same before they married? She believed Luke was different, but he would interfere with her focus, her goal of independence and security, and she couldn't afford that. But, oh Lord, she wanted that man!

Still poleaxed by the passion Kate unleashed in him, Luke walked into his town house co-op and looked around. He'd purchased it a year earlier when he'd gotten a bonus along with his promotion to captain. He had loved its uncluttered serenity and charm, nestled as it was in a grove of willows and dogwood trees. Its simple masculine elegance pleased him and complemented his need for freedom. In his living room, soft beige leather chairs and a matching sofa sat on a Turkish carpet woven of orange, beige, and brown fibers. Books filled the wood paneling that covered one wall from the floor to the cathedral ceiling. The paintings of little-known but gifted African-American artists adorned another. From windows the height of the room, he could see willows swaying in the breeze and dogwood blossoms that smiled arrogantly in their aristocratic glory.

He flicked off the light and climbed the stairs, winded from the weakening force of his desire. The flame she'd ignited still burned in him. In his forty-two years, he hadn't had a woman lose every semblance of inhibition with him as Kate had. He didn't want to think of what she'd be like if he had her naked in his bed. Where would it take him? He couldn't imagine not going all the way with her, because it wasn't in his nature to leave anything half done. He shook his head. What kind of man had she married who could have lived with her for a decade without assuring her fulfillment? Laughter spilled out of him—partly in frustration, but mainly in self-mockery. His chances of walking away from her were practically nonexistent, because he didn't believe for a second that she'd let him do it. He needed a strategy, and he had to walk carefully.

Chapter Five

"I'll be away approximately ten days. These are my orders, and I want every one of them enforced. When I get back, I want a report on that case of suspected arson on my desk. Signed. Any questions?"

"You don't want much," Axel said. "If I have to run the shop, how am I going to get that report ready?"

Luke looked toward the ceiling, let out a long breath, and threw up his hands. "That report was due over a week ago, when you didn't have anything else pending. I don't care how you manage, as long as you do it."

He looked into Axel's narrowed eyes and stared at the man, unflinching, forcing Axel to blink first. The man's opinion of himself could stand diluting. He leaned back in his chair and laced his voice with authority. "I'm sure you can handle it, but if you don't think so . . ." He let the alternative form in Axel's imagination.

"Sure, man. Nothing to it. Say, who's going to handle the kids in PAL? Other than Jenkins, I mean."

Luke stared into Axel's eyes. "You are, Lieutenant." He

made a ceremony of locking his desk drawers, cabinets, and computer. "I've got a few stops to make, so it's time I got out of here."

He wondered at the look of disappointment on Axel's face until the man said, "Suppose I need some records?"

Savoring the sweetness of it, Luke let himself grin. "The only records in my office are yours and your colleagues, and you're not entitled to see those. Sergeant King has all other records. Let's go. I have to lock up."

"You . . . You're locking your office?"

Luke forced himself not to grin. "Why not? Everything in here's locked up, and you'll be using your own office."

He locked the door and patted Axel on the shoulder. "I'm depending on you to keep everything straight." As he gazed at Axel, he knew his eyes conveyed his double meaning, including his warning not to crowd Kate. "See you."

"Yeah," Axel said, the word coming slowly. "See you."

Luke called a taxi and rushed out of the precinct headquarters just as the cab drove up. "Airport, please, but I want to make a quick stop at eighty ninety-one Forest Street."

He loved the way she had of greeting him at the store's door, as though he were entering her home. "Hi. How's it going today?"

"Business is good. What time does your plane leave? I could run you to the airport."

"Thanks, but you'd have to close up. Anyway, I have a taxi waiting. Where's Randy?"

"In my office."

"Come with me." Holding her hand, he went in the office, where they found Randy studying.

"What's INTERPOL, Captain Luke? Mom said you're going to INTERPOL."

"Its real name is *International Police Cooperation*. Police forces in its member countries—and there're one hundred and seventy-seven of them—cooperate in apprehending criminals."

Randy gaped in awe. "Gee. Is it in Nairobi? I've been checking my map to see where you'll be."

"No, it isn't in Kenya. That's where the conference will be held. INTERPOL'S headquarters is in Lyon, France."

"What are you going to talk about, Luke?"

He looked at his watch. "Apprehending drug couriers." *Wonder what caused that?* he asked himself, when a quick frown creased Kate's forehead. Probably his imagination. "I've got to get out of here. Randy, I expect you to cooperate with Officer Jenkins and Lieutenant Strange over at PAL, and be good to your mother."

Randy buried his head in his work and didn't answer, but Luke didn't have time to sort it out. He kissed Kate on the cheek and left.

Kate imagined that Luke couldn't have gotten to the airport before Axel Strange walked into her store. She pretended not to see him, and busied herself with her customers. "When's the first meeting of the reading club?" he asked after walking to within two feet of where she stood. At least he had the grace not to get overly friendly with her in front of her customers.

"Haven't gotten around to scheduling one, Lieutenant. There doesn't seem to be much enthusiasm for one."

The last of the customers paid for his purchase and left, and the triumph of Axel's smile shouted as loudly as a blaring trumpet. She whirled away from him and headed for her office. If he followed her there, she'd tell him a thing or two.

He followed her. She'd temporarily forgotten about Randy studying there. She stopped short, and Axel almost stumbled over her.

"What are you doing?" Randy yelled at Axel. "Take your hands off my mom."

"It's all right, Randy," Kate hastened to say. "I stopped short, and he tripped over me."

She couldn't believe the hostility reflected in her son's eyes as he glared up at the six-foot-three-inch officer. "Go on with your work, Randy. Lieutenant Strange only stopped by to see how we're getting along."

Randy's astuteness stunned her. That the boy had discovered Axel's Achilles' heel was clear when he said, "Captain Luke came by to see how we are a couple of minutes ago."

When she saw Axel's lips curve into a snarl, she didn't utter the words of reprimand she'd planned for Randy. In a flash, however, Axel replaced his snarl with his patented smile.

"Actually, I wanted to ask you to have dinner with me, Kate."

"She can't," Randy said, " 'cause I got a upset stomach, and I don't feel so good."

Kate didn't laugh, though not doing so took a good deal of self-control. "I'm sorry, Lieutenant. Not tonight."

His lips quivered, and she noticed that his Adam's apple bobbled rapidly. Too bad. She wasn't going to have dinner with him just to make him happy.

"I'm in charge of the department for the next ten days, you know," Axel said, as though indicating his status would salvage his pride.

"Yes, I know," Kate said. "Captain Hickson told me you'd be in charge. Now, if you'll excuse me, I'd better see to those two customers who're wandering around out there."

Three afternoons later, she gazed in horror at Officer Jenkins's sheet-white face, when he walked into the store, stopped in front of her, shook his head, and didn't say a word.

"What is it? What's the . . . *Officer Jenkins, where is Randy?*"

Jenkins shook his head, more slowly this time. "Ma'am, I was hoping I'd find him here with you."

"What happened?"

Jenkins dropped into the lounge chair that she had placed opposite the cash register for tired shoppers. "He got into it with Strange, and—"

Her mind shut down, and she looked down at her fingers. She couldn't feel a thing, and the shelves full of books blurred into a mass of rainbow colors. Why didn't she panic? "What do you mean by that? Did he sass Lieutenant Strange?" Surely that calm voice didn't belong to her.

"He refused to make rounds," Jenkins told her. "Said he wasn't doing anything for Strange. And when Strange tried to force him, he turned and ran off. What got me was he seemed to have planned to do that."

She sat down on the other end of the sofa. "Randy told me that he wasn't going to do anything Lieutenant Strange asked him to do, and I said that if he didn't obey Strange I'd lift all of his privileges for the next three months."

"Uh . . . I don't think I like what I'm hearing. Randy is strong-willed, but he's a good kid. Strange doesn't know a thing about kids, and they don't like him. He yelled at Randy and told him he was Luke's pet."

Needles and pins attacked her toes and fingers. She sprang to her feet. "I have to find him."

"I told Strange to put out an alarm on him, but he said it was too early. I'm off duty, so I'll go with you."

She grabbed her pocketbook, remembered the cash register, and stored the day's take in the safe. "I don't know what I'll do if—"

Her heart nearly stopped as the telephone ring jarred her into immobility.

Jenkins answered. "She's right here, sir."

She grabbed the phone, anxious to tell Axel Strange what she thought of him. *"Hello!"* She all but screamed it.

"Hi. Don't be upset. He's probably just hi—"

"Luke! Where are you? How did you know? Axel won't let anybody—"

Luke interrupted. "I'm in Nairobi. Jenkins telephoned me about twenty minutes ago. Stop worrying. I've talked with the Chief, and he's got a search out for Randy. Try to calm down. Everything that can be done will be done."

"But he's never done anything like this before."

"We'll deal with that after we find him."

She wanted to tell him that she'd be more confident about that with him in charge, but with Jenkins standing a couple of feet from her, she couldn't say anything personal. Her thoughts must have reached him telepathically, for he voiced them.

"I hate being so far away from you right now, and I ought to be there looking for him. Hell, if I'd been there, it wouldn't have happened."

"You . . . you did what you could." A glance at Jenkins as he moved away let her know that he might have caught the intimacy of her tone. She was certain of it when he walked out of the office and closed the door.

"Yeah. But if I had been there . . . I had a peculiar feeling about this whole trip, and I shouldn't have come."

"Luke, please don't punish yourself. This isn't your fault."

"He's all right. You understand that? I'll see you soon."

"I hope so. Bye."

He hung up. Maybe he was one of those people who didn't like saying good-bye. She flicked off the light, walked out of the office, and joined Jenkins. Nothing had changed, but somehow the situation didn't seem so ominous.

"He took care of it, didn't he?" Jenkins asked as they left the store.

"Thank you for calling him. He phoned the chief."

"That's what I thought he'd do. I can think of a hundred reasons why Luke was promoted over Strange. That man thinks with his ego."

They searched until after midnight, and Jenkins finally prevailed on her to go home. She went for his sake, because he hadn't eaten or seen his family since morning. Pains stabbed her feet as though splinters pierced them, but that didn't stop her from walking the floor the whole night. And by morning, the dry sockets of her eyes guaranteed that she could shed no more tears. She didn't know how she could open the store. To her relief, Officer Cowan phoned to tell her that he had put a sign on the door, and he suggested that she remain at home.

She had fallen asleep on the living room sofa, and she jumped up, startled by loud knocking on her front door. The events came back to her, and she raced barefoot to answer it and yanked it open without waiting to see who knocked.

Luke had hung up and started packing. She'd sounded scared, and he didn't blame her; too many cases on lost children were left unsolved. He phoned the conference secretary, thanked her for the invitation and the opportunity to address detectives from around the world, checked out of his hotel, and headed for Swissair. He didn't ask himself why he'd aborted the best networking opportunity he'd ever get. The chief had promised he'd take care of it, Axel Strange be damned. His luck held, and he got a business-class ticket on the next Swissair flight from Nairobi to Zurich to New York. In New York, he took a flight from LaGuardia to Portsmouth, and nineteen hours after talking with her, he knocked on her apartment door.

"Luke!"

He stared at the woman in front of him, and his vital organs seemed to seesaw in his body.

"Hi. You gonna let me in?"

She stepped aside, her lips slightly parted and her face the picture of wonder. "How did you get here? Lord, I'm so glad to see you."

He pushed his tired frame through the doorway, dropped his bag at his feet, and took her into his arms. "I had to come back here. They didn't find him yet, I take it."

She didn't speak, but he gleaned her answer from the movement of her head against his chest. Her fingers clung to his jacket, telegraphing to him the measure of her desperation, and he had to push aside the urge to love her, to shield her from the world while she held him in her womanly cocoon. Her arm went to his waist, and she guided them to her living room.

"Can I get you some coffee or something?"

"I wouldn't mind a sandwich. I slept all the way from Zurich to New York, and I missed the meals on Swissair. I didn't expect anything to eat on the flight from New York to Norfolk. You know the airlines in this country don't give you anything but peanuts and pretzels."

He watched her trudge to the kitchen, her jerky movements all the evidence of her tortured state that he needed. His mind had told him not to go to Nairobi, but he'd gloried in the recognition that the invitation to address an INTERPOL conference represented and ignored his inner wisdom. And when she'd needed him, he hadn't been there for her. Fighting back the bile of déjà vu that furled up in him, he walked to the window, looked out at the garden, walked back to the sofa, and returned to the window. Many men in his field would envy his achievements, and he viewed them with pride, but would he forever be accursed by an inability to protect those dear to him?

She placed a tray on the coffee table, and he walked back to the sofa and sat beside her.

"Thanks." The chicken salad sandwich might have been delicious, but he chewed it without tasting it. She sat closer to him, and he tried to concentrate on the sandwich and on all the reasons why he had to keep his hands off her, but her warm body touching his and her faint perfume arousing his bedeviling libido made a mockery of his common sense. He put his free hand on her right one, and she turned over her palm and caressed his with her own, welcoming his overture. That had been the wrong move, he knew, as his need for her began to stab at him. He withdrew his hand and held the sandwich with all ten of his fingers, not caring how foolish it might seem to her.

From the corner of his eye, he saw her lean back and lock her hands together in her lap. "You weren't due back until next week, six days from now. Why are you here?" The sharpness of her tone was proof, if he needed it, that he'd displeased her.

"It's . . . well, it's my duty to see that my department uses every resource available to it in solving every case, and especially one involving a lost child. That wasn't being done."

"Your *duty*? Listen to me, Luke, I don't want to hear about your duty. I want to know why you walked away from the most important honor of your life and came back here."

Before he could answer, she glanced toward the foyer and the telltale truth that sat on the floor in the form of his luggage. "Look at that. You haven't even been home. You came straight to me from the airport. I want to know why you're here in this apartment with me this minute."

He sipped the cool coffee and let time pass, knowing that she had the patience to sit quietly until he answered. He supposed she had a right to an explanation, though he'd have thought she'd guess enough to satisfy her. He couldn't fault her for wanting the record straight.

"I . . . couldn't stay away knowing you needed me."

She got up and faced him. "If you'd never met the principals in this case, would you have done the same?"

If she wanted a confession, he'd disappoint her. He'd tell her how he felt about her if he came to the point where he knew he wouldn't turn back, not before. Yet, he wanted her to need him, depend on him, and trust him. His head wrestled with his heart and his body's needs, creating an ambivalence, a frustration, that pounded at him like a river rushing downstream to flood everything in its path.

He patted the cushion beside him. "Come sit down." The guilt that had nagged him ever since the death of his wife six years earlier spilled out of him, and he confided to her the battering he'd taken from his conscience from the minute Jenkins told him Randy had disappeared. Once more, the woman he cared about had needed him, and he hadn't been there for her.

"I'm sorry about your wife, Luke, but I don't believe she would want you to punish yourself about something you couldn't control."

"I appreciate what you're saying, but this is the way it is, and I can only be myself. I can't and I won't risk a deeper involvement with you as long as I'm responsible for your safety—and now, for Randy's. I don't believe in jinxes, because I'm not superstitious, but I need a clear head, and—"

Her chin went up, and he didn't feel any of the warmth that had embraced him when he entered her door. "However you slice it," she said, "Randy's disappearance has nothing to do with the lucidity of your mind, and you must know that. If you want to distance yourself from me, say so. I'm not about to let it kill me."

He dropped his head in his hands, the weight of it all hitting him forcibly for the first time. "Well, it certainly won't leave me unscathed. Let's be friends, Kate. Close friends. And once we get Randy home and I find out who's pestering you, I'll . . . we can see where we stand with each other."

She stared into his eyes for a long time, so intently and with such apparent coolness that he thought she might ask him to leave.

"I don't know whether you care enough for me that I can hurt you," he told her, "but I do know that I don't want to cause you any kind of discomfort. Not now. Not ever. So, can we be friends for now?"

The slow nod of her head wasn't the solace he needed right then, so he waited for her words. "We can be friends, but I don't see myself developing a sisterly attitude toward you, so be prepared in case I slip up sometime and treat you as though you're a man."

He stood and lifted his right shoulder in a quick dismissive shrug. "For that matter, I may remember that you're a desirable attractive woman. I'd better get out of here. Strange needs to know that I'm back at work."

"I'm not sure I'll forgive him for telling Jenkins that a certain amount of time had to elapse before he could send out an alarm for Randy—and just because he doesn't like the child."

"You can't hold that against him, Kate. He merely followed precinct guidelines. Don't forget, Randy probably provoked Strange, and the man doesn't know how to deal with children. I'll call you as soon as I get a line on what's happening."

She walked him to the door and stood looking up at him, letting him know that if there was to be any distance between them, he'd have the responsibility of creating it *and* maintaining it. And as if to prove he'd read her right, she stood on tiptoe and pressed her lips to his in a fleeting kiss. Tremors shook him as whispers of her breath attacked his resolve. Without taking her gaze from his, she reached for the doorknob. Still staring into his eyes, tampering with his resolve, toying with his self-control, she opened the door and stepped aside to let him pass.

"Don't forget to call and let me know what's going on."

He nodded, picked up his bag, and walked off.

Kate couldn't turn on the radio or the television, for fear she'd get bad news. She wondered why, if Axel Strange was so hot for her, he hadn't bothered to call either to console her or to tell her he was doing everything possible to find Randy. Thank God she hadn't paid attention to his declarations of passionate interest. Absentmindedly, she ate the untouched half of Luke's chicken salad sandwich, heated the coffee, and took a few sips. She wanted to call someone, anyone, but to what end? Luke was on the job, and when he knew something he'd telephone her. She looked in Randy's desk drawer and found the twenty dollars she kept there for him in case of an emergency. If he'd run away, he hadn't planned it. She walked through the apartment aimlessly, and when her fingers began to tingle she realized she'd twisted her hands until they ached. She sat at her piano, something she'd rarely done since moving to Portsmouth, and began to play, hoping to lose herself in the music.

She played until tears blurred her vision and her fingers hurt. Desperate, she dialed Luke's cell phone. Then she remembered that he hadn't been home and didn't have the phone, because he hadn't taken it to Nairobi. She went back to the piano, her only solace as it had so often been during her childhood. Finally, she let herself look at her watch. Thirty-five hours since anyone had seen her child. Her briny tears slid over her lips and splashed on the ivory keys, and her fingers began to shake so badly that she had to stop playing.

Get a hold on yourself, girl. She started to the bathroom to wash her face, and when the doorbell's familiar sound assaulted her ears, she raced to it, slipped the lock, and flung it open.

"Luke, what—"

She looked down, and the small boy who stood there holding Luke's hand filled her gaze. "Randy! Randy! Where . . . I'm almost dead with worry." Her arms wrapped around him, and for once he didn't seem to mind being petted, as he called it. She didn't try to stop the tears that cascaded down her face as she rocked her child.

"Mom, I'm . . . I'm kinda hungry. Captain Luke was going to get me a burger, but I told him I'd maybe better be getting home."

She looked at Luke, her heart bursting with what it held for him. "Come on in, while I get Randy a glass of milk and a piece of toast. You haven't eaten, either. I can fix the three of us some scrambled eggs, quick grits, bacon, and toast in about twenty minutes while Randy's washing his face and hands." She smiled, not caring if she betrayed her feelings. "Will you stay?"

The lights danced in his wonderful eyes, and he patted his stomach, playfully she thought, obviously to drain the air of the tension that simmered between them.

Randy gulped down the milk and barely browned toast and left them alone.

"If you'll give me what I need, I'll set the table while you cook."

She got the dishes, flatware, and place mats and gave them to Luke. In all the years of their marriage, Nathan Middleton hadn't performed a single chore at home. She put the food on the table within the promised time and, at eleven forty-five that night they sat down to eat. Luke helped her clean up, and Randy insisted on helping them—Randy who never wanted to do chores—though he had to be exhausted.

"I'm sure you're tired, Randy," Luke said as they repaired to the living room, "but before you go to bed you must tell your mother where you were, and apologize for frightening her."

Was this her Randy, neither pouting nor behaving obstinately? "I'm sorry, Mom. I ran down in the basement at PAL to get away from Lieutenant Strange, and I got lost down there in all that stuff. Then somebody turned out the lights. I was scared, and I guess I cried myself to sleep. When I woke up the light was on, and I was scared to scream, 'cause he was really mad with me. I kept hoping somebody would come down there and find me. Captain Luke woke me up. I . . . I thought I was dreaming when he picked me up."

Randy had one more surprise for her. He hugged her, paused, then hugged Luke. As though ashamed of his gestures of sentimentality, he ran from the room.

"He was certainly glad to see me," Luke said, "but not more than I was glad to see him. We'd combed this city. Then I remembered to ask whether anyone at PAL saw the direction in which he went. Canyon, who'd been at the desk, swore he didn't see Randy leave the building, and on a hunch I went down to the basement. Kate, that place is a morass of nooks, corridors, tiny passageways, storage rooms, boxes, barrels, old office furniture, sporting equipment, you name it. There's even a connecting tunnel to the precinct. He's a brave kid not to have screamed his head off. Thanks for the supper. I'd better be going." He stood, took her hand, and walked with her to the door.

"How long since you stretched out in a bed?" she asked him.

"Day before yesterday."

"Luke, I don't know how to thank you, but you know that I do." Her hand drifted upward to his face, and she didn't try to hide what she felt.

He stared into her eyes, aware that his own must be fiery orbs of passion. "Listen, honey, what you're feeling right now is gratitude."

She pressed her thumb into his bottom lip. "Is what you're feeling gratitude?"

"Kate, I won't go that route again. I couldn't bear it twice in my lifetime."

Feminine want shouted to him from every pore of her body as her finger traced first his bottom lip and then moved up to close his eyelids. Every nerve in him screamed in frustration, and when she lifted her arms to him and parted her lips, he seized her to him and found in her mouth the sweetness for which he yearned. She opened to him, and he drank in her frustration, yearning, and, yes, her loving. Her body moved against him, and she battled him with her tongue until he surrendered to his rising passion and rose against her.

Every movement she made told him that she was his, there for him, but he couldn't accept what she offered, not when he had to keep his own counsel. He put as much space between them as he could without offending or hurting her.

"Honey, we agreed to control this thing. Of all times, this isn't the one to lose our heads."

She stepped back as if to give him the benefit of her attitude as well as her voice. "I haven't lost my head, but I'm sure that after almost three days without sleep, you must be tired. " She bit her bottom lip and let what passed for sympathy flood her face. "You need your rest."

He couldn't help laughing. At times, he forgot how good she was at mugging. "I'm tired, baby, but when I get *that* tired I'll be ready for a box. Now, mind your manners," he added for levity. "I'll call you tomorrow." He left, but this time he knew his stride didn't bespeak his usual confidence. Kate had just served notice that it was she who called the shots in their relationship.

Chapter Six

Kate sat down and read the letter a second time. After her thirty-six hours of terror during Randy's disappearance, the prospect of two weeks of her cousin Jessye's company loomed more like misery than pleasure. If she'd ever known a more affected human being, right down to the way she spelled her name, Kate didn't recall it. In the small South Carolina town in which they'd grown up together from babyhood, Jessye wore an invisible crown. The local African-American population expected Jessye to have the latest styles, wear the best, and most attractive clothes, the latest hairdo and the most dazzling Flo Jo fingernails. Nobody knew how Jessye managed this, since she was reasonably virtuous. Looking back, Kate concluded that setting oneself apart wasn't too much of a stretch in that Bible Belt town of only three thousand people. She hadn't envied Jessye; admiration more nearly described her feelings for her flamboyant cousin, but sharing a bedroom with her for two weeks would probably drop Jessye a few notches in her esteem. Frivolity could wear on a person.

She couldn't help feeling sorry for Jessye, who'd walked away from an unwholesome marriage, straightened out her life, and now was once more crying the blues. For the first time in Jessye's life, a man had dumped *her*. Kate didn't let that fact concern her, for she knew that all Jessye needed was a target. The next man would heal her wounds, and quickly. She went to the phone and called her cousin.

"Sorry about you and Ed," she told Jessye after they'd greeted each other. "Come on up. You'll have to share my room, because I don't have a guest room, but I can handle that for two weeks."

"I knew you'd come through for me, honey. I can't face the gossip. I must have been the only person in town who didn't know he was making out with Wanda Morton. I'll be up day after tomorrow. Only the Lord and I know how much I thank you."

She'd forgotten Jessye's penchant for drama and over-statement. "Add me to that list," she said dryly, "and don't bring too many clothes, because I'm short of closet space."

After they talked a few minutes longer, Kate hung up and moved half her clothes into Randy's closet. He'd raise a commotion about it, but she had no other solution; Jessye wouldn't come to Portsmouth without half of what she owned.

"This is one fab-u-lous spot," Jessye crooned as they entered Kate's bookstore the morning after Jessye's arrival. "What a great place to meet men!"

Kate tried to ignore the chill that snaked down her spine at those words. "Don't get used to that chair," she said as her cousin sat down and crossed her long shapely legs. "You need to get your mind off yourself, and work will do that, so prepare to help me shelve books."

"Sure. Show me the childrens' section. Maybe I'll pick up on something new for my third graders. I can't find anything much more taxing than *Barney Google* down there in Bates, South Carolina. And I want some books on Native American children.''

Jessye quickly classified the books in the children's section, rearranged them accordingly, and put up a sign featuring the new books. Before noon, half a dozen of them had been sold. Kate saw that a second person in that store could help her promote and improve her business. She'd have to examine her books to see whether she could afford an assistant.

She answered the phone, and a weight settled in her chest when the voice she heard was that of her book distributor and not Luke. The door of her store opened, and her heart leaped, but it returned to its normal place when she saw Axel walking toward her. She finished the conversation and beckoned to Jessye.

"Over here, Jessye. I want you to meet one of Portsmouth's finest, Detective Lieutenant Axel Strange.''

As she'd expected, Axel beamed at them. He took both of Jessye's hands, as though he'd waited all of his life to meet her. But Kate couldn't dismiss her sense of wariness: Axel didn't impress Jessye. That didn't mean she wouldn't play with him, but she was still looking—still on the make. And Jessye was never without a man.

"I'm happy to meet you, Jessye,'' Axel said with unmistakable sincerity. "I hope we'll get to know each other better.''

"Me too,'' Jessye replied airily, and Kate had to wonder if Ed, back in Bates, South Carolina, had really done a job on her cousin.

She thought Jessye would get Axel out of *her* hair, but he immediately turned to her with his usual plastic smile. "We're all giving thanks that Randy is safe.''

"Now *that* is a nice surprise,'' she said. "I hadn't realized you cared, Lieutenant.''

He stepped closer to her, signalling his intention to

continue his pursuit. "Now, Kate, you know I'm deeply concerned about anything that affects you." He meant his smile to dazzle her, but it shone to no avail.

She stared at him with the full measure of her displeasure until he fidgeted, his arrogant demeanor temporarily vanished. "Concentrate on someone else, Axel, you're wasting your time."

"Honey, don't be so hard on this nice man. He looks to me like the answer to a girl's dreams."

Axel whipped around and looked at Jessye. He didn't smile, only gazed at her. Kate shook her head in wonder. Jessye had hooked another one, and she wasn't even interested. When Axel turned back to her, his charm once more at work, Kate wondered what he wanted. Surely, he wouldn't try to tell her that she interested him after ignoring her at a time when he knew he could have helped her. She went into her office and left them alone. They deserved each other.

Keeping his distance from Kate Middleton wore on Luke until he began to look for excuses to call her, reasons that wouldn't seem personal. He had to talk to her. He got up from his desk and went out of his office to the water cooler.

"Met Kate's cousin?" Axel asked him.

He didn't know Kate had a cousin, and he'd as soon Axel didn't know that. "How'd you like her?" he bluffed.

He couldn't help being amazed at Axel's subdued manners. When the man replied, "I don't know. She's . . . she's really something," he knew he had to find an excuse to visit Kate's Friendly Bookstore.

He read Cowan's report. The officer had frustrated two men in their attempt to break into Kate's store, the two had fled when the squad car came into view, and he hadn't been able to catch them. If he knew what the thugs were after, he'd know how to find them. Sooner or later, they'd make a blunder, and he'd be there.

Jenkins wanted to get home early, and Luke readily agreed, seeing an opportunity to take Randy to the store after he finished at PAL. As usual, Kate met him at the door. Her quick kiss, virtually a public statement, left him nonplussed, until his gaze caught Jessye. The woman walked up to him, introduced herself, and linked arms with him as though Kate didn't exist. He looked from one woman to the other, from the tiger to the kitten, and decided not to laugh. Kate knew Jessye, he surmised, and didn't plan to put up with her foolishness.

"Hello, Jessye. I'm glad to see that Kate has some help. I've been concerned about her being alone here, and especially after dark." He slid an arm around Kate's waist and extricated himself from Jessye's clutches. "Where're you from?"

He hadn't meant to rip out her feathers, only to clip them, but the woman appeared crestfallen. "I'm Kate's cousin. We grew up together."

"Yes," Kate added, her voice drier than usual, "she's staying with me for two weeks." He noticed that she emphasized the two weeks.

"Good. Then you and Randy can go to Caution Point with me for a weekend, since you have someone who can mind the store." He'd planned to take them soon, but mentioning it now was a statement for Jessye's benefit, though he guessed she didn't care to whom a man belonged if she wanted him.

"Does anybody have an aspirin?" Jessye asked, holding the side of her head. "I declare y'all have got to do something about the air in this town." A deep long sigh poured from her. "Clean air's about the only thing good you can say about my small town."

"I don't have anything here for headaches, Jessye, and

if the air's going to bother you I suggest you buy a few bottles of pills before we head home."

"I can go get some, Mom," Randy said.

"Anything to postpone studying. Right?" She hugged him, thankful that he was alive and healthy. "Go do your homework, Randy. Jessye will be fine."

Luke glanced at Jessye to see how she took Kate's brush-off and found her gaze settled on him, open and vulnerable. Her blush confirmed that her interest in him was anything but sisterly. He'd been the target of many women, but this one was a master, and she meant business. He'd have to watch his every step.

"Think you can make it next weekend?" he asked Kate. "Jessye'll be gone the following Saturday, so let's take advantage of this one."

"I don't want to go to Caution Point," Randy said.

"Why not? You can fish, walk in the woods, swim, and have a great time with my family."

"But what about my clients? Who'll deliver stuff to them while I'm gone?"

"You'll only miss Saturday, and Officer Jenkins will take care of that for you."

Randy didn't seem satisfied with that. "Okay. I'll ask him and let you know what he says."

Luke stifled a grin. The boy was shaping up quickly. He already had a sense of responsibility for the senior citizens to whom he delivered lunch six days a week.

Letting Randy know that he respected the boy's concern for his clients, Luke replied, "Good. Let me know as soon as possible." He'd make sure Jenkins cooperated.

"Nice to meet you, Jessye." He looked at Kate. "Walk me to the door?"

"She's quite a number," he said of Jessye, "but her type gives me the willies. Don't get any notions in your head."

She stared into his eyes. "I thought you'd backed off."

"Yeah, but how I feel hasn't changed. How about

another one of those little kisses you laid on me when I walked in here?"

Wicked fire danced in her eyes, and he figured he'd just made a mistake. When she placed a hand on each side of his face and pressed her parted lips on his, he was sure of it. The scent of her perfume filled his nostrils, and the hardened tips of her breasts pressed into his chest while her tongue flicked against his lips. Heat roared through him, and he had to turn sideways to prevent his certain arousal. She opened her mouth and he plunged in, mindless of his vows to himself and the whipping his common sense poured on him. His arms tightened around the warm sweet bundle in his embrace, and he lost himself in her loving.

"I see I'm gonna need a lot of aspirin, what with you laying it on the captain like that," Jessye said after Luke left them. "Honey, that scene made a living goosepimple out of me. Girl, I sure hope he's not monogamous."

Kate hadn't expected Jessye to make such a brazen play for Luke, though her act hadn't been a complete surprise. Her cousin flaunted her sexuality, but back in Bates she'd always employed some discretion. Apparently, the anonymity of a city gave her *carte blanche* to be her real self.

Kate gave Jessye what she hoped was a withering look. "Jessye, the men in Bates, South Carolina, are not the standard for this world. So mind your act. And put on a bra, for goodness' sake."

Jessye looked toward the ceiling and let out another of her long deep sighs. "Don't be silly. That's like locking up your guard dog when you're expecting prowlers. Why do people have ammunition if they don't plan to use it? Next thing I know, you'll tell me to wear a girdle."

Kate couldn't help laughing. "Not on your neck. Walking behind you is too much fun."

"Go ahead and laugh. I don't remember missing out on a man I wanted. Can you say that?"

Kate shrugged as if to dismiss the argument. "I wish I'd missed out on the one I got. I thought he was the man for me, but he disabused me of that notion before we'd been married six months. I'm not going to scale any walls to get a man, no matter how much I want him. Even if he's eaten up with desire, he can still be as disappointing as a wet match."

Jessye walked around to face Kate, who'd been dusting a shelf of books. "You didn't used to be like this. You're pretty sure of yourself. It doesn't bother you that I might decide to go for Luke, does it?"

Kate spread out her hands, as though she didn't care what Jessye did. "Go ahead, girl. Shoot your best shot. Scrambling over a man is a waste of time. Men go for the music that makes them dance. Cover the cash register, will you? I have to see what Randy's doing."

Though she'd behaved nonchalantly about Jessye's designs on Luke, Kate knew she was anything but unruffled. She'd meant it, though, when she said she wouldn't demean herself by fighting for a man. Luke wanted space, and she planned to give it to him no matter how Jessye acted.

She looked over Randy's drawing of a distiller for his science class. She never had to urge Randy to do his science and art homework, but faced with social studies he could be obstreperous.

"That's a perfect sketch. You have any more homework?"

He shook his head. "No, but I have to work out a plan for my clients."

"What kind of plan?"

"Well, the precinct has all these vans, so why can't my clients have a picnic? They can walk."

Why not, indeed? "Have you discussed it with Captain Luke or Officer Jenkins?"

"Can we go by Captain Luke's house tonight, and I can show him my plan?"

"But, Randy—"

"Each group has to have a plan for its clients, and my group expects me to help us win, Mom. *Please!*"

If she drove him to Luke's house, she'd have to take Jessye along, too, and she'd had as much of Jessye's gushing over Luke Hickson as she could stand for one day.

"We're going home. You may call him and ask him to come over to our place."

"I can?"

She gave him the phone number and left the office, because she didn't want Luke to think she'd prompted Randy's call. Still, she knew he'd come, and her heart had already begun its wild boogaloo in anticipation of the minute she'd lay her eyes on him.

Luke had his own misgivings about the visit, but he didn't want to discourage Randy. The boy had done an about-face since he'd found him huddled in a dark corner of the basement of the Police Athletic League building, and he had to encourage him. But he didn't relish another encounter that day with Jessye-whatever-her-name-was. He pointedly chose a time after dinner, but everything inside of him seemed to droop when Randy, not Kate, opened the door. At least Jessye hadn't opened it.

Randy presented him with a good plan, one that he was fairly certain neither of the other groups would equal, and he accepted it. As he prepared to leave, he said to Randy, "Would you please ask your mother to come here for a minute?"

"You wanted to see me?" Kate asked him.

"Yeah. I want my kiss in private, and I don't want to hang around the door while your cousin practices her lasso technique."

Her hearty laughter, twinkling eyes, and scintillating perfume shouted *Stay, don't leave.* He let his lips brush hers, and when she grinned, all feminine allure, he capitulated, gripped her tightly in his arms, and swallowed her sweetness. Undone by the swift peaking of her passion that threatened to drag him into fullblown desire, he stepped back and looked down at her. He couldn't be the servant of his libido every time she was near him.

"What is it about you that I can't . . . Look, I've got to go."

Quiet and seemingly unruffled while his blood raced madly, she gazed up at him. "Are we still going with you Friday afternoon?"

He wanted to shake her until she screamed that she felt what he felt, needed what he needed. But he acted the lie, just as he knew she did. "Of course. I'll pick you and Randy up at home around four-thirty."

"Is your sister-in-law very formal?"

He stroked his stubble-free jaw. "Formal? Amanda? I'm trying to figure out how many times I've seen her wear shoes in the house."

"Uh . . . do you like her?"

What was she getting at? "Kate, I couldn't love my own sister more. I think of her as my sister."

He could see something akin to peace settle over her. "That's wonderful. I'll look forward to meeting her." Seeming puzzled, she chewed on her bottom lip. "Luke, what will they think about you taking us there? I mean . . . well, we're just friends."

He grinned, more out of habit than amusement. "Then that's what we'll tell them. Not to worry." He kissed her cheek and headed for the front door, where Jesse stood, waiting for him.

"Thanks for looking over my project, Captain Luke."

He gave thanks for Randy. Whatever Jessye had planned, the boy had just botched. He stood between them and, in an uncharacteristic act, held both of Luke's hands.

"Any time, son." He nodded to Jessye. "Good night, miss."

"Whew!" That had been close. From fresh makeup to flowing hair, jersey top, and tight satin pants, the lady had been ready for all-out war. Not that she was unattractive. She wasn't. She was just so damned obvious. He got in his car, turned on his Max Bruch tape, and headed home.

They reached Caution Point at six o'clock as he'd figured they would, and he drove slowly through the town, pointing out places of interest to Randy and Kate. He promised to take them to the museum that housed the remains of a boat in which runaway slaves had escaped from a Charleston plantation and won their freedom, and to the church in which a piano once owned by Hall Johnson still supported the choir each Sunday morning.

"Does your brother have any children, Captain Luke?"

"Three of 'em." He turned into Ocean Avenue and parked in front of number thirty-seven.

"You must be Kate. I'm Marcus. Come on in."

"I'm happy to meet you, Marcus. I hope we're not putting you out."

What a disconcerting wink! "Of course not. Luke doesn't do things like that. He'd never bring you where you wouldn't be comfortable. Where's your boy?"

She looked around. "I suppose he's back there with Luke helping him put the car into the garage," she said, and winked right back at him.

He treated her to uproarious laughter, and she had the kind of comfortable feeling one experiences when getting home.

"Where's Amanda?"

"She's feeding Todd, my younger son. Go on upstairs."

"I see you've met." Luke and Marcus clasped each other

in bear hugs. "This is Randy. Randy, this is my brother, Marcus. You may call him Mr. Marcus."

Randy looked Marcus up and down. "But you're not a detective?"

At that moment, Amy came barrelling down the stairs with Marc in her wake. Kate's eyebrows shot up when Amy walked up to Randy, offered to shake hands, and said, "I'm Amy, this is my brother Marc, and Lady is nursing my other little brother. Wanna come see?"

Randy looked at the three adults for permission. "I think he can watch some other time, Amy," Luke said.

As though anxious to assure his status with Amy, Randy said, "Amy, this is my mom, Kate Middleton. You may call her Miss Kate."

Kate gave silent thanks that Luke and Marcus didn't seem amused at Randy's mimicking of Luke. He had needed a role model. She saw that now. He couldn't have a better one than Luke, but she didn't want Randy to become too attached to a man who'd told her, for whatever reason, that he intended to keep a distance between them.

Luke's gaze as she shook Amy's and Marc's little hands set the marbles in her belly to rocking. His gray eyes sparkled with the fire of desire, and she didn't imagine it, for Marcus looked from Luke to her. And though she knew she blushed, Luke didn't shift his gaze. She swallowed furiously, aware that she failed in her effort to hide what she felt. The blaze dancing in his eyes drew her as a flame draws a moth and, like a zombie, she stepped toward him. If he burned her she didn't care, so long as he made it all that it could be. She didn't know what would have happened if Marcus hadn't suddenly taken Randy and Amy by the hand and walked toward the back of the house.

With trembling fingers, she reached out and he was there, flesh, sinew, and blood, a man who cared about her and who wanted her. The tips of her fingers touched his warm body, and she gazed up at him.

His posture a rigid contrast to the swirling heat in his eyes, he said, "Don't test me right now, Kate."

Shivers coursed through her. For that moment he was hers to do with as she pleased. Power and passion leaped within her, battling with her common sense. But reason had deserted her. Frantic for a way to indulge her passion, she let her gaze sweep the foyer.

But he second-guessed her, slickly divining her thoughts. "There's no privacy in this foyer, and it's just as well, because I'd give in to you all the way. And I'd regret it."

"I'm . . . I'm not trying to seduce you. Can't you see that I'm just as susceptible to you as you are to me? What do you think happens to me when I see you look at me as if you want to—"

"Don't say it." He shook his head as though in wonder. "God made us like this, but I wish he'd posted a cure someplace where I could find it."

Not till after I've had my way with you. Aloud, she said, "Lord Forbid!"

Sparkles lit the wonderful gray eyes that she adored, and a grin slowly took possession of his face. "Honey, you're one heck of a piece of work. A woman with the guts to say what she thinks and feels. I'm not going anywhere. Trust me on that. But I'd appreciate a little patience."

Say whatever she thought? Humph! She wondered how he'd take it if she blurted out everything about him that worked its way into her mind? A smile formed around her eyes. "You like that, huh? Then you won't mind knowing I think you ought to have danger signs posted on you in big letters, going and coming." She poked her tongue in her left cheek and looked at him through slanted eyes. "No, honey, you are definitely not going *anywhere.*"

He glanced downward and dug the toe of his shoe into the carpet before staring into her eyes. "Cut it out, Kate. If I believed that kind of talk, I'd be as asinine as Ax . . .

as some other people you know." He looked down again. "Marc, for Pete's sake, stop pulling out my shoelaces."

He hunkered before the little boy, who sat on the floor bubbling with giggles. *Yes,* she thought, *he loves children,* and her mind immediately conjured up a vision of him holding *their* child. Luke stood with Marc in his arms and looked down at her for a long time, obviously shaken. His eyes let her know he'd read her thoughts. His own expression became unreadable. Then, as quickly as lightning streaks the dark, his mood changed.

"It's time you met Amanda." He took her hand with his free one. "Come on," and they climbed the stairs together.

"Where are they?" Amanda asked Marcus. "You think they're still standing in the foyer?"

"Bet on it. Considering the sparks I saw flying between them, I wouldn't be surprised if they were glued to the spot."

Amanda loved her brother-in-law. She often fretted over his aloneness and his inability to put the circumstances of his wife's death behind him.

"What did you think of Kate?"

"I liked what I saw. A good-looking, intelligent, and frankly feminine woman. She has a sense of humor, too, and anybody living around Luke needs that. Randy's infatuated with Luke."

When she reached up and brushed her husband's lips with her own, his eyes promised her heaven. She'd learned not to play with him unless she meant business, because he'd lock the door, and they'd eat supper when they ate supper.

"I think I'll put Todd in his crib and run down and welcome her."

She got no further than the top of the stairs. After hugging Luke, she opened her arms to Kate. "Thank you for coming down to see us, Kate. I've wanted to meet you and Randy. Would you believe my daughter is already besotted with him? Come see my baby."

While Kate watched Todd play with the gadgets strung across his crib, Amanda fixed her gaze on Luke. His eyes blazed with passion as he looked steadily at Kate, but she also saw more in his regard of her, unaware that she watched him. Warmth and caring shone in his face, open and unguarded. Kate smiled at Luke, and blushed at the intimacy of his expression—unsmiling, with a look of love and longing. Amanda relaxed, satisfied, and glanced at her husband. He, too, had witnessed the couple's silent communication. Nobody had to tell Amanda that Marcus liked what he saw, for a smile covered his face.

"Drinks if anybody wants them, and supper in half an hour," she said. She started down the stairs, turned back, and spoke to Kate. "Why don't you come down with me, and let's get acquainted."

A woman without guile or pretense, Kate concluded as they descended the stairs.

"I want you to visit often, Kate. Luke spends every weekend with us, but I expect that's about to change."

Let her spell it out. I'm taking nothing for granted. "Why do you say that?"

Amanda skipped down the last three steps and waited for Kate. "He won't need us as much as he does now. Luke loves Marcus, all of us, in fact. But he needs his own life, and what I see when you two look at each other tells me he's going to get that. It gives me a nice warm feeling."

Kate laughed inwardly, reluctant to tell Amanda that she hoped it also gave Luke a warm feeling. "Luke's biding his time. He isn't ready for a commitment, at least not to me."

"Don't expect a man with Luke's intelligence and sense of responsibility to surrender easily. If he promises you anything, you can bet your life on it. Of course, such a man would be careful." Amanda took a pan of apple turnovers from the refrigerator and prepared to fry them.

"When Marcus and I married, I wouldn't have bet a nickel on our being together today. But Marcus fell in love with me. Oh, he fought it like Don Quixote did his windmills, but, honey, love is powerful, and I didn't hide mine from him."

Must be a family trait. "I don't think he's scared of what he feels. I believe whatever I represent to him is something he doesn't want. Simple as that."

Amanda flipped a turnover. "Pshaw! I know he doubts himself because of what he experienced with his wife. And don't get me wrong, it's something he can't seem to shake. But you're the one woman I've seen him with, the only one he's brought here, and a man who looks like that one, who has his status, can get just about any woman he wants. Right now, he's with you."

"I'm not going to pressure him. He roared into my life like a souped-up locomotive less than a year after I swore I'd never look twice at another man. One look at him was enough to make me eat my words. I can't believe such a powerful attraction is one-sided."

Amanda put the turnovers on a sheet of brown paper to drain. "I don't give people advice. Smart people don't need it, and the rest can't use it." Twinkles flashed in her soft brown eyes. "But in this case . . . well, honey, learn to make gingerbread, ginger snaps, and ginger rum cake."

Kate couldn't restrain the mirth that poured out of her as she joined in Amanda's sparkling laughter, amused and happy that she'd found a new friend. She wanted to hug the elfin woman. When she could stop laughing, she said, "I knew about the other two, but ginger rum cake?"

Only wickedness could describe Amanda's slow wink. "I'll give you the recipe. I made it up when I got sick of gingerbread."

As naturally as if she'd done it for years, Kate opened her arms and embraced Amanda. "I'm so happy that I know you."

"Where's all this good stuff I smell?"

Kate looked at Marcus, so like Luke and yet so different. It crossed her mind that Marcus enjoyed a happiness, a contentment that she didn't see in Luke.

"I like your family, Marcus. Amanda is . . . well, a very special person. But of course you know that."

He seemed to rise above his six feet four inches, his pride in his wife almost a tangible thing, and she got a good dose of Hickson charisma when he treated her to a broad grin.

"The credit for our life together goes to Amanda. She withstood plenty, and she gave me the family and the home I wanted and needed. Amanda's pure gold. Morning sunshine and evening shade." He shook his head as though unable to believe his good fortune. "I'll never know how I got so lucky."

"Where's Randy?" Kate asked him.

"Luke's reading stories to the children."

Kate mused over that for a second. "But there's such a difference in their ages."

Marcus shrugged first one shoulder, and then the other. "That's no problem for Luke. He makes up things as he reads and puts in something for all of them. Besides, Amy will enjoy anything Randy likes. She's just six, but she's the best student in her advanced second grade class. And I can thank Amanda for that, too."

"I've never known Randy to take to anyone so quickly."

"No? She wants him to stay here with us for a while. Said she needs a big brother."

Both of Kate's eyebrows shot up. "I doubt he'd consider

that. He hates being away from his clients, computer, paint-ing things, and all the other stuff he has in his room.''

Marcus winked mischievously. "Don't bet on it, Kate. Amy's got almost as many feminine wiles as a thirty-year-old woman, and she's already working on him.''

Luke strolled into the kitchen, bringing the three older children with him, and sniffed with pleasure at the aroma that greeted him. Amanda set out a meal of roast pork and dressing, candied sweet potatoes, string beans, biscuits, and a salad of sliced tomatoes with basil dressing. Randy watched Luke to see what he did, for which Kate was grate-ful, because Luke didn't lift his fork until Marcus said grace. She marveled that—though Randy claimed to dis-like everything on Kate's table at home except the biscuits—he ate everything with gusto. If she could have, she'd have taken Amy home with her.

"We're having apple turnovers for dessert, Randy," Amy said. "Every night, Lady makes something with apples, 'cause my daddy loves apple things. Uncle Luke loves gin-ger in everything.''

Randy stopped eating and looked at Amy. "In every-thing? *Everything*? Yuk!''

" 'Course not. Just gingerbread, gingersnaps and ginger rum cake," Amy explained.

"That's different. I'm crazy about gingerbread, too, and my mom sure knows how to make it.''

Amy looked at Kate and let an angelic smile light up her face. "When you come back to see us, Miss Kate, please bring me some. I love it, too.''

With the children asleep, the four adults talked long into the night. Luke held Kate's hand as she sat beside him on the velvet sofa, and Amanda sat on an ottoman beside Marcus's knees while he occupied a lounge chair, his left hand draped over his wife's shoulder. Everything about Amanda seemed natural, Kate silently observed— Her bare toes peeping out from beneath the orange caftan, her hands relaxed in her lap, her serenity. Marcus looked down at her, smiled, and Amanda seemed to catch fire. A glow covered her face, her lips parted, and her eyes drank him in, welcoming him.

Kate counseled herself not to envy the woman, but in her mind's eye she saw Marcus carrying his wife to his lair, loving her, flying with her on an ecstatic voyage to heaven—a voyage that she had never taken, one that she longed with every fiber of her being to experience. The hot fire of desire swirled in Marcus's gaze. Frankly. Openly. And the woman he adored reached for him. Kate had to close her eyes.

"Where are you? You haven't heard a word I said," Luke told her, his knowing gaze fixed on her. She worked hard at shaking herself out of the trance into which witnessing the couple's frank desire and need had thrust her. "I'm over here. Look at me," he persisted.

She turned her face toward him, but couldn't make herself open her eyes, because she knew what he'd see, and she wasn't ready to give him access to her soul.

"I think it's time I turned in," she announced to no one in particular, certain that Marcus and Amanda, wrapped in their own world, wouldn't hear anything she said.

Her shaky fingers found the light switch at the bottom of the stairs that led to the new wing of the house, and as she stumbled up the first few steps she realized that Luke followed. Beneath the surface of her skin, her scrambled nerves battled each other, testing her. She fought to keep going. What she wanted was to turn back to that living room and see for herself how a man loved a woman he cherished.

Her steps faltered, and Luke came up beside her, draped an arm around her shoulder, and took her weight.

"This way, Kate," he said, and turned them into a wide hall hung with paintings and art objects. He pointed to a doorway. "That's your room," he said, his rueful smile

making a lie of his cool facade. "And this one's mine."
He leaned against the door that faced hers and crossed
his ankles, his gaze fixed on her. His gray eyes were without
their fire and sparkles—lackluster, haunting.

She wondered what he'd say if she invited him into her
room, and oh, how she wanted to! She pinned him with
a searching accusing stare—healthy, virile, as good-looking
and sexy a man as she'd ever laid eyes on. Couldn't he see
her loneliness, how much she needed him? That dull ache
she'd lost when Nathan was no longer a part of her life,
promising and forever withholding, once more pummelled
her chest, exacerbating her longing for the man before
her. At the moment, she wished she had never seen him.

"Good night, Kate."

She managed a smile, opened her door, went in, and
closed it. She was doggoned if she'd cry! She hadn't sunk
to that even when Nathan had stayed out nights and
ignored her for days. She showered, pampered her body
with the lotions she found in the bathroom, and got into
bed.

"He'd better not wait too long," she said aloud. Then
she turned out the light and went to sleep.

Luke paced from one end of his room to the other and
back. The passion between Marcus and Amanda could get
hot enough to make a dead person fan. Kate had wanted
from him what Marcus was giving Amanda, but he didn't
walk in his brother's shoes. He hoped the time would come
when he and Kate could explore the depth of their feelings
for each other. *And it had better be soon, too,* he mused,
because he wasn't Superman, and she showed signs of
wanting to push him. A low soft whistle expressed his exasperation. If she knew him as well as he knew himself, she
wouldn't worry. That woman had his number. He got ready
for bed. Whoever was out to get her was becoming impatient, and that was precisely what he wanted. If he caught
them, he'd start getting his life in order.

Chapter Seven

"You got a couple of guys, out of towners, hanging around here, Luke, who don't seem to live anywhere. Looks like they just drive in, or maybe ride in, since I haven't seen them in a car. What do you think?" Cowan asked Luke.

He was still trying to get the past weekend with Kate down at Caution Point out of his system. As he'd expected, he'd been spending more time thinking about her and wanting her than was good for her safety.

"What do they look like?"

Cowan fingered his chin and appeared puzzled. "Well, that's just it. They wore suits and ties, but didn't look right in them, like they weren't used to wearing them. And one was a lot older than the other one."

"Father and son, maybe?"

"I don't think so, because it didn't occur to me. The tall one slouched noticeably. They wore hats, would you believe that? So I didn't get a good look at their faces. Neither time."

Luke stopped taking notes and tapped his pen on his desk. "Were they black or white?"

"Not sure, Luke. If they were black, they were light skinned."

Could be anybody. "Thanks. Keep an eye out. I want them tailed."

"Right."

Luke phoned Rude Hopper. "Rude, this is Luke. Seen two strangers strolling around your way?" He gave Rude Cowan's description of the men.

"I haven't seen 'em around here, but I'll get the word out. Somebody comes around here wearing a business suit's not suspect, but if he sticks a Sunday-go-to-meeting hat on his head to boot, he'll stand out like a splash of red paint on a white house."

"Thanks. I'll be in touch. See you." A look at his watch told him he'd better get over to PAL and give the boys their fencing lesson.

As he walked in, Randy ran up to him. "Can I have your cell phone number, Captain Luke? My mom said if I get into any trouble I have to call you."

A dizzying sensation attacked him as though his blood had curdled. There it was again—that blind trust, as though he were omnipotent.

"Listen to me, Randy. If you get . . . If anything happens to you and your mother's not home, call nine one one. It's their job to rescue people. I'm—"

"But, Captain Luke, my mom said—"

"I don't care what she said. I'm telling you, if you get into trouble, call nine one one. I may be thirty or forty miles from here, and you could die waiting for me to get to you. Do as I say."

Randy hadn't heard that last part, and he hadn't seen the boy leave, because the picture before him had been of his wife, when he'd gotten to her too late. He slumped on the bar of an exercycle, praying he could make the child understand.

Kate walked back into the office, where Randy sat with his elbows on her desk and his hands supporting his chin. "Why aren't you studying, Randy?"

After she'd asked him the third time, he got up as if to leave, but she stopped him. "Didn't you hear me?"

"I'm not studying 'cause I don't want to."

"Randy!"

"I hate social stuff, and I'm not studying it."

Something had happened to turn him into the old disrespectful Randy. "What happened at PAL today?"

"Nothing, and I'm not going there any more. Captain Luke said I'm not to call him for anything. I have to call nine one one. I don't like him anymore."

So that was it. He didn't want responsibility for Randy. "You're going back to PAL tomorrow, and that's that." She walked back into the store. She didn't need Luke Hickson to look after her child. She could do that just fine without help from him or anybody else.

The door buzzer rang, and she looked that way. Axel Strange. She wouldn't have believed she'd rather see him than Luke, but at the moment she wanted no part of Luke Hickson.

"When are we getting the reading group started?" he asked after greeting her with such effusiveness that she felt she needed a shower.

"When enough people have signed up Jessye will take care of it."

He looked around. "Where *is* the lady?"

Hmm. So that accounted for his restlessness. She looked into his eyes. "She's hunting for an apartment."

"Really?"

His casual response didn't fool her—Axel wanted Jessye.

But in that case, why was he still tomcatting after her? Like a blaring light, the answer flashed before her: Axel Strange didn't want her, and never had. He made a play for her because he didn't want Luke to have her. But why? Well, he'd boxed himself in, because Jessye had set her cap for Luke. She shrugged.

"She's decided to stay for the summer and help me in the store. Did you encourage her not to go home? To stay here?"

"You do me a disservice, Kate. It's you who won't let me sleep at night."

Sure, and the Mississippi River empties into the Pacific Ocean. "Fortunately, I don't take that kind of talk seriously, Lieutenant. Better spend your efforts on Jessye. I've had my fill of that sort of thing."

He narrowed his eyes, and she waited for the snarl, but instead he ground his teeth. "I suppose the captain understands this and accepts it? In that case, why'd you go away with him last weekend?"

"What? Don't you think you ought to be minding your own business? How dare you ask me such a question?"

"What do you expect? I don't like seeing the woman I want going off with another guy. And the local stud, at that."

Stud! She threw back her head and laughed. "You're kidding."

"I don't see a thing funny."

"Well, I do," she said. "Excuse me. I have to take care of a customer."

Jessye burst in, bringing her usual air of irreverence. "Lieutenant, honey, where've you been? I thought you'd given up on us."

He rushed to her. "Here, let me help you with those packages." Surprised at their weight, he raised an eyebrow. "How'd you manage to carry this stuff? What's in here, bricks?"

Kate didn't know when she'd gotten so much pleasure from another person's embarrassment. Axel found those packages heavy, and they probably were, but Jessye had breezed in with them as though they didn't weigh a pound.

"Didn't anybody tell you about us Southern girls?" Kate asked him. "We're as fragile as a butterfly, tough as nails, and strong as . . . as most anything you can name."

Jessye repaired her makeup, occasionally fanning herself. "Speak for yourself, honey"

Kate smothered a laugh. "I am, and you were always tougher and stronger than I. If a man can't accept that, it's his problem, not mine."

"Oh my, does anybody have an aspirin?" Jessye said. "All this philosophy gives me a terrible headache."

"I'll be right back," Axel said.

"Shame on you, girl. You could teach philosophy, and you know it."

Jessye's headache quickly abated as she fanned vigorously. "Where'd he go? I declare, these men—"

"To get an aspirin," Kate said dryly. "Where do you think he went?"

Jessye stopped fanning and stared at Kate. "You're kidding. He must be from up north some place. It takes a southern man to understand a woman. I declare—"

The door opened, and Axel rushed in with a large bottle of Bayer aspirin, his eagerness to get it back to Jessye so great that he hadn't waited to have it wrapped.

"Where's some water?" he asked Kate.

She nodded toward the unisex bathroom. "Back there, and don't forget the paper cups on top of the cooler." He stopped and glared at her for her audacity, remembered the urgency of his mission, and rushed to the bathroom.

Jessye let out a sigh of resignation. "Just my luck. If I told that handsome captain I had a headache, he'd merely suggest I take something."

"Since you know that, you ought to save yourself some trouble and like the one who likes you."

"Honey, that's not something you can mix up like biscuits. A guy has to turn you on, and just thinking about the captain ignites my engine."

"What about your 'unbearable grief for the pig' who cheated on you with Wanda what's-her-name?"

Jessye sat on the edge of the desk and positioned her crossed knees to her legs' best advantage as she awaited Axel's return. "Girl, that was almost a month ago. The best way to forget a man is to concentrate on another one."

Axel rushed to Jessye and handed her an aspirin and a paper cup of water. "That ought to make you feel better."

Jessye swallowed the pill, grimacing as she did so. "Thanks. You'd think they'd have sense enough to put some sugar in these things." She smiled at Axel. "You're a prince."

"Oh, it was nothing."

Kate looked at Axel, a peacock with his plumage on full display, and shook her head. If she were mean enough, she'd expose him. The gnat-head thought he could court both women and neither would notice. Well, if he wanted a chance with Jessye, she'd give it to him.

"Jessye, I'll be away this weekend. Would you take care of the store Friday and Saturday? You can be off Monday and Tuesday."

"Sure. I love having a four-day work week. We can fix that permanently."

Instinctively, Kate knew that Axel had fixed his gaze on her, but with Jessye as his real goal, he had to keep his thoughts about her and Luke to himself.

Kate drove home that night with a sullen uncooperative Randy. She knew Luke's refusal to give Randy his cell

phone number had hurt the boy. Maybe she'd been wron
in telling him to call Luke if he got into trouble, but sh
hadn't remembered Luke's terrible trauma over his wife
death. She fixed a simple meal of beefburgers, baked pot
toes, and green salad, and they ate in silence, becaus
Randy wouldn't talk. When she thought he'd gone to be
she heard him talking on the phone and prayed that he'
called Luke. She stood by his room door long enough
discover that he'd actually called Amy Hickson in Cautio
Point, and her heart ached for him. He'd needed an eg
boost, and had known he'd get it from Amy. She tiptoe
to her room and prepared for bed.

Later, she answered the telephone reluctantly, for sl
didn't relish speaking with either Axel or Luke. "Hello

"Hello, Kate. This is Luke." As if she wouldn't kno
that voice anywhere, and at any time. "Randy left PAL ar
didn't come back. I'm sorry I upset him. I shouldn't ha
been so blunt. But—"

"I understand, Luke. Or at least I think I do. And
know it all harks back to your experience with your wif
I should have remembered that, but I didn't, and I'
practically ruptured Randy's relationship with you."

"That's what I'm worried about. Kids can be unforgivin
and he and I had begun to develop a good relationship."

What an understatement. Randy had idolized Luk
"He'll get over it, but it'll take time. He doesn't want
go back to PAL, but it's the best thing for him, and I'
going to make him attend every day. Let me know if yo
don't see him there."

"All right." Silence interrupted their awkward convers
tion, and the pain of it tore into her. She wanted to han
up.

"I see I have some mending to do with you, as well,
he said, "but I'll let that wait till we're together. For no
believe that I'd no more hurt you than I'd sever my righ
arm from my body. I mean that, Kate."

They said good night. She'd give a lot to know how their song would play out. Ten years of living death in a vapid unfulfilling marriage had left her unduly cautious and overly sensitive. And, for this strong man of principle, the legacy of marriage was agonizing self-doubt. For Randy's sake, she hoped they could bridge the chasms that kept them apart.

"It's time I opened up my place in Biddle," Luke said to Marcus, referring to his summer house on the Albermarle Sound. "So I won't get to see you this weekend. Last fall, I boarded up the windows and doors, tied down the lawn furniture. There's plenty to do."

"I'd help you, but I promised Amanda I'd get these lawns and this garden into shape. Maybe next weekend."

Luke pulled up to his house in Biddle shortly after dark, unboarded the front door, and walked in to find everything as he'd left it. He turned on the refrigerator and went back to his car for his luggage and supplies. After working late into the night, he heated two slices of pepperoni pizza, got a bottle of Heineken, and sat out on his back porch to enjoy his supper. Waves roared in the Atlantic and sloshed ominously against each other. Still, the sound carried with it a peaceful quality, a guarantee of life; it had roared in that spot from the beginning of time, and it always would. He propped his feet against the banister and took a swig of beer from the icy bottle. This was his place, where he could be himself, free of the problems and personalities that he had to deal with every day at the Second Precinct. Not that he minded. He loved his job, and had no problem controlling his men. Even Axel would cave in if he showed him the hatchet. He got up to go inside, glanced at the house next door, and stopped. The place had been empty for the two years he'd lived there, but a light shone in every room. He'd go over the next morning and introduce himself.

Around ten the next morning, he knocked on his new neighbor's back door. The door wouldn't open, so he went around to the front and waited.

"*Luke!*"

"*Kate!*"

They spoke simultaneously, and he figured that if his surprise was as obvious as hers, they made a bizarre sight. "What are you doing here?" Again, they spoke in unison.

"I own the house next door. Bought it a couple of years ago," Luke said. "Are you renting this for the season?"

Clearly nonplussed, she shook her head as though in disbelief. "I bought it a few weeks after I settled in Portsmouth. I had no idea you—"

He cut her off with a wave of his hand. "Of course not. You didn't even know me." He noticed that she didn't ask him to come in. "When did you move in?"

"Last night. We're just trying to get the place in shape."

"Who's that, Mom?" Randy asked, and Luke could hear him running toward the front of the house. "*Oh!* What's he doing here?" He spun around and left them.

The best antidote for that was to ignore it. "Maybe we could have a cookout this evening," he said.

"Uh, if I'm not too tired."

"Look, I can fix that back doorknob for you, and maybe most things you want repaired."

"Thanks, but I was planning to go to the village, get a handyman, and let him get the place in order."

"The only things in the village are a filling station and a place to buy milk, charcoal, and the newspaper. I doubt you'll find a handyman in Jarvisburg, and that's the only built-up place near here." If she didn't want his help, fine. He wasn't going to impose on her. "I'll be next-door if you do need me."

Kate closed the door and tried to deal with her shock.

A house next to Luke Hickson's, and she had paid cash for it. She walked to the back porch, where Randy struggled to open the door. "Captain Luke said he'll fix that for us. I'd rather you cleaned up the debris around this house. Seems like everything but whales washes in from the ocean."

She tried the doorknob, and it came off in her hand. "I know you're upset with Captain Luke, Randy, but we can't sleep here tonight with the door in this shape. I can't tell whether it's locked or unlocked. It's dangerous."

"I don't want him here."

She rubbed her hands up and down her sides, took a deep breath, and let it out. "You do not tell me what to do. I'm going to ask him to fix this door, and that's that."

She knocked on Luke's front door a few minutes later. Seeing him nude from the waist up, as he was when he opened the door, rocked her. She stared at his thick chest, prominent pectorals, and washboard belly, and couldn't open her mouth. Heat flushed her body, and when it settled she didn't dare look at him, knowing that her face would carry the telltale signs of desire.

"Need me for something?" He said it airily, but he didn't fool her. The man knew he'd poleaxed her.

Get yourself together, girl. She made herself look at him, expecting a roguish grin, but she'd never seen him in a more serious mood.

"I said, do you need me?"

"I . . . Yes, I do. It's the door. Randy tried to fix it, and it's a total mess. Could you—"

He held out his hand. "Kate, are you angry with me? I know I've disappointed Randy, but surely you understand why."

"I'm not . . . I'm not angry with you, Luke. I'm—"

He grasped her hand. "Then come in here. Kate, come in here. I have to hold you."

She didn't want to need Luke, didn't want her world

to revolve around him, because she hadn't planned on learning a lesson a second time. But she did need him, and she hated herself right then because she wanted to be in Luke's arms. And he wanted her there. She looked up into his impatient desire-filled eyes, the fiery gaze of a lover, an impatient lover fit to explode, and opened her arms. He lifted her to him, stepped inside, and kicked the door shut.

One of his arms wrapped around her shoulders and the other clamped her hips, straining her to him. She slid her arms to his shoulders, clung to his naked flesh, and waited, waited while he gazed into her eyes—searching for she didn't know what—and fighting himself, her, and the heat exploding between them. Her lips parted, and his mouth claimed them. There was no gentleness in the way he kissed her, but she didn't want civilized loving. She wanted him with his defenses down, without his public persona and his refined passion. She wanted the raw man without the smoothness and the charisma, and she needed him to show her his deprivation and his awful hunger. He squeezed her to him until she began to ache, and his mouth trembled against hers as his tongue plunged into her. She held him and loved him until she thought he'd snatch her soul. Frightened by the consuming power of her feelings, she tried to break the kiss. But he intensified the heat of it, squeezing her to him while his tongue savored every crevice of her mouth, promising, teasing, sapping her willpower.

"Luke!"

Still holding her off the floor, he buried his face in the curve of her neck. She called his name several times before he set her on her feet. This Luke was not the disciplined detective that he'd always presented to her, but primal man from whom an aura of wildness emanated, who had an earthiness, a raw texture that both excited and frightened her.

"Luke, I didn't mean for anything like this to happen. I just wanted you to—"

He interrupted, his voice winded and gravelly. "Don't tell me that. I don't believe it. It's been eating you just like it's been gnawing at me since we stood in my brother's foyer Friday before last. You wanted to get to me just like I wanted to get to you. It's this way with us, Kate. I feel as if I'm standing here digging my grave. I have to find who's after you, but I can't concentrate on the problem, because anytime I'm alone I'm thinking about you. And every time I yield to what I feel, I'm in that much deeper. *But, my God, I want you!*"

She looked around, searching for a way out while her trembling body betrayed her longing. "Luke! Oh, Lord. Randy could come over here any minute."

He removed his hands from her body. "Don't I know it? I'll be over to your place shortly to fix that door, and anything else that needs fixing. And you tell Randy I don't accept rotten behavior from kids, not even if they're angry with me. I respect him, and he'd better do the same for me."

"Luke, he's hurt. He's using anger as a cover."

He let out a long breath. "I know, and I have to find a way to patch it up, because I care about him. But I won't give him my cell phone number. That's out." She stared as he leaned against the doorjamb, his arms folded across his chest, his hard biceps emphasizing his masculinity. With his relaxed appearance, he looked as if he'd never had a concern in his life, while the tornado he'd let loose in her still roared in full furor.

"I understand," she said. And she did. She turned to go back to her house, then stopped. Who did he think he was, charging her up as if she were a human battery and then letting the unused electricity trickle out?

She whirled around and faced him. "How can you act so . . . as if nothing happened? You want me to believe the world didn't stop two minutes ago when you went at me as if I were the last woman alive?"

His naked chest sprouted beads of perspiration, and he raised himself to his full height, his feet wide apart, his balled fists dangling loosely at his side and his eyes narrowed.

Her nerves went on a rampage, but she was damned if she'd back down. "The rest of us humans should show our feelings, but not you. Is that it?" she said, unable to control the tremor in her voice.

"What do you want, Kate? Should I show you what I'm feeling right now? You want me to let it all hang out? Is that it? Well, listen to me, baby. If I ever lose control, you don't want to be there. I'm as full of fire for you this second as I was when I picked you up and pulled you in here. You want me to send my fist through that window as proof? Huh?"

Her heart thundered, and her lips quivered at the prospect. Yes! She wanted him just like that. Out of control. For once, she wanted him minus his mask. But she didn't dare risk pushing him further.

"I'd . . . better get back."

"Yeah. You do that. I'll be over in a minute to fix that door."

Luke gazed after Kate as she crossed the narrow strip of lawn between their houses, and wondered which of them owned it. He had to watch his step with her, because the next time, if there was one, he knew they'd go all the way. And if he did that, he'd as good as commit himself to her. He had to learn to keep his hands off her. He went inside, put on a yellow short-sleeved T-shirt, selected some tools, closed his front door, and headed over to Kate's house.

An enormous burden fell from his shoulders when Kate told him Randy had decided to remain in his room and paint. He preferred to straighten out his relationship with the boy when Kate wasn't around.

"Let's have a look at that door," he said as he entered, hoping to set the tone of their relationship. He repaired the doorknob, the stove, electric sockets, several electrical fixtures, and rehung a window.

"Anything else around here that doesn't work?"

"Plenty," she said, "but you can't fix it with a hammer, nails, and pliers."

He didn't look at her. "I have a power saw and a hatchet over there. Think either one of those would work?"

When he felt a towel strike the back of his neck, he wished he *had* looked at her. He gazed at her for a second before letting a grin settle around his mouth. "Feeling violent, huh? I've been told there's a relationship between that and what you'd *really* like to do to me."

She could give as good as she got, he saw, when her face bloomed into a smile. "And did your informant tell you what to do when you're expecting a warm greeting and get an arctic blast instead?"

His grin took over and spread into a genuine laugh. "Give me some credit. I know how to start a fire. Wouldn't you say?"

"What would impress me right now is how you put one out."

He knew she'd get mad, but he couldn't help laughing. "Come on, Kate, lighten up. If I was perfect, you wouldn't like me any better than you like Strange."

"Who told you I don't like Lieutenant Strange?"

"The way your body moved into me over there at my house. Besides, Randy can't stand him, and kids have a way of reflecting their parents' attitudes."

She raised an eyebrow and propped her left hand on her hip, and he knew what was coming. "Right now, Randy isn't crazy about you. Is he reflecting my feelings?"

"That's not what you said a few minutes ago. Come on,

honey." He didn't know what made him do it, but he stepped closer and opened his arms. "Sweetheart, come here. I know we need to find out where this thing's going, but my priority right now is protecting your life. For that, I need a cool head."

She put her arms around his waist, hugged him, and stepped away. "When you can stop blaming yourself for something that couldn't have been avoided, you'll see this differently."

He shrugged. "Maybe. Two strange men have been seen around town. One's tall, and the other's older and barrel-chested. If you see them, be certain they don't see you." He closed his eyes as reality hit him. "If I'd been thinking straight, I'd have told you about those guys immediately. I can't afford to lose my edge, Kate. So I'm going to try to avoid scenes like the one over at my place this afternoon. If you're patient, I won't have to worry about an arctic blast when I get this thing solved."

"All right. But don't start anything."

His smile had to be wan and unconvincing. "I'll work at it, Kate. And I'll need all the cooperation I can get."

Two weeks later, Kate concluded that Luke didn't intend to weaken in his resolve to keep his hands off her. She found that she didn't mind, though he managed it by staying away from her. She had as much as she could handle with Randy having reverted to his old, disobedient self and Axel constantly in her way. If he wasn't sidling up to her, he was hitting on Jessye when he thought she didn't see him. Luke stayed away, and she could count on Jenkins taking Randy to PAL every afternoon and bringing him back to the store at five-thirty.

"How does he behave at PAL?" she asked the officer after Randy had gone into her office.

Jenkins displayed a reticence to talk that she figured was

somehow related to Luke. "Well ... he does what he's supposed to do, and keeps his group ahead of the others."

So he didn't intend to mention Luke. All right, she'd ask him. "What about Captain Hickson? How does Randy get along with him?"

"Kate—if I may call you that—Randy's not an easy child. He nurses a grudge the way old people hold on to their youthful memories. He won't go near Luke."

"Just as I thought ... and of course, you may call me Kate."

Jenkins ran his hand over his hair. "I can't figure him out. He's devoted to those ten old folks that he takes a hot meal to every afternoon, even refers to them by their names, knows what they do and don't like to eat, and puts on a stink if there's a mix-up in their meals. He's a good kid. But—"

"I know, and I can't figure out what to do about it."

Jenkins leaned against a row of shelving. "Luke was magic with Randy. He didn't indulge him, and he made some solid demands on him, but Randy loved him." He shook his head. "I tell you, it beats me. See you tomorrow."

Kate helped a woman who'd planned a vacation in Italy find an English-Italian dictionary, then went in her office to speak with Randy.

"Did you see Captain Luke at PAL this afternoon?"

He kept his gaze on the desk. "I haven't been looking for him."

She slapped a hand on each side of her head, looked toward the ceiling and rolled her eyes. "Randy, I'm tired of this attitude. I made a mistake when I told you to call him rather than—"

"Will you please can it, for Pete's sake? I'm sick of hearing about him. I'm going to find Grandma Middleton. She won't like him, either."

Kate stared at her son, and Nathan's stories about his

parents' low esteem of her once more crowded her mind. "How do you know they won't like him?"

" 'Cause Daddy said they were rich, and people had to look up to them."

She grabbed his shoulders. "People don't *have* to look up to anybody, and certainly not because the person is rich. If you want respect, Randy, you earn it with honesty, integrity, and common decency."

"But Daddy said so."

She didn't want her son to lose faith in his father, so she changed the topic. "These little doodles you're always making. Miss Martha Jessup wants to include some childrens' art in her gallery. Pick out the ones you like best, and we'll drop them at her place on our way home."

"Where's your boss?" she heard Axel ask Jessye, a hopeful ring in his voice.

"In the back with Randy," Jessye said. "What can I do for you, handsome?" After a brief silence, she went on, "Want something to read, honey?"

"Now, Jessye, quit fooling around. Why won't you give me a break? I'd settle for a movie tonight."

"With me? Lord, and here I thought you were hot after my little old cousin. Men up north where you come from sure must play it close to the chest."

"But, Jessye, that's only because she was here before I saw you, and she expects me to pay attention to her."

Scoundrel! Not even he believed that line. And if he thought Jessye was from the sticks and had a head full of hayseed, he had a surprise coming.

Jessye didn't make him wait for it, either. "Honey, just because I left South Carolina less than a month ago doesn't mean I was born the day before I got here. You're after Kate, but you want me. I'm dying to see how you plan to manage that."

Met your match, buddy, Kate said to herself. *When it comes to two-timing, Jessye wrote the book.*

"Don't tell me you're chasing that stud."

"What stud? I never have to go after a man. Honey, you got bats in your belfry. I do declare! If you're not one big laugh."

"You know who I'm talking about. Hickson." The seductiveness went out of his voice. Even listening through the door, the words came across with a snarl.

"Captain Hickson? A stud, huh? Well, sugah, if he's a stud, I haven't seen any evidence of it. I'll have to check that out."

Enough of that. Kate ambled casually out of the office. "Well, Lieutenant. How's it going?" She squelched a laugh. If the man had been caught stealing, his face couldn't have had a more guilty expression.

"I uh . . . How about the three of us taking in that Will Smith movie?"

"Oh, I wouldn't crowd your date with Jessye. Besides, I promised Randy I'd take him somewhere. You two have a good time."

Jessye's deep sigh heralded a piece of acting worthy of Katherine Hepburn or the great Ethel Waters, and Kate primed herself for some first-class entertainment. Axel looked at Jessye, his real target.

She sighed again, this time more deeply, and swayed slightly for good measure. "One of y'all please hand me my aspirins. I do declare these headaches have got to stop."

Axel showed more guts than she'd have credited him with when he said, "Aw, Jessye, you didn't have a headache a minute ago."

Jessye stopped wilting and narrowed an eye. "A minute ago no man had ever asked me to go out with him and some other girl. Last time I did that was when my daddy made my big sister go with me and my date to Sunday evening Baptist Training Union. Kate, hand me my aspirins in that drawer, please."

Kate gave her the bottle. Axel rushed to the water cooler

and returned to find Jessye sitting down with her head thrown back and eyes closed. He gazed down at her with such longing that Kate couldn't watch. If he'd never had a broken heart, he was about to learn how it felt.

Luke strolled through Jessup's gallery, as he frequently did, searching for good paintings by unknown African-American artists. He couldn't find anything that interested him, and started out just as Kate opened the door. He greeted her and Randy, but fixed his gaze on the boy, who averted his eyes and barely mumbled a greeting. What had given this child such a hard heart at so early an age? He suspected that the boy had suffered too many disappointments. No matter what it was, he'd find out.

"We came to give Miss Martha some of Randy's drawings. I hope she'll agree to hang at least one of them."

"Mind if I have a look?"

As he expected, Randy didn't want to release them. "She has a couple of my things on that back wall, Randy."

"Which ones?" Randy asked—the first words the boy had said to him in three weeks.

He told him and decided not to press further for a reconciliation. Less often proved to be more. When he looked at Kate, he knew he'd been wise to stay away from her. Her soft greenish-brown eyes mirrored a longing that he, too, felt, and that opened up that hole in him, that awful pit of loneliness that made a mockery of his strength and his accomplishments. Beneath it all, he was merely a man who needed the love and caring of his woman. A churning began in his belly as if his insides were under attack.

She took his hand. "I hope you're all right, and . . . and everything's fine."

He nodded. "Me, too." Aware that she'd had a need to touch him, he squeezed her hand. "I'll be in touch."

As he stepped out of the gallery, his cell phone rang. "Hickson."

"This is Rude. One of the brothers just saw those two goons on Deep Creek headed toward Race Street."

"Anything stand out?"

"Yeah, man. They're still wearing those nineteen fifties fedoras. We're tailin' 'em to see where they go."

Luke raced to his car, paged Cowan, and gave him the information. Deep Creek and Race was only five blocks from Martha Jessup's gallery. He went back inside and looked around until he saw them. Randy stood staring at one of Luke's eleven-by-eighteen color doodlings. "It's awesome," he heard the boy say as he approached them.

"Thanks. Did she accept one of yours?"

The boy's eyes widened in surprise at seeing Luke. "Two of them, but she has to frame them."

"I'll drop by and have a look in a day or so." He didn't want to alarm them, but he couldn't risk leaving them alone. "Kate, remember those two men I told you about?" He said it softly, so that Randy wouldn't hear. "They're not too far from here right now, so we'd better leave."

Randy didn't want to go. "I'm not going anywhere till I look at all this stuff."

"Randy, please. I don't want a scene here."

"Let him go by himself," Randy protested. "I want to stay and look at the paintings."

He didn't have time for Randy's histrionics. "Do you want me to pick you up and carry you out of here? Your mother wants to leave, and you're going. I thought we agreed that you're old enough to put your mother's interest before your own. Let's go."

"Oh, all right. I'm sorry, Mom."

"You drive, Kate, and I'll tail you. And park in your garage." Something didn't make sense. How had those guys known where Kate was? He slapped his forehead with his left hand. Of course! They'd been around town buying spies, human tracking devices.

He followed Kate and Randy to the door of her apartment. "Thanks, but I won't come in tonight. Kate, I want you to call Cowan tomorrow morning when you're ready to leave. He'll tail you to the store. And I think it's a good idea to lock the front door and use the buzzer from now on. Okay?"

When she swallowed, her eyes had that wide-eyed vulnerability in them that he'd noticed the morning he met her. He knew that for all her bravery, fear was eating at her like termites in a neglected building, undermining the foundation of her independence. He wanted to hold her and never let her out of his sight, but if he so much as touched her . . .

"Don't worry about this, honey. I'll—"

"Ju . . . just hold me, Luke."

He stared down at her, and all he could think of was the way her body caught fire when he touched her. "Kate, this isn't the . . . ah, baby . . ."

He had her in his arms, rocking her as her fingers caressed his face and her lips pasted their sweetness on his neck.

"I missed you. You don't know how I missed you."

Knowing what would happen next, he held her away from him. "I imagine it's the way I've felt not seeing you, but hold on, honey. Try to be patient. If we're lucky, our day will come."

Chapter Eight

Luke surveyed the surroundings as he stepped out of the building that housed Kate's apartment. Trees were great for shade and for giving a street an upscale appearance, but they could be one big problem if you had a criminal on your tail, or if you were looking for one. The bright moonlight made him an easy target for a marksman, but he searched the area, nonetheless. He couldn't take it for granted that whoever was after Kate didn't know where she lived. Satisfied that there were no prowlers near the building, he got into his car, locked the door, and paged Cowan.

"What have you got for me on those two?"

"Nothing, except I discovered why they're always walking. When they realized I was trailing them, they practically flew in different directions. I suspect they're both track stars, and I'd bet my last dime the fat guy isn't fat, that he's made up to look as if he is. A heavy man can't run as fast as he did."

"Where'd you last see them?"

"About a block from Jessup's Gallery."

"So they had a tip."

"I'm not so sure, Luke. They might have some kind of listening device."

"Yeah. Or a wiretap. These days, electronic eavesdropping is as easy as falling down. Thanks, and keep an eye out."

"You bet."

He drove into his garage and parked. He loved his house, but right then he didn't care to face its emptiness. He moseyed around to the front of the house. How beautiful it all seemed in the quiet night! He leaned against a dogwood tree at the corner of his driveway and gazed at his shadow, a sinister thing a quarter of a block long, and thought about the times he'd pursued men to their criminal ends. The women hadn't been serious law-breakers, mostly prostitutes and petty thieves, but in his rookie years, he had spared none of them. And he didn't regret any of it. Still, one case came back to him time after time: the poor Joe wasn't a hard criminal, only a foolish man who saw an opportunity to make a fast buck, didn't question the source, and now had ten years to stew about it.

He went inside and raced upstairs without turning on the light, and the flashing red button on his private telephone caught his eye immediately. He switched on the light and checked his messages. Martha Armstrong. He blew out a long breath and dialed her number.

"Mrs. Armstrong, this is Captain Hickson."

"Oh, thank you so much for returning my call, Captain. I wanted to reach you before anyone else on the committee did. You know we're having the annual Urban League party the end of May. Mrs. Commonwealth of Virginia has agreed to come as a . . . a sort of, you know attraction, and . . . well, I just couldn't entrust her to any man in this town but you. Besides, if you escort her, I'm sure she'll agree to attend our gala in December."

He closed his eyes and told himself to sound pleasant. He'd spent more than enough hours in the company of Mrs. Joshua Armstrong's female celebrities.

"It's for a good cause," she added hurriedly, sensing his reluctance. "We only have two fund-raisers a year, you know."

"All right. I suppose you'll give me the particulars in due course."

"Oh, Captain, you're simply won-der-ful! I knew I could count on you."

He wasn't going to lie and say it was his pleasure, because it wasn't. "The Urban League is a worthwhile organization, and its fund-raisers are money and time well spent."

He got her off the phone as quickly as possible and remembered that he hadn't eaten dinner. Pizza would have to suffice, so he defrosted a slice, got a bottle of Pilsner and an apple, and ate in front of the television. And still, a restlessness suffused him. After showering, he put on his favorite music and found himself pacing his living room, occasionally examining a statuette, painting, or simple art object that marked a special time in his life. What had happened to the contentment he knew whenever he heard Max Bruch's violin concerto? He kicked off his house shoes and slipped into bed, but the feel of the cool sheets against his flesh irritated him. He looked at his watch. Ten o'clock. He didn't have an excuse to call her. Hell, he didn't need an excuse. He dialed her number.

"Hello." Her sleepy sexy drawl sent heat plowing through him, and he would have hung up, if he hadn't realized that an anonymous call would frighten her.

"Kate, this is Luke."

"Luke? Oh, hi—"

"Sorry I woke you up. I . . . Kate, I called you because I—"

"You saw somebody?" She was fully awake now, no

longer soft and sleepy. "Are you all right? I mean, nothing happened, did it?"

"I'm okay, and nothing happened."

"Luke, why are you calling?" With that strong voice, she had to be standing or, at the least, sitting upright. He wished he hadn't yielded, hadn't tried to fill that awful emptiness by calling her, when he knew better than to follow through on what that call signified.

Though he tried, he couldn't make himself lie to her. "This big empty house gets next to me sometimes. I needed to hear a human voice. I hadn't thought you'd turn in so early." Now, what would she say to that?

A long, cold, and silent minute ate at his nerves. Then she said, "A weak moment, huh? I'll probably have some of those, too, and I hope you'll be understanding."

"Let's pray they don't coincide," he said, imagining the speed with which he'd get to her when that happened.

Her laughter struck him as cynical. "Sorry, but I don't think you'll catch me praying for *that.*"

No. He didn't suppose she would. "From the time we met, I've had the impression that you don't want to be involved with me or any other man, but you don't act like it when . . . when we get into clinches."

"What that means, Luke Hickson, is that I am human and healthy and you're . . . you're like the trigger on a Saturday-night special. I don't start these fires." He was sure he heard laughter in her voice, a wicked kind of mirth. When she said, "But, honey, when *you* start them, I sure do enjoy all that warmth," he was certain of it.

"I'd better let you get back to sleep."

"Why? I'm wide awake now. You accused me of being inconsistent, but what about you? You keep saying you want us to cool off, yet you make that almost impossible. What am I supposed to think?"

"Beats me, Kate. I've never been so wound up about

anything in my life. How about a kiss, so we can get some sleep?"

She made the sound of a kiss. "Now close your eyes and dream. I'll be there." She hung up.

Damn! She had a way of getting next to him, down to the marrow, in the loneliest part of him, where he lived and hurt. He turned out the light beside his bed, slid down between the sheets, and started counting sheep.

He got to work the next morning feeling as if he had a hangover. Before he could drink his coffee, his secretary buzzed him. "Ms. Patterson on two."

He didn't know a woman named Patterson, did he? "This is Captain Hickson."

"Good mawnin', Captain. This is Jessye Patterson over at Kate's Friendly Bookstore."

His antennae shot up in anticipation of news of Kate or Randy. "How may I help you, Ms. Patterson?"

"Oh, Captain, why don't you call me Jessye? All my friends do. I'm in the biggest fix imaginable." He steeled himself for some southern conning. "I want to go to that Urban League party that everybody who's anybody goes to, and I'd just love for you to go with me. I haven't been here long enough to have a regular date, and I'm just dying to go to that affair."

Thank God for Martha Armstrong. "Sorry I can't be the lucky man this time, Jessye. I've already promised Martha Armstrong that I'd escort Mrs. Commonwealth of Virginia. She'll be a special guest at the fund-raiser."

"What a pity! Some other time."

"These things happen. Be seeing you."

He couldn't tell her he'd go with her some other time, because he planned to avoid that. Now, if he could just swallow the rest of his coffee in peace. He checked the police log for the night before, saw nothing interesting or unusual, and decided to concentrate on the unsolved case of a missing husband. He suspected the man was probably in Mexico, avoiding alimony and child payments.

Kate checked off the newly arrived cartons of books with the UPS delivery man and gave Jessye her assignment for the day. She found her cousin's unusual crestfallen behavior worrisome. Jessye loved coffee, so she made a fresh pot, filled two cups, and gave her one.

"If you're not feeling well, Jessye, why don't you take the day off? I can manage."

"I worked myself half to death in my place last night. A woman needs a man to do all those heavy things like hanging curtains and cleaning refrigerators and . . . all that stuff." She waved her right hand airily.

Ever the southern belle, Kate mused, over Jessye's flimsy explanation, disbelieving every word of it, because no one could make her believe Jessye had done any heavy work. "Did you get the tickets to the Urban League party?" Maybe that was the problem.

Jessye released a long sigh. *Now we're getting to the real issue,* Kate told herself. "Were you planning to go to the party with Luke Hickson?" Jessye asked.

She didn't like the tone of that. "He hasn't asked me. Why?"

"Oh, so you didn't turn him down. I hear he's squiring Mrs. Commonwealth of Virginia to the party."

She'd forgotten how catty Jessye could be. She'd been on the receiving end of Jessye's meanness when they were kids, but those days were over.

"So you asked him, and he said he was taken? Jessye, I told you once that I'm not tangling with you over Luke or any other man. And don't expect your little nastiness to upset me. Luke Hickson is forty-two years old, and nobody's going to choose a woman for him, so leave it to him, will you?"

"You changed a lot," Jessye said, her voice conveying an inflection of awe. "You didn't used to be aggressive."

Kate had wondered when they'd have that conversation. Jessye had a sharp mind and a blunt tongue; she had to have noticed that the meek Kate, who'd withstood her childish taunts and unfair comparisons about their respective feminine attributes, no longer existed. Jessye knew that she and Luke had more than a passing interest in each other. But she had always thought herself the more attractive of the two, had acted as if she were, and wanted to believe it, still. Kate knew that one reason she'd married Nathan had been to prove to Jessye that she could get a man, and a rich one at that. Well, Kate was grown now, had learned her lesson, and was not interested in such shenanigans.

She gave Jessye a level stare. "You mean, I was meek, and you pushed me around. Let me tell you, cousin, you weren't nearly as gifted at that as my late husband. Since I don't care what you think of me, I am not, and cannot be, your victim. I will never again be anybody's victim. So chisel yourself down to size, and behave like a grown woman."

"My, my. Aren't we testy today? Sorry, Cousin Kate, but I refuse to fight with you. We're blood kin. Don't forget that."

A good feeling washed over her, like a cool refreshing breeze on a hot humid day. Jessye couldn't upset her and knew it, but she'd compensate by going to any lengths to get Luke to chase her. Inwardly, she laughed. Jessye had better pull out her big guns and do it fast, because Luke showed signs of weakening and cementing their relationship, and she intended to give him plenty of help.

It hadn't occurred to her that Axel might shove Luke in her direction. He burst into the store that evening minutes after Jessye left. "I've got two tickets to the Urban League party. Everybody who's anybody attends that. Would you go with me?"

A refusal settled on the tip of her tongue, but she quickly swallowed it. She didn't have to take a back seat to Mrs. Commonwealth. "Sure you hadn't planned to ask Jessye?"

Eagerness sparkled in his eyes, giving him a boyish appearance. "I wasn't going to ask her unless you said no."

Whatever his game, that had a ring of truth. "Well, if I can get a sitter."

"Then you'll go, because my housekeeper will stay with Randy."

She knew Madge would gladly stay with Randy. "I'll let you know tomorrow."

She didn't want to give him the impression that, by asking her to attend that party with him, he'd presented her with a new world. His rush from the store was no doubt meant to prevent her reconsidering, and maybe she should. As she watched him go, she wondered whether Luke would tell her that he'd be escorting a celebrity.

And why had Axel asked her, when he'd really rather take Jessye? She shrugged. Axel and Jessye deserved each other. She wanted to go to the party, and she would.

On the way home she stopped at a dressmaker known for high fashion creations and ordered a red chiffon strapless dress with a full circle skirt, the flare of which was reinforced with inset panels. The locals just called it a party, but the invitation clearly stated black tie. Axel might be a prune, but he'd look fantastic in a tuxedo. "Let it all hang out, girl," she sang as she darted into Ferragamo's. She left with three-inch-heeled silver sandals and a tiny matching purse. Luke would walk in there looking like a prince among men, and even if Mrs. Commonwealth was a goon, she'd look great hanging on Luke's arm.

Kate laughed as she walked into her apartment. She

couldn't be jealous of somebody she'd never seen. Could she?

"Randy's already had his supper," Madge announced. "I gave him baked ham, turnip greens, and candied sweet potatoes, and he ate every bit of it. He just loved the sweet potatoes, Kate, so you'll have to learn how to make them."

Kate stared at the woman. "Which Randy are we talking about?"

Madge flipped off the TV. "Your Randy. I got to get going, cause Bugs will be on in half an hour and I got to get my clothes in the washer before then."

Kate thanked her. "Uh, Madge, are you sure Randy ate all that?"

"Of course I am. That child just loved those sweet potatoes."

Kate nodded. "I see."

Madge rushed out, and Kate headed for Randy's room. "So now you like candied sweet potatoes? What's different about hers?"

"Hi, Mom. Oh, you've been talking to Miss Madge. She gives me points, depending on how much I eat. When I get enough points, she'll take me to the planetarium."

"Randy, I am not going to let her bribe you to get you to eat. You know you're supposed to eat your meals."

"It's okay, Mom. She's a real good cook, so I'd eat it anyway. I just don't let her know that, and I get my points."

She forced herself to glare at him, though she could hardly suppress the laughter that tried to spill out of her. "You little con artist."

His questioning look bespoke the purest innocence. "You got it wrong, Mom. I'm learning how to survive."

"You *what?*"

"Yeah. Lieutenant Strange was our lecturer at PAL today. He said you have to start early if you don't want to be lost in the ... er, scuffle, I think he said. And he said if we plan to be millionaires by the time we're twenty-one we ought to have our first hundred in our piggy banks right now. Officer Jenkins said that was crap. Is it?"

When Kate could stop laughing, she said, "I have enormous respect for Officer Jenkins."

She loved her time alone with Randy, even when he misbehaved, because she always learned something else about him and about herself. She was loathe to leave him when the phone rang.

"That might be Captain Luke," Randy said. "He called maybe half an hour ago, I guess."

She controlled her urge to race to the phone, and got to it by the fifth ring. "Hello."

"Hello, Kate. This is Luke. How are you?"

She'd been better, but didn't say as much. "Fine. You?"

"Do I detect a bit of frost?"

Frost? She'd like to smack him, but she didn't say that. Instead, she poured on the sugar. "Honey, how could you ask such a question? Don't you know the sound of your voice is sweet music to me?"

"You're laying it on a little too thick, Kate. I assume Jessye told you I agreed to escort Mrs. Commonwealth of Virginia to the Urban League party. At any rate, that's what I called to tell you."

"Mrs. who? Well, since you'd asked for a cooling-off period it didn't occur to me that you'd invite me to go with you, so I made other arrangements."

He let a period of silence pass, to indicate that she'd annoyed him. "How's Randy doing?"

Now, that was a topic she could embrace. "When I last spoke with him, he was learning how to survive."

"He was *what?*"

"You heard me, and apparently conning is the appropriate technique. Lieutenant Strange's lecture at PAL today made a remarkable impression. Fortunately for all concerned, Officer Jenkins assured Randy that what he'd heard in that lecture was—in his word—crap."

"Strange needs another set of brains. I got a report on those two guys, and we're not sure you're their target. Still, I want you to be careful and continue to wait for Cowan. You went home tonight without waiting for him."

"I guess I forgot. I was anxious to stop by the dressmaker and do some more shopping. I'll try to remember."

"All right. I need to know I'm doing everything possible to keep you safe. I have a couple of leads, but I can't share that yet. Just be careful."

"I . . . I will, Luke."

"Kate, you're important to me. I . . . I can't let anything happen to you."

"I know."

"Good night."

She stared at the receiver. He'd hung up. A flare of anger shot through her, then quickly subsided. The man's emotions were waging a war with his head. If he'd taken the pains to ask her, she'd gladly have told him which would win, because every chance she got she intended to stir up his emotions like a poker teasing hot coals.

Luke tied his red bow tie—he hated tying the things— checked his tux jacket for lint, brushed it, and finished dressing. He'd forgotten his vow that he wouldn't squire another of Martha Armstrong's celebrities. During the winter season, she'd roped him in seven times, and he hadn't once enjoyed himself. Add to that Kate's flippancy and cool pretense about the matter, and he wouldn't mind getting one of Jessye's convenient headaches. He laughed. Imagine canceling a date because of a headache! Well, that would certainly whittle away his reputation as a ladies' man.

It hadn't occurred to him to wonder what she'd look like, and he realized with a laugh of self-derision that he didn't care. Age had its virtues. However, Mrs. Commonwealth of Virginia proved to be a forty-five-year-old knockout.

He took the elevator to the S level of the Renaissance Hotel and rang the bell at number S-110.

"I'm Detective Captain Luke Hickson."

She looked him up and down, and he wondered about the Mrs. The lady had a roving eye. "When we're alone," she drawled, "call me Kendra. Otherwise you have to use this silly title."

He was having none of it. "Surely you have a last name," he chided.

She looked at him through slightly lowered lashes. "Rodgers. Are we going to fight all evening, or are you going to be . . . er . . . cooperative?"

He looked down at her and grinned. She was one audacious woman, and if she pushed him he'd enjoy telling her so. "Mrs. Armstrong asks me to escort her celebrity guests." He made a show of rubbing the back of his neck as though searching for an answer. "She hooked me seven times last winter, because she claims she can trust me to keep my hands off them."

Her eyelids raised slowly. "And can she?"

He guided her toward the limousine he'd rented for the evening. "I don't get paid for it, but I consider it a night's work, nonetheless. All of these occasions are held for charitable purposes. I believe in supporting charity."

"You didn't answer my question," she said, adjusting her crown after he'd helped her straighten her white silhouette-style evening gown.

He joined her in the limo and offered her a glass of cold wine, which she accepted without hesitation. "I thought I did. But if you want it more bluntly, beauty is ephemeral and often doesn't go below the surface. Furthermore, I don't consort with other men's wives."

"You're very sure of yourself."

"Let's just say I've lived long enough, hard enough, and well enough to know who I am."

"And you like yourself, don't you?"

So she was disappointed with the rules he'd laid out. He turned to face her. "Damn straight I like myself. Don't you? Where's your husband?"

"He's at home."

"Take my advice and ask him to travel with you. Keep you out of mischief."

"You have a point. Friends?"

He made himself smile. "Sure. Friends."

When they arrived, Luke greeted Mrs. Armstrong and let his gaze sweep the room while she gave Kendra her effusive thanks. He caught sight of—*It couldn't be!* What the devil was she doing with her arm linked with Axel Strange?

"Something wrong?" Kendra asked.

He couldn't believe what he saw. No wonder she hadn't complained when he told her he'd agreed to escort Martha Armstrong's guest.

"Who is she?" Kendra asked, obviously having followed his gaze. "She's stunning in that dress."

"She's stunning, period," he said without weighing his words. He knew he wouldn't have a long wait for Axel's triumphant smile. And the man guided Kate directly to him, all but ignoring the guest of honor.

"Up to your old tricks, I see," Axel said. Turning to Kate, he added, "Trust this fellow to be where the action is."

"Ms. Middleton, this is Kendra Rodgers, the guest of honor," Luke said, ignoring Axel. And with what he hoped was his most steely expression, he said to Kendra, "Mrs. Rodgers, this *gentleman* is Lieutenant Strange, my deputy."

The queen of Virginia matrons raised an eyebrow. "Hmmm. That must be some office. How do you do, Lieutenant?" She winked at Luke. "I teach elementary school, and when my kids get out of line I send them to the blackboard and make them write one hundred times: *I am ashamed of myself*. I don't suppose you can do that."

Luke let himself enjoy a good laugh. "By the time they get to me, it's too late."

He looked at Kate, the personification of elegance. He'd never seen her so lovely, and here she was wasting all that charm and feminine softness on Axel Strange, a man who'd let himself in for a trouncing by a beauty queen.

"Kate, you're ... You look beautiful. Just ... You're lovely."

He knew Kendra stared from Kate to him, but he fixed his gaze on Axel, who'd begun to sulk, his face sullen and angry.

"You look great, too," Kate told him, momentarily diverting his attention from Axel.

"Do you have any children, Mrs. Rodgers?" she asked Kendra, in an obvious effort to engage the woman in friendly conversation.

He let the women talk, stepped aside, and warned Axel. "If you ever attempt to demean me again—even if no one else is present—you look for another job. If you'd been outside just now, I'd have flattened you in a second. And from now on, stay out of my way. Got it?"

"You sure you're not jealous because I have Kate with me?"

"Axel, I wouldn't be jealous of you if I were dying and you were in perfect health. I've warned you. Don't speak to me unless it has to do with your work, and even then, be careful what you say."

"Look, I'm sorry. I was just—"

He didn't want to hear more. "Have a good time," he said to Kate. "I'll be in touch."

"You have a good time, too," Kate said, and she clearly

meant it. "I enjoyed meeting you," she told Kendra, and extended her hand to the woman for a generous shake.

He winked at her and walked on, eager to get out of Axel's presence. He had angered Kate by agreeing to take another woman to the party, but she had been the epitome of graciousness to him and to Kendra. He couldn't help wondering whether she'd dress Axel down for having been rude.

Kate didn't mention Axel's faux pas; she figured Kendra had done a thorough enough job of putting him in his place. But Axel couldn't drop the matter.

"That guy thinks he's the be all and end all."

She ignored the disparaging remark. "I liked Mrs. Commonwealth of Virginia. Didn't you?"

"All that business about Mrs. Armstrong asking him to escort the guest of honor. Not a word of it's true. The guy's a stud. I told you that. And now maybe you'll believe me."

Kate stopped herself before her fists touched her hips. "Lieutenant Strange, if you say one more word about Luke Hickson tonight, I'll leave at once, and you won't be going with me. If you hate him so much, why don't you transfer out of his department?"

"Say, I didn't mean to upset you. I mean ..." He shrugged. "He gets everything I want. But not this time."

Kate stared at Axel. He had definitely heard what she'd said, but he was so obsessed with Luke that he couldn't refrain from calling her bluff. She rested a hand on his arm and whispered in his ear.

"Excuse me. I don't intend to spend the evening listening to you lambaste Luke. Good night, Lieutenant."

"But we just got here."

She looked him in the eye. "Stay as long as you like. Good night."

"You can't—"

"I warned you. *Good night*, Axel."

"Sure."

He hadn't believed her, probably still didn't. She looked around for Luke, and found him in a far corner of the ballroom in a group of five people, but she couldn't catch his attention. She went to the ladies' room, dropped a quarter into the pay phone, and called a taxi. She waited until five minutes had elapsed, then slipped out of the lodge, got into the taxi, and went home.

And for that, she'd bought a five hundred dollar dress. She thought about that for a few minutes, and decided it had been more than worth the money. She'd felt the equal of Kendra Rodgers with all her statuesque beauty and regal crown.

"Randy! What are you doing out of bed this time of night?"

"He refused to go to sleep until you came home," Madge said. "Something about the Lieutenant. I couldn't figure it out. Well, I'll see you tomorrow. Better give him a dose of bicarbonate—he's been eating steadily ever since you left."

She told Madge good night and rushed back into the living room to deal with Randy. "Why didn't you go to bed? If you don't obey Mrs. Robinson, I'll get someone else to sit with you."

Randy's bottom lip protruded as far as she'd ever seen it. "I don't like him, and I don't want you to be friends with him."

"Lieutenant Strange? And that's why you stayed up?"

"I figured if I was up he'd leave."

She didn't laugh, because Randy needed a reprimand. "That isn't your business, Randy, and if you ever do this again I'll punish you. That's a promise."

"I called Amy, and she said he'd kiss you when he brought you home."

She stared at him. "Randy, Amy is six years old, and that hardly makes her an authority on adult behavior."

"Yeah, but she knows a lot. She said her daddy's always kissing her mother. How come he didn't come in?"

"Stop worrying about that man, Randy. I told you he's not important in my life."

"Is Captain Luke important in your life?"

"Randy, go to bed. This minute."

He hung his head. "All right, but is he, Mom?"

Whatever happened between Luke and her would affect Randy, so she told him the truth. "I care a lot for him, Randy, but anything else is way in the future."

A weight seemed to drop from his shoulders, as he raised his head and half smiled. "I'm mad at him, but he's nicer than Lieutenant Strange. He's real different."

Didn't she know it! She kissed his forehead and patted him on the bottom. "Now go to bed and stop worrying."

She couldn't banish the notion that Axel was trying to use her in order to hurt Luke. The man's words suddenly thudded in her head: *He gets everything I want.* So that was it. Axel wanted to get even. He wanted to possess what he thought Luke craved, and he wanted the victory so much that he'd sacrifice his chances with Jessye. *Don't hold your breath, pal.*

Axel leaned against a marble column of the ballroom of The Grand Scenic Lodge and watched the dancers. She'd been gone a while, but who knew why women spent so much time fixing and powdering themselves. He looked at his watch. *Forty minutes!* He walked around the ballroom and, not finding her, went toward the ladies' room.

"Did you see a woman in a red dress in there?"

Her smile acknowledged his masculine presence, but his annoyance simmered close to the surface, and he couldn't appreciate the woman's interest.

"There's no one in there, but I'm sure she's around. She'd have to be stupid to walk out on *you.*"

Kate's words came back to him like a blast of arctic air. He hadn't believed she'd leave, but she'd done it. The heavy pounding of his heart nearly frightened him, and the embarrassment of his suddenly chattering teeth sent him dashing to the men's room, where he struggled to control the anger that boiled in him. *She'll pay for it. If I do nothing else for the rest of my life, I'll find a way to make her pay.*

Luke took Kendra back to her hotel and declined her invitation for a "nightcap."

"What's the matter? If you're unhappy, try to solve it with your husband. Talk with him and let him know you hurt, but don't fool around."

He didn't let her expression of longing touch him. "You're right, of course," she said, her words soft and slow to come. "He's successful, handsome, and charming, and women envy me." Her eyes glistened with unshed tears. "But, Luke, he's an absolutely lousy husband. Well, it's my problem, isn't it? Have a great life, and tell Kate I think she's lucky."

Kate. She and Axel had left early, and he'd spent the last two hours telling himself not to wonder why. It was too much to hope that she'd become fed up and insisted Axel take her home. He left the hotel, got in the limousine, and headed for his town house.

After listening to his messages, he made a note to call Marcus in the morning and meet him for lunch. If only he could talk with Kate for one minute, assure himself that she was all right and that the evening hadn't been a disappointment for her. But he didn't dare telephone her after midnight.

He slept fitfully, awoke early, did thirty pushups, showered, and dressed. After working a couple of hours at home, he went to work.

Axel greeted him at the water cooler. "Luke, I'm sorry about last night. I must have been out of my mind."

"You were."

Luke made a wide path around Axel, giving him plenty

of room and, he hoped, sending the message that he'd meant everything he'd said the previous evening. He went back to his office and put on the red light above his door: Do not disturb. Ten o'clock was a long time coming.

"Hello, Kate, this is Luke."

"Good morning, Luke, how are things?"

He wondered why she sounded breathless. "Fine. You left early. Does that mean you didn't enjoy the party?"

"Is the antagonism between you and Axel irreparable? It's becoming a bore."

So that was it. "If that's what you detect, it's one-sided. I don't spend my time thinking or worrying about Strange. He's . . . well, he's like he is."

"Hmm."

"I didn't think he'd continue it after I walked away. A smart man doesn't focus a woman's attention on another guy. I don't suppose I'm entitled to know why you went with him."

"No, you definitely are not, since I didn't figure in your plans."

"Ouch! Are you going to forgive me?"

"I'll think about it."

"I couldn't have a kiss, could I?"

"You think you deserve one?"

"I sure do. I didn't embarrass you by knocking Strange flat on his back last night, and that took some willpower."

She blew a kiss over the wire. "There. I have to get to work. Bye."

He told her good-bye and took solace in the fact that she wasn't angry with him. A bulletin sticking out of his in basket caught his eye, and he pulled it out. Mutt and Jeff, the code names for the two strangers who spent their days in Portsmouth and their nights elsewhere, had recently been seen in Charleston, South Carolina. He phoned Kate.

"Did you tell me you grew up in South Carolina?"

"Yes, why?"

"No special reason as of now. Where did you grow up?"

"Orangeburg."

"I'm looking for clues as to who's after you."

"Why don't you believe my in-laws are involved in this?"

"Because they don't fit the profile of people who'd try to harm the mother of their only grandchild. But not to worry. One slip, and I'll catch him. You stay sweet."

He phoned Marcus. "How about a quick lunch?"

"Great. Meet you at the River Café at one."

The waiter led them to their usual table. "So, what's going on with you and Kate?" Marcus asked him.

"The same. Why?"

Marcus sipped his lemonade, explaining that he had a tedious job to do after lunch and wouldn't drink beer. "Why'm I asking? My six-year-old daughter is worried. She said Randy is afraid Strange will kiss Kate, and he doesn't like Strange. He's unhappy, and Amy, being the woman she is, doesn't want her man to be unhappy. She told me to tell you to keep that strange man away from Kate."

Luke had to cough for several minutes before he could speak. "Tell her Kate's particular about who she kisses."

Marcus eyed him straight on. "Is she?"

"If she kisses Strange, I expect it'll be under duress."

"Glad to hear it. How is old Strange?"

"Probably somewhere pounding out the dents in his integrity. If he's an example of the way a rich only child turns out, give me poverty."

"What's he after?"

"Right now? Kate. Or whatever else he thinks I want."

"Do you want Kate?"

He finished his coffee and stood. "Does the sun rise in the east? Let's go."

At three o'clock, he steeled himself for another confrontation with Randy. He didn't expect the boy to enjoy a half hour lecture on altruism. He'd become attached to his clients, as he called the senior citizens to whom he delivered hot food, but he didn't associate that with helping others in general.

Randy surprised him. "Captain Luke," he said before the lecture began, his voice filled with warmth as if there had been no enmity between them. "I have a new plan for my group. I'll get my clients' phone numbers. Each boy will be responsible for three seniors, and he has to call them twice every day to see if they're all right."

I will definitely recover from this, Luke told himself. "Let me see your chart," he said to Randy. "Looks good to me. Instead of my lecture on this topic, why don't you explain it to the boys?"

"Yes, *sir*."

"Great job," he told Randy later, and suggested that they talk.

"Sorry, sir, but I have to meet Officer Jenkins now to take the dinners to my clients."

When he rested his hands lightly on the boy's shoulders, Randy turned, smiled at him, and ran off. Now, what had happened to cause that turnabout? He rubbed the back of his neck as he watched Randy run off. Marcus's story flashed into his mind. He could hardly believe it. Randy didn't want his mother with Axel Strange, and he had concluded that—because he had been rude to Luke— Kate had decided he didn't like Luke and had gone out with Axel. Randy was now removing himself as an obstacle to his friendship with the boy's mother. He shook his head. Randy and Amy. What a pair of minds.

Later, in his office, Luke swung around in his swivel desk chair and slapped his hands over his knees. Seeing Kate wasn't smart, but Jenkins couldn't take Randy to his mother's store, and all other officers were busy. Strange was free, but Randy would rather spend the night alone down in that dark basement than go any place with Axel. He'd have to do it himself.

With Randy beside him, he reached for the door of Kate's bookstore and stopped. Gashes around the lock suggested that someone had attempted to open the door without a key. He didn't want to alarm the boy. Without mentioning it, he opened the door and went in.

To his disgust, Axel's jacket lay on the arm of the sofa that faced the cashier. He looked around and spied his deputy on his knees shelving books. At five-thirty in the afternoon, the man could do as he liked, for the office had closed. He could only ignore him.

"Sorry, Luke," Kate whispered. "I asked him to leave that for Randy, but . . . well, you know him better than I do."

Randy was less charitable. "Why can't he open his own store?" Randy asked her. "Mom, tell him to stay out of here."

At least the boy's honest, Luke thought.

"We've had this conversation before, Randy, so please don't persist, and don't be rude."

"How are you, Kate?" he asked as Randy left them to go into his mother's office.

Though obviously surprised, she let him know her pleasure at seeing him. "I'm making it."

He raised an eyebrow. "That all? Say, looks as if someone tried to jimmy your lock. When did that happen?"

Her eyes widened. "Are you serious? I haven't noticed a thing. Good Lord, what next?"

He meant his words to comfort her, so he spoke softly. "That lock will hold, so don't worry. Going to Biddle this weekend?" He hadn't gone there for the last few weeks, avoiding the temptation that being near her presented.

"I'm planning to," she said. "I go every weekend, and I've missed you."

A stack of books tumbled over, and he watched Axel deal with them. Something had gone amiss at the party, and Axel felt the need to make amends, but surely he could have found a more dignified way.

At that point, Jessye strolled out of the stockroom and walked over to Axel. "Lieutenant, honey, you'll break your back. Randy'll do that."

Axel rested on his haunches. "In case he doesn't, I don't want you to be stuck with it."

"You're such a sweetheart." She turned, and, seeing Luke and Kate for the first time, gaped in embarrassment. "Captain Hickson, I do declare. Honey, you give a girl heart palpitations."

Hearing her address Luke, Axel stood, got his jacket, and put it on as one would a royal vestment. "Didn't see you guys." With his gaze on Kate, he said, "You must have fifty copies of something called *Watermelon Time*. What's that book about?"

Luke knew Axel deliberately ignored him, and he couldn't have been more pleased.

"The book's about a small-town Southern lynching in the nineteen thirties. That's my third shipment. It's very popular."

"Good evening, Lieutenant," Luke said, forcing Axel to recognize him.

"Good evening," Axel replied, his gaze never wavering from Kate. "Why do people keep bringing up that old stuff from sixty years ago?"

In a voice minus inflection, Kate replied, "There must have been ten books published about Thomas Jefferson in the last couple of years. Wonder why people keep bringing up *that* old stuff from two hundred and fifty years ago?"

Luke let himself smirk, and enjoyed it until his glance caught the expression on Jessye's face. She'd been making a play for him, but he was used to that, and it hadn't concerned him. But this woman wanted him, and she had the audacity to wet her lips and gaze at his mouth when he saw her naked desire.

What the devil was going on? Axel stared from Jessye to him, his lips curled into a nasty snarl of hatred. Luke shook his head. Did the man want both women, or had Jessye's indiscretion aroused Axel's competitiveness with him? Whatever! He wasn't going to sweat it.

"I'll see you this weekend," he told Kate, letting his hand clasp hers briefly. "And keep that door locked at all times." With a smile, she could get him completely discombobulated. Unable to resist touching her, he stroked her chin with his right thumb. "Be sure to get there early. I'll plan a cookout. OK?"

She nodded. He looked down at her for a moment. "See you." He couldn't help glancing in the direction of Jessye and Alex, for he knew they had locked their gazes on Kate and him. He shrugged it off and got out of there.

Chapter Nine

"Get up, Mom. I wanna go swimming." Kate rolled over and looked at her watch. Nine o'clock in the morning. Saturday morning.

"Randy, I'm sleepy. Can't you find something else to do until I get up?"

"Oh, all right."

She dragged herself up an hour later, dressed, and went into the kitchen. "What did you eat?" she asked Randy.

"Milk and cereal. Now can I go swimming?"

"Seems awfully windy." She went to the back porch and looked out toward the ocean. "It's too windy. Too rough out there. Wait till the wind dies down. I'm not going out there now."

She hadn't expected him to have a tantrum, but his almost sullen quietness disturbed her. "We'll go out this afternoon," she assured him. "So why don't you go in your room and work on that watercolor until lunch? I'm going to write a letter, and then I'll paint the woodwork in the kitchen."

She wrote a short letter to her father, something she did at least once each week. Then she covered the floor with newspaper, put a shower cap on her head, got her work gloves, and went to work.

Luke got his lawn furniture out of the garage and carried it around to his back lawn. He loved lying on the old chaise lounge late evenings and nights listening to the water and the night sounds.

He looked out toward the ocean, and stopped cold. Where was Kate? Surely, she wouldn't allow Randy to swim alone in the ocean, and especially not in windy weather. He looked toward her house, but didn't see her following the boy. Randy had reached the water. He stared in horror as the boy plunged in and began to swim.

"Of all the knuckleheaded—" He jerked off his belt, emptied his pockets, and raced to the water. Where on earth was Randy? *Calm now,* he told himself. Then he saw him, already too far out, fighting the wind and the tide to get back to the shore. He kicked off his sneakers and dived in, glad he hadn't eaten because he'd never been able to swim with a full stomach. He swam as fast as he could toward the spot where he'd last seen the boy, pulled himself up and looked around. He didn't see him.

"Help." Though faint, the sound was not far away. He turned to his right, swam a few paces, and caught Randy trying to keep his head above the water.

"Do as I tell you, or we'll both drown."

It seemed as though hours passed before he got them back to shore. Randy could hardly stand, so he picked him up and carried him home. Not to Kate's house, but to his. He had a few things to say to that boy, and he didn't want to be interrupted.

He handed Randy one of his T-shirts. "Go take a shower, dry off, and put this on. Then come back here."

"Yes, sir."

He washed himself down with the lawn hose, dried off,

put on a T-shirt and a pair of Bermuda shorts, and waited for Randy.

He didn't believe the boy had Kate's permission to swim alone in the Atlantic Ocean, on even the calmest day. Randy's erratic behavior distressed him. He heated some milk in a saucepan, and made some hot cocoa.

"Drink this," he said when Randy came into the kitchen. "I'm not going to ask if you had your mother's permission to do that, because I know you didn't. If I hadn't seen you running to the beach, you'd be dead right now. Why do you disobey your mother?"

"I don't—"

"You're going to sit here until I'm satisfied you won't do anything like that again. Why do you do it?"

" 'Cause my daddy said she didn't know what she was talking about, and he said my Grandpa and Grandma Middleton didn't think much of her."

Luke sat down facing Randy. "Your daddy did not tell you that."

"He told my Mom that. Lots of times."

"I understand your father got killed test-driving a sports car. Right?"

"Yes, sir."

"You don't want to hear what I think of daredevils. If he'd used better judgment himself, he'd be alive today. Your daddy said those things to your mother when he was angry. Right?"

"Yes, sir."

"When you get angry with your friends, you say things you don't mean?"

"Yes, sir."

"Good. Let's understand each other. Your mother is an intelligent clever woman who is smart enough to take excellent care of you. You owe her obedience and respect. The next time you do a stupid thing like you did today, I may not be around to save you. If you were my own son,

I promise you I'd put you across my knee and paddle you, because that's what you deserve.''

"I'm not going to do anything like that again, Captain Luke. Cross my heart.''

"Fine. Are you going to obey your mother and respect her? If you can't answer yes, I don't want anything else to do with you. I mean that, Randy.''

"Yes, sir. I mean, I'm not going to be bad to her anymore. I'm . . . I'm sorry about everything this morning. And . . . and thanks for coming and getting me. I was scared.''

"I know you were. Next time, ask your mother.''

"I did, and she told me not to go.''

Luke shook his head. "You learned a tough lesson, and I want you to remember it.''

"Yes, sir. I sure will.''

"*Luke! Luke!* Have you seen Randy? I can't find him anywhere!''

Luke opened the screen door. "He's here. Come on in.''

Shivers coursed through him, and he couldn't account for his skin's cold dampness. He walked out into the bright sunlight, hoping to get warm, but he had to lean against the gate to steady himself. He closed his eyes, and the waves headed toward him, huge waves that could pitch him to the bottom, and with him Kate Middleton's child. He gasped for breath and clung to the gatepost.

Get your act together, he chided himself. It had been close. Close for Randy, and close for him. He couldn't figure out how he'd done it; he'd never before been in a swift moving tide, and he couldn't imagine having swum against one.

Kate stepped out of the house, clearly shaken. He walked toward her with his arms open and she dashed into them, tears flooding her face. "He told me. I could have lost him. If it hadn't been for you, I wouldn't have him.''

When his arms enveloped her, he realized that he

needed her as much as she needed him. If he had lost
Randy, he didn't think he could handle it. Tremors seemed
to possess her body, and he held her tightly to reassure
her and to steady her, and because he needed to protect
her.

"It's all right, baby. He's safe. And he won't do it again.
Let's put that behind us. He told you everything, I take
it?"

"He said he didn't remember your swimming back with
him, only getting his feet on the shore. He's still scared."

"Yeah. And if he knew what I know, he'd stay scared a
long time. Why don't I fix lunch? I've got plenty of hot
dogs."

"I can make potato salad." Her wide bright smile
warmed his very soul. He stared down at her, and her soft
greenish-brown eyes returned his look of longing.

"If I . . ." No, he couldn't ask her that. *Not now.* But one
day soon, he'd take her away with him and love her as he
longed to do.

"Sweet," he whispered. "You're so . . . so sweet."

She hugged him closer and kissed his left cheek. "I
could be with you like this forever."

Let Randy worry about who kissed his mother. Beside,
the boy owed him one. Several, in fact. He squeezed her to
him, so close that air couldn't penetrate the space between
them. "Put your arms around me and kiss me, honey."

"But Randy—"

"Owes me big time." He lowered his head and drank
in the sweetness from her parted lips. Her arms tightened
around him, but he had to break it off, lest it get out of
control, because when she got started, there was no stop-
ping her. He hugged her.

"I don't want us to be the subject of Amy and Randy's
analysis tonight. When does he call her?"

"According to my phone bill, any time and often."

"Go get your salad and I'll roast the franks and warm the buns."

He watched her walk away, and the rhythmic sway of her hips sent heat flying through him. Yeah. She'd be an armful, all right.

Kate swung around and went back to where Randy sat in his catatonic-like position. Still as a statue. "Come home and get some clothes, Randy. You're lost in Captain Luke's shirt." He sat so motionless and so quiet that she feared he'd become depressed.

"Randy?"

"Mom, can I just stay over here with Captain Luke?"

She examined his face carefully. "Are you feeling all right?"

He nodded. "He almost got killed on account of me."

Guilt and shock. Not a good combination. She hugged him, and his fierce return stunned her, for he disdained exhibitions of affection.

"You may stay. I'll bring your clothes over, honey."

She kissed him on the forehead and looked up into the searing gaze that told her more than Luke had ever said with words. How could he expect her to be immune to his passionate kisses and desire-laden glances and expressions? It no longer mattered that neither of them had wanted to become involved. They *were* involved, because they cared deeply for each other. If he denied that, she wouldn't believe him.

Later, after they'd eaten lunch, the ring of Luke's cell phone interrupted what had been for them a season of bonding, of quiet togetherness. Randy had fallen asleep, and she and Luke sat on the sofa, not speaking, only gazing into each other's eyes and holding hands. She'd been at peace, had known an unfamiliar tranquility, something with which she'd had such little experience in her marriage.

He answered the phone. "When was that?" After listening for a few seconds, he said, "Yeah. It smells, all right. I know someone who'll take care of it. I'll call you in an hour."

Kate had a premonition that the call concerned her or her store, and she waited to hear what he'd say. Minutes passed, but he didn't share it with her, and she fought back the anger that threatened to obliterate the bond they had so recently cemented.

"Randy's asleep, so I'll carry him over to your place. We'll get together and make plans for dinner. Maybe a cookout. Okay?"

So he needed privacy for that phone call. She nodded. "I'll take a nap, " she said, making it easy for him. "This fresh salty air makes me sleepy."

She tried to shake it off, to push it aside, but anxiety gnawed at her, nonetheless. She'd trust him with her life, but she wanted the decisive voice in whatever affected her and her affairs.

Luke paced from one end of his back porch to the other. What did the guy want? Papers? A particular item? Certainly not drugs. The man hadn't touched the cash register, and hadn't trashed the store, though he'd obviously gone into Kate's office and searched her desk. At least they now had a description of him.

He telephoned Rude. "Luke here." He told him about the break-in at Kate's store. "See if you can get a line on this guy, Rude. I'll have my men out, but this fellow is slick." He gave Rude Cowan's description of the man. "I think we're looking for a very ordinary citizen."

"Or somebody who passes for one. You say he cut the glass?"

"Yeah. It's being replaced."

Rude swore softly. "Look, brother, from what you've been telling me, the guy you're looking for probably isn't black, just made up to look as if he is. That's not your ordinary criminal. Too sophisticated."

"Right. I've thought of that, and we're proceeding as though he could be either. Give me someone I can trust. That guy probably recognizes every detective in the state."

"Gotcha. Ernie's your man. Clean as boiled water, and no record."

"Suppose I meet him at your place Monday at noon. And, Rude, keep a lid on it, please."

"You bet."

He had to let Kate know that someone had gotten into her store, but he didn't want to do that until he could tell her something positive, as well. He phoned Cowan and learned that the glass had been replaced. At least she wouldn't have to look at a huge hole in the front of her store. He prowled around the house, waiting for suppertime, when he could see her. After all, a man couldn't chase after a woman every minute like a lovesick teenager. If he wasn't careful, his feelings for Kate would get out of hand. He laughed.

After supper when Randy had gone to sleep, Kate crossed the narrow strip of lawn to Luke's house and knocked on his door. She wasn't going to get mad until he'd had his say. Cavemen had to protect their women from wild animals, but that was eons ago, and most dangerous animals had long since been herded behind fences or hunted to extinction. Luke meant well, but he had no right to withhold information from her about her store, maybe her life.

"Hi, I was just going over to your place."

How could she remain annoyed when he was trying to protect her?

"It's safe to leave Randy alone here," she said. "I'd like to walk along the beach."

She supposed from his frown that he didn't like the idea. "Maybe we could save that for tomorrow afternoon.

After his experience this morning, Randy might have a nightmare and wake up scared, so let's stay nearby. I'd as soon sit with you on your back porch and listen to those waves."

She hadn't thought of that. His smile told her that the thanks she'd expressed with her eyes had reached him.

He took her hand, walked with her to the back of her house, and stopped. Holding her right hand, he gazed into her eyes as though seeking the answer to some mystery. Drenched in moonlight with the black waters of the Atlantic looming loudly behind him, an eerie backdrop, he made an awesome figure, at once a dangerous and a sexy exciting animal. The aura of imperilment that swirled around him scared her just enough to make her want to test him. He enticed her, drew her as a magnet lures a nail. He smiled down at her, his wonderful gray eyes promising her everything. In that moment, she knew he would be hers if she had to swim an ocean to get him. And she knew, too, that she had to wait till he freed himself from guilt about his former wife's death.

His left hand rested on her shoulder, light and gentle. "Kate, someone got into your store last night. He cut the glass."

So that was it. The accelerated beating of her heart thundered in her ears, deflating her ballooning desire for him. "What happened? I knew that call had to do with Randy or me. What was . . . the damage?"

"He got in by cutting the glass next to the door. An obvious professional, who looked at the lock and knew he couldn't pick it. Except for riffling through your desk, there's no evidence of tampering. Apparently, money wasn't his objective, because there's some in your cash register. Any idea what he'd want?"

"No. Maybe he thinks I keep my keys in that desk drawer. Remember the last man who accosted me as I was closing the store? He asked me for my house keys."

"Why would he want to get into your house? Certainly not to harm you. He has plenty of opportunities to do that, which is why I have Cowan trail you home and meet you in the mornings."

She rubbed her arms to ward off a sudden chill. "Luke, I think we ought to go back."

"Cowan had the glass replaced, and I've got a man in an unmarked car right in front of your store. I don't think you need to leave here now."

She took a deep breath. Being a dependent of the Portsmouth Police Department was not in her plans. She intended to be independent, and that meant paying her way. "How much did it cost to install that glass?"

"I don't know. Cowan's brother's in the business, and he did the job."

"Thanks. I'll ask Officer Cowan. It's my responsibility, and I'll take care of it. Your friend cleaned the graffiti off the store and wouldn't charge me. Now, Cowan's brother has replaced that entire glass front. As things go, I don't know what I'd do without the bunch of you wonderful guys. But I'm paying for this."

"That's between you and Cowan. If you want to pay for it, I can't blame you. It's right, it's what I'd do, and I wouldn't expect less of you."

Without thinking, she moved closer to him, grasped his arm, and rested her head against his shoulder. At last, he understood her, and for the first time she felt completely comfortable with him, able to share her goals and her dreams with him. Yes, and her disappointments. He didn't ask her to be what she wasn't.

He must have sensed what she felt, for he held her loosely and kissed her forehead. She stepped back, looked at him, and knew her smile matched the one that blazed across his face. They shared a togetherness, a blending of mind and heart that she'd never experienced with anyone else. He walked to the swing, sat down with her, and rested her head on his shoulder while his left arm protected her.

"Kate, I know I'm ready for something solid with you. Right now, I feel closer to you than I've been to anyone. But I don't want these feelings I have for you to take over my life at a time when I need all my wits to save you. Can you be patient, sweetheart?"

She sat up and looked him in the eye. "What will I be waiting for?"

He grinned. "Baby, you shoot from the hip. You'll be waiting for me."

He wasn't going to have his cake and eat it, too. "You can make that plainer, can't you?"

He laughed. "All right. Could you put Strange on your back burner?"

"Strange?" She caught herself. No point in giving him the idea that he didn't have any competition. She let herself appear to give his question deep thought.

"Come on, Kate. I know you're not crazy about him, but as long as he wants you he'll be after you. I want you to give him the boot."

"I can't keep him out of my store." His fingers combed through her hair until his hand rested at the curve of her neck, soft and affectionately. She resisted snuggling closer. "Wouldn't it be against the law to tell him to keep out if he hasn't done anything wrong?"

"Are you trying to make me think you're dense? Come off it, Kate! If you're not interested in the guy, I wish you'd tell him."

"If I do that, who'll take me to the mayor's Fourth of July barbecue when some top-heavy dame comes to town sporting a rhinestone tiara?"

"*Ouch!* You know where to stab. I get your point. Next time Mrs. Armstrong and her gang ask me to do my civic duty, I'll say I'm busy."

She moved back to his shoulder. "Good. I'll see what I can do about Lieutenant Strange."

They swung quietly on the porch while the rising wind chilled them with the Atlantic's cool and salty air. She watched the stars dance in the heavens in a wild flirtation with the brightest moon she'd ever seen. No sound from creatures of the night reached her ears, only the loud and boisterous cavorting of ocean waves.

She hated to bring their moment of peace and her sense of belonging with him to an end, but she had something to tell him, and he'd probably object to it.

"I . . . uh . . . I have to attend a regional booksellers conference in Baltimore week after next. Jessye will take care of the store."

"What about Randy?"

"I thought I'd leave him with Madge Robinson. Jessye can be flighty."

"Let him stay with me."

Her head spun around. "You're serious? Suppose you have an emergency?"

"The conference is on the weekend. Right?"

"Uh, yes. Well, if you're sure you want to."

He tipped up her chin and gazed into her eyes until a strange dizziness washed over her and she wanted to know him, to experience him in all his maleness. With as much willpower as she'd ever exerted, she pulled back, because she'd promised herself and him that she wouldn't push him.

And still his gaze pierced her whole being, shattering her emotions. He stood, raising her with him, and held her close. "Don't you trust me to look after him? If I didn't want to do that, I wouldn't offer. Our weekend together could be a constructive time in Randy's life—and who knows, maybe mine, as well."

"Of course I'd trust you with my child's care. You saved

his life, and I'd trust you with mine. You ... You're a wonderful man."

Again, he stared at her, penetrating the essence of her, dismantling her defenses. "I can't help it, I ... Honey, open your mouth for me. Kiss me. *Kiss me.*"

She swayed to him, entranced by his lover's eyes, and her parted lips trembled in anticipation. He moved toward her, so slowly that she almost screamed in frustration. His lips touched hers at last, hot and sweet. Oh Lord, how she needed him! His arms tightened around her, and frissons of fire shot through her as his tongue plunged into her, loving her and staking his claim. She knew he could hear the wild crazy thudding of her heart as it threatened to fly from her to mate with his.

He spread his legs and tucked her hips between them, and she could feel him. For the first time, he was hard against her, letting her know who he was. Tremors possessed her body when he moaned aloud and trembled in her arms. Uncontrollably. Her hands went to his buttocks to hold him closer, to feel more of the man in him, and she undulated helplessly against him.

"Kate, honey, I need you. I'm out of my mind wanting you. Kate. Kate, love me ... lo—"

He broke the word as wrenching screams reached them through the window.

"Randy! Just as I feared."

She stood where he'd left her when he charged into the house. Rooted to the floor. Unable to move. Shackled by her need of him. After a few minutes, she opened the screen door, went inside, and walked slowly to Randy's room. She found her child tight in Luke's embrace with tears cascading down his face.

"He'll be all right. He may have these for a while, but he'll be okay, " Luke said in what she knew was an attempt to set her at ease.

"I thought I was drowning," Randy said.

"You weren't going to drown, not as long as I had breath enough to swim. You understand that?"

"Yes, sir."

She watched Luke Hickson stroke her son's shoulders and head, reassuring him, giving him a father's strength, and she couldn't speak. Stunned at her reaction, she walked back to the porch and sat down. How had she let herself do it? With her arms wrapped around her middle, her head lowered, and her eyes closed, she rocked back and forth in the swing. She'd sworn never again, and she'd meant it. But God help her, she loved him. *She loved him!* He'd become her life. Her second nature. *Everything!* But as much as she knew he cared for her, Eunice Hickson still possessed his mind, if not his heart. She couldn't do battle with a dead woman. He might *never* be hers.

Luke stood beside Randy's bed looking down at him, once more asleep, in precious oblivion. When and how had that boy crawled into him? What he felt for Kate didn't explain it. If she went out of his life, he'd still love that kid. He saw much of himself in the boy, a version of himself as a youth—the stubbornness, refusal to compromise about a principle, faithful execution of responsibility at all costs. He shook his head in wonder. That youthful rambunctious swagger that was so much like his, and the willingness to stand up for what he wanted and believed in, no matter the stature or size of his opponent.

He stepped out of the room, took out his cell phone, and punched in Cowan's number. The only way out of that morass of conflict was the arrest and conviction of whoever was after Kate. And he'd swear that her in-laws had nothing to do with it.

"Any news on that break-in?" he asked Cowan.

"This beats me, Luke. We've received calls identifying a man corresponding to both the white and the black police sketch. We're still running fingerprints but, so far, nothing. The guy obviously wears gloves. He's a professional."

"Thanks. That doesn't surprise me. Stay on it." He hung up.

He didn't want Kate to go to Baltimore, but he couldn't ask her to give up her freedom. He found her on the back porch and didn't like her demeanor one bit, but he didn't think she'd want him to comment on it.

He sat down, and took her right hand in his own. "I think we have a problem with electronic eavesdropping. I know you want to go to that conference in Baltimore, so I'm not going to ask you to reconsider. But please don't tell anyone, not even Randy."

"But I can't—"

"Please, honey. A couple of hours before you leave, tell him you'll be out of town for a few days and that he's staying with me. I'll make all your reservations from my private office phone, because I know that's not tapped. Just give me your dates and preferred departure and arrival times."

Taking over again. Exasperated, she didn't look at him. "Life would be easier for all of us if I just moved overseas. I'm tired of this whole scene. I came here with such hopes, anxious to make a life for Randy and me, to be my own woman, independent of in-laws and away from—" She stopped, shocked at what she'd almost revealed. "Away from the past," she said, hoping to foil any suspicions her lapse may have aroused.

His deep resonant voice lacked its usual authority. "I imagine how you feel, and it troubles me all the more because I'm the guy whose job it is to find those crooks."

Immediately, she released his hand, and her arms enveloped him. "You're doing all that can be done, and I know you'll find the culprits. I know it down deep in me. You'll succeed."

His hand stroked her back, idly, slowly, as if he were in a reflective mood. "You have such faith in me? But how can you, when I haven't been able to do the one thing you needed me to do? Don't invest me with more than I deserve. I'll never let you down if I can avoid it, but I'm just a man."

And what a man! "And I'm not doing that." She didn't like the direction in which the conversation was headed, and decided to change it.

"Did it occur to you that we're wasting good moonlight? I could have been getting into your business. You said you're forty-two. Height and weight, please."

He pursed his lips as though figuring out a difficult formula. "Uh ... I'm six feet four, and two hundred pounds right out of the water. What else?"

She quickly erased her mental picture of him rising like the Greek god Poseidon from the swirling waters of the Atlantic, proudly bare, and shook her head, clearing it of passion's debris.

"Let me see your palm." She made a ceremony of looking at the lines in his right hand. "What's your birth date?"

He raised both eyebrows and cast a skeptical glance at her. "November the fourth. Why?"

"My Lord! A Scorpio. I never could get along with Scorpions. Me and those things just do not mix."

His voice, low and gentle, almost businesslike in tone, might have been directed to a stranger. "Baby, what the hell are you talking about?"

She ignored his apparently serious mien. "I am trying to understand you, and that's something you should appreciate. Men are always grumbling about not being understood."

Why was he grinning? She hadn't said anything funny.

"I think you're mistaken. It's usually a certain class of married ones who aren't understood, but that only occurs to them when they're hitting on another woman."

"Great. So you're understood?"

He'd stopped grinning. Now what? "What's wrong with your English today? You didn't phrase that right, either. If you want to know whether I think you understand me, the answer is, well enough for now. When I need you to understand me better, I'll help you."

He'd maneuvered them back to shaky ground. "I wish you wouldn't be so obtuse," she grumbled. "Tell me straight out that you don't want me digging into you and your personality."

He winked his left eye, putting her off. "You don't have to dig. I want you to know me. I said you understand me, and I don't think I need to explain the rest of it."

Thank God for her dark skin. A rush of blood heated her face, and she wanted to bite her tongue. *He'd practically said that when he made love to her, he'd teach her to understand and meet his needs.*

Flustered, she hedged. "Whatever you say."

His resolve to free his mind for the work he had to do, to limit their involvement while he solved her case, had begun to demand of him more than a man should have to sacrifice. It mocked him, for he knew himself. If he gave in and surrendered to his need of her, nothing else would matter. Having her and loving her would become his zeal, his only passion. All else would have to take what was left of him.

He stared down into the soft greenish-brown eyes that could so easily mesmerize him, at her flawless complexion, face free of makeup and full sweet lips, and he had to divert his gaze as his hunger for her racked his body. He'd give anything to know how long he had to wait.

"Will you let me take you to the airport and meet you

when you come back from Baltimore? It's important to me, Kate."

"All right, if you want to. Thanks."

He let himself relax. If she'd told him it wasn't necessary, he wouldn't have been surprised. "I'd better say good night. It's been a long day."

"Yes, and what a day!"

She looked at him expectantly, but he didn't want another trip to the brink, as it were, so he kissed her cheek, jumped over the porch railing, and went home.

Kate had never attended a booksellers conference, and she reveled in the excitement of being among so many authors and representatives of major publishing houses. Being a member, one of the sellers, heightened her confidence in her ability to succeed with her store. If only Nathan were there to see her making deals with publishers and arranging booksigning engagements with famous authors! She knew she had to stop caring about the way he'd demeaned her and lessened her worth in her son's eyes, and she would. With each day, she grew more like the Kate she'd been before she met Nathan Middleton— proud, competent, and ready to take the world by the horns. And she was going to prepare herself to resume teaching if she had to go to the university at night and practice the piano until her fingers hurt. Who said she couldn't teach and own a store, too?

No programs were scheduled for Saturday afternoon, so she rented a car and headed for the Chesapeake Bay Bridge. After driving about an hour and forty-five minutes, she pulled into a rest stop and consulted her map. She took Route 32, exited onto Route 50, and headed for Cambridge, a fishing, canning, and shipping town of about twelve thousand people. She wanted to visit the place where she and her beloved father had known so much joy in days long past once more. He'd taken her there every summer to spend a few weeks with an army buddy and his wife to swim, fish, sail, and go crabbing. Tears nearly blurred her vision as she mourned what her mind remembered.

She became aware that she saw no road signs, stopped and checked her map. She must have taken the wrong road. She drove several miles, saw an old farmhouse, and stopped there to ask directions.

"How do I get back onto Route Fifty?" she asked an old woman who swung an ax like a woodsman as she cut logs.

"Ain't nowhere near here. A good twenty to twenty-five miles over yonder." She pointed south.

Kate looked at her map and couldn't find a road eastward from Route 50. "Could I use your phone, please?"

The old woman's cackle gave Kate a shiver of unease. "Phone? I ain't even got 'lectricity. Wait'll the storm passes, and I'll lead you over there."

Storm? Kate didn't see a cloud, but she didn't think it wise to question the old woman's wisdom. "How long do you think that'll be?"

She spit out her snuff. "Storm'll be here in about half an hour, and it'll be heavy rain even if it don't last long."

"I see. Maybe I'd better get started."

"A flash flood could wash out the road, and you with it. Better stay till it's over. I got plenty to eat. She pointed to a garden filled with vegetables. "Chickens and pigs, too. I love to have plenty to eat. Come on in. Place is clean." She pointed to an outhouse about two hundred feet downhill. "That's clean too, if you need it."

Deciding to take a chance rather than risk possible drowning, Kate followed the old woman into a clean, neat, and attractive, if old-fashioned, setting.

The old blue eyes twinkled with amusement. "You worried 'cause you don't see no clouds, but they'll be here. My husband been gone over fifty years, and I keep the place just like it was when he was here, God rest his soul."

"I appreciate your hospitality, ma'am."

"Lucy. Lucy Monroe Watkins. I introduce myself so seldom, it's a wonder I don't forget my name."

"I'm Kate Middleton."

Lucy nodded. "I got beef stew, baked cornbread, string beans, and tomatoes. If you want, I'll cook you a potato."

After refusing the potato, Kate consumed what was probably the tastiest meal she could remember having eaten. "I'll help you clean up."

"Not now. I don't touch things like knives and forks when its thundering and lightning."

She didn't want to offend the woman, but she couldn't help frowning. "But it's not—"

"No, but it will be before we finish. If you have to go to the house out there, you'd better go now."

Deciding not to trust too much, Kate took her pocketbook with her as she headed outside. By the time she got back to the farmhouse, clouds, ominous in their darkness, covered the sky, which minutes earlier had blazed in brilliant blue. Lightning streaked wildly across the horizon, and she dashed inside. She quaked at the earsplitting sound of roaring thunder, the lion of the universe. What kind of place *was* that? She'd never heard such thunder.

Her gaze took in the old woman sitting peacefully, her eyes closed. On the table beside her chair lay an old humidor and a box of matches, as if Mr. Watkins had used them only minutes earlier. She imagined that the cigars inside had long since dried and crumbled.

Kate studied the old woman, who dared relax and close her eyes while a stranger sat in her home. "How did you know you were marrying the right man?" Kate asked her.

Lucy opened her eyes and peered at Kate. "Because he loved me. Any fool could see it. She closed her eyes again. "You got a real man, a good one, sure as my name is Lucy Monroe, and he's exactly the father your son needs. Don't push him. He's already practically yours."

Kate gaped, her mouth wide open, and couldn't force a word from her throat. "How did you—"

"I'm gifted. You won't get out of here till morning, 'cause the road's flooded and it's still pouring."

As the wind howled, the thunder bellowed, and lightning sprinted wildly across the sky, the storm increased in fury. The old woman gave Kate a nightgown, washcloth and toothbrush. "I'll put a lamp in your room. Might as well get some rest, 'cause you sure need it."

Kate's eyes widened, and her breathing accelerated. Suppose something happened to Randy, and Luke needed her. She walked the floor, wringing her hands. "I . . . Suppose my son needs me? Nobody knows where I am."

Lucy shook her head as though in wonder. "Nothing's going to happen to neither one of them, but your man will go out of his mind. That's good for him. Sleep well."

Kate got ready for bed and crawled in as the wind seemed to shake the house. They'd be worried about her, and no one knew where she was. Still, she was grateful that she hadn't been caught in that deluge, perhaps drowned in the flooded roads. She didn't expect to sleep. How could she?

Luke prowled around his house in Biddle. He'd called her every twenty minutes for the past nine hours. Where on earth could she be? Randy stuck close to him, and he knew the child sensed the gravity of his concern.

"Where do you think she is, Captain Luke? She said she was going to a meeting."

"She probably went to a party or some kind of reception," he told Randy. "There's usually something going on every night at these big meetings." But, heaven help him, he didn't believe his own words.

He got Randy to bed and poured himself a beer. Why didn't she phone? If he got his hands on her he'd . . .

No, he wouldn't. He'd love her until they lost themselves in each other. He shouldn't have let her go.

He walked out onto the porch and looked into the black night. "I love that woman more than I love my life," he said. "Where in heaven's name is she?"

Chapter Ten

"The roads is all closed," Lucy told Kate Sunday morning, "so you going to have to wait till the water goes down and they clear the roads of tree limbs and things. Might as well make yourself comfortable."

"But they'll think I'm in some kind of trouble, and my son—"

"He's in good hands. Do you know how to knit?"

Knit? Was she serious? "I never learned."

"Too bad. It's very soothing. When you and that man have a misunderstanding, instead of quarreling with him or maybe just folding up, you just rock and knit, knit and rock, and you don't have to say a word. It cuts through 'em like a knife. They can't stand not being answered. 'Fore you know it, they're begging you to forgive 'em. Works every time."

"Are we going to have misunderstandings?"

"Sure as your name is Kate."

Kate took a long look at the old woman. "How long has Mr. Watkins been gone?"

Moisture floated in the ancient blue eyes, but not a tear fell. "Twenty years come Friday. Just like yesterday. You finally accept it, but you never get used to it."

Did she dare? "Uh . . . How old were you when you married?"

"Nineteen. I'm ninety-three, child."

"And slinging that ax as if you were twenty? I couldn't do that, and I'm only thirty-eight."

"I'm blessed. I can lift anything."

She must be losing it, because this was getting more eerie by the second. "Mrs. Watkins—"

"Call me Lucy. Nobody never called me anything else."

"Uh . . . Lucy, why did I miss my turn on Route Fifty? I couldn't find this road on my map."

"Who knows why things happen the way they do? Route Fifty floods every time we get a storm like the one we had yesterday, and far as you were from Cambridge, you'd have been lost."

"I don't remember telling you where I was headed." *And come to think of it, she didn't remember turning off Route 50.*

"I know. I told you I'm gifted. Take my advice and never pick a blessing to pieces. We can go now. Bring that handsome man to see me, but don't wait too long. I won't last forever."

The best meal she'd ever tasted. What in the name of Kings was this all about?

She got back to Baltimore too late to make checkout time at the hotel and had to pay for an extra night. And if that weren't enough, she missed her flight back to Portsmouth. Her calls to Luke in Biddle got no response, and she figured he and Randy were on their way to meet the flight she'd missed. She got a flight leaving immediately for Norfolk and phoned them again when the plane landed, but got no answer. No one had to tell her that Luke and Randy were upset at not seeing her get off that plane. Finally, she called Officer Jenkins at home and got Luke's cell phone number. He answered on the first ring.

"Kate! Where on earth are you? Are you all right?"

She gave him a brief summary of her bewildering experience. "I'll rent a car here at the airport, so I should be home in an hour."

"Oh no. We're coming to get you. Stay right there."

"But—"

"Listen, Kate, you said you'd call Saturday evening around six. In the twenty-eight hours since then, I have paid for every single sin I ever committed. Can you imagine all the possibilities—every one of them negative—that went through my mind? I want you to stay in that airport lounge till we get there. Please do as I ask."

"All right, I'll wait."

Luke tightened Randy's safety belt and turned the Buick toward Route 135 leading to Norfolk. He hoped he'd never have another night and day like the ones he'd just gone through. In his mind's eye, he'd seen her kidnapped, murdered. He'd believed that she had fallen into the hands of whoever had been pestering her, that once more he'd been unable to save a beloved when she needed him. Shudders raced through him. She was safe, and he intended to keep her that way. He glanced at his speedometer and slowed down.

"Where was she all this time, Captain Luke?"

He explained as best he could without telling the boy all. "She'd have called, but she couldn't get to a phone."

"I thought they had phones everywhere. I sure will be glad to see her."

Luke blew out a long deep breath. "You and me both."

He put his official plate on the dashboard where it could be seen, parked in front of the airport, unbuckled Randy, and went inside.

"I don't see her, Captain Luke."

But Luke did see her, and had to stop himself as he grasped Randy's hand with the intention of running to her. "She's over there." Randy dropped his hand and ran, and he chucked his reserve and raced to her.

With Randy's arms locked around his mother, he couldn't hold her, couldn't appease the hunger that pummeled his body. He stared down at them loving each other. Then, unable to bear the separation any longer, he lifted the boy, set him aside, and wrapped her in his arms.

"I almost went crazy. Crazy, do you hear me? I'd have died if anything had happened to you." Her arms held him tight, and he felt Randy's hand gentle on his waist.

"I know, and I'm sorry. It's what worried me most, because I knew Randy would be happy with you."

He wanted to taste her, to love her, but this wasn't the place, and Randy's trusting hand patted his back. "Think of a time and place where we can be alone," he whispered. "I am starved for you."

Her soft lips pressed against his cheek, and he searched her eyes for the meaning of what she'd done. If he could have squeezed her any closer, he would have. He didn't know if she loved him, but what he saw in her eyes tempted him to believe that she did. Randy pulled on his belt, and he looked down at the boy.

"What is it, son?"

"I though you were going to kiss her. Amy says her daddy is always kissing her mother."

He stared at Randy, then looked at Kate, whose amused expression set off a reckless feeling in him. "Don't worry, I'm going to do just that."

Immediately, she raised on tiptoe and parted her lips as her arms tightened about him.

"Baby, don't pull me under. I need more than a Band-Aid. It's you I need. *All of you!*"

"Shhh. Just kiss me."

Her soft sweet mouth opened for him and, as if it were gasoline, ignited a fire in his loins. He could make himself wait no longer, and at last his lips touched hers, rocking him to near ecstasy. He plunged his tongue into her mouth, then withdrew, for he was at once threatened with arousal. He put an arm around her and took Randy's hand.

"We'd better be going."

"Gee," Randy said, "a real kiss, just like Amy said."

"I do not want to hear that you reported this to my niece, Randy. Surely, you can keep a man's secret."

"Uh . . . yes, sir," Randy said, but his protruding bottom lip told what he really thought about that secret.

"Come on, now," Luke said, his heart now lighter and his sense of humor once more at work. "Be a sport, Randy."

"Yeah. All right, since I had such a good time with you while Mom was at that conference."

"I know you hate lectures, Randy, but you need them. For instance, loyalty is important in relationships with people."

"Gee whiz, Captain Luke, you already gave me a lot of lectures. I don't know if I can remember it all."

He got them in the car, reached in the backseat, and checked Randy's seat belt. "You're doing fine, son. I'm proud of you."

He heard a mild gasp. "You are? Gee!"

At Kate's apartment door, he waited until they were inside, heard her bolt the lock, turned, and headed home. He wasn't getting into Kate's bed with Randy in the apartment. But he hurt. He could define what he felt no other way. Something gnawed and chewed at his insides, and he knew it wouldn't stop until her body fulfilled its promise to him. He drove into his garage, parked, and went into his house—an empty manor that begged for a woman's warmth and the patter of children's feet. He shook his head in puzzlement. Maybe playing father over the weekend had set him off. He showered, dried off with a beach towel, and slipped his unclad body between his brown-and-beige tiger's-paw sheets. In his dreams, she nestled beside him.

"How was the trip?" Jessye asked Kate the next morning shortly after she'd opened the store. "I know I'm not due here on Mondays, but I left some tickets on your desk. Business sure was jumping on Saturday. Wait'll you see the receipts."

She'd seen the tickets and figured Jessye had left them there as some kind of a statement. "Really?" she asked Jessye. "That's music to my ears. Who's going with you to Repertory Theater?"

Jessye put on an air of disgust, shrugging her shoulders and rolling her eyes skyward. "Wouldn't you know, Axel. He's like the poor—everywhere you turn, there he is."

"He's not such a bad fellow."

Jessye propped her left hand on her hip. "No? I don't see you wasting a lot of time with him."

"That's because it's you he wants. Oh, he tomcats after me, because he's got some kind of agenda where Luke is concerned. But, girl, you're the one he wants, and you know it."

Jessye let out a bitter laugh. "Reminds me of Jean Paul Sartre's play, *No Exit*. Locked in a room for all eternity were a lesbian, a nymphomaniac, and an impotent man. A wanted B, who wanted C, who was incapable. And that was their eternal hell. Thank God, this isn't eternity. Were you with Luke?"

She didn't want to tell her cousin that she wanted Luke for herself, and that as long as Luke wanted her she'd put stones in the path of any woman who went after him. Fight over him? Never! But she'd make it tough for the competition.

"Luke was in Biddle. I was in Maryland."

Jessye maneuvered herself to a place where she could look Kate in the eye. "Where was Randy?"

If you can't find out one way, try another. Anybody as devious as Jessye would be clever at that. She walked to the cash register, waited on a customer, went back to Jessye, and looked the woman in the eye.

"Luke Hickson kept Randy for me while I was away. Why?"

She didn't doubt that Jessye's seemingly careless shrug belied her real feelings, as did her words. "Just checking."

"I didn't think it fair to encumber you with taking care of Randy and possibly blocking your chances of a date with Axel or one of your other men friends."

"You always were so thoughtful."

Kate saw no room for gloating. Caring for someone who didn't reciprocate your feelings could be devastating. She'd been there.

"I'd better get to work on those accounts while traffic in here's slow," Kate said.

"You need an accountant."

The door opened and Axel strode in. Kate ducked behind a bookshelf to give the man an opportunity to be honest.

"You're not working again today," Axel said to Jessye, his voice gentle and solicitous. "Not after the workout you had in this place Saturday."

"I stopped by for the tickets. I'd left them on the desk in there."

"Good." His arm went around her shoulder. "Let me take you to lunch."

"Axel, honey, I was going shopping."

"Shop this afternoon, sweetheart. I need to be with you, if only to watch you eat."

"I wasn't planning to ... Oh, all right. Axel, honey, I do declare sometimes you're like a bad penny. Now, I'm going to gain weight."

"You're perfect, baby, and you'll always be perfect to me, no matter how much you eat. Honey, I'm crazy about you."

"Oh, you go 'way from here. You're just saying that to make me fall into your big strong clutches. Remember Little Red Riding Hood." She laughed seductively.

"Aw, Jessye, you're not calling me a wolf?"

"Now, Axel, honey, you know you have just a wee bit of wolf in you. Hmm." She giggled. "All of you big handsome men are wolves in disguise."

His laughter was that of a satisfied man who'd just had his ego oiled. Kate breathed a deep sigh of relief when the door buzzer announced their departure. What a woman! If Jessye knew a man wanted her, she couldn't resist exploiting him. And if one to whom she was attracted ignored her, she marshalled every one of her feminine wiles in her campaign to hook him. Once she succeeded, she drank from other springs. But Kate suspected that Jessye had actually fallen for Luke, and it was time for her to pay the piper. Too bad. The phone rang, and she raced to answer it.

"This is Luke, How are you?"

Every time she heard his voice, her whole being jumped for joy. She told herself to cool off. "I'm okay," she said in as casual a tone as she could muster. "What about you?"

"Fine. I told Jenkins I'd bring Randy to the store this afternoon, so I'll see you later on. Any idea when and where we can spend some time together? I know I said we should back off till this case is solved, but my head can't get any fuller of you than it is now, and you can't occupy my thoughts any more. Are you willing to . . . to find out what we have going for us, Kate?"

Anticipation kicked her heart into runaway sensations; he'd just declared his readiness for the next step. But her mind shut down, and she couldn't think, much less speak.

"Well? You're so quiet. What . . . what's the matter?"

She pulled herself out of her mental vacuum. This was what she'd prayed for. "Uh . . . maybe Randy would like to spend a weekend with Amy. That way, I'll be able to afford my phone bill."

"Jokes aside, sweetheart. Do you want us to have a weekend together?"

"Yes, I do."

"All right. I'll phone Amanda and ask if they can keep Randy this weekend. Whatever experiences you've had in the past, forget them now, sweetheart. They never happened. I'll do the same."

"I'll try my best."

"I can't ask for more."

She'd hardly been able to release the words. At last she would know who she was; she'd be a different woman at the end of their idyll.

At around three-thirty that afternoon, Randy raced into her office bursting with excitement. "Mom, Captain Luke said you're going to let me spend the weekend with Amy."

"Yes, if you want to."

"Hot dog! *You da man, Mom.*"

He grabbed the phone and dialed, and she couldn't believe it when he said, "Amy! Amy, guess what? My mom's letting me stay with you for the whole entire weekend. Get Robert's mother to let him go fishing with us."

A long silence ensued. "He does? All the time?" His ebullience subsided somewhat. "Then ask your mom to tell your dad to take us fishing." He listened for so long that she decided Amy had to be quite a talker.

"Okay, I'll ask your uncle to bring his violin. He can really play that thing, Amy. I heard him last weekend. Yeah. Okay. Bye." He hung up. "Mom, Amy is my very best friend in the whole entire world."

She hugged him. "I'm glad you're happy. Where's Captain Luke?"

"Right here. Hi."

She turned around slowly, embarrassed to face him after what she'd all but promised. When she looked at him, he tortured her with the hot gleam in his eyes. She swallowed hard, and her shaking fingers knocked over a container of pens and pencils. She closed the desk drawer on her hand, and he needed only two long strides to get to her.

As though oblivious to Randy's gaze darting from one to the other, Luke leaned over her and slung his right arm around her shoulders.

"Easy, sweetheart," he whispered, "I'm feeling this, too. We need this as much as we need air."

He kissed the top of her head, and she moved it to rest against his arm. "If you're as shook up as I am, you don't look it."

He grinned, but it wasn't one of his practiced grins. "I've been a wreck ever since I first looked at you."

Maybe, she thought, *but he's not knocking over everything he touches the way I am.* "A wreck, eh? In that case, I want to see you when you're put together."

Sparks flashed in his gray eyes, firing the gaze that bored into her, promising her that he'd fulfill that wish. She looked away from him, aware that with her careless words she'd whetted his appetite.

"How about a lasagna supper?" he asked her.

"Please, Mom. Mom, please? He makes the best lasagna. Crazy stuff, Mom. Honest!"

She settled her gaze on the man she loved and let her smile tell him that she thought him wonderful. "I love it, too," she said as passion leaped out from him, drawing her to him, and her heart bloomed, a rose unfolding its petals, preparing itself for love.

He handed her a package. "Honey, I want you to take this everywhere you go, including your walk-in closet."

She opened the package. *A cell phone!* I don't know how to thank you. I—"

"I don't want any thanks. If you'd had it this past weekend, I wouldn't have gone out of my mind. It works anywhere in this country."

She read the writing on the box and remembered a strategic question. "Don't get upset now, but is it registered in my name?"

From his facial expression, you'd have thought she'd shot at him. "Of course it's in your name. And you pay the monthly bills. Did you think I had the gall to put it in my name? I understand you well, Kate."

"Let's go cook the lasagna, Captain Luke."

She looked at her watch. "I can close early. Mondays are usually so slow that I often wonder if it's worth opening at all."

Kate let her gaze sweep the living room of Luke's town house. Modern paintings graced one sand-colored wall; oversize sofa and chairs in soft beige colors provided seating; a glass-top coffee table and end tables rested in strategic places. Scattered Bokhara carpets revealed a highly polished wood floor that complemented the curtainless windows. The cathedral ceiling and the windows that matched it were fitting reflections of the man who lived there.

"Let's eat in the kitchen," Randy said. "I hate dining rooms, 'cause you have to sit up straight and not drop stuff on the tablecloth."

He put place mats on the kitchen table and arranged the glasses and flatware perfectly, dancing around the table as he did so. Was this her Randy? He had changed so drastically in such a short time. The past weekend with Luke had given her child a polish she'd been unable to impart. She'd have to give that serious thought.

Luke put the lasagna in the oven to bake, and she watched her son look up at the big man with adoring eyes.

Kate lowered her own eyelids and shook her head, praying that those moments of peace and the love that vibrated between the three of them now wouldn't cost too much in days to come.

Kate noticed that Luke said grace before the meal and told herself she had to do the same when Randy closed his eyes and waited for Luke to finish before diving into the food as he usually did.

"What do you say we take Randy to Caution Point and drive straight on to Biddle?"

She nodded. "Then could we leave at noon?"

His gaze sent streaks of heat plowing through her. "Barring something I don't anticipate, I can't see why not. We could be in Biddle by dark."

He'd almost lost his breath during that minute when he'd waited for her decision to go alone with him to Biddle. He leaned against the doorjamb of his balcony, seeing in his mind's eye the wheels of his life finally rolling into place. He didn't regret his first marriage; in it, he'd grown as a man and as a human being. It was its ending that stripped him of his sense of accomplishment, and his pride in his life's work. He had to trust that it wouldn't happen again, because he could no longer shove aside his need of Kate—a need that dogged him every waking minute of his life. He'd left his cell phone in his briefcase, and when the telephone rang, he raced to the dining room to answer it.

He would have expected just about anything but a telephone call from Jessye Patterson. "To what do I owe this call?" he asked, rejecting her sweet, Southern come-on.

"I do declare, Captain Hickson, you're plain murder on a girl's morale."

"Sorry about that. Why are you calling?"

"Well, I want us to be friends, and instead of sitting around moping about it, I just said to myself, Jessye, call that sweet man and invite him to a good home-cooked meal.''

''Thank you, Miss Patterson, but I'm sorry I can't accept.''

''Why not, for goodness' sake? It's just a meal.''

Might as well give it to her straight. ''I don't cross my wires, and that's what you're asking me to do. Furthermore, you know it. I wish you well. Good night.''

He didn't wait for her to respond. Getting caught between Jessye Patterson and Kate wasn't his idea of a smart move. Besides, he didn't like scheming women, or men.

He phoned his brother. ''Kate and I won't stop long enough for a meal, Marcus. We want to be in Biddle before dark.''

''Sorry you won't stay awhile, but we can visit another time. I hope this goes well for you, brother. Amy has flipped over Randy. I don't know whether she sees him as a big brother, a buddy, or a future husband. Would you believe she told Amanda she didn't want to wear braids when Randy is here? 'I want my hair to hang down long and loose like yours, Lady,' were her exact words. And no jeans. She wants some new caftans. I caught myself as I was about to ask her for the wedding date.''

Luke shook with laughter. ''At least it's mutual. Randy nearly sprouted wings when I told him he was spending the weekend with her. He called her as soon as he got to a phone.''

He hung up and telephoned Kate. ''Hello, girl of my dreams.''

''What number are you calling?''

He laughed. Somehow, he had accumulated a belly full of mirth, and he let it roll out. When he got himself under control, he said, ''Sorry, wrong number.''

Her laughter, a pure joyous release, flew to him through

the wires, and he could feel her sweetness wrap around him.

"I'm expecting a call from my . . . er, S O. So, whoever you are with the seductive voice, please say good-bye."

"Hang Mr. S O, baby. I'll make waves while that brother's still treading water."

"Oh, my. You're not serious, are you? Can you do that?"

"Sweetheart, do eagles fly?"

"Last I heard, those devils soared. But I can't be talking to you like this, 'cause my guy doesn't tolerate hanky panky."

"That so? I had something quite different in mind. How about racing the moon with me this weekend? While we're at it, I'll pluck a few twinkling stars for you, wrap you in the softest cloud, and let you drink heavenly champagne from the Big Dipper. You want to fly with me?"

"Sounds like a lover's offering to the gods. But what can I do? I already have a date with a guy who's bought me a ticket to paradise. Anyway, you be sweet."

"Do my best, baby. And I know it's difficult, but try to stay out of mischief."

"I'll try. Here's a kiss."

He heard her blow it through the wire. "Good night, sweetheart."

He stepped out on his balcony and looked across the horizon. He loved the night, always had, for it was more peaceful, quiet, and conducive to meditation and self-examination. Clouds covered the moon, and his thoughts went to Kate. He counselled himself to let her take the lead during their weekend, and he'd do that, difficult though he knew that would be. Only great pain in a relationship could sour a young, healthy, feminine woman on love. She'd become willing to accept him because she cared for him, but she wouldn't allow him many mistakes. And he didn't intend to make any.

* * *

Sitting at the desk in her office at the rear of the store, Kate felt her patience dwindling. She wrapped the gingersnaps, one package for Luke and one for Amy, who would share with Randy. Then she divided the gingerbread squares into similar packages.

She let out a deep sigh. If only Axel would go away.

"Why can't you have lunch with me?" he asked her for the nth time.

"Because I have a date with Captain Hickson," she replied in exasperation, immediately sorry she'd identified Luke and exacerbated Axel's jealousy.

"I should have known. Are those gingersnaps for him? Sure they are, and that gingerbread, too," he said, answering his own question.

She wished he'd leave. Luke would be there in fifteen minutes with Randy to begin their weekend, and he had asked her not to spend time with Axel.

"Lieutenant," she said, swinging around in her chair to look him in the eye, "I am not required to explain my behavior to you, and I wish you'd stop acting as if you're entitled to get personal with me."

"Hickson. The man's a stud, a womanizer, and you're like all the rest of the women around here."

She'd known that he'd eventually make her mad. "I want you to leave. You may come in the store, but be sure you don't say one word to me. My patience with you has just about expired."

His eyes widened. "You're evicting me?"

She threw up her hands. "For goodness' sake, don't be so melodramatic. I'm telling you to get out of here, and stay out, unless you want to buy a book or see Jessye."

She'd never seen such ugliness in a man, but in a flash his charming mask reappeared. "Kate, how could you? We're friends. I'm sorry if I stepped over the line, but I'm intoxicated with you. I . . . Sometimes it nearly bends me double. Have pity, and at least let me come in here and look at you.''

"Well, I'll . . . be . . . damned!''

Her head snapped up, and Axel whirled around at the sound of Luke's voice. But Randy charged into the office and saved the moment.

"You ready to go, Mom? I told Amy we'd be there by one-thirty, and she'll be expecting me.''

"In a minute, hon.''

None of them could vent their ire in Randy's presence, so she put an arm around him and effectively imprisoned him. Axel's long stare at Luke sent chills down her back. She glanced at Luke, who stared back at Axel, cool and challenging. Tension radiated from him. His left fist hung at his side, but she knew it signaled his readiness if Axel made a foolish move. She hadn't known that Axel disliked Luke so intensely. They stood that way for a long minute. Then, as if by mutual agreement, Luke stepped away from the doorjamb, and Axel walked out. She gave silent thanks that nothing untoward had happened, and that Axel hadn't created a scene.

Luke parked in front of his brother's house at one-thirty that afternoon. During that hour and a half drive, he must have told Randy the correct time on at least fifty occasions. She'd marveled at his patience and understanding. Randy jumped out of the car and ran up the walk to where Amy waited at the door. They grinned at each other, then hugged excitedly and ran into the house.

Luke shook his head. "Be careful how you deal with her. I'll take bets she's your future daughter-in-law.''

Now that was a thought. As if her own love interest hadn't turned her brain into quivering blubber, she had to worry about Randy's puppy love. Luke took her hand as they started up the walk, and when she looked at him, his stern expression told her that he was making a statement.

Amanda and Marcus greeted them at the door. "Sorry you won't stay a while," Amanda said, "but at least come get some coffee or ice tea. I packed a lunch for you."

"Thank you," Kate said, though she knew Luke was anxious to leave. "Some ice tea would be wonderful." She gave Amanda the package of cookies and gingerbread. "These are for Amy. She can share them with Randy."

"She said you promised to bring her some gingerbread, so I know she'll be delighted."

"Since you're here, Luke, how about checking this violin?" Marcus said. "I'm not often asked to repair a left-handed fiddle."

"Sure thing," Luke said.

With the two men out of earshot, Amanda said to Kate, "I was hoping we could have a minute to ourselves."

With three young children, how could the woman exude such serenity? But she knew the answer: Amanda was deeply in love, and her husband reciprocated that love. "Of course," she said, "I want us to be friends, and I'm glad to have a chance to talk."

"I sense a change in the way you and Luke feel about each other. Am I right?"

Kate nodded. "I'm in love with Luke. Totally and irrevocably."

Amanda's smile lit her brown face. "I thought so, and this weekend is *it* for you. Kate, Luke is strong and he's tough. But inside, he's tender and a little raw. He needs you. Don't hold back on him, don't think of yourself and what you'll receive. Think about how much you can give him. If he knows you love him and need him, he'll try to give you the world."

Kate stared at her. She'd been wondering, hoping that Luke would show her what she'd missed, hadn't thought of what she would give him, and that would have been a gargantuan mistake.

"Keep talking, friend. Something tells me you're my guardian angel."

Amanda draped her long tresses over her shoulder to avoid sitting on them and sat down. "Honey, forget the disappointments of your first marriage. This is a new life, a second chance. A friend once told me to pull out the stops, to bamboozle my man, and not to let anything happen by chance. You get my message?"

"Do I ever!" Kate said, enveloping Amanda in a loving hug. She looked at her watch. "I'd better put a fire under Luke. I think he's forgotten he wanted us to be in Biddle before dark." Strains of Suk's *Meditation* reached her ears, and she gaped at Amanda.

"Is that Marcus playing like that?"

Amanda shook her head, and a smile played around her lips. "That's Luke, and you'd better break it up right now, because once he and Marcus get started he'll play for hours and won't know a minute's passed."

Amy and Randy met her in the hallway as she went to find Luke.

"Sh," Amy said. "Uncle Luke is playing the violin."

Kate looked at the two children holding hands. Happy. Free to express their feelings for each other.

"Yeah," Randy said. "He's cool. *Real cool.* My mom plays the piano."

"My daddy does, too, and my daddy's taking us and Robert fishing tomorrow."

Kate hugged them both and followed the strains of Luke's violin until she found the two men, Marcus watching enraptured as his brother played.

"You're wonderful," she told him when he finished.

"Thanks. I . . . thanks." A slight frown marred his handsome face as he put the violin in its case. His modesty surprised her.

A few minutes later, they stood at the front door, ready to leave. Luke cautioned Randy, "I want you to obey Amy's parents, and take good care of Amy when you're playing together."

"Yes, sir. I know she's not like a guy," Randy replied, still holding Amy's hand.

"He's never had a friend, a boy or a girl," Kate said in an aside to Luke. "He needed a friend. A playmate."

She wanted to kiss Randy good-bye, but figured that would embarrass him, so she hugged first Amy and then her son, waved to them from the car, and headed for the unknown.

They reached Biddle at sunset. "What the—?" Luke said after inserting the key in the lock on Kate's front door. He turned and looked at her. "You sure this is the right key?" She nodded. "It doesn't work."

He went around to the back porch and tried the back door. Someone had attempted to break in and had failed, but he'd ruined the lock. For once, he appreciated the storm windows and doors that all Biddle residents had installed. But she needed better protection. The next time the crook came, he'd bring the proper tools. He went to his car and got several different screwdrivers, a knife, and hammer. The front door wouldn't yield, but he opened the back one.

"Stay behind the car," he told Kate, "until I check out the place." He walked into the house with his revolver ready and gave the place a thorough search. Satisfied that no one had gained entrance, he got a Segal plate lock from the shed on his back porch and put it on Kate's back door.

He got the impression that she'd rather not go into the place when she hung back, her face the picture of resignation. "No point in being upset about this. The crook couldn't get in, and before we leave I'll make sure the place is secure," he said in an effort to comfort her.

"But they know where my house is."

"That's true. Maybe we ought to put metal grills on the doors and windows. That could keep us busy this weekend. But right now, let's forget about those crooks. I could eat a horse."

He didn't want her distracted by that attempted break-in. It wouldn't take much for her to wrap that shell around her as tight as a ball of wax—the way she'd been when he met her. And if she did that, he didn't know if he could get her to take a chance on him again.

"How about a quick swim before dinner?"

Her smile signaled her desire to make their weekend a beautiful experience. "Be ready in ten minutes."

He gently detained her with a hand on her arm. "I put your things in my house. Is . . . that all right with you?"

He knew he'd surprised her when she gaped at him. "Luke, I bloom best in my own garden."

He handed her the key to her back door. "Be right over with your bags."

Her smile of appreciation for his understanding sent fiery ripples of anticipation spiraling through his body. Thinking that he could be in for a hard night, he turned and went to get her bags. She trusted him. There was no way that he'd let her down.

They frolicked on the beach, teasing, testing. With every move she made, her body telegraphed an invitation to lose himself in her entrancing beauty. Not classic beauty in any sense, but flawless, even-toned skin from head to toe, eyes that challenged him to drown in her, an intelligent countenance, a luscious bosom, beautifully rounded hips and a bottom lip that . . . Hell, he had to straighten out his mind or he'd be sunk before the voyage began. But in that skimpy one-piece bathing suit, she was woman personified. Hot. Approachable. *And* his! A handful of sand hit his chest.

"I'll get you for that," he said as she headed for the water. She jumped in and swam with a kick the strength of which astonished him, and he raced to catch her.

"Don't go too far out," he yelled.

In the next minute he grabbed her, flipped over on his back, and swam beneath her. She raced toward the shore. What a woman! They reached it simultaneously, but she jumped to her feet at once and ran to her house.

He'd never seen the beat of it. She hadn't said one word. Shaking his head, bemused, he walked slowly to his house, where he showered, dressed, and dragged his electric barbecue station out of the shed. By the time she joined him in a billowing, red, sleeveless dress, the smell of grilling chicken legs and country sausages perfumed the air.

"You're one heck of a swimmer," she said.

"Me? You're the one. Where'd you learn to swim like that?"

"I was intramural swimming champ my senior year at Howard U."

Seeing her silhouetted against the light of the rising moon, he couldn't take his gaze from her. "You look lovely. Beautiful."

He wouldn't have thought her so modest, but she lowered her head in apparent embarrassment. "I know I'm not beautiful, Luke. But thanks."

He walked over to where she stood beside the grill, a dream shrouded in moonlight. "You are to me."

"*Luke.*"

"And . . . and precious." The last word came out in a whisper, as if he'd torn it out of himself, and maybe he had. The fork in his hand clattered against the grill. *Steady, man.* He wondered if he loved her so much that he wasn't his normal self. He didn't wait for her reaction, because he had to control his emotions, to discipline the desire that bellowed for relief, to quiet that horrifying thumping of his heart. Back at the grill, he cut off a piece of grilled sausage and carried it to her in his fingers.

"Open your pretty mouth."

She did, and fire shot straight to his loins. He pushed the bit of met between her parted lips and quickly found something that needed tending at the grill. He had to finish that meal and get down to business, or he'd be a basket case.

"I'll clean up," he said when they'd finished eating. "Won't take me but a few minutes. I'll just dump the leftovers, wash the utensils, and clean my grill." He threw the dish sponge up and caught it. "Can I come over?"

"I'll be disappointed if you don't," she threw over her shoulder as she walked away.

He brushed his teeth, washed up, splashed on aftershave, put on a fresh shirt, locked his door, and struck out across the lawn. He stopped as he was about to step onto her porch. Why was he whistling, "Bess, you is my woman now?" If he'd ever whistled it before, he didn't recall it. He snuffed out a laugh and knocked on the door.

"Hi. Come on in."

She took his hand and walked with him through the kitchen to the living room. "Would you like some wine?"

She sat on the sofa and he joined her. Wine? He lifted the bottle of Moet et Chandon champagne and filled their glasses.

"What a lovely thought. Champagne becomes you, Kate."

He couldn't think of an appropriate toast, and decided to skip it. He wanted to ask her if she loved him. He wasn't prepared to make a declaration, so he couldn't ask it. But suddenly he needed to hear her say those words. *Slow down, man,* he cautioned himself. He slid his arm around her shoulder, and she snuggled up to him. When he kissed her forehead, she raised her face and looked at him.

"Kate, I am not, as Axel would have you believe, the reigning stud of Portsmouth, Virginia. I'm here with you because I care for you . . . a lot. And I . . . Kate, do you care for me?"

Her fingers caressed his face. "Yes. Yes. Don't you know I do?"

Her head lolled on his shoulder, and her left hand caressed his chest. He hadn't wanted to rush her, had promised himself that he'd let her take the lead, and when her fingers brushed his right pectoral, he grabbed her hand.

"Baby, you're treading on dangerous territory."

As if she hadn't heard him, she repeated the gesture.

"Kate, sweetheart."

Her hand grasped his nape, and he cradled her body and gazed into her limpid eyes, eyes dreamy with rising passion. When her tongue rimmed her parted lips, a harsh groan sprang out of him, and he took her mouth, at last tasting her sweetness. She opened to him, and he wanted to plunge into her, but he made himself hold back and tested her, letting the tip of his tongue brush her inner lip. As though greedy for more, she tightened her hold on him, pulled his tongue into her mouth and sucked on it, feasted, her motions a promise of things to come. He stopped and looked at her. Was she sophisticated, or innocent? He got his answer when she kissed his cheek, and he locked her to him with his left hand. With the other, he held her head while he gave her *his* notice of what she could expect, thrusting rhythmically into and out of her mouth. She fought him for his tongue, but he denied her until soft groans escaped her, and he let her have it.

Changing tactics, he kissed her eyes, the tips of her ears, and the corners of her lips. Her restlessness excited him, and he kissed the pulse at her throat and let his tongue trail down to her cleavage. She grabbed his hand and placed it on her breast, and he rubbed its turgid point through the thin fabric that separated it from his bare hand. With his tongue searching every crevice of her sweet mouth, he rolled the tiny bud between the tips of his fingers until she put her hand on his to increase the pressure. When she crossed her knees, he slipped his hand into her dress and freed her breast for his mouth. He bent to it, kissing around the sides until she grabbed his head and forced him to suckle her. He closed his mouth over her nipple and she cried out, gripping his arm as though to steady herself. He circled it with his tongue and began the sucking motion that he knew would bring him her sweet surrender.

"Luke," she whispered. "Oh, Luke, Can't you . . . Honey, please take me to bed. I . . . I waited so long, so long."

"Do you want to make love with me?"

"Yes. Oh, Lord, I'll die if you don't . . ."

He settled his mouth on hers. Then he picked her up and carried her to her bedroom.

Weak with passion, she clung to him. At her bedside, he set her on her feet, unzipped her dress, and let it pool around her feet. He stared at her until she covered her naked breasts with her arms.

"My Lord, you're exquisite," he said, lifting her and laying her on the pink satin sheet. She gazed up at him as he quickly disrobed and reached for the G-string that cupped him.

"Let me," she whispered, stripping it from him, and letting him swell in her hands. Liquid accumulated in her mouth as she caressed him, awed by his magnificence. He placed a knee on the bed, and she lay back and opened her arms to him. He leaned over her, pulled her hands over her head, and held them there, kissing her eyelids, her ears, and her neck. Why didn't he kiss her mouth? She wanted his tongue in her mouth.

"Kiss me. Luke, kiss me."

His lips brushed the corners of her mouth, and when she opened to him he plunged his tongue into her, claiming her. She squirmed beneath his onslaught. He freed her hands and she rubbed her right breast until he moved her hand and settled his mouth on her, sucking, teasing. Fire shot to her loins, and she spread her legs. He suckled her other breast while his fingers teased, rubbed, and tortured the left one.

"Luke, for God's sake, what are you doing to me? I'm aching for you."

"We've just started," he murmured. He flicked his tongue over her nipple, pulled her aureole into his mouth, and sucked it. His fingers skimmed the inside of her thighs and his lips caressed her waist, then her belly, while he worried her left breast with his fingers. Her hips began to sway, and his mouth pressed to her belly. Moisture covered her forehead and her arms, and suddenly his fingers touched the folds of her love passage, and she couldn't hold back the scream that came from her. His bold fingers parted her folds and stroked her until she thought she'd die of pleasure.

"Luke, please. I want you in me."

"Shhh, love. You're not quite ready."

He hooked her knees over his shoulders, and his warm tongue stroked her nub of passion.

"Luke!"

"Don't deny me this, baby. I have to have every last bit of you." Jolt after jolt of electricity flashed through her, as he loved her, kissing, sucking, and stroking. She tensed, as a strange tightening gripped her.

"Honey, something's happening to me. Something's—"

"It's all right, baby. Give yourself to me."

Then at last, he rose above her and slipped on a condom to protect her. "May I?"

"You want to . . . oh, Lord, yes."

"Take me. Take me in." He took her hand, wrapped it around him, and let her lead him to her lover's gate.

Sensations she'd never experienced swirled in her as he touched her for the first time.

"Look at me, baby. It's me, nobody else." His velvet steel lingered there until she raised her hips and he plunged into her. Immediately her body flamed like molten lava as he stroked her.

"Do you feel that? Do you? Am I in the right place?"

"Yes. Yes. Every stroke." She caught his rhythm and moved with him. Suddenly heat flashed at the bottom of her feet, and a tightening began. She reached for it.

"Relax, baby. We'll get there. We can't miss."

Hard now, and faster, he stroked, until she thought she'd die if she didn't burst. Then he bent to her breast and sucked it hard, pulling the essence from her. Pulsations started, and she undulated wildly beneath him, the rhythm forgotten. Only the powerful loving, and the hot tremors that shook her were real. The clenching and squeezing possessed her, and she cried out.

"Luke. Luke. Oh, Lord. I love you. I love you."

"Sweetheart!

He gripped her body and stroked furiously. "There's more, baby. A lot more."

She thought life had gone out of her. Then he put his fingers between them, circling and teasing while he stroked her. She grabbed his buttocks, raised her body to his, and buckled beneath him as the tension began again, more furiously, faster, dragging her under as the hot fever of climax plowed through her like a cyclone, sucking her into a vortex of ecstasy.

Her screams split the air. "Luke . . . I . . . I'm dying."

She was in him, all around him, a part of him, as he

writhed in the clutches of violent tremors and the shudders that possessed him. His moans gripped her like steel bands as he shivered helplessly in her arms.

"Kate. My love. My love."

Chapter Eleven

Luke propped himself up on his elbows, gazed down into Kate's face, and then covered his own face with his hands.

"I don't know what happened to me. At the end there, I . . . I was out of it. Are you all right? I mean . . . are you . . . did I . . . I want to know if you're satisfied."

The brilliance of her smile made it unnecessary for her to speak, but he still welcomed her words.

"Darling, I've never been so happy in my life. Now, I know what it's all about." Her hands went to the sides of his face, and she released her words haltingly as tears pooled in her eyes. "Thank you for . . . for this precious gift."

"Are you telling me—"

She nodded. *"Ten years.* Nathan was the only man I knew. He boasted about his way with women, and I think he tried, but the love wasn't there. So he wasn't as caring or as . . . as loving as he might have been. I finally gave up, closed off my heart, and stopped feeling."

He squeezed her to him, his heart aching for her, and for the pain of those ten hollow years. And though he battled against his pride, his heart swelled with it, and he gave in and let himself revel in triumph.

"At a point back there," he said, "I thought as much, but I didn't want to believe it."

He rolled over on his back and gathered her to his side. "Kate, this was special for me, too. It was . . . I can't think right now. I do know we have to consider where we're going from here."

She stretched languorously like a sated feline, and his pride shot up as he watched her. "Wherever I go, honey," she purred, "I want to find you there."

He let his fingers skim her thigh. "I'll do my best to accommodate you, and that won't be much of a stretch, because I want the same. I can't go any further than that now. Can you . . . Will you be patient?"

Her fingers frolicked through his chest hair, teasing in an idle, almost absentminded way. "I know we're together now against your best judgement, Luke, and I don't know why you made an exception. But I'm happy that you did."

She had told him she loved him, and he ached to tell her what he felt, but if he spoke the words he'd have to go the next step, and he couldn't do that. If he did, he'd soon be totally enmeshed in the barbed wire of his passion and desire. He'd lose focus, and she'd be exposed, a sitting duck for anybody who cared to take a shot at her.

"I didn't change my mind, sweetheart. I just couldn't do without you any longer."

Her left index finger drew circles in his chest hair, then tripped down to his belly. He stiffened. "What about now?" she asked him. "Can you do without me now?"

He spread his legs and lifted her on top of him. "I know the answer to that. It was torment before, but now that I'll know what I'm missing, what I could have, it'll be plain torture."

He jerked upward where the palm of her left hand rolled over his right pectoral. "That'll get you into trouble."

She pinched his flat nipple. "Maybe trouble for you, but for me it'll be a trip to paradise."

He wrapped one arm around her shoulder, the other around her hips, and pressed her to him as he rose beneath her, ready and eager for what he knew awaited him.

"Paradise, huh?" He gazed at her face, wreathed in smiles above him. "I think I could walk away from you— if I had to. But believe me, baby, I'd be back."

Her face showed none of the feminine triumph that he'd seen on other women who—aware that he'd found release with them—couldn't resist gloating. Her demeanor was that of a happy woman, properly loved, who wanted more and didn't mind asking him for it. Her eyes expressed the vulnerability that he needed to see, that let him know her need for him tied her in knots, just as his need for her did him. Need real and raw. Desire coursed through him, a fever running wild.

He rolled her over. "Kiss me?" His voice, hoarse and shaking, startled him. He was overboard. For the first time in his life, he was up to his neck in a powerful wave that he didn't control. But right then, he cared only for the woman beneath him. Her lips parted, and he dipped his tongue between them to sip the nectar she kept there for him alone. Her legs sprang up over his buttocks and locked themselves between his thighs. Anxious now to reach his goal, his fingers darted down to the seat of her passion and found her ready for him. He reached to the floor beside the bed, found the protection, and shielded himself. Impatiently, her hips bobbed and weaved beneath him until he wrapped himself in her fingers and she guided his silken steel to her love portal. Out of his mind with desire, he drove home and took them on a journey to that place where only they had been. She soon laid claim to him when her rhythmic spasms began to clutch him and, once more, he came apart in her arms as, together, they flew to paradise.

The following Monday evening, Kate kissed Randy good night, turned out the light beside his bed, and went to her room. As she'd done weekly for the past four years, she took a photograph from its home beneath the lingerie in her dresser drawer, set it on her desk, and began to write.

Dear Papa,
I wish you'd let me visit you, but since you won't, please answer my letters. In all these many months, I've had no news of you, and I want so much to know that you're well. Randy is growing like a wild weed, and, thank goodness, he's becoming more manageable and more loving. For that, I have to thank a man I've met, a wonderful man whom I love deeply. I wish you could meet him. My prayers are with you.
Your daughter, Kate.

She addressed it, sealed the envelope, and stamped it. She wouldn't know whether he received it, because he had forbidden her to put her return address on letters to him.

She thought back to her weekend with Luke, the joyous fulfillment she'd found with him and the blissful contentment that had begun then and still bloomed within her. With him, she'd been a whole woman, giving and taking, loving and receiving love. She wrapped her arms around herself, and kicked up her heels. He wanted her to be patient. Well, she'd be so patient she'd drive him crazy. He could erect as many fences as he pleased. They wouldn't do him one bit of good. Case solved or not, he was hers, and she'd knock down any barrier he put up. He gave himself to her when he splintered in her arms time and again those nights in Biddle. She would offer him the space he claimed to need, but she'd love him so much he wouldn't use it.

Her thoughts sobered, and she rubbed her forehead, astonished by the memory of what she'd felt when he'd been hot and firm within her. Surely Luke knew she belonged to him for all time. Her father would love Luke, but she had little hope that they would meet.

As she got ready for bed, her musings shifted to incidents and happenings to which she'd given little attention while she looked forward to her weekend with Luke. For one thing, Jessye had become more receptive to Axel's overtures, even seemed to encourage them. Knowing Jessye's capacity for deviousness, apprehension pervaded her. When it came to men, Jessye didn't countenance failure. The woman had an agenda, and Luke Hickson was its focal point.

By Friday of that week, she had become convinced that Jessye and Axel were in cahoots about something that wasn't quite savory. Each afternoon that week, Axel had come to the store, supposedly to see Jessye. He had been pleasant to her, so that she couldn't object to his presence.

"Here, let me grab that," he said when a stepstool on which she stood teetered toward him. "I must be good for something," he jested. "Can't get a woman to give me a second look."

She thanked him, but ignored his comments.

"Maybe you oughta take lessons from some of these Romeos," Jessye said. "A little extra *sugah* never hurt, honey."

"Wouldn't help. I cherish my women. No bumblebee stuff for me. Sweetheart, you're not saying I need *lessons*, are you?"

Kate cocked an ear. What was going on with those two?

"Not me, lover. *You da man.*"

Kate moved to the other side of the store, out of earshot. That conversation was aimed at her. Jessye definitely hadn't been in bed with Axel, because she wanted Luke, and she had sense enough not to give Axel ammunition with which to trap her. What a mess!

"Mom, look at this. Look, Mom," Randy called as he charged into the store. In his excitement, the boy's words tumbled over each other. "My group won the Altrusa award. It's for helping other people. Captain Luke said he's going to take us for an excursion on the Elizabeth River Ferry. Mom, he's taking us to Norfolk, Mom."

Her lips formed a large O as she gaped at her transformed son, speechless.

He jumped up and down, tugging at her arm. "Mom, did you hear me? The mayor's even giving my group a medal."

When they came to Portsmouth, she wouldn't even have prayed for all that. She wiped the dampness from her cheeks, pulled him into her arms, and held him as tightly as she could. "Randy, I'm so happy."

He kissed her cheek, and she had to fight back her tears.

"Why don't you join the Boy Scouts?" Axel asked him. "That's more appropriate. Policemen don't have time to raise kids. We're not a correction agency. We're supposed to apprehend criminals."

Randy gaped at Axel for a long minute, as if deciding whether and how to answer him. Finally, he walked away. Then he stopped.

"Maybe you'd rather put us in jail after we do something wrong."

Kate decided not to upbraid Axel for his callousness toward Randy, because she understood that it was aimed at her. Besides, Randy's reply had been to the point.

"I'm so proud of you, Randy," she said.

Her son's expression showed that he wanted to be certain of his ground. After looking at her for seconds, he said, "Does that mean you'll take me and my group to see *Tarzan?* I mean, Mom, I'm the leader, and I have to treat."

The little con man! In times like that, Nathan's genes made themselves felt as Randy took advantage of every opening.

"We'll see," she said. "I'll have to ask their parents."

"I already did that. I got the notes right here."

"You have the—"

"He's gonna grow up to be just like his grandpa, a regular opportunist," Jessye said. "Uncle Jethro always had an eye for a deal."

Kate closed her mouth and told herself not to react, that the old Jessye was inching out of the closet. She'd deal with that when Randy wasn't around. If she commented, Jessye would have the opening she wanted. Her silence would outwit the woman. She put an arm around Randy's shoulder, took him to her office, and closed the door.

"Talking about the wind stripping somebody's sails," she heard Axel say when she walked out of her office into the store. Like partners in crime plotting the perfect offense, they seemed aware only of each other, though she worked only ten feet away in the reference section.

"Now, you behave yourself, honey," Jessye replied. "I don't want to have to go to confession on account of you."

His voice lowered and took on that sultry tone he used so skillfully. "Baby, if you go to confession on my account, I want it to be because you quit dodging me and accepted what I'm offering you."

After a lengthy silence, she heard a note of exasperation in Jessye's voice. "Honey, let's not get into that again. You're after Kate. Remember?"

Kate moved father away, to the children's book section where she couldn't see them, but Axel's voice followed her, its charm no longer evident. "And you're after Hickson. Both of you are chasing that stud. I can't figure what you see in him."

"I don't expect many men would. But you can relax, honey, because he is definitely not chasing *me.*"

Bitterness laced her words, and Kate cringed at her memories of Jessye on the prowl.

"The captain can be had, though," Jessye said, as though reassuring herself. "I've never met one who couldn't be."

Axel's very presence had begun to antagonize Kate, but she hurt for him, nevertheless. A man couldn't help feeling emasculated listening to the woman he wanted tell him she desired another man. She wished they'd whisper or keep their conversations for times when they weren't in the store. She didn't want them to know she heard them. She had to work, and their voices reached her wherever she went.

"Why don't you open your eyes, Jessye?" Axel said. "You'd rather pine for a man who's looking in another direction than take a chance on one who can't see anybody but you? I'm being straight with you, baby. I care for you."

Kate couldn't see her cousin's face, but her voice didn't convey a modicum of compassion. "Lover, you've wasted your share of sistahs. You said so yourself. And I've gone through a few brothas—not that they didn't deserve it—but, honey, we're all out here for number one. You'll forget about me as soon as Kate stops running from you."

"I wish I thought it."

Kate walked to the cash register a few feet from where they stood and completed a transaction with a customer. Then she tapped the bell to alert them to her presence. From what she'd heard, she was certain that their individual agendas didn't bode well for her, and their guilty faces when they glanced toward her strengthened her suspicion. But then, she'd swum in infested waters many times. That hadn't destroyed her, and neither would they. She needed to have a talk with Jessye, though, because she'd hate to see her cousin self-destruct.

Kate got home that evening and stopped short. Her heart seemed to jump from her chest, and chills streaked through her body, when she saw it.

"Mom! Mom! What's that?" Randy wasn't in the habit of running to her for refuge, and his young arms clutching her told her how frightened he was.

She remembered the cell phone Luke had given her the week before.

"Hello, Kate. What's up?"

"How'd you know it was me?"

"Caller ID. What is it?"

She described the appearance of her front door and the walls beside it. "It's awful, Luke. Frightening. Red paint sprayed to give the appearance of blood. Just looking at it makes my flesh crawl."

"Where's Cowan?"

"He walked with us to the lobby as usual, and left."

"Don't go in. I'm on my way there."

She thanked him and considered leaving the apartment building, for fear the culprit might be hiding there. However, Madge rushed into the hallway, out of breath, as if in shock. She looked at the door and screamed.

"Captain Hickson just called me. Would you just look at that! It'll cost a few hundred dollars to paint it over." She wrung her hands, shaking her head from side to side. "Now who could have done such a thing?"

Kate didn't think the question deserved an answer, but she told her she had no idea.

"Not a soul came in that door who didn't live here."

Kate nodded. She could believe that if Bugs Bunny wasn't on TV. "What about delivery people?"

Madge waved her hand in dismissal. "Oh, them. I get five or ten of them every day. Why?"

Why, indeed? Well, she wasn't a detective. That was

Luke's job. She was about to ask Madge if they could wait in her apartment when Luke walked into the hallway.

To her amazement, Randy left her and dashed to Luke, who immediately put an arm around the boy. "Don't worry, son. We'll get to the bottom of this."

"But what about the door?" Madge asked him. "Who's going to pay for it?"

Luke looked at the woman from the corner of his eye. "Call your insurance company, Mrs. Robinson. They'll be glad to take care of it." Holding Randy's hand, he walked over to where she stood marveling at her son's restored calm. "Don't worry about this. If you want me to, I'll help you secure the place, including your garden. In fact, it's necessary, and we can get it done tomorrow if you like."

She noticed the care he took not to order her to do it, but sought her agreement, and she appreciated his sensitivity. As vulnerable as she was to him, she'd show him no mercy if he tried to order her around.

"Thanks, but I'll call a security company tomorrow morning."

He asked for her key. "All right. I think you'd better stay out here till I check the place out."

When he came back, he handed her the key and leaned against the doorjamb. "How will you react to my posting someone out front? If that company you call strings sensors on top of the fence surrounding your garden, you won't need more protection back there. But the front—"

"What about delivery men in disguise?" Kate asked him.

He shrugged his left shoulder. "Good point. I'll place my man in the lobby where he can see your front door. Can you handle that?"

She nodded. "A few more weeks of this, and I'll be paranoid."

"I doubt that," he said dryly. "I haven't met many women with your strength. I'll amend that to many *people.*"

"You gonna spend the night with us, Captain Luke, so

nobody can get in the door?" Randy asked, his voice pitched high with anxiety.

Luke fastened his gaze on her as he spoke to Randy. "I'd give anything if that were possible, Randy. Anything. But I'll have a man stationed here to make certain you're all right."

"You will? Gee! I sure am glad you're our friend."

Still looking at her, he said, "So am I. And, Randy, I wouldn't tell Amy about this, because she'll worry."

"I guess I won't, then."

He closed the door, stepped close to her, and spoke in low tones. "It's not smart, but I'm not leaving here until you kiss me."

She glanced toward Randy. "No? In that case, I could keep you here indefinitely."

His grin and flashing gray eyes nearly undid her. "Give me some credit, sweetheart. If I want a kiss, I know how to get it."

She gazed at him through lowered lashes and then winked. "Careful, or you'll soon need a bigger pair of pants."

His grin broadened, and it occurred to her that he didn't consider Randy a deterrent, but an ally. His left index finger circled the tip of her nose and then brushed her bottom lip. And then the teasing stopped as the hot blaze of desire darkened his gray eyes.

"Randy, I want to speak with your mother alone."

"Yes, sir." Seconds later his room door closed.

"Come here to me, baby."

She didn't know how she got there, but she knew once more the strength of his powerful arms as his tongue slipped into her mouth, and she held him. Live blazing fire shot to the seat of her desire, demanding the essence of him, stripping her of all pretense as her hot blood raced in her veins like molten lava gushing down a mountain. She clung to him for strength, for a sating of her passion, and for the love of him. She wrapped her arms around him and pulled his tongue into her mouth. More—she wanted, needed, more of him. More of his strength, his sweetness, and his loving.

"Baby, hold on there. Good Lord, woman, in another minute, we'd ..." He backed away. "Honey, I know I shouldn't hold you to it, but you said you'd—"

She couldn't help laughing. It wasn't funny, but she had to laugh, anyway. "I should've added the condition that I'd be patient and mind my business if you did the same."

He gathered her back into his arms. "I get your message. Kiss me good night." Her arms went to his shoulders. "No. No. Just a little one. I can't handle any more of your TNT right now."

He touched her lips with his own, kissed her on the cheek, opened the door, and left.

She opened Randy's bedroom door. "Maybe you can come and visit me, Amy. I'll ask your uncle. He's my friend, so maybe he won't say no. And I know my mom won't mind. She's real cool. I'll call you day after tomorrow."

Kate walked into the room as Randy hung up. "I think it would be a better idea if she spent a weekend with us on the island. She'd have a lot more fun."

"Oh, that's cool. I'll ask her when we talk tomorrow."

"How often do you call Amy?"

"I call her one day, and she calls me the next. She said that way her daddy's bill is big as yours."

Kate hugged him, hoping and praying that he'd always be that straightforward and honest. But she knew well enough that innocence fled along with youth.

Two weeks later, she watched Randy strut proudly out of her apartment on a Sunday morning, resplendent in one of his group's new PAL uniforms—a gift from Officer Jenkins. It was his first venture without her. A dull thud began its slow rhythm in her chest. She knew it was the beginning of his maturity, so she kept her eyes dry, kissed his cheek, and let him go. As she straightened to her full height, she looked into Luke's loving eyes.

"I'll take care of him, you know that. The boys will be talking about this outing for months."

"It's the first time he's gone anywhere without me, and I'm so glad he's with you."

His gaze caressed her. "I'm taking them to dinner, too, so we probably won't be back until around seven or so this evening." He looked over his shoulder at Randy, who stood talking with the officer he'd posted near their door.

His gazed darkened, and his hunger sprang out to her as he wet his lips and stared into her eyes.

"Luke. Luke, you'd . . . you'd better . . ."

He swallowed the rest of her words in his mouth, as his marauding tongue claimed her. He stepped into her apartment and closed the door, all the while loving her mouth and claiming her body with his possessive hands.

"Luke. Luke, what will that officer think?"

"I don't care what anybody thinks, Kate. I ache for you. I—"

"I'm glad, because I need you, too."

He stared down at her for a long time, opened the door, and walked out.

Nothing was going as he'd planned. He couldn't seem to put the brakes on his feelings for Kate. Indeed, ever since their weekend in Biddle his desire for her had threatened to spiral out of control. He couldn't figure out how she could act so calm about it, when he knew she was boiling inside, too. He let Randy sit in the front seat, buckled their seat belts, and headed for Waterside. With four seven- and eight-year-old boys to care for, he knew he'd better get his mind off Kate Middleton. But she wouldn't release her hold on his mind. If he could just eliminate one or two main suspects, he'd . . .

The Middletons. Her in-laws. He didn't believe they were involved. It would take some doing, but he was fairly certain that he could prove it. He'd get to work on that first thing Monday morning.

Kate didn't believe that Luke wanted Jessye. She sympathized with her cousin, a woman who would never be happy, and would wreak havoc in the lives of those around her. She telephoned Jessye.

"Randy's gone on an excursion with his group at PAL, Jessye, so why don't we meet for brunch? Unless you'd rather do something else."

"Now this is a surprise. Makes me think gray-eyed lover boy is busy doing whatever he . . . er . . . does."

She was through playing games with Jessye. "He took Randy's PAL group on an all-day excursion. How about brunch?"

"Honey, I haven't had my bubble bath. This is my day for pampering myself. A real woman keeps herself fresh and sweet. I don't mean to insult you, but—"

"Come down to earth where the rest of us are, Jessye. Brunch or not?"

"All right. What time and where?"

"Eleven o'clock at River Café. And, Jessye, please be on time. If you're not there, I'll start eating."

"Oh, all right. I'll be there. I've never seen the point in keeping a woman waiting. A man? Now, that's another thing."

Jessye arrived on time, dazzling in a burnt-orange linen suit, white linen blouse, white shoes, gloves, and broad-brimmed hat. Guaranteed to get attention.

They served themselves from the buffet and returned to their own table. Kate decided to get to the point.

"Jessye, I wanted to have a really personal talk with you and, for once, I want you to pay attention to what I say."

Jessye shrugged. "Methinks this has something to do with his majesty the captain."

"Only indirectly. Since we were kids, you've always behaved as if the boys—and later the men—who liked you were stupid for being attracted to you. You went after the ones who ignored you, and on at least one occasion that I know about the man was married. You get these men to want you while you play hide-and-seek with them. Then you forget them. Too bad for them, because pretty soon you've found another good-looking man who doesn't want you, one you just have to have. Look back over your life, and see if I've misrepresented you. Don't you like yourself, Jessye?"

"How can you . . ." Jessye's voice thickened, and she shook her head from side to side, denying the indictment. "I need love just like you do."

Kate reached across the table for Jessye's hand. "You need to conquer, honey. That's why you always go after the men who don't pay attention to you."

The waiter came to take their order and Jessye treated him to her most seductive smile.

"See what I mean?" Kate said after the waiter left. "You couldn't resist flirting with that twenty- or twenty-two-year-old boy, even though you know this is the place we eat most often, and he may be expecting you to follow through the next time you come here."

"You can talk. Nobody ever loved me. You were the apple of Uncle Jethro's eye. Nothing was good enough for you."

"You always look for love where you're least likely to find it. Honey, you look in the wrong places. You've gone after Luke, because you can't bear his disinterest, though you know from what you've seen of him that he isn't going to change. And you'll pursue him and open yourself to pain and rejection."

Jessye's shoulders sagged, and she closed her eyes as

though fighting for dignity. "You're hitting me where it hurts, Kate. It's like I can't stop myself."

Kate leaned forward, hoping to convey her compassion along with her words. "Why don't you stop and have a good look at Axel? He's not a bad person, just wants to get the better of Luke. Axel cares for you, Jessye, and he's been attracted to you since you met. You saw that, but you turned your attention to Luke, who isn't attracted to you. Luke wants children, a family of his own, and you don't act as if you'd hold still for that."

"And you would?"

"Yes, Jessye, I would. I'm not saying you should give Axel a chance to keep you away from Luke, because no matter what you or I do, Luke will want the one to whom he is attracted. Axel's not attracted to me. Whenever he thinks I don't hear him, he lets you know how he feels. But you know he cares, and you exploit him. When he's had enough, you'll start chasing *him*, and it'll be too late. That's not a healthy sign, Jessye. Stop, and let him love you. You'll never be the same."

Jessye stared at her. "So it's progressed that far, has it? I guess I ought to thank you for warning me. I just don't know what to look for."

"Look for sincerity. The little things—gentleness, tenderness, examples of caring—and a need that goes beyond desire. That's why you ought to give Axel a chance. He's a gentleman, handsome, educated, and has an excellent family background. But I think he's wounded, just as you are. He needs love, too. Give him a chance."

"Suppose the chemistry's not there?"

"If you let yourself get to know him and let him see who you are deep inside, know you as I do, you'll see him as a different man."

The waiter served their food, and Jessye didn't even glance at him. *Hallelujah! Hope prevailed.*

Jessye took a lace handkerchief from her purse and

pretended to blow her nose, but Kate knew the woman was afraid she'd cry. "I always thought I was more attractive than you and I could get any man I wanted, including yours. I didn't really care. Like you said, I just wanted to see them crawl. I never dreamed it was because my papa ignored me from the day I was born. He sent Mama money to take care of us, so we didn't want for anything, but he never showed up except at Christmas and Fourth of July, when all the townspeople would see him. I'm gonna try. If not Axel, then someone else. I expect I've loused up things with him."

They left the restaurant arm in arm. "Look at that!" Jessye exclaimed. "My Lord, that's smoke coming out of that window."

Kate slowed the car and looked in the direction toward which Jessye pointed. "My goodness, Jessye, that's Miss Fanny's house."

She curbed the car, parked, and unfastened her seat belt. "Where're you going?" Jessye asked her, alarm robbing her of her Southern drawl.

"In that house, if I can get in. Who knows? Miss Fanny could be sick."

"Wait. I'm going with you."

As Kate expected, the door was locked. Seeing that the smoke had thickened, Kate picked up a flowerpot, stepped back, and threw it against the window. Fortunately, she realized, she had exposed the tab that locked the window. She pulled it back, opened the window, and climbed in.

"You can't go in there. The place is full of smoke."

"Look in my pocketbook in the car, get my cell phone, and call nine one one. Hurry!"

Kate ran to the living room, where she found Miss Fanny in front of the television. Her heart was beating, but Kate couldn't detect a sign of consciousness. She began to cough, grabbed a doily that decorated the back of a chair and tied it across her nose and mouth. Then she dragged

Miss Fanny to the front door, unlocked it, and pulled the frail woman through it. She tried to breathe, couldn't and collapsed.

"Kate, for goodness' sake, get up!" Jessye pleaded. "Girl, I won't let you do this. I won't have it."

Somewhere in the vague recesses of her mind, Kate heard her cousin's voice, then a man's words. "I'll give her some oxygen. She'll be fine in a second."

She sat up and looked around. "Where's Miss Fanny?"

"We sent her to the hospital in an ambulance. Poor woman passed out with a high fever, probably from pneumonia. They'll take good care of her."

Poor woman, indeed! Pneumonia could take a heavy toll on an octogenarian. Kate looked at the window and the splinters of glass on the porch. "What about that window?"

"We'll board it up. Stop worrying, Miss. You're a hero."

Kate jumped to her feet, reeled forward, and then got her bearings. "Not one word of this goes any further. I'm not a hero. I was scared to death. Thanks for helping."

The EMS driver winked at her. "My pleasure."

Kate remembered the fire. "How'd it start?"

The man shrugged, almost reluctantly, she thought. "When she passed out, her cigar fell on that broadloom carpet. That's all you need to get a fire started."

Kate looked steadily at the man. "Cigar? Well, I'll be."

"You sure fooled me," Jessye said as Kate drove her home. "I wouldn've thought you'd have the guts to run into a house that was on fire."

"It was mostly smoke, because it began in the carpet."

"All the same. My nerves have shrunk to nothing just thinking about it."

"Forget about that, and call Axel when you get home."

"Honey, I just might. If I don't get settled down, you'll probably have to send an airplane after me. I tell you, child, seeing you jump through that window into that place full of smoke just about did me in."

"I'm fine," Kate said as she brought the car to a stop in front of the apartment building in which Jessye lived. "Now go home and start straightening out your life."

And she'd better do the same for her own. With the apartment to herself, she wrote a letter to her father and sat down to practice the piano. Her father had loved to hear her play. She'd wanted to learn how to play so much that he'd bought an old upright piano for her at a time when money had been tight. She'd proved an apt pupil and quickly learned the rudiments well enough to play hymns and popular songs. He'd sat quietly and listened for as long as she played. She told herself not to dwell on the past—a time that could never return—but to build on what she had right then.

Several days later, she closed the store at the usual time and, with Randy in the backseat, headed for her apartment. She didn't much care for the constant protection of the police department. On a whim, she turned off Elm Avenue onto Highland, testing Officer Cowan's attentiveness. Seconds after she completed the turn, her car swerved into the wooden fence that bordered someone's well-kept lawn. Thank God for good brakes. She looked back at Randy. Anxious.

"I'm okay, Mom. What happened?"

As her hand reached for the door, it occurred to her that she'd better not get out of the car, that she might be in danger.

"Randy, hand me the cell phone out of my pocketbook, please."

He did, but at that instant Officer Cowan's police car pulled up beside her. Assured that neither she nor Randy had sustained an injury, he checked the car.

"But how could my rear wheel come off?"

"That's what we'll find out. I suspect some tampering,

but if that's the case I want to know when anybody got a chance to do it."

A tow truck took her car to a mechanic, and Cowan drove her and Randy home.

"Mom, I sure am glad nothing happened, because my group is going on the excursion Sunday."

Nothing happened? She'd love to know what he considered a happening. She answered the phone in her bedroom. "Yes, Luke. We're fine. Well, I admit I was naughty when I made a sudden turn into Highland, but at least we know Officer Cowan is on his mark."

"It's nothing to make light of. If that wheel had come off when you were making that left turn, the car would probably have turned over. Will you wait for Cowan to pick you up tomorrow morning? I'd do that myself, but I'm in Richmond right now. I got here in response to an emergency call a couple of hours ago. Did Jessye tell you?"

"She may have left a note somewhere, but she was waiting at the door to leave when I returned from lunch."

"I'll see you tomorrow. Remember to wait for Cowan in the morning. Good night, sweetheart."

She blew him a kiss. "Night, hon."

Sunday arrived, and she luxuriated in the peace she found in being alone. Randy, Jessye, and her customers had their place in her life but, as much as she cared for them, she needed time away from them. She practiced the piano until her doorbell rang. Her watch told her it was seven-thirty, and that she had played all afternoon. She planned to apply for a teaching job in another six months, provided she passed the summer school courses.

Randy bounded into the apartment, bringing with him the smell of ocean air and Luke. "Mom, this was the best day of my life. Mom, it was just awesome. Captain Luke took us to the museums, the naval base, and we saw some baby sharks and a lot of fish and things under the water, a lot of stuff. And, Mom, I'm not hungry. I gotta call Amy.''

"Would you like some coffee or something cold?'' she asked Luke, not wanting him to leave.

"I'll take a glass of water. Do they talk to each other every day?''

"You got it. Seven times a week.''

"No, I won't sit down,'' he said when she suggested it. "I've done some thinking today, and I want you and Randy to go with me to Honolulu to see Randy's grandparents.''

She nearly choked. "You're not serious.''

"Deadly serious. What can happen to either one of you when you're with me?''

"I . . . I'll have to give it a lot of thought.''

"I have to eliminate false possibilities, sweetheart, and the most obvious red herring is that your in-laws are behind this. It's well after midnight there. I'll be at the store early tomorrow morning, and we may call them. All right? I'll be with you all the way. Remember that.'' His lips warm and velvety against hers only whetted her desire, but he quickly moved away. "See you in the morning.''

Luke walked into Kate's store minutes after she opened it. Her approaching talk with her in-laws and the range of its possible consequences weighed so heavily on him that he'd hardly slept the night before. From what Kate had told him of Nathan Middleton, he'd sized the man up as selfish, self-centered, and possibly untruthful, and he was betting that if the Middletons didn't like Kate it was because they didn't know her. Nathan had misrepresented either Kate, or his parents. He greeted Jessye in passing and went directly to Kate's office.

"Don't worry about this, Kate. The worst that can happen is that we'll know for sure that what your husband said of their estimation of you is true, and we'll take it from there." He dialed the number and handed her the phone.

At her questioning look, he said, "Kate, I'm a detective. It's my business to know everything about a possible suspect."

She nodded and took the phone. "Mrs. Middleton? This is Kate Middleton. What? Oh. Randy's fine. Me, too. We're getting along fine. I, uh . . . I thought it was time Randy got to know his grandparents, so I . . . Are you all right, Mrs. Middleton? Uh, just a minute."

She turned to Luke. "I don't know what to make of this. She's crying. Said they're dying to see us."

"Tell her you'd like to visit her."

"School's out now, and I was wondering if we could visit you. Randy, a friend—Luke Hickson—and myself."

"Next weekend?" When she looked at him for confirmation, he nodded in agreement, and she continued. "Randy helps a group of senior citizens, but if he can get someone to substitute for him I guess we could go next weekend. I'll call you tomorrow morning after I talk with Randy. I'm looking forward to this, too. Good-bye."

"Well? What do you think?"

"I . . . I don't know. Unless she rivals Cicely Tyson as an actress, she was touched by the call, and especially by the prospect of seeing us."

"What did she say when you told her I would be coming?"

"She said, 'No problem. Just come. We have plenty of room.' "

"Then we'll go? Jenkins will see that Randy's clients— as he calls them—will be taken care of."

"I would have thought I'd be miserable at the thought of visiting them, but I'm not."

She looked at him for a long time—silent, her countenance unreadable. Then the fire of desire suddenly blazed in her eyes, and her stare promised him all that a man could want in a woman. The scent of her perfume mingled with her own feminine scent, and he had to fight the temptation to take her into his arms. With all the strength he could muster, he did the only thing that he could safely do. He slung an arm around her and gave her the barest of hugs.

"Communication is a powerful thing. I'll be glad when we get this straightened out."

"So will I," she said in a voice thick with desire. "Oh, Luke, so will I."

Chapter Twelve

Luke parked the rented Chrysler in front of the rambling yellow villa and looked at the white, wrought iron fence that loomed before them, its height such that the average man needn't dream of scaling it. Blooming bougainvillea and an assortment of tropical plants softened the fence's forbidding presence. Palms swayed in gentle rhythm around the house that they adorned, and several birds battled the breeze to flit from one tree to another.

He got out, walked around, and opened the doors for Kate and Randy. "Just be your normal self, son," he said. "Your grandparents will love you."

Still, Randy took his hand, as if for reassurance. The boy hadn't wanted to come. First, he gave his elderly clients as an excuse, and once that was settled he claimed his father said his grandparents didn't like him and his mom. It had taken Luke nearly half an hour to calm the boy's fears. Kate hadn't been able to reason with him.

She stepped out of the car, regal and poised as usual, and he wouldn't have expected less of her, though she had to be aware that the next hour could challenge all of them.

After receiving permission to enter, he opened the gate and walked with them along the winding brick path until they reached the house. He stopped, as did Randy and Kate, and stared at the petite woman whose outspread arms welcomed them. Tears gushed down her face, though her smile sought to make a lie of them. They started toward her, and she ran to meet them. A small woman, she clasped Kate to her, seemingly unmindful of her body's trembling. She stepped back and gazed at Kate as though searching for some truth, something fundamental to hold on to. Then she looked at Randy, whose young face mirrored his confusion.

"Randy. How handsome you are! I've wanted to see you for so long. So long." She wiped the moisture from her eyes, and he gave her credit for not embracing Randy, much as she might want to hold him.

"I hope you'll forgive these tears," she said to her grandson, "but I just can't help it." Her gaze turned skyward. "Thank you, God, for answering my prayers."

"I can't . . . I . . . Just let me get myself together," she went on, wringing her hands, obviously flustered. "I'm not usually like this. I'm . . . But you don't know what this means to us. We didn't even know whether you were alive."

He'd never loved Kate more than when she put an arm around her mother-in-law and said, "Mom, this is Luke Hickson. Why don't we go inside?"

"Yes. Yes." Ellen Middleton extended her hand to him and, in less than a minute, read him to her satisfaction. He did his best to help her. She dusted her sides with her hands. "What am I thinking? Come on in." She took Randy's hand, and Luke expelled a long breath of relief that the boy hadn't balked, and was actually holding his grandmother's hand.

"Asa—that's my husband—had to go to a funeral this morning, but he'll be back soon as the service is over."

When they entered the house, the woman put her free arm around Kate. *If she's acting, she ought to have an Academy Award.* He told himself to keep a sharp eye and an open mind. So far, Ellen Middleton was batting one thousand.

Kate couldn't have hidden her shock if she'd tried. Ellen Middleton wasn't the cake of ice that Nathan had made her out to be. She walked with Luke behind Randy and Ellen through the breezy foyer to the living room. As rambling as the house was, it fell short of the palatial palace that she'd expected. Covered sconces on the yellow stucco walls, large, potted, desert plants, rattan furniture, and an occasional art object gave the room a cool, expansive, and peaceful air. Here and there lay a hooked area rug, floor coverings that she suspected were Ellen's creation.

"Kate, I'll send someone out to the car for your bags. Do you want to share a room with Mr. Hickson?"

Whew! She averted her gaze to hide her feelings from Luke. Of course she wanted to, but what she said was, "Thank you, but if you have another room, I'd—"

"Certainly, dear. I noticed there was something between you, but I didn't know what stage it was in. You may face the ocean or the courtyard."

"The ocean. I love the water."

Settled in her room, Kate put on a pair of espadrilles and walked out of her bedroom door, which led to the garden and faced the Pacific Ocean. The runaway train beating in her chest nearly winded her when she saw Luke standing at the window of the room that joined her own. Then desire fled, and panic set in. Where was Randy? Had this been a ruse to steal her child? Luke opened his room door and stepped outside.

"Where's Randy? What has she—"

"Sh, sweetheart. Randy's room is next to mine, but his door doesn't lead to the beach. It leads to my room. He's already into the Internet."

She let herself relax. "I wouldn't have guessed that Nathan's mother was a modern woman. She floored me with that question."

"Me, too," he said, a grin forming on his lips. "From the way she arranged this, I don't think she believed you. What do you think?"

"So far, I'm getting good vibes."

His grin broadened to a laugh. "So am I, but that isn't what I meant. And you know it."

"Luke Hickson, it wouldn't be appropriate for me to share your bed in Randy's grandparents' home with my son a few feet away, so don't even think it."

He laughed aloud, and she wanted to shake him. "The place bears little resemblance to the world around it, but what the heck, baby, it's not a convent. I don't care whether you share my bed as long as you don't mind my sharing yours."

He took her hand and walked with her through the garden—through the patches of blooming bird-of-paradise, calla lilies, and blossoms of breathtaking beauty and seductive fragrance that she'd never seen before. The perfumed flowers teased her olfactory senses, all but seducing her. Beyond, wave after gigantic ocean wave spent itself at the shore's edge. And not a sound could be heard other than the water and the rustling breeze.

"This is about as close to paradise as one can get."

He stopped walking, gazed down into her face, and raised an eyebrow. "You couldn't be serious. I thought paradise was—"

Wanting to redeem herself, she interrupted him. "In your arms? That it is. But I was talking about earthly paradise, things in nature. You know."

"Yeah."

She didn't like his pensive demeanor as he looked into the distance. In seconds, he'd drifted far away from her. He did that frequently, but she didn't want to question him about it. He was entitled to the privacy of his thoughts. She stroked the back of his hand, and it seemed as though she had anticipated his feelings, for his right arm went around her, and he pressed her head to his shoulder.

"We've got to make it, sweetheart. I don't know what I'll do if we miss."

She didn't ask him what he meant. The aura of his desire began its now familiar swirl around her, slowly building her passion to match his. She knew she should move, but tremors raced through his body, shaking her up and weaving her into the web of his hot desire.

"Tell me you love me," he whispered, "and that you need me. I want you to need me."

How did she know what eyes were trained their way? She resisted the temptation to wrap her arms around his shoulders and lift her mouth to his, but it wasn't easy. "I love you, Luke, and I need you in every way a woman can need a man." The blazing need in his eyes shook her, and frissons of heat shredded her nerves. "Luke. Luke, for heaven's sake."

His lips, gentle, then hard, firm and demanding on hers, fired her libido, and her willpower scattered to the winds. She grabbed his hips in an effort to feel him against her, but he stepped back. His nostrils flared and his breath came short and fast. Then he parted his lips, and she reached for him.

"Sweetheart, hold on. I'm past making out. If you think I needed you in Biddle, you can't imagine how I need you now."

"I know, and Randy's window is right there." She pointed to her son's room.

He ran his fingers back and forth over his hair in what she now recognized as frustration. "You're right. And we're in another time zone. So let's get some rest. I'll check on Randy. Then, I'll get a nap.''

He stepped inside and went directly to Randy's room. It didn't surprise him to find the boy talking with a child in Denmark. And what else had he done and seen? Luke pulled up a chair and sat down beside Randy.

"Tell your friend you'll talk with him tomorrow." Randy signed off, and, for the first time Luke appreciated the difficulty of being a father.

"Randy, if you get an E-mail message that tells you in blue letters to click, delete it at once. You understand?"

Randy turned his head slowly to face Luke, a quizzical expression on his face. "Yes, sir. I know I'm not supposed to look at those sex pictures."

He digested that, shook his head, got up, and went to his room. He needed a nice long rest. When he'd been weeks shy of eight years old, the word sex wasn't a part of his working vocabulary.

He'd been asleep two hours when he felt Randy's hand on his shoulder. Alert to possible trouble, he sprang up. "What's the matter?"

"How can I call Amy from here, Captain Luke? She doesn't know where I am."

He'd never seen the beat of it. Those kids had taken to each other like two doves caught up in spring fever. "It's almost dinnertime in Caution Point, son. We'll call her tomorrow morning. Aren't you sleepy?"

"No, sir. I wanna see the Pacific Ocean. Is it like our ocean at Biddle?"

"It's not so rough. In fact, it was called Pacific because it was considered peaceful compared to the Atlantic. Maybe we'll go for a swim later on, after your mother wakes up. Right now, Randy, I want to sleep."

"Sleep? In the daytime? Gee!"

During their nine-hour flight the previous night, Randy hadn't opened his eyes, but he hadn't slept one wink. He wanted a family, but he wanted his kids to sleep when he slept. Feeling righteous as well as put-upon, he rolled over and got up.

"What's your mother doing?"

Randy lowered his gaze, took a sudden interest in the carpet, and stabbed at it with his toes. From that, he guessed that Kate was asleep, but he didn't even want to think about her in connection with a bed. The fire in him hadn't cooled, though a good two hours had elapsed since he'd left her. His phone rang.

"I'll get it," Randy said. "Hello? He's right here."

Luke dashed to the phone before Randy could call his name and identify him as a detective.

"Hickson speaking. Yes, ma'am. I'll be there in fifteen minutes." He turned to Randy. "Excuse me, I have to shower, and you might do the same. Then, we're meeting your grandfather. Fifteen minutes, Randy."

"All right." His bottom lip protruded, but considering what he was going through, who could blame his reticence? "What about Mom?"

"When she wakes up. Now, get a move on."

As he and Randy entered what he assumed was a study, Asa stood—a man of about six-feet, three-inches in height, with a full head of salt-and-pepper hair, skin the color of pecan shells, and fierce brown eyes. He merely shook his head from side to side, his gaze glued on his grandson.

"I didn't think I'd live to see you, to witness this day." His voice shook as the words escaped his lips. "Come here, son."

Randy walked to his grandfather, and the old man stumbled backward and sat down. Luke hardly believed his eyes when Randy stepped to the chair.

"Are you all right, Grandpa?"

The man's attempt to smile dissolved as tears cascaded down his cheeks. "I'm ... I'm fine. It's a blessing," he managed at last. "After all these years, I'm looking at the only grandchild I'll ever have."

Luke walked over to them. "I'm Luke Hickson, Mr. Middleton. Kate's asleep, and we didn't want to awaken her because she didn't sleep during the flight."

Using the chair arm for support, the man raised himself to his full height and extended his hand. "For as long as I live, I'll be in your debt. I know Kate had no idea what she faced, because my son never brought her to meet us. I thank you for coming with them, and I can see she's a better judge of men than she used to be. You're most welcome here."

Luke thanked him. Questions tumbled over themselves in his mind, but he'd wait for a more opportune time to voice them. He'd been right. Asa and Ellen Middleton knew nothing of Kate's harassments, and he hoped that before they left Honolulu she'd realize how baseless her suspicions were.

Dinnertime revealed the first unmistakable indications of the Middletons' wealth. The rich meal of drawn lobster nuggets, crown roast of pork, wild rice, asparagus, field greens salad, French cheeses and Grand Marnier soufflé didn't surprise or impress Luke. He expected that in a wealthy household. But he almost did a double take when the butler carved the crown roast of pork in his morning coat and white gloves—and in a tropical climate, no less. He couldn't help wondering about their lifestyle in Grosse Point, Michigan, the other six months of the year.

Kate and Ellen quickly formed a bond, but Asa wanted only to talk with Randy. "Come over here with us, Luke," Kate said in what he supposed was an effort to prevent his feeling left out. He joined her, though he'd rather have observed Randy and Asa.

Ellen didn't bite her tongue. He learned right away that the woman spoke her mind. "Luke, I hope your relationship with Kate continues to develop, because you'd be a wonderful father for Randy. I can see that, even now, he's very much attached to you."

Some people figured that age licensed them to say whatever they liked. He fingered his chin and looked her in the eye, letting her read his expression. Then he'd tell her that she wasn't going to back him into a corner. "I'd as soon not comment on that," he said in as gentle a voice as he could muster. Then he softened it with a smile, though he knew she understood him.

Her own smile assured him that he hadn't unsettled her, and, in truth, he hadn't wanted to. But she'd needed a reminder that he was grown, and she'd delved into his personal life. He looked at his watch, then at Kate.

"Feel like taking a stroll toward the bright lights?"

"Me, too," Randy said, abandoning Asa and running to Luke. "I haven't seen anything yet."

Not a bad idea, Luke thought. "Okay with you?" Luke said, looking at Kate. She nodded in agreement.

Luke took Randy's hand. "Ask your grandparents if they'll excuse you."

As anxious as Ellen was for the three of them to become a family, he was certain she wouldn't object, and she didn't.

They walked along Kahala Avenue and Diamond Head Road, past evening joggers and carousers of every nationality until they reached the big hotels.

"Aren't you tired, Randy?"

"No, sir. I have to see everything, so I can tell Amy when we call her tomorrow morning."

"It's time you were in bed," Luke said, and hailed a taxi.

Randy's increasing attachment to Luke worried Kate. As they'd walked toward town Randy had chosen to walk beside Luke, and had held his hand all the way. She consoled herself with the knowledge that Luke knew how Randy felt about him, and that he wouldn't hurt the child.

Randy went to bed, and it didn't escape her that Luke locked the boy's room door from the inside and left the door between Randy's room and his own open. She didn't comment on it, and neither did he. She walked out in the garden, knowing he'd join her.

"Moonlit nights such as this one have caused many men to act in ways they later regretted," he said, his voice soft but his tone deliberate, as he joined her in the garden.

"Who seduced whom?" she asked. "Don't tell me. Frail wispy women led those poor defenseless men straight to their ruin? The women hypnotized the poor guys?"

He took her hand out of her skirt pocket, where she'd put it in order to keep it off him. "Tell me about it. I think I've been hypnotized since the first time I saw you." He put an arm around her waist. "I'm under your spell, all right."

"Don't say that. Spells are temporary."

He turned her so that the moon shone in her face and he could see her eyes. "How long do you want us to last . . . to care for each other? To be together?"

What was he getting at? She wanted her hand back, because he was making her jittery, and she didn't get jittery. "Are we . . . er . . . talking serious here?"

"As serious as I've ever been in my life."

"You told me not to push you. Well, not in those words, but that's what you meant."

"I won't regard what you say as an attempt to push me. I need your answer."

She looked into his eyes—soft dreamy eyes—the eyes of a vulnerable man. She took his other hand and pressed them both to her breasts. "Forever, Luke. My whole life long."

He didn't shorten the distance between them, but stood

his ground as he stared into her eyes. "You're certain of that? You don't have any doubts?"

"Yes, I'm certain. And no, I don't have any doubts."

"You love me." It wasn't a query, but a statement of the wonder of it.

"Oh, yes. That's not in question."

His smile curved around his mouth and began a slow journey to his eyes. Then he grinned. Seconds later, his arms enveloped her, and his mouth came down on hers in an explosion of passion. As quickly as he began that onslaught on her emotions, he backed away.

"It's hard to believe that I can love you like this, and I do love you, Kate. There isn't a second of the day that I don't need you." He slapped his hand on the back of his neck and walked away from her, then retraced his steps. "I love you, Kate. Will you agree not to see any other man?"

Her blood plowed through her veins like a runaway train, but she controlled her excitement and restricted her reaction to a raised eyebrow. "After the way we came together in Biddle, did you think I wanted to see other men?"

"No, I didn't think it, but if I don't state my case you'll be free to do that if you want to."

"Are you seeing other women?"

He laughed, though she'd missed whatever it was that amused him. "I wasn't seeing other women, as you put it, when I met you, and my head's been so full of you since then that there hasn't been room for anyone else."

"Not even Mrs. Commonwealth?"

"Am I never going to live that down?"

"I suppose you will, but that hurt."

"You were jealous?"

"Not one bit. I was mad."

He slung an arm around her shoulder and walked with her to the white gazebo in the far corner of the garden, and they sat on a bench that seemed to have been placed there for lovers.

He leaned back, resting his head against the bench. Holding her hand, he told her, "I'm glad we came here. It's been years since I had this feeling of . . . of contentment. Do you feel that you don't want or need to look any further?"

Maybe he needed to talk to seal it with words, but she didn't. The shifting breeze blew over them, bringing with it the scent of hyacinths, roses, snapdragons, and numerous tropical flowers, teasing and seducing her. White doves cooed loudly as they made love, and she rested her head against his strong chest.

"Honey, I'm way ahead of you. I've known for weeks that you're that special man."

He turned to be able to look her in the face. "Kate, you beat all at obscuring the meaning of your words. What the devil did you mean?"

She shrugged. "Randy could figure *that* out. Surely you—"

The word landed in his mouth for, as he bent toward her, like a sensor her lips automatically parted to receive him. He lifted her to his lap and buried his face in her cleavage.

She tried to stay focused on her visions of her future and Randy's, and on the lesson she'd learned when she'd placed her trust in Nathan, but his delicious masculine scent furled up to her nostrils, she thought of what he represented as a man and how he could make her feel. Moaning in surrender, she opened up to him, hooked her hands at his nape, looked at him, and let her eyes tell him that she was his. His arousal pressed into her hip, and her head spun as though drunk with vertigo. She let go. If he peeled her clothes from her hot restless body, she wouldn't care.

"What if I lock my room door?" tumbled like a hoarse growl from his throat.

"No."

"Yes."

"No . . . I . . ."

"You want me as much as I want you. What will you feel when you have me inside you? Huh? Tell me."

"Luke, you said we should cool off."

"And after that I told you I love you, and you said it was mutual, and that you needed me."

"I do," she groaned. "Oh, Luke. I do. I do. I'm aching for you."

His fingers toyed with her right nipple and, when she gasped, his tongue plunged in and began to stroke the inside of her mouth. She tried to get closer to him, to feel more of him, and her hips began a wild dance against him as he cradled her in his lap.

"Sweetheart, you're . . ." His big hands stilled her hips. "Randy's asleep, and he's too exhausted to wake up."

Why should she deny herself the loving she knew they'd find together, the sweet fire he would build within her? She stood, took his hand, and squeezed it. "Come with me."

"Are you sure?"

For an answer, she started walking toward her room door. He locked the door behind them. "We don't need a light," he said, but on the dressers in her bedroom half a dozen beeswax candles burned slowly, casting their soft glow over the room. He closed the shades, went to his room and opened the door to Randy's room. Finding him asleep, he locked it.

He slipped her caftan from her shoulders, let it pool at her feet, threw back the bed covering, and she lay back on the pale yellow sheet. She watched him strip off his clothes, and fluid accumulated in her mouth when at last he was bare before her—masculine, big, strong, and powerful. She crossed and uncrossed her knees as he stared down at her, his eyes ablaze with hot desire. Her arms opened to him, and he removed her bra and panties and leaned over her.

"Baby, you'll have to cooperate with me, because I'm near the point of explosion."

She'd have agreed to most anything right then if he'd wrap her in his arms and love her. She nodded. "Hold me."

At last, his fingers stroked her naked flesh, and his lips brushed her eyes, her face, and the sensitive pulse of her neck. Why didn't he kiss that place where she longed to feel his mouth? She put his hand on her breast, and he toyed with it until she writhed beneath him.

"Please, honey. Stop teasing me. You know what I want."

His thumb twirled her nipple. "What? Tell me."

"My breasts. Kiss them."

Her body surged to him when his lips circled an aureole and began to tug at it, rhythmically, as he'd learned she liked it. Her hands went to his buttocks, but he escaped her clutches and continued his assault on her breast. She spread her legs, welcoming him, but he ignored her, and let his fingers travel slowly, tantalizing, promising, heating her blood on their way to the nub of her passion. She couldn't help the involuntary movement of her hips, and spread her legs for him. His fingers toyed with her belly, making her want, until at last, frustrated with need, she reached for him and began to stroke his velvet steel. Fiery needles raced through her blood when his fingers found their goal and began their talented besiege of her love nest. She cried out, but his lips subdued her. She felt his body temperature rise as she went after him, caressing him rhythmically and mercilessly, but he increased the pressure and pace of his stroking until tension gathered in her loins and that awful deathlike tightening began. Tremors shook her body. He rose above her, and she sheathed him with a condom.

"Take me in, baby. Take me."

She raised her hips, led him to her lovers' portal and he drove home.

He had to find more for her. Her belly and hips wiggled beneath him, demanding, begging, for the essence of him. "Be still, honey. Don't make a move, or I'll explode."

He stroked powerfully, but the tiny quivers, the sweet signs of her surrender, nearly drove him to climax. The way she opened to him, cradling him with her arms and legs, kissing him, stroking. Her quivers exploded into a wild and powerful squeezing, and she gripped his buttocks as the pinching changed to pumping and her moans begged him for relief. He stroked with everything he had, and she began to suction him into her, like quicksand, and he couldn't . . .

She erupted all around him, over him, and in him, and he couldn't fight it, couldn't hold back the rushing swell, the terrifying release that overpowered him. When she screamed and went limp with relief beneath him, he exploded into her and fell helplessly into her arms.

He fought for his breath, lodged somewhere in his belly, as he pulled himself out of the vortex into which their tumult of passion had pitched him.

"Are you okay?" he asked, though he didn't see how she could be otherwise after the way her body had responded to him.

She opened her eyes and gazed at him through heavy lashes. "I'm in heaven. What about you?"

"If I didn't think you might take it the wrong way, I'd ask you to give me back myself. "I'm . . ." He shook his head, awed by the power of his emotions. "I'm drunk on you."

She moved beneath him. "Wait a while before you sober

up. Who knows when you'll decide to ignore your will-power again?''

He grinned, delighting in her wickedness. "You mean you're storing up?''

"I plan to try, though it probably won't work.''

He felt himself stirring within her. Her desire for him excited him like the potent aphrodisiac that it was, and he gloried in the knowledge that he satisfied her, saturated her body with pleasure, and left her with the feeling that she was a whole woman.

She kissed his neck, undulating beneath him until he hardened to full arousal. On cue, she swung her legs across his hips. But he wanted her to have her way, so he flipped over on his back, bringing her atop him.

"I'm all yours," he said.

Her eyes glowed and she licked her lips as though antici-pating a feast. Her fingers frolicked on his chest and settled on his right pectoral. He tensed and she bent her lips to him, biting and sucking.

A riot of sensation plowed through him, and he steeled himself for a battle with his control. "Kate! Sweetheart, hold on there.''

"Don't give me the keys if you don't want me to drive,'' she murmured as her lips teased his belly. She kissed his thighs and skimmed her fingers over them. Then she sud-denly attempted to hook his knees over her shoulders, as he'd done to her. God, he'd give anything to feel it, but as far gone as he was, he couldn't risk it.

He pulled her up, locked her to him, rolled over, and settled between her legs. With his lips, he tortured her breast while his fingers worked their magic at the seat of her passion.

She lifted her hips to him. "Can't you ... please, I ... I can't stand this," she said.

Love's liquid flowed over his fingers, and he sheathed

himself quickly with a condom, found his home within her, and loved her until they collapsed in a whirlpool of ecstasy.

After a few minutes, he separated them, but lay above her and gazed into her face. How had it happened that he'd gone head-over-heels, irrevocably, in love with this woman? Never in his life had anything or anybody captured him as she had. But he didn't feel like communicating that. He raised himself up on his elbows.

"I'd like to stay here with you, but it wouldn't be wise."

"No. Suppose Randy's nightmares return, and he wakes up." Her eyebrows shot up. "Would you believe I didn't think of that earlier?"

"Sure I can believe it. A one-track mind will do that to you, and that includes mine."

She kissed his neck and licked his collarbone. "Be careful, sweetheart. A little more of that, and I'll be here all night."

He rolled over, sat up, and sprang out of the bed. She watched as he dressed, a lazy sleepy glow of contentment on her face, and he wanted to get back in that bed. But he finished dressing, leaned over her, and loved her mouth.

"See you in the morning. Sleep well."

"You too." Her voice carried that low sexy drawl that always raised his heat index.

"Behave. You know I can't stay here all night, but if I get back in that bed, that's what I'll do."

She raised her arms above her head and stretched. He couldn't help grinning. "I owe you one, sweetheart, and I plan to pay."

"Be too glad to collect, honey. Night."

He didn't know when he'd had such a great feeling. "Good night, sweetheart." He blew out the candles that glowed on her dresser, careful to prevent the wax from splashing, and went to his room.

* * *

Kate all but skipped along the hallway to breakfast, letting her nostrils lead her to the bacon and buttermilk biscuits. She wanted to fling her arms above her head and shout to the world: *He loves me.* "Ah, Sweet Mystery Of Life," she sang as she rounded the door and entered the breakfast room.

"Good morning, dear," Ellen sang out. "You must have slept well. I'm so glad."

She greeted them all, served her plate from the buffet spread on the sideboard, and sat down. They spoke to her as if they found nothing out of the ordinary, but Randy eyed her quizzically, and Luke managed to greet her without looking into her face. Not so Asa, who scrutinized her as if he, not Luke, were the detective. Immediately, she was on guard, though the smile she gave him disguised her thoughts.

"Soon as I call Amy, can we go sightseeing, Mom?"

"All right." Randy gulped down his milk and the remainder of his breakfast and looked at his grandfather.

"Grandpa, can I make a phone call to Caution Point?"

"Sure," Asa said, "but where is it?"

"North Carolina," Randy flung over his shoulder as he raced out of the room.

"How old is Amy?" Asa wanted to know. When told she was almost seven, he nodded slowly. "I didn't start that business till I was thirteen. Things have changed."

"That's Diamond Head over there." Luke pointed up later, on their morning tour. The huge rock couldn't be considered a mountain, yet it was one of the island's major tourist attractions. They journeyed to Pearl Harbor, viewed the structure resembling a covered bridge over the hulk of the *USS Arizona,* the ship that sank with 1,177 American servicemen aboard when the Japanese attacked Pearl Harbor on December 7, 1941.

"It's a memorial to the servicemen who died here," Kate explained to Randy.

Randy wanted to see tropical fish, and Luke rented a boat whose pilot took them over the reefs and the clear green water near the shore on the lush leeward side of the island. They watched the blow whales, saw the pineapple farms, and witnessed a quick downpour of rain during bright sunshine.

Kate couldn't help comparing the relaxed, laid-back demeanor of the locals with the tourists' galloping pace, so like what she'd known in Grosse Point—that all-consuming drive to be first and accumulate the most. Luke's intuition had served them well, and she was glad she'd come to Hawaii, that she and Randy had been disabused of the false notions they'd had about Ellen and Asa Middleton. She wouldn't mind staying a few days longer, but the next morning they would board a plane for Norfolk. *Please, God,* she prayed, *don't let anything happen before we leave here*.

Luke took Asa aside, told him about the persistent harassment against Kate, and watched Asa closely for his reaction. Liking the man's response, he related his role as a police detective, assured Asa that Kate and Randy were safe, and told him of the measures taken to assure it. It pleased him that Asa offered money for around-the-clock bodyguards, though he rejected the offer as unnecessary.

Kate's in-laws wanted to take them to the airport for the flight home, so Luke had Hertz pick up his rental car. With Ellen beside him, Asa drove their guests to the airport for their trip home. "We won't go in with you," Asa said, "because we'd have to park so far away." He got out and handed Kate a large manila envelope. "Handle this with care, and be sure and come back. It's been many a year since we've been so happy."

When Kate assured him that she and Randy would visit them again, Asa said, "And I hope you'll bring Luke, too." He turned to Luke. "You're a fine man," he said, "and it's my pleasure to know you. My grandson is fortunate to have you in his life."

"He'd be a lot more fortunate," Ellen said, "if he could call you daddy."

"Now, now, Ellen. Meddling is the best way I know to ruin a good relationship," Asa said.

She looked toward the heavens and raised both hands, palms up. "No point in pussyfooting around the truth with all that business about how fortunate somebody is. I believe in calling a spade a spade. Bless you all." She hugged the three of them and got back into the car.

After embracing each of them, Asa remained standing beside the car as they walked into the terminal.

"Two fine human beings," Kate said.

"Absolutely! Glad you came?"

She nodded. "Yes, I am. I wish we lived closer to them."

In the airport gift shop, chills streaked down her back when Luke watched while she bought a tourist card that had a color picture of Diamond Head. Momentarily flustered, she went to the ladies' room, wrote her father a short note, addressed and stamped it, and put it in a mailbox. She felt as if she'd betrayed Luke by not sharing that important part of her life with him, but she couldn't do it.

They'd been away for two whole days. If anything untoward had happened in Portsmouth during that time, he hadn't mentioned it. But she couldn't help wondering whether things had gone amuck—her house, her apartment, and the store. Whoever had set out to plague her had to know that she and Randy were out of town, and Luke, as well. She wondered what she'd find when she got back there.

Jessye hadn't expected Axel's fast rush any more than she would have believed herself capable of tolerating it, but she hadn't forgotten Kate's words. She hadn't given up her campaign to get Luke, but its seeming hopelessness made her insides sag. She did her best to search for whatever good there was in Axel. And Axel surprised her, for she hadn't thought she'd find in him a man who would actually listen to her, see her as a person and not just as a soft place to lie, as most men did. Something about his attitude and his patience with her brought her down to earth and let her open up to him. He just held her hands and listened quietly as she told him of her life in Orangeburg, her envy of Kate, who got all the best roles in school plays, made the highest grades in school, and graduated at the top of their class.

"She wouldn't believe how jealous of her I was, because I never let it show. Instead, I put her down. I'm not proud of that now, but it looks like she's still getting the best of things."

"I know what you mean," Axel assured her. "It's the same with Hickson and me. He gets everything I go after. He may be a good detective. I'll give him that, but just because he busted up a crack ring doesn't justify his rise from rookie cop to top detective in eight years."

Though she tried to concentrate on Axel, Jessye still wanted to know everything about Luke. "He busted up a drug ring? That must have been dangerous."

Axel shrugged. "Maybe, but not risky enough to merit the payback he got. It's time to close up. Let's go to dinner and then take in some jazz."

She took a mirror from her pocketbook, found her makeup and hair in perfect condition, smiled at him, and said, "I can't think of anything more exciting than doing the town with you."

Chapter Thirteen

Axel seated himself at his favorite table in the River Café, leaned back, and stared at Jessye. "You mean Kate spent the weekend with him out of town?"

Jessye shifted in her chair and lowered her lashes. "I don't know where they were. I just know I couldn't find either of them, and I've been trying since Friday afternoon when she left the store early."

Axel narrowed his eyes. In spite of the attractive things she'd discovered about him the past few days, she got a queazy feeling when he showed anger.

"Why would you be trying to find Hickson? Are you hot after him, too?"

Jessye allowed herself a long sigh. "Honey, no southern gentleman would let such words slip off his tongue. I declare you northerners are something."

"Answer my question, Jessye."

She supposed the expression on her face would pass for a smile, but he'd better know it didn't mean anything. "Honey, my papa didn't boss me around, and he had a right to. You're not my husband, and I'm not sleeping with you, so if you want to be friends, cool off.''

His shoulders drooped. "Sorry."

Axel defeated? She didn't believe it. "Axel, honey, Luke's not after me. He wants Kate."

He straightened his posture. "And you?"

She shrugged, almost as if she had no voice in the matter, not that anyone who knew her would believe that possible. "Which one of us do you want, Axel?"

"You, and you know it."

"I'm not convinced."

Later, he parked in front of the apartment building in which she lived, walked around the car, and opened the door for her. With her hand in his, he walked with her to her apartment.

"I'm at my worst when I think of Hickson. I'm sorry if I got out of line back there, but I . . . I care so much for you, Jessye."

She searched his face. "Earlier this evening when you were so gentle, I believed you. If you ever get over your fixation about Luke, you'll be a . . . a super fellow. Good night."

As quickly as a flash of light, he pulled her to him, and she didn't have time to escape his embrace. His soft, delicate, and worshipful kiss stunned her, and she stepped back and stared at him. Goo . . . good night.''

She stumbled into her apartment, closed the door, and leaned against it. Not only did he care for her, he'd just showed her how a man treated a woman when he cherished her. She'd been used to passion hot and heavy, blazing fiery stuff that had always petered out, but this . . . She blew out a long breath. *Who would have thought Axel Strange capable of that?*

Axel got into his car, slapped the steering wheel, and mused over the quandary his life had become. He loved Jessye, but she wanted Luke. Kate wanted Luke, and he supposed Luke wanted her, but he didn't intend for him to have her. Why should the man have everything, while he got nothing? And Kate. A woman who'd had the temerity to tell him to leave her store, a miserable little bookstore, when his family owned Fortune 500 companies. Hickson. Kate. It was time he got some of his own. While Jessye had reminisced, he'd added two plus two and come up with four.

Later that night, unpacking her bags, Kate remembered the manila envelope Asa gave her. She'd stuck it in her flight bag.

As she opened it her eyes widened and her belly clenched, then erupted in spasm after spasm. After a while, she clutched her middle, took a deep breath, and forced herself to examine the contents—a packet of Series E United States Savings Bonds in Randy's name. She counted fifty of them in five-thousand-dollar denominations, a small fortune, because she wouldn't give them to him until his twenty-first birthday. She looked at the envelope addressed to her, hesitated, then opened it and read:

Our dear Kate,
Nathan punished us by not letting us see our grandchild or bringing you to us. It was our fault, because we spoiled him, and when we finally denied him something he got even by withholding his family from us. We can imagine the pain he caused you, too, for we know how selfish he was. From our copy of his will, we are aware that little of his estate went to you and his son, and we want to begin to make amends for that. You and Randy are all we have in this world. Please let us be a part of your lives.
Love, Ellen and Asa.

She unfolded the green slip of paper and gasped. It was a certified check made out to her for two hundred and fifty thousand dollars. Dumbfounded, she telephoned Luke.

"What's up?" he asked, his voice conveying a wariness that suggested he expected a problem.

"You won't believe what's in this envelope."

"Yes, I would," he replied, his tone urgent.

She explained what she'd found, and read the letter to him. "I'm too weak to stand up."

"I can imagine. I suspected something like that, because they convinced me within the hour after we got there that they wouldn't consider abusing anybody."

"I'm going to put these bonds away for Randy until he's twenty-one."

"Right, and unless you need some of that money I'd invest all of it conservatively and forget about it. You have a nest egg."

"I'm glad you twisted my arm about going to Hawaii. Anything happen to the store, or out on Biddle?"

"I just got the reports. Not a thing. And I have to admit that puzzles me."

"But you posted guards around, and they weren't taking chances. Any news about Miss Fanny?"

"She's back home. Fine. Seems she fell asleep in front of the TV and the cigar dropped out of her hand and started that fire. When you found her, she was suffering from smoke inhalation. In another half hour it would have been curtains, because the poor woman had just recovered from pneumonia. I'm proud of you, sweetheart."

"Don't be, Luke. If I'd stopped to think about it, I might not have risked it."

"But you didn't. I know an idyllic spot upstate New York. What do you say we give Randy an opportunity to see Amy, and we fly up there next weekend?"

"I'd love it."

"And me?"

She blew him a kiss. "Does a morning glory love the sun?"

His voice seemed wrapped in a smile. "Works for me. I love you, Kate. Good night."

He hung up. She wished he hadn't done that—she hadn't blown him a kiss.

At the bank the next morning, she invested in a mutual fund and put Randy's bonds in a safe-deposit box. Her long steps made little of the three short blocks to her store as she strode along, greeting passersby, her stride lithe and her heart light.

Kate contemplated a weekend with Luke—a tryst where they'd be alone as they had in Biddle the first time she knew him, had him locked within her, tight in her arms. She opened the store and said a word of grace, thankful that there'd been no tampering in their absence. Looking to the street, she saw Officer Cowan's car and waved her thanks. It crossed her mind that having to trail her wherever she went had to keep the man in a state of boredom. She locked the door, flicked on the buzzer, and got to work checking Jessye's receipts. Her cousin had become an excellent salesperson, something to which her days' receipts always attested.

At the sound of the buzzer, she glanced toward the door, saw Axel, and pushed the buzzer.

She didn't bother with small talk. "Jessye's off today, Lieutenant. May I help you with something?"

To her amazement, he took a seat on the sofa that faced the cash register, stretched out his legs, crossed them at the ankles, and treated her to a display of self-satisfaction.

Dampness accumulated on her brow and forearms, and he sat there enjoying her discomfort. His grin displayed his perfect white teeth, and his eyes sparkled as though in triumph, reminding her of an operatic tenor who glories in at last having hit a defining high C, or a relief pitcher after he's struck out the other side. Crafty too—an animal ready for the kill. She braced herself.

"What do you want, Lieutenant?"

His grin broadened, and he crossed his right knee and swung his foot as though to some imaginary jazz tune. "I don't want anything, babe. I'm just enjoying the prospect of seeing your royal highness take a fall."

Tendrils of fear raced down her spine. With his streak of meanness, she wouldn't put anything past him. And he strung out the torture, making her imagine every conceivable horror, rubbing in it with his disrespectful tone, calling her babe to denote her plunge in his esteem.

She stood straight and proud. "Say whatever you've got to say, please, and leave. I have work to do."

"With the greatest of pleasure. Did you ever find out who apprehended Jethro Raven and set him up for a fifteen-year stretch?"

She nearly choked, and fought back a swirl of dizziness as she clutched the cash register. "Where'd you get . . . I have no idea what you're talking about."

He jumped up, took two strides in her direction, and loomed over her, menacing and threatening.

"Sorry. I didn't know you disowned your own father. My research didn't disclose that. But when lover boy's hot after you tonight, babe, ask him how he met your old man."

She resisted covering her ears with her hands and pointed toward the door. "Get out! And don't you ever come back in here."

She watched him saunter out, heard the door slam, and crumpled in a heap behind the counter. Long minutes later, the door buzzer alerted her, and she dragged herself up. How had he known? Only a few relatives in Orangeburg knew of her connection to the case, and of her father's misfortune.

She made it through the day, all the while procrastinating about asking Luke if he had indeed been the officer who accused her father—a man the whole of Orangeburg knew as an upstanding citizen. *Call him and ask him,* insisted the jealous inner voice that begrudged her Luke's love, but she couldn't force herself to do it. Yet how could she join him for their weekend idyll if she was unsure and suspicious? She tried to figure out how Axel had known, and could only conclude that he'd checked the records. Her father hadn't been apprehended in Richmond, but he'd been tried there.

If only she'd gone to the trial. She hadn't been there to support her father because Nathan forbade it, and, without a credit card or sufficient cash, she couldn't defy him. That was another reason why she'd never again be dependent on a man.

She couldn't muster enthusiasm for Randy's success with his clients' picnic and, for once, she was glad that Jenkins, and not Luke, brought Randy to the store that afternoon.

"Luke told me to let you know he has an emergency, and he'll call when he can."

She thank the officer and wondered if Luke realized that in sending her such a message by one of his officers, he'd made a statement.

With Randy in bed and the apartment quiet, she couldn't settle down. She wandered from room to room, opening closet doors, moving books from one shelf to another, making trip after trip to the refrigerator. Unable to shake her blue funk, she got out the flour, eggs, baking powder, Crisco, and buttermilk, and made biscuits. Their aroma perfumed the apartment, an odor that she loved, but she barely noticed it. She put some raspberry jam on one of them and walked out into her garden, but the scent of roses as they teased her nostrils, bright moonlight, frolicking stars, and soft breeze all reminded her too much of nights with Luke. She went inside and flung the uneaten biscuit in the refuse basket.

Then she suddenly stopped and snapped her fingers. *Jessye!* The only person in Portsmouth who knew Raven was her maiden name. She looked at her watch. Eleven-fifteen, but she didn't care.

"Jessye, this is Kate. Why did you tell Axel Strange about my father?"

"What? I didn't do any such thing."

"Then how'd he find out? Only you know my maiden name."

"Good Lord. Honey, you know I wouldn't do that. That's something our family doesn't speak about to outsiders. I told him my maiden name when he asked me. And when he wanted to know where my papa was and what he did for a living, I told him he runs that little old biweekly newspaper. Later, he asked if my papa was an only child, and I told him that my papa and yours are brothers. I guess he did some research and drew his own conclusions. Has Axel—what did he do?"

"*Do?* Jessye, he implied Luke is the officer who apprehended Papa and set him up." Unshed tears dampened her eyes, but she wouldn't let them flow, and her lips trembled until her words were little more than warbles. "Jessye, I love Luke. Do you hear me? I love that man."

"Honey, settle down. Maybe Axel's wrong."

"No, he isn't. I never saw a man more sure of his ground."

"Well, if that's true, it's sure 'nuff awful. You have to stick your chin out and ask Luke about it. Honey, I declare, if it's not one thing, it's another."

"Tell me about it." She hung up.

At a quarter past one in the morning, she dialed Luke's cell phone number. It might not be fair, but she couldn't help it. She couldn't stand not knowing any longer.

"Hello." The velvet sweetness of his voice rolled over her like a soft lover's breath, and she almost put down the receiver. "Yes?"

She could tell that he was no longer lying down, that he'd sat up, clearheaded and alert. "Luke, this is . . . Kate."

"What's the matter?" The urgency in his voice spoke of his protective nature and his concern for her, but she couldn't backtrack.

"I'm sorry I woke you, but this is killing me. Axel said I should ask you who apprehended and accused Jethro Raven."

Icy pellets fought a battle in her belly as she listened in horror to his long silence. When she thought she could stand it no longer, he said, "I did. Why do you ask?"

She pressed her lips together in an effort to control her chattering teeth. "Jethro Raven is my father."

She hung up.

Bent double with the pain of it, she rocked herself, seeking comfort she knew she wouldn't find. Of all the towns in the United States, why had she chosen to return to Portsmouth?

Luke Hickson had done his job, but, in her mind, that hadn't involved determining whether the man was a courier or merely a victim of his own naivete. Maybe to a police detective, that didn't matter. By morning, she'd walked until her feet ached, and she'd eaten nearly a dozen biscuits.

Get your act together, girl, she admonished herself. One night's loss of sleep was enough of her life to waste on any man. After wasting the better part of ten years on Nathan, she knew better than to expect miracles to last. And that's what Luke had been to her. A miracle.

She showered, awakened Randy, and started preparing breakfast. Though her relationship with Luke was history, she would have Randy stay with PAL, because those officers had turned him around.

Kate knew from the sound of the doorbell that Luke was the caller.

"I don't need this," she said, thankful that Randy was in the shower and wouldn't hear their exchange.

He walked in, haggard and obviously out of sorts. "You hung up on me. You didn't care enough to hear me out."

"What did you expect?"

He stared down at her, his gray eyes devoid of their flashing charm, dull and lackluster. "I expect the woman who said she loves me, who gave herself to me as if doing so glorified her, who, in the name of love, held me inside her body, I expect that woman to want to hear what I have to say no matter *who else* is involved."

She hadn't known she could hurt so much. Numbness attacked her fingers and toes as Luke continued to stare down at her without warmth or passion, judging her as she'd judged him.

"Well? May I sit down?"

"I . . . Randy will be in here in a minute, and I don't want him to hear this."

He raised both eyebrows. "But it was so urgent that I had to be awakened at almost two o'clock this morning and deprived of the remainder of my night's sleep." He took a seat on the sofa. "We might as well get this over with. Let Randy eat in the kitchen. Do you want to hear me out, or not?"

"All right." She sat in a chair facing him.

He shrugged, as if he didn't care. Then a grin settled around his mouth, though it didn't reach his eyes. "Two days ago, you sat in my lap. Now, with all this space beside me on this sofa, you're over there. Time changes things, doesn't it?"

His sarcasm restored her equilibrium and poise. "All right, Luke. Tell me for what reason an innocent man should be convicted."

He rubbed his chin, and she could see that he struggled

for self-control. "I was neither judge nor juror. I hand-cuffed Jethro Raven after I found a twenty-five-pound box of cocaine on the floor in the back of his car. Every courier claims he or she didn't know what the package contained." He crossed his left knee and leaned forward.

"I've sworn to uphold the law, and if I had caught Marcus with that load, trust me, I would have arrested him. Should I have broken the law for someone else?"

"But you knew he was innocent. Anybody can look at my father and see that he's an upstanding citizen, that he would never knowingly break the law."

"If you have such power as that, Kate, we need you on the force. I've caught sweet little old ladies trucking heroin. Why don't you ask your father why he let himself get into that mess?"

He stood, and she saw the door closing on her life. "To you, it's black-and-white, with no extenuating circum-stances," she whispered.

She hardly recognized his voice, thin and strained. "If you can walk out on me because I did my job as best I knew how and according to my lights, you're the wrong woman for me."

"But—" She wondered if he could hear her heart breaking.

"No buts. I should have known you were too good to be true. One of the officers will pick up Randy at three-thirty today, as usual." He walked a few paces toward the door and stopped. "I won't be in touch, but if you need anything, anything at all, you know how to reach me and I'll be there for you." Before she could react, the door closed behind him.

Gone. Finished. She snapped her finger. Just like that. He'd taken her heart and left behind an empty spot in her soul. Somewhat dazed, she looked around her and couldn't see anything different. The sofa and chairs retained their olive-green tone and buttery soft leather fabric; her Turkish carpets still graced a highly polished parquet floor; her paintings and flowers stared back at her as if to say, we are still here.

She picked up a magazine and tossed it across the room. *To hell with it.* "Randy, would you hurry up and get in here and eat your breakfast?"

Luke prowled around his office, knocking his right fist into his left palm. He looked at his watch. Another twenty minutes. He ought to get some work done while the place was still quiet. He sat down and leafed through the papers in his mailbox. After a minute, he threw up his hands, got up, and began walking around his office. He rubbed the back of his neck, went to his desk, and started to dial a number. He thought better of it, and hung up. A glance at the clock on his desk, which faced out to call visitors' attention to the importance of his time, told him that only five minutes had passed.

Enough. When he heard Axel's voice at the water cooler he locked his desk and charged out into the corridor.

"Come in here, man."

"You addressing me?" Axel asked.

He hoped the man wouldn't pick that time to fool with him, because his tolerance for Axel Strange was nonexistent. "Yes, I'm talking to you, and I said come in here."

Axel sauntered in, and Luke slammed the door shut, causing the more junior officer to spin around wearing a look of terror. "Uh, what's up?" Axel asked Luke.

"I don't see that Langford report on my desk."

Axel backed up and extended his hands palm out. "Look. Don't get uptight. I'll have it in here tomorrow morning."

Luke stepped closer to him. "It was due Thursday, and today is Tuesday. If you had been doing your work instead of disclosing the content of confidential files, you wouldn't be in trouble right now. I could unload you for that."

"You can't prove I did that. You and I both know what you're so heated up about. You didn't win this time, did you?"

"You're obsessed with getting the better of me. I don't know why. But to accomplish that you'd have to show that you're better than I am at what I do, and you don't have a snowball's chance in hell of pulling that off. So you tried to break up Kate and me. For myself, I don't care what you do, but you inflicted a load of pain on her. And for that, I'd like to smash your face."

"You can't prove one thing. It's my word against hers."

Luke grinned at him. "Did you remember to wipe your fingerprints off those files that you're not cleared to see?"

Axel stopped himself just before he clutched his belly, realizing that he'd indict himself with such a gesture. "Uh . . . I—"

Luke allowed himself a laugh. "See what I mean? So what'll it be? Walking papers, or a transfer to the Third Precinct, where I won't have to look at you but once a month?"

"I'd rather transfer, but I don't see why we can't work this out."

"And along with your transfer, I'll send your quarterly evaluations. Look, Strange, if your exalted social status places you above this kind of work, I suggest you go back to your family's shoe factory and work there."

"We own a conglomerate, and we make a lot more than shoes."

Luke shrugged. "Good. So if you get fired from Third Precinct, you won't have to look for a job. That's all. You're transferred as of now."

The door closed, and he'd only have to see Axel Strange at the monthly citywide law enforcement meetings of senior officers. The man wasn't a bad detective. Indeed, if he'd concentrate on his work he'd probably be a good one. Maybe in the long run, the transfer would drive Axel to prove himself.

"Come in," he said in response to a knock. Jenkins walked in and dropped himself in the chair nearest the door.

"Strange said he's moving to Third Precinct. Mind if I ask what happened?"

He considered Jenkins closer to him than his other men, and he trusted him, but he'd rather not discuss Axel Strange. He sat back in his chair and made a pyramid of his ten fingers.

Finally, he said, "Axel made a couple of wrong turns, bad ones, and I didn't care to put up with his style any longer."

Jenkins didn't bother to camouflage his glee. "Past time, man. Strange is too opaque for this job. The guy's a walking secret. We used to wonder if he was somebody's undercover agent."

Luke raised an eyebrow and half smiled. "Strange? No way. He just has a hard time loving the common man."

"Well, the common man sure didn't fall in love with him. Did he do any damage?"

He leaned forward, and—with his left elbow on his desk and his hand supporting his chin—he looked Jenkins in the eye. "Remains to be seen." Jenkins knew that both he and Strange had an interest in Kate, and he hoped the man was smart enough to know that he'd never regarded Axel Strange as competition. Besides, anybody but Axel could see that Kate didn't want him.

That afternoon he tried not to think of Kate, but Randy stayed so close to him at the PAL session that he finally had to ask the boy if he had a problem.

"My mom says I'm not going to see Amy and Robert this weekend. She said I'm not going back there."

He patted the boy's frail shoulders. "Perk up. I'll speak with her."

He wasn't perked up himself, and he'd rather not have the sound of her voice remind him of what he'd lost, but after the boys left PAL, he called her.

"Hello, Kate. This is Luke."

"I know. How are you?"

"I'm making it. What about you?"

"The same."

How could they talk to each other as if they'd never flown to paradise in each other's arms? As if they didn't love each other?

"I assume you're breaking our date for this weekend, but can't you let Randy go to Caution Point along with Marcus Friday afternoon? He'd be back Monday morning."

"Luke, I'd . . . rather not."

"Please, Kate. Don't do this. Will you let him go if I take him?"

"If you . . . You mean you'd change your plans and drive all the way to Caution Point because Randy has to see Amy?"

He closed his eyes and took a deep breath. "No. I'll do it because we told him he'd go, and he and Amy are pumped up for it. I don't want what happens between you and me to hurt the child. I . . . I care about him, and—"

"You're right. This isn't his problem. He can go with either one of you."

"All right. He'll go with my brother. I'll pick him up at two-thirty and take him over to Marcus's office."

He didn't know how she'd take the news about Axel, whether she'd think he'd done it as an act of revenge. Well, she might as well hear it from him. "This morning, I transferred Lieutenant Strange to the Third Precinct, on the other side of the city."

"You're kidding." Pure merriment tinged each word. "What for?"

"He broke a couple of the department's strictest rules, and I was in no mood to overlook it."

"Too bad. I hope he learned a lesson, but what Axel Strange does and where he goes are immaterial to me. I don't know about Jessye, though. They seemed to have become rather close recently."

She had to be kidding. "Jessye's an opportunist. If she did fall for him, Lord help her, but I'd be surprised if she did. See you Friday."

"I might not be here when you come. I got roped into jury duty starting tomorrow."

"You might find it interesting. Be in touch."

Kate didn't see how she could be so sure someone had committed a crime that she could vote for a guilty verdict. However, the woman who sat beside her waiting to be called had no such compunctions.

"I love jury duty," the woman said. "I'm a mystery writer, and this is my best source of material. Boy, I hope we get a drug smuggling case with lots of murders. My editor loves those." Kate eased away, opened her copy of *Obsession,* and concentrated on the romance novel. With luck, neither the prosecuting attorney nor the lawyer for the defendant would accept her.

Luck wasn't with her, and when the jury was seated she took her place among them. She listened as the assistant state prosecutor accused the man of smuggling rubies and sapphires from Thailand into the country. Though the government's records showed that the man had entered Thailand, halfway around the world from Portsmouth, Virginia, seven times in eight months, the man insisted that someone had planted the jewels on him. He'd had no idea what the packages contained.

She struggled to keep her bearing, fighting the pain that settled around her heart—pain for her father, for Luke, and for herself. How could the man not have asked what the sealed packages contained?

The arresting officer took the stand, and, to her surprise, gave only concise answers and didn't volunteer any information. Her thoughts went to Luke. Had he also attempted to be fair, and treated her father's case with the same honest dispassion?

Luke. She recalled little things about him that set him apart and made him so special. The way he mixed gentleness with his strength, and used his power for good; his dependability—always there when she needed him. She could see him rubbing the back of his neck while he figured something out, loving and tutoring children, grinning that slow seductive grin that could make her heart tumble backward, his unbelievable . . .

"Are you all right, madam?" the judge asked, looking directly at her.

A glance at her surroundings let her know that everyone in the courtroom was gazing at her. "I'm fine . . . as far as I know."

"But you're crying," the judge said.

She wiped her eyes and looked at her wet hand. "I . . . uh . . . I didn't know it. My eyes do that sometimes."

Corralling her thoughts, she concentrated on the proceedings. After listening to a dozen witnesses, she'd never been more uncertain about anything. Two weeks later, having listened to the defense and seen the mounting evidence against it, she had to vote.

"If he wasn't smuggling jewelry, how could he afford a round-trip first-class ticket to Bangkok once a month?" one woman asked in the jury room.

"Simple," a man replied. "He could have had a rich Thai woman who wanted to see him."

In the end, Kate's conscience forced her to vote guilty

along with the eleven other jurors. She had no doubt as to the man's guilt. Still, her voice shook when she said, "Guilty, Your Honor," in response to the jury poll.

As she was leaving the courthouse she thought about Luke. He'd said he only arrested her father and presented the charges, that the jury had rendered the verdict. Once more, her loyalties warred with each other—her faith in her father battling her confidence in Luke's honesty and integrity.

"Hello, Kate."

She whirled around. Her blood plowed through her veins like a runaway thoroughbred, but she did her best to hide her excitement at seeing him.

"Hello, Luke," she said. She looked up into the storm of passion that raged in his fierce gray eyes. "I . . . Why are you here?"

"I attend trials whenever I can. It's sort of like research. Is this your last week of jury duty?"

"Unfortunately, I have to serve a total of four weeks, so I have one more."

He stepped closer. "Is it too much to ask whether you learned anything important from that trial?"

She wanted to look him in the eye to reinforce the sincerity of her words, but a glance showed that his gaze had become personal. Intimate. She had to get away from him. In her haste to move away, she stepped back, and he grabbed her to him.

"Luke! For heaven's sake!"

He stared down at her. "Would you rather have fallen backward down those concrete steps?"

She glanced over her shoulder, and shuddered as fear streaked through her. "My Lord. I almost . . ." She couldn't utter the words. "Thanks."

That captivating seductive grin formed around his mouth. "I'm glad I was close enough to catch you." He pressed his lips together, as though savoring fine wine. "Having you in my arms again wasn't bad, either."

She wasn't anxious to get out of his arms, but propriety dictated that she move. He released her slowly, as though to convey his reluctance.

"Cowan's waiting for you." He nodded toward the unmarked blue Chevrolet that stood in front of the building. "Take care of yourself."

She greeted Cowan and got in the car, but she couldn't enter into a conversation. All she could think of was how she'd felt in Luke's arms, what she'd missed all those lonely days.

As Luke watched Kate move down the steps, he was tempted to fantasize, to let himself believe she hadn't wanted to move out of his arms. But what was the use? If she pined for him, she certainly didn't show it. And unless she could understand why he'd had no choice but to arrest Jethro Raven and to file the charges, it didn't matter what she felt.

She'd voted guilty on the first round, and that meant she'd based her decision on the case, and hadn't been persuaded by other jurors. He knew he shouldn't hope, but he couldn't help himself.

The following Monday morning he stepped onto the witness stand, took the oath, and looked toward the jurors. As he'd hoped and prayed, she was there, sitting on the far right. If things went as he wished, she wouldn't disqualify herself, but would have faith in him and in her own ability to judge fairly. When he gave his evidence about a national ring of credit card thieves, he didn't look at her as he spoke. He hadn't been that nervous even in his rookie days. He wanted her to be proud of him, whether she agreed with him or not. Perspiration beaded on his forehead and above his upper lip, but he ignored it and focused on the prosecutor's questions and his own answers. To avoid the temptation to speak with her in violation of court rules, he left before the judge recessed court. But it wasn't over. He testified the next day, and the next.

"Your honor, Cox and Reddaway have criminal records," Luke said. "McClendon doesn't, at least not so far as I've been able to determine."

His furtive glances at Kate let him know that she took copious notes throughout his testimony. A good sign? In his heart, he knew that if it proved otherwise he could forget a future with her.

He had a week during which to stew about it. A week to dig into himself and find his ultimate truth—that he wanted her for his wife and the mother of his children, and that he wanted Randy. And in what seemed the most important week of his life—six torture- and doubt-filled days—he'd once again had to deal with Axel Strange. The man lodged a written complaint, claiming that Luke had transferred him because of their contention over a woman. He wouldn't have expected it if Jessye hadn't warned him.

"Luke, honey, I think you ought to know Axel's filing charges against you. I don't believe a word of it, and neither does he. I just thought I'd tell you."

As if he didn't have enough on his mind. He sat on the corner of his desk. "What's his gripe, Jessye?"

"He's claiming you transferred him so he won't be near Kate and you'll have a better chance with her, that both of you are dating her."

He almost laughed. "Portsmouth isn't *that* big. If a few extra blocks would put him at a disadvantage, he didn't have much of a chance to begin with."

"I'm not ratting on him, Luke. I'm telling you because he admitted he'd do anything to knock you off your pedestal, as he put it."

"The guy's crazy. I'm not on any pedestal."

"Luke, he's a friend, and he's not a bad fellow. He just

has this . . . this thing about you. I do declare, I never saw the beat of it. I told him he wastes too much of his life worrying about what you're doing.''

"Good advice. Is he going through with this . . . this charge?"

"He's already done it. Well, I hope you're able to refute it. I'll be glad to witness for you."

He shook his head. Never! But he said, "Thanks, Jessye. It's a cinch. But why are you telling me this? I understood that things between you and Strange had . . . well, tightened up."

"I got to know him better, Luke, and he's showed me that inside he's not a scoundrel, but a decent guy. He hurts like the rest of us."

"If you feel that way about him, why warn me when you know he'll lose face?"

"Don't misunderstand me. There's nothing between Axel and me, though I know he wants that. He's not interested in Kate, and never was. He just doesn't want you to have her. Kate knows that."

She'd made it reasonably clear, but he had to be sure. "Where does that leave you?"

Her sigh, long and harsh as though she stared at the personification of futility, told him more than her words. "You know how it is with me."

He also knew better than to pursue it further.

When the review board confronted him with the charges, he had Axel's record ready for their examination. The complaint was thrown out. So much time and energy frittered away.

The smuggling case went to the jury. He had expected that they'd reach a verdict in three days at the most. But two weeks passed, and he wondered if Kate was the one who wouldn't yield. He hadn't expected a hung jury, nor had his officers.

Finally, he got the call and raced to the courthouse in

time to hear the jury foreman read the verdict. *Guilty on all counts.* The clerk polled the jury, and when he addressed Kate she answered in a voice that, to him, had the sound of a temple bell—clear and loud. "Guilty, your honor." He dropped his face in his hands and said a prayer of thanks. The one barely audible voice belonged to a matronly woman whom he'd seen on juries a number of times. In his view, she had to have been the holdout.

When the judge excused the jury, though, Kate almost ran from the courtroom. Had he been wrong?"

Chapter Fourteen

"Why did you run from me? You knew I was there and that I'd want to see you, talk with you. Why did you ... Kate, talk to me."

Kate sat on the edge of her bed and looked at the telephone receiver that brought his voice to her. What could she say to him? That she couldn't think? That pandemonium had broken out in her head like a herd of wild horses racing in different directions?

"I didn't run from you, Luke, but after that harrowing exercise in the jury room I had to get somewhere and find some peace."

"And you couldn't find it with me?"

"Not on the level that we both need it. Some moments with you would be wonderful, but I'd only put a bandage on a wound that needs cleansing. Luke, I have to come to terms with ... with this whole business of guilt and innocence."

"Then you *did* learn something? Let me in on what you're saying."

"I learned a lot, and not all of it pleased me. I hope when I piece it together, if I can, that you'll still want to talk with me."

"Kate, I'm here for you, and if you ever change your mind and your heart about my role in Jethro Raven's incarceration, I'll embrace you with all I have, all I'm holding inside of me. Holding for you."

"I can't promise anything right now, Luke, but you have to know after what I've just been through, I'll do all I can to get rid of ... of this awful thing that stands between us."

"Everything is there for us, except your faith. We're good together, whether playing, teasing, scrimmaging or—"

She interrupted him because he could sway her with the mere sound of his voice. "Luke, give me a chance."

"You want a chance? If I walked into your bedroom, you'd be mine in five minutes. It doesn't hurt to acknowledge the truth of your feelings. In fact, it's damned liberating. You know where you stand in this matter, and I don't doubt it for a second. There are no immovable forces between us. You only have to believe in me, Kate."

"You mean you still question that?"

She could imagine that her question surprised him, for he hadn't mentioned the jury's verdict. "I know the jury's vote was unanimous. It had to be. But I don't know which juror held out for fifteen days."

She sat forward, and her blood began to warm with the spurt of anger that curled up in her like smoke on a still morning. "Luke, if you need the answer to that, you only have to read the record. I wouldn't expect you to make a hasty conclusion."

"And I haven't made one. If you're suggesting that you're trying to deal with your father's imprisonment, I'll gladly give you the space you need. I want it cleared up. And, Kate, if you love us both, try to be fair to each of us.

I know that learning about my role in this was a blow, but I hope you can see it now from a new perspective."

She looked at the piece of hair on her fingers and realized that she'd been yanking on the strands that dangled over her left ear. "I'm doing my best. While we're speaking, I'd like to ask a favor of you. Could you keep Randy for me this weekend? I have to make an important trip, and I don't want to take him with me."

His silence told her that he'd prefer to have more information, but that he didn't intend to ask for it. "Of course. We'll both enjoy it. If you're going where I think you are, we need to ensure your safety. Could you come to my office and make your travel arrangements on my secure phone? It's the only one I trust."

"All right. May I come tomorrow around noon?"

"Sure, and bring Randy with you."

The empty silence hung between them like an ominous shadow, and her heart cried out, but she couldn't say what she felt. And she realized that he, too, remained captive to pain and pride.

When she could, she said, "Uh . . . see you Saturday."

She went to her desk and looked at the notes she'd taken during the trial. Half of the jurors had been anxious to get home, but the other half had held out for justice, for proof of innocence or guilt. But in the end, all of them, even the woman who used the court system as the source of her mystery novels had taken it seriously. That woman believed the man had been duped, that he hadn't known what the packages contained, while Kate had argued that the man was a courier, that each time he traveled airline personnel had asked whether he'd packed his own belongings, and he'd answered yes. It had been her argument that prompted the woman to vote guilty after holding out for fifteen days.

At least, she now knew that Luke hadn't locked her out of his heart. From the time they'd gone their separate ways, she'd longed for him. Loyalty to the father she loved so much, who had been the delight of her young life, hadn't let her exonerate Luke from responsibility for her father's fate. But every morning when she opened her eyes, Luke Hickson was her first thought, and every night she closed them thinking of him, loneliness eating away at her, digging an ever bigger hole in her.

After watching Luke on that witness stand and hearing his testimony, she wanted to embrace him, to tell him that she'd misjudged him, but what if her father maintained his innocence? She threw up her hands. She didn't know if she could make it without Luke, and she didn't see herself presenting her father with a grandchild sired by a man who'd railroaded him to prison. Oh Lord, what had she done to deserve such a dilemma?

Luke got up and opened his office door. He'd never seen her looking so good. "Hello, Kate. Come on in. Hi, Randy."

She gazed up at him for a few seconds. "Hi. You didn't get taller, did you?"

Nervous small talk. Barely able to steady his voice, he knew the root of her nervousness. An hour alone with each other would cure both of them. He read the longing that blazed in her eyes, and his body threatened to revolt against its prison of denial. Lord, but he wanted her in his arms, where she belonged. He looked down at Randy, who gazed from one to the other. As clever as he was, the boy had to have sensed the distance between them.

He put an arm around Randy's shoulder. "Let's go down to the lounge, son. Your mother has some calls to make."

When they returned half an hour later, she stood at the window in rapt attention. He couldn't imagine to what.

"Sit over here, son," he said to Randy, and pointed to a chair beside the door. She was too still, ramrod straight.

He walked over to her, put his hands on her shoulders, and turned her to face him.

"Good Lord. Baby, what happened? What's the matter?"

She squeezed her eyes shut and groped for him—blindly. And, dear God, she was in his arms at last. In his need, his yearning to comfort her, his lips caressed her face, and he sipped the brine that streamed from her eyes. Though nearly undone by her sadness and his overwhelming desire to protect her, soothe her, he had to settle for holding her and stroking her back. And in spite of his concern, he couldn't help glorying in her obvious need for him and in the feel of her close to him.

"Tell me what it is. What can I do to help you?"

She burrowed into him, and he absorbed her tremors and stilled her shaking body. "I just don't know what I'll do if this doesn't come out right."

"Listen to me, baby," he whispered. "You know the truth. I realize that accepting it isn't easy, but you have the courage and the strength."

"He was always there for me. Always. And you ... oh, Luke!"

"Easy, sweetheart. Do what you have to do. When you get back, I'll be here."

He'd never seen her cry, never seen her without her composure. If he could just ...

He glanced toward the door and, as he expected, Randy had locked his gaze on them, an anxious expression on his young face. It was then that he realized the extent of Randy's trust in him, for the boy hadn't run to his mother when he realized her distress, but had left it to him.

"Did you eat lunch?"

She shook her head.

"The three of us could go out, or I can have something delivered here. What would you like?"

"I'm not hungry, but Randy hasn't had lunch."

He couldn't stand to see her so down, and it occurred

to him that he ought to change the scene. She wouldn't slouch in the presence of strangers. "Then maybe we'd better go out," he said. True to her fashion, she stepped away from him, put a smile on her face, and laid back her shoulders.

His heart skipped a beat when she wrinkled her nose in an effort to make light of what had just transpired. "All right. Give me a second to repair the damage I did to my eyes."

"I don't see anything wrong with them. What'll it be? Hot dogs, hamburgers or—"

"Crab cakes," Randy said. "My mom likes them."

So the boy would offer concessions to brighten things for his mother. All wasn't lost. "Works for me, Randy," he said.

At the door, Randy took his left hand, and Luke wanted to put his other arm around Kate, but he couldn't. No matter that he loved her to the recesses of his soul; he knew he wouldn't go any further with her unless she accepted his integrity in what he did for a living. His life's work as a police detective demanded that his woman and his family accept and respect that he had to do what the law and his conscience dictated, that he could do nothing less.

At least he knew the worst of it, that her father was doing a fifteen-year stretch at the Federal Correction Institution in Cumberland, Maryland. She wouldn't have given in to the pain that seared her if Luke hadn't put his hands on her and offered her his body's comfort. She'd needed him. For years, she'd stood on her own, alone in spite of the husband who'd vowed to put her above all else. She'd never cried on a man's shoulder, not even Nathan's, and she wasn't proud of losing her cool in the presence of Luke and her son. But how many women were forced to chose between their beloved father and the other man they loved? She snapped the small case shut, unplugged her computer, closed her piano, checked the back door, and walked out of the apartment. Head high, she told herself that what she'd learn in Cumberland—or anything else—would not break her.

She hadn't expected Luke to take her to the airport, because she hadn't given him her confidence, hadn't told him where she was going though he'd guessed. But when she saw that Jenkins waited for her her heart lightened and her steps quickened. She tipped the taxi driver and let him go.

"He said phone his cell number and let him know what time you'll get back."

She thanked him. "Wish me luck."

He frowned, and she wished she hadn't said it, but immediately he smiled, flashing white teeth against his honey-beige complexion. "You got it, Miss Middleton."

"Thanks, and I think it's time we switched to first names."

He walked with her to the boarding gate. "Have a good flight, Kate."

At the prison she told the guard in reception, "I'm here to see Jethro Raven, please. Tell him his daughter, Kate Middleton, is here."

The guard scrutinized her, flipped through a folder, and said, "Sorry, but Raven doesn't accept visitors."

"But—"

"I said he doesn't accept visitors."

She refused to give up. "Would you please tell him it's a question of life and death? I have to see him. Ask him please not to do this to me." She fought back the moisture that threatened to cloud her vision.

"Let me see some official ID."

She showed him her driver's license, and he let his gaze roam over her. Finally, apparently having made up his mind about something, he lifted the phone receiver on his desk.

"Send Raven out with a guard. I think this visitor's okay, but who can be sure?"

She'd have to ask Luke why the guard seemed to be protecting her father. Or was he suspicious of her?

She gazed around her and shuddered, seeing drabness personified and an enormous lock on a metal door that she imagined protected the world from the men behind it. She thought of her father's love of gardening, plants, and sunshine, of his early morning walks. And she remembered the tale he told her as a child about the stars—Jack Star and Mary Star—who lived above in the heavens and lit the sky each night with baby stars to brighten the world. At age twelve, she had no longer believed it, but she'd loved hearing the story's singsong rhythm in her father's mellifluous baritone. Now, at thirty-eight, she could still be soothed by a sonorous male voice, like Luke Hickson's.

"I'll smile if it kills me," she promised herself.

After a routine search, a guard escorted her to a small room, sparsely but serviceably furnished with comfort at a minimum. She supposed it served as the visitors' room.

She stood when he walked in as erect and proud as ever, and a glance at the guard told her not to expect privacy. They stared at each other until she could stand it no longer. Realizing it was her move, she ran to him with arms outstretched.

"Kate. Oh, Kate," he moaned, holding her to him. "I didn't want you to see me here like this. I didn't even answer your letters, because I didn't want my grandson or anyone else to know you received mail from prison."

She stepped back and let her eyes behold him. "I . . . I didn't expect you to look so . . . so much like yourself. You look good."

"So do you. Lord, so do you. Child, you're just like a flower in full bloom." He shook his head as though in wonder. "You knew I didn't want you here. So why have you come?"

"Papa, I ..." She looked at her watch. Only twenty-three more minutes, so she took a deep breath and told him about Luke.

"When I learned he was the detective who arrested and accused you, I confronted him, and we broke up. But, Papa, I love him, and he loves me. I want you to tell me your side of it."

"Kate, he only did his job. I was guilty, because I didn't use my head. I let money get in the way of my good sense. You know that I started a courier service right after you left Orangeburg. Strictly legitimate. I handled everything from packages to pets to kids. A man asked me to deliver a package personally because it was valuable. I was so carried away with the money he said he'd pay that I forgot to ask him what was in it.

"Fifteen hundred dollars plus transportation costs to rush a twenty-five-pound package from Orangeburg to Portsmouth didn't seem outrageous, so I did it.

"After I got caught, the man sent word that if I breathed anything to anybody, his friends would finish off every one of my relatives. And he still sends me a reminder from time to time. I took the rap. It's a tough lesson, but even in this place I've managed to find some rewards."

She clung to his hands. "What do you mean?"

"I teach Sunday school classes, and I'm helping some of these men learn to read."

"But, Papa, you're not guilty of any wrongdoing."

"I am, and don't you forget it. I've asked myself many times why I didn't question the man. That package could have contained a bomb. I have to be honest with God and myself, Kate. I didn't ask because, deep down, I didn't want to know."

Her mind brought back to her the case she'd heard as

a juror. Was it only the act that mattered? Didn't intent count for anything?

"What about Luke Hickson?"

"The arresting officer? Very respectful, but no nonsense. Not one iota. He's standing his ground, is he?"

She nodded. "He isn't likely to budge. If I can't believe he was right in arresting you and pressing for your conviction, it's over."

Her father stood, signaling that their time was up. "And he shouldn't budge. The man did what he had to do. I didn't, so don't let me stand between you."

"Time's up, miss."

Quickly she kissed her father. "If I get a post office box, will you answer my letters?"

He didn't speak, but she remembered that whenever something pleased him a lot he'd just light up his face with a big smile.

With Saturday night and Sunday morning waiting to be used up, she called a taxi, went back to her hotel, and wrote her father a note thanking him for the visit. Then she stretched out on the bed and faced some truths.

Luke took his prized pizza from the oven and cut hefty slices for Randy and himself while the boy finished setting the table. Then he got a pitcher of fresh lemonade and a can of beer from the refrigerator, sat down, and said grace.

Now who could that be? He got up and went to answer the doorbell. "Miss Patterson!" Just what he needed with Randy in the kitchen. "Is something wrong at the store, or with Kate?"

Jessye tossed her head, and her hair spread out like the points of a Japanese accordion fan. "Luke, honey, I'm not used to such a cold reception from a gentleman."

He didn't doubt that, but if she didn't lay off him he'd give her cause to wonder if he was a gentleman. He ran his hand over his head and told himself to be patient. "Jessye, will you please stop playing games? My dinner's getting cold."

Years ago, when he was nineteen or twenty, he might have been challenged by the promise of her seductive smile, but he was forty-two. And where women were concerned, he'd fought and won more battles than Jessye could incite.

"Well, you could invite me to join you, since I haven't eaten."

Ease up, man, he admonished himself. "I'm sorry. I can't invite you in. I have a guest. So if you'll ex—"

"Well, I just wanted to give you a chance to get to know me. Will you be free tomorrow evening?"

Her posture slackened and, instead of looking him in the eye as she usually did, her gaze settled on a spot to the left of his head. She hurt. Her entire demeanor shouted it.

"I'm sorry," he said as gently as he could without inviting her further interest, "I have to meet Kate at the airport tomorrow night."

Her eyebrows flew up. "I didn't know she went out of town. Where'd she go?"

Glad he could tell the truth, he replied, "Your guess is as good as mine."

Her hands went to her hips. "Why don't I believe you?"

He couldn't help grinning at the reply that came to his mind. "Because you'd prefer something more melodramatic. More sensational. I'd better go eat. See you."

He watched her walk slowly down his walkway. A waiting taxi told him that she hadn't had much faith in the success of her visit. He wished she'd give up. He went back to his pizza.

"What did Cousin Jessye want, Captain Luke?"

His hand stopped just as the pizza reached his lips, and he focused on Randy. "How'd you know that was Jessye?"

Randy finished chewing his mouthful of pizza. "Nobody else talks like that. All that honey and sugar stuff. What'd she want?"

Now, there was a good question. "Just a friendly visit, I guess. Nothing special."

"Oh! What time's my mom coming back?"

Clever little mind. He'd associated the two. "She hasn't called me yet, but I expect she will tonight. Don't worry. We'll meet her."

"Sometimes I don't like Cousin Jessye. Not all the time, but sometimes."

He couldn't accept that. "She's a good person, Randy. Give her a chance. I know she's not like your mother, but Kate's exceptional." He swallowed the rest of his beer and stood. "Let's clean up. The National Spelling Bee is on TV in a few minutes, and I want you to watch it."

He went up to his room and dialed Jenkins. "Russ, did you tell Kate to call me?"

"I sure did, Luke, and she said she would. She . . . uh, seemed a little shaky to me. Nervous, like."

That didn't surprise him, but it wasn't like her not to hide it. He didn't want to ask Jenkins the destination of her flight, though he was sure that Jenkins, being the smart detective that he was, had noted the plane's destination and any scheduled stops en route.

"I doubt she'd ever fly for pleasure," he said, fudging the truth.

"Oh, I hadn't thought of that."

"Thanks for seeing her off, friend. Be in touch."

"You bet."

For heaven's sake, why didn't she call? Didn't she know he'd be out of his mind with worry until he heard from her? He went into his den, got his briefcase, and tried to study her case, to piece together the bits of evidence. One by one, he discarded the leads. If only he had a motive. He'd never suspected her in-laws, and after visiting them he'd scratched them off the list. He couldn't keep three shifts of two men on watch—one at her store, and the other at her apartment—indefinitely. The department wouldn't support it, and very soon, he wouldn't be able to justify it. He looked down at what he'd been doing with his right hand—swirls of clouds and flocks of birds in flight beneath them. He laughed at himself. Maybe he ought to give up chasing criminals and doodle for a living. Seven-thirty. He dialed Rude Hopper.

"Rude, this is Luke. Did your man have anything to report?"

"Not a thing, Luke. He says we're looking in the wrong places. He doesn't see any logic to this pattern."

"And he's right, Rude. I suspect each one of these guys was hired by the same person. My problem is the motive."

"Maybe somebody wants to frighten her?"

"They've done that. Seen or heard anything of those two goons?" Luke asked.

"Not a thing, brother. Not since that night we headed them off on their way to Jessup's Gallery. And if they'd been around, the brothers would have seen them."

"Thanks, brother. Be in touch."

"Right on."

He hung up. Why didn't she call? He checked on Randy, sent him to bed, and went out on his balcony. Within a few minutes, his T-shirt clung to his body and breathing the still air seemed to weigh him down as the late July heat added to his discomfort. The ringing phone brought him charging into the house. He waited. His cell phone.

"Hello." He never identified himself when he used that phone.

"Luke, it's—"

"Kate. Thank God. I was on my way out of my mind. How are you? Where are you? No, you don't have to tell me that. Just say you're all right."

"I'm fine, Luke. I'm . . . I think I'm fine. I—"

"Listen, honey, save that till you get back here. I want us to be together when we talk. I . . . I have so much to say to you."

"Me too. I'd have called earlier, but I fell asleep. I'm in my hotel room. I'm glad I came."

"If you are, then so am I."

"Are you meeting me tomorrow? I'm getting in at three-ten."

"We'll be there."

"How's Randy?"

"Fast asleep. He's a good kid, and I've enjoyed having him here."

"He's so attached to you."

"What's wrong with that? Such things are never one-sided. If you're not on that plane tomorrow, I'll send out an FBI search, bloodhounds, the works. Kate, I need to see you."

"Not more than I need you, but I realize we have to straighten things out. Maybe we could take that weekend we'd planned."

"I hope it'll be possible, sweetheart, but let's not cross that bridge yet. All right?"

"I know. I'd better hang up. We said we'd wait till we're together."

"Yeah. But if you can't hold it, let it out."

"I . . . Just be there, please, when I get off that plane."

"You betcha, baby."

"Night."

"Hey, wait a minute. You mean you're not blowing me a kiss?"

"I didn't know whether you wanted one."

"Do I need to breathe, Kate?"

He listened as the sound of a kiss caressed his ears. "Good night, sweetheart."

He hung up. She hadn't said she needed to see him, but that she needed him. And she'd made the distinction deliberately. Something had changed. He didn't know what, but she seemed close to bursting. If her old man had played on her sympathy, it was probably over for them, because he wouldn't back down. And suppose the man had been honest. Well, he'd rather she'd believed in him without the benefit of his exculpation. But if she could convince him that she understood, appreciated, and respected his attitude toward his work, could he ask for more? And should he? He didn't know.

He answered his telephone on the first ring. Who'd be calling him on his official line at one o'clock Sunday afternoon?

"Hickson."

"Hello, Luke. This is Jeb Baker in Cambridge. I've got a fellow over here who may be the one you're after. He's tight-lipped, and we can't get him to budge. We can't hold him longer than tomorrow morning at seven without evidence. Can you come over tonight, have a look at him, and see what you can get out of him?"

Could he miss meeting Kate's plane? Out of the question. "How late can I get there?"

"Eleven. Can you make that?"

"Do my best." He jotted down the address and trip directions. "What's the guy's name? I'll give him a run-through." He made a note of the man's name and features, hung up, and called Rude.

"Does he ring a bell?" Luke asked Rude.

"The name does, way off somewhere in my mind, but it doesn't match the description. Maybe our man's been using disguises. But, heck, brother, it's pretty hard to disguise your height that much. Who knows but some guy's invented a way to do it? I'll pass the word."

"Not this time, Rude. Keep it under your hat."

"Will do."

He opened his laptop computer, which was connected to the department's system, and entered the suspect's name and description and waited. No information matched, but that didn't rule out the man in Cambridge as a possibility. He packed a few personal items, called Cowan and Jenkins to let them know he'd be away overnight, and got ready to meet Kate's plane. The opportunity to mend their relationship that evening had just been taken from them. He'd sweat out another long day, at least, before he stood a chance of loving her again.

"Come on, Randy, we'll be late for your mother's plane."

"Soon's I finish this."

He looked over the boy's shoulder at a drawing of the view from the window beside the desk where Randy sat. "That's a very good likeness."

"I wanted to give it to my mom, but I guess I have to finish it next time I stay here."

"You can come over one afternoon and work on it. Let's go."

His heart began a wild thudding in his chest, and moisture covered his forearms as he counted the minutes until she'd walk off the escalator. He looked around for the wall, found it, and let it take his weight, lest he double up from the pains that ripped through his belly. He hadn't had such a case of nerves since the day his college football coach told him he'd be quarterbacking the team on Homecoming Day. The expression on her face would tell him whether she loved him, but he also needed to know if she believed him, and in him. And it was the latter that had him strung out. For the nth time, he looked at his watch. The plane had been on the ground more than twenty minutes.

And then he saw her, her face wreathed in smiles and her eyes sparkling as though happiness suffused her. Swift feet took him to her, and she came to meet him halfway. She stopped and hugged Randy before straightening up and staring into his face, her own a solemn mass of questions. Then she smiled and opened her arms to him. "Just hold me," she whispered.

With one hand at the back of her head and the other across her shoulders, he drew her into his arms and held her close. He didn't speak, couldn't speak. She was in his arms where she belonged, where he needed her to be, and right then he wasn't about to tempt the angels. They'd face the rest when they got to it. She leaned back to observe his face, and her lips parted to welcome his kiss, but, with Randy's gaze glued on them, he couldn't risk arousal. He squeezed her tightly.

"I just found out I have to go to Cambridge tonight to check out a suspect. I wanted us to spend the evening together, but we'll have to wait till tomorrow. If I don't go, the man will have to be released. Understand?"

She nodded but—though he could see that she tried to hide it—disappointment was evident in the droop of her mouth and the way in which the light faded from her oval brown eyes.

"We'll see each other tomorrow?"

"I'll be here tomorrow evening, so let's be together then."

"Maybe Jessye would keep Randy."

He shook his head. "That might not be the best solution, so I expect we'll have to be patient."

He drove them home, parked in front of her door, and went with them to examine her apartment for safety. "I'm on my way to Cambridge. Call my cell phone if you need me."

Good Lord, the need in her eyes! Hot shivers of desire roared through his body. Heaven help him, he had to taste her. "Kate. Baby, come here. She flew into his arms, parted her lips, and he had his tongue in her mouth, savoring her, loving her. His blood pounded in his head when she gripped his arms and then his shoulders, and finally pulled his buttocks tight to her body. Too late. His full arousal jumped against her, and her moans sent thrill after thrill through his whole being. Her eyes widened in surprise when he held her away to avoid a rush to completion. Never in his life had he come so close to losing total control. Then gently, he pulled her back to him to dispel the feeling of rejection that he knew his sudden movement had caused her.

"It's okay, sweetheart," he whispered. "You came around on my blind side and powdered me. I had to . . . to get it under control."

"When will you be back?"

"Sometime tomorrow. I'd better go. Randy will bring you up to date. Call you later."

In Cambridge, he sat on the edge of Jeb's desk, one foot on the floor and the other swinging free as he concentrated on the suspect, a tall, thin, young man who looked him in the eye and didn't waver in his testimony. He examined the man's arms for evidence of drug use. None. Three hours later, he had no choice but to recommended his release.

"I think he's clean, Jeb, but he shouldn't leave town just yet."

"Why're you so sure?"

"I can't shake his story. And he didn't recognize me. Whoever's after Kate Middleton knows who I am, and what I look like. I'd bet my neck on that. If you get any more leads, call me. Any place around here where I can get a night's sleep?"

"Yeah. Come on to my place. The kids are on their own now, and the house is empty."

An hour later, after a good home-cooked meal and a warm shower, he got into bed and called Kate on his cell phone.

"I'm spending the night," he said after they'd greeted each other. "If I leave around six in the morning, I should be in Portsmouth by nine at the latest. Save this evening for me."

"I will. Drive carefully. Night."

"Say," he growled, "didn't you forget something?"

"No. It just seemed so inadequate. But . . . well, here's your kiss."

"Sleep well, sweetheart."

Five-thirty the next morning found him on Route 50, headed for Salisbury and on to the Scenic Highway that would take him into Norfolk. Early morning driving provided a peacefulness that he enjoyed. Summer rains had blessed the surroundings with lush foliage. Rows of brilliant green corn laced the fields; huge green heads of cabbage and field after field of red tomatoes stood ripe for picking. He marveled at the faith of the American farmer; one month without rain could lay waste to all that beauty and prosperity. He slowed down to pay a toll, and got his first morning's smell of carbon monoxide from the big truck that pulled up beside him. He didn't like Route 13, but it represented the fastest way home.

Suddenly he slowed down. Holding out a cane with a red scarf tied to it, an old woman sat beside what was obviously a disabled car, commanding his attention. He pulled up behind her and, mindful of treachery, felt for his revolver, put on his coat, and got out.

"Something wrong, ma'am?"

Fierce old eyes peered up at him from under the wide brim of a tattered straw hat. "There certainly is, young man. I've got a flat, and I'm practically out of gas."

"Do you have a spare?"

She nodded toward the back of the car. "There's a tire in the trunk, but I don't know what good it is, because I've never looked at it. Could be rotten, for all I know."

He looked hard at her. "Do you have a driver's license?"

"Of course I have. If I didn't, I'd be a fool to flag down a cop."

He nearly slammed the lid of the trunk on his hand as he spun around and stared at her, ready for any necessary action. "What makes you think I'm a policeman?"

"Because you are."

He walked back to her and faced her. "How do you know, and what are you doing out here this time of morning?"

"I have a message for you. But first, you please fix my tire."

Goosebumps popped out on his arms and hands, and shivers shook him. "Look, ma'am, I'll help you if I can, but you give me an eerie feeling."

"Nothing to be afraid of. Hurry up and finish it before that big truck comes along here weaving in an' out as if the driver's on something."

He shook his head. The woman must be loco. He finished changing the tire and checked her gas level. "How far are you going?"

Suddenly, she grabbed his arm and yanked him out of the way. A big eighteen-wheel truck missed him by inches. Horrified, he backed up and stared at her. "Who are you, and how old are you?"

"I'm Lucy Monroe Watkins, and I'm ninety-three."

"With that kind of strength?"

"That's the same thing your Kate asked me. I live right."

"Wait a minute. What do you know about Kate?"

"She got lost and asked me for directions. Ended up spending the night at my place while you worried yourself silly. When you catch that fellow, he'll be driving. You're going to get the ringleader, because his flunkies have been missing the mark. And something's just happened to make your man real anxious. I told her to bring you to see me when you get yourselves straightened out, but I knew she'd forget all about that. Well, I'd better be getting on." She

got in, turned the ignition key, and looked at him.
"Thanks."

He stared unbelieving as she checked the traffic, eased
into Route 13, and headed toward Salisbury doing a good
sixty miles an hour. Had he just seen an apparition? No,
he'd spoken with her, and she'd talked. Made sense, too.
He recalled Kate's tale of an old woman after her atten-
dance at that booksellers convention. Same woman? Possibly. He got in his car and tried to shake it off, but her
words hung in his mind. *The man would be driving.* He didn't
believe any human being knew the future, but he'd take
all the help he could get. From now on, two men would
tail Kate everywhere she went. If the old woman knew
so much, why hadn't she told him what to expect in his
relationship with Kate? Maybe she had, and he hadn't
been listening carefully enough. But he'd figure it out. He
relaxed behind the wheel of the big Buick, flipped on the
cruise control, and headed for Norfolk.

She'd done everything wrong. Jessye heaved a deep sigh,
hooked the strap of her white pocketbook over her shoulder, and went in the lobby of her apartment building to
meet Axel. Right then, she doubted she had the strength
to handle an eager man with Axel's temperament. She'd
done as Kate suggested and paid closer attention to Axel.
As far as she could see, the man's one big shortcoming
was his reaction to Luke, but that one packed a wallop.
None of it mattered, though, because understanding was
no substitute for chemistry. She shook her head. That
wasn't it. She'd always craved the unattainable, and Luke
Hickson had put himself out of her reach. She wondered
if she'd want him if he was as hot after her as Axel was.
She couldn't figure it out.

"Hi. Every time I look at you, my blood runs faster."

"Oh, Axel, you sure do know how to make a girl feel

special." With her help, his kiss missed her mouth and caught her cheek. "Where're we going, honey?"

"I got us two tickets to Buddy Guy, but rain's threatening, and there's no shelter for the park concerts. Maybe we'd better just have a nice dinner." He looked at her, hopefully, she thought. "Unless you want to go to the movies."

He wanted to please her, so she said what she knew he'd prefer. "Honey, dinner's just fine. You know I love to eat. If this town would just get some good old butter beans, the place might grow on me."

His ready smile told her she'd pleased him. "I'll get you some butter beans, sweetheart, if I have to grow them myself."

And he would, she realized. Why couldn't it have been him, and not Luke?

They finished the meal at the River Café, and he leaned back in his chair, more pensive than she remembered having seen him. "Axel, honey, are you depressed?"

"Not more than usual. You're everything I want, and something tells me I don't stand a ghost of a chance."

"I haven't always been honest with men, Axel. I'm just learning that fellows hurt just like I do, and I'm sorry for a lot of the selfish and inconsiderate ways I've acted with them. Axel, I think the pill I'm going to swallow is as bitter as yours."

"You mean Hickson?"

She nodded. "But you have so much, honey. All you have to do is go home like your folks are begging you to do, and run the family businesses. Look what's waiting for you. Position, power, and money." She rolled her eyes skyward. "Honey, I've walked away from some tidbits in my life, but you're throwing away a fortune."

He shook his head. "Try to understand, Jessye. I don't need that. If I had it, it wouldn't complete my life. For that I need you."

She leaned forward. "You're saying you'd take me over the Strange position and fortune? Lord, how could you have done this to me?"

She had to get used to this Axel. Cool. Dispassionate. As if he had nothing to push for. "Money isn't everything, Jessye."

She raised an eyebrow as she imagined herself serving tea in the Strange family drawing room. "Of course it isn't, especially when you've got plenty of it."

He called for the check. "Come on, babe, let's go. You're not giving up on Hickson, and I can't give up on you."

She stood and placed a hand gently on his arm. "You're a terrific guy, Axel. Forget about Luke. He's never showed a speck of interest in me. Not once."

He stared down at her, and she could see skepticism splashed across his face. "You're kidding."

"I'm not. And when I made passes at him, he brushed them off. Axel, he's not a ladies' man. Trust me, I would definitely know."

"You want me to believe—"

"I wouldn't lie to you. There's no point. And if he got every promotion you applied for, like you said, ask yourself why."

He took her hand as they left the restaurant. "Let's walk down by the water for a while. I'm not ready to leave you."

At the promenade, he sat with her on the wrought iron bench, still holding her hand. "You hit pretty hard, Jessye, but I can take it. When I first took this job, I cruised. In recent years, I've done my best to make up for it, but nothing comes my way. I'm a good detective, a damn good one, and I know it." His sigh bespoke his puzzlement. "Hickson could have fired me and rid himself of me for good, but he didn't, and I'm still trying to figure out why."

She stroked his arm in a gesture of comfort. "He's a decent man, and he took himself out of your way. At Third Precinct, you have a chance to start over."

His hand squeezed hers and she wished—oh, how she wished—that the chemistry would lock them together. "But can I start over with you?"

No woman could want a more handsome or masculine specimen of the male gender, and she responded to that. "Let's be friends, Axel. Only the Lord knows what's in our future."

Chapter Fifteen

Kate read and reread the results of her father's trial from the record she obtained from her father's lawyer. She'd done the right thing, and, no one, Luke included, could convince her otherwise. Her father hadn't intentionally broken the law, though he admitted having closed his eyes when his common sense should have warned him to open them wide. A phone call to her father's lawyer left her with little or no hope of a retrial, or that if one were granted the verdict would be reversed. She put the court papers where Jessye and Randy wouldn't find them, and settled down to work.

At that moment, her cousin breezed into the shop. "Kate, honey, Axel found me some good old southern butter beans cooked down with some good old smoked ham hocks, and I knew you'd want some. I stopped by the wharf and got some crab cakes and corn muffins, some spoons and things so we can eat lunch right here."

What had gotten into *her*? "Wonderful. How're you and Axel getting on?"

Jessye set the bag of food on the desk. "Let's say we have an understanding."

"Oh? Really?"

Jessye focused her gaze on the bag of food. "We're friends, and if I ever decide the sight of him shakes me up and wrings me out we'll take it from there."

So it hadn't worked out. "I see, but did you at least try?"

"He's a sweetheart, Kate. A few spikes here and there, but we all have those. I'm just going to let nature do her own thing." She laid out the food. *"Her* own thing? Humph! Anybody who screws up things like this is bound to be male."

Kate let herself laugh, though realizing that Jessye still had designs on Luke saddened her. What would Jessye do when it all came to a head, as it surely would? Her cousin could be trying, but she was one of only three close relatives and the only female one, so she accepted her shortcomings.

Later, Jessye wrapped the remains of their lunch and put them into an empty shopping bag, waved airily, and left. *It would help a lot,* Kate thought, *if Jessye would touch earth occasionally.*

"Cousin Jessye left some crab cakes for you," she told Randy, who came from his French class shortly after Jessye left."

I don't want any."

She looked closely at him. "You feeling all right?"

"Yes, ma'am. I don't think I like her. She came to Captain Luke's house Sunday, and I heard her whispering her stupid talk. What did she want, Mom?"

His words struck her like a blow to the solar plexus, but she managed to smile her best smile. "I don't know, dear. Why didn't you ask her?"

"She didn't come in. I heard her at the front door with her silly talk."

So she'd started an undeclared war. Same old Jessye.

Always after whatever stood beyond her reach. She looked at her watch. Twelve-thirty. Where on earth was Luke?

"Randy, go shelve those books, please. And you're not to talk about your cousin that way," she admonished him, but her mind was on Luke. Maybe he hadn't gotten back. She threw up her hands. Worrying about a man, after she'd promised herself never to do it again. She put on a Louis Armstrong cassette and worked at changing her mood.

She hummed as she worked, posting the weekend receipts and answering mail, until the scent of musk and lavender reached her nostrils, bringing her head up sharply.

"Luke!"

"Hi. You spoiled my fun, sweetheart. I meant to plant a kiss on your ear."

She opened her mouth, but not a word escaped from it as she gazed on him. Satchmo's horn screamed in frenzied passion like the joyous coming together of long-parted lovers. Her heart's rhythm adopted a pattern of its own choosing, and the fingers of her right hand trembled like chattering teeth. God forbid that their verdict, the test of their love for each other, should come so soon, but he had the appearance of a man with a mission.

"How'd it go?" she asked in a tone more subdued than usual, and she corrected it at once. "Did you get what you wanted?"

Even before he spoke, she knew his answer from the furious way in which he rubbed the back of his neck. "No, I didn't, but I met an old friend of yours."

She pointed a finger at her chest. "Mine? Who?"

He looked hard at her, obviously to gauge her reaction. "Lucy Watkins Monroe."

Her loud gasp brought a rush to protect her, and his arms rested briefly around her shoulders as though to steady her. "You're not serious," she said, and she supposed that her face bore a stunned look.

"You bet I am."

"Did you get lost?"

He raised and lowered each shoulder in rapid succession. "I definitely did not. She was waiting for me on Route Thirteen at six o'clock this morning." He slapped his forehead. "I never take that highway. Never. Is she a real live human being?"

Kate couldn't help grinning. At one point during her visit with Lucy, a similar question had plagued her. "Real as rain. When we parted that morning I hugged her, so I'm certain. She's alive and breathing."

A sharp whistle flew from his lips. "Well, I'll be. Incidentally, I'm putting a double tail on you." She nodded, and he continued. "Do we still have a date this evening?"

She pushed her chair back from the desk and got up. "We do indeed, and I have a lot to tell you."

"And I want to hear it. Suppose I come by your place around seven."

The place and the time told her he hadn't relented. For two cents, she'd outfox him, but knowing the man, she figured he'd still come out on top.

"My place?" she asked, aware that her face and her tone communicated her disappointment. She didn't set out to build a fire in him, but her need was so intense that her whole being had to telegraph it to him. She thought of the cataclysmic eruption he'd drawn from her in Biddle, when he'd destroyed her sanity and her will to be other than his. Her memory of it must have shown on her face, for the hot fire of desire sprang forth in his eyes, gray, stormy, and wildly possessive.

Her right thumb trailed across his full lower lip, and his eyes blazed with passion and something else. He'd make her pay for that audacity, but she didn't care. She wanted him, and she'd pay the freight.

"Don't tamper with what you don't understand, Kate," he said, his tone harsh as though it pained him to utter the sounds. But the uncertainty of his voice only served to embolden her.

"I'll understand it later," she replied, heedless of her inner warnings. "I'm hungry, and I need you. Luke—"

A steely grip held her, and he stared down at her, a storm brewing in his eyes. "You want me, damn the consequences. Is that what you're telling me?"

"Luke, your arms—"

One hand grasped the back of her head, and the other tightened around her hips. Her breathing came in fast spurts, and he stared down at her, a blazing mute furnace.

"Kiss me or let me go," she moaned as his heat drew a hot feminine response from her, a quickening within her love nest. She rimmed her lips with her tongue, and she could see his Adam's apple bobbing up and down while he fixed his gaze on her mouth and gritted his teeth.

"Luke!"

Nothing, not even their nights in Biddle, had prepared her for the seductive force of his mouth on hers. Strong. Demanding. Stroking. Drugging. Had she pushed him too far? His hands, big and powerful, pressed her hips against his hardened flesh, and his tongue, thrusting deep into her mouth, commanded her total capitulation. Strong masculine fingers found her left nipple and toyed with it mercilessly. She tried to hold back, but her moans and whimpers escalated in volume and intensity until, as if dragging himself back to reality, he forced himself to pull away from her. Abruptly, he released her and stepped back.

He looked down at the floor and stabbed at it with the toe of his left shoe. "By now, you ought to be able to predict my response to any move you make, and you shouldn't have to prove to yourself that I want you." He trained his gray eyes on her, serious, but, thank goodness, not accusing. "I take it you didn't feel a need to prove it to *me.*"

She threw up the first defense that came to her mind. "What was Jessye doing at your house Sunday evening?"

Taken aback by her own words and the temerity of uttering them, she slapped her hand over her mouth, furious at herself for having let him know she cared about it.

He stepped closer. "If Jessye told you about that, you should have laughed, and if Randy told you, you should have ignored it. Do you consider me a philanderer?"

His heat still captured her, and she couldn't help responding to it. She wanted—she needed—to be back in his arms, but if she attempted to seduce him again, she knew she'd regret it.

"You didn't answer my question."

She swallowed hard. "No, I don't think that of you."

"And you know Jessye. Right?"

She nodded.

"Case closed. Your place at seven?"

"All right." So he was staying with his agenda. Well, she had to stand by hers, and only the Lord knew where they'd end up.

Why the devil would she concern herself with Jessye's antics? Didn't she know when a man loved her, adored her, and couldn't see another woman? He laughed at himself. He'd had a few anxious moments after seeing Kate with Axel at Martha Armstrong's fund-raiser. He nodded to the officer stationed in the lobby of the apartment building in which Kate lived. At her door, he raised his hand to knock and left it suspended in the air. How much was he prepared to yield? He shrugged, and tapped the doorbell. Best to play it by ear and let the chips fall where they would.

He had to laugh when she opened the door in a white shirt buttoned to the neck and a pair of navy blue pants. Nobody was going to accuse *her* of being seductive. What a scenario! She'd get mad, but laughter poured out of him.

"Hi. What's funny? Do I have a fly on my nose?"

He ran a finger over that nose. "You can't hide it, sweetheart, at least not from me. Your allure has nothing whatever to do with your clothes."

"Oh, for goodness' sake. Come on in and have a seat. I sent Randy to bed."

He looked at his watch and raised an eyebrow. "Kinda early for that, isn't it?"

She ignored the remark, went to the kitchen, and returned with a tray of coffee and gingerbread. He let his gaze sweep the tray of goodies.

"That'll seduce me as sure as you're born." He savored the dessert. "This is . . . wonderful. Thanks for thinking of it."

To his astonishment, she plowed right into a discussion of their immediate concerns. "Luke, I saw my father last Saturday for the first time in the six years since his arrest."

How could she say it that casually, when she hadn't even told him where she was going, though he'd guessed. He chewed more slowly, so as not to miss a word or gesture.

"You don't visit him?"

"He's forbidden it, and he doesn't answer my letters or make phone calls."

He set the cup and saucer on the coffee table and focused on her. "Did he say why?"

"Same reason why he clammed up and took the rap at his trial. If he revealed the name or description of the man who hired him to deliver that package, every member of his family would suffer. Luke, unless you count a couple of other cousins, that's only Jessye, her father, Randy, and me. Since he's been in prison, he's had a dozen reminders. He also said he didn't answer my letters because he didn't want anyone to know that I got mail from a prisoner."

He spread his knees, leaned forward, and propped his elbows on them. She was telling him something important and relevant to her case, but he couldn't grasp it because his thoughts were on her and how she must have felt at that prison. It was there, right in front of him, and he couldn't pull it out. But he would. He stopped himself as his hand started toward the back of his neck. "Go on. What else?"

"I got him to agree to answer my letters if I got a post office box. It wasn't . . . I mean—"

"What is it? Tell me."

"A guard stood there while we talked, and my father signaled me to whisper. But I had the feeling that, in spite of our whispers, every word we said was heard somewhere else."

"Yeah. I wouldn't be surprised."

Suddenly, she sprang up and hovered over him. "Luke, he was wrongfully convicted, because he didn't know what was in that box."

His blood seemed to stop flowing. "Wait a second. If we're back to that, I'm wasting time here. Ignorance is no excuse for breaking the law."

"But can't you understand what it means to a man—"

He pushed the tray farther from him and held up both hands, palms out. "I don't want to hear it, Kate. If Jethro Raven told you he was falsely arrested and convicted, I withdraw any sympathy I had for him."

She sat down. "No. He said he should have asked what he was carrying, that in his subconscience he suspects he didn't want to know because the money looked so good."

He got up, walked away, and then back to her. "Then why in king's name are you telling me he was falsely convicted, when he and I know that isn't true?"

He stared, almost transfixed, while she wrapped her arms around her middle and rocked backward and forward, her face marred with pain and her eyes dry and haunting.

"He's not guilty." Her voice thinned like the fading chirp of an aging parakeet. "That place is drab and bare and ugly. He loves long walks at sunset, nature, flowers, gardening. And fishing. He loves fishing. It's his passion. He'll be a broken old man when he gets out of there.''

He wanted to hold her, to comfort her, but he couldn't. She'd resurrected that barrier between them. "Kate," he whispered, "I want to hold you so much, but it would be a lie." His voice strengthened. "When you called me from Cumberland, Maryland, and when I met you at the airport, I believed you'd straightened it out. I need to know you understand that I'll always try to do my duty as best I know how." He shifted his glance from her eyes, unable to look at their failure to connect with him, to show him that she was with him.

"You haven't accepted my obligation to be faithful to my profession."

"But, Luke, you should have seen him—a man who'd enjoyed the respect of everybody who knew him—wearing a number on his plain battleship-gray shirt. I nearly died. It's not right."

He stood. Why couldn't she see the truth, understand it and him? "If you change your mind and your attitude about this, I'll be waiting with open arms."

He stared down at her, the vessel of his hopes, dreams, and all that he longed for, and she gazed back at him, open and honest, hiding nothing. Poles apart. He wished she wouldn't look at him with pain and vulnerability etched in every pore of her face, and he grabbed at his chest as the weight in his heart nearly shortened his breath.

"I don't think it's too much to expect that the woman I love and hold above all others, who professes to love me, should believe in me and trust my judgment in matters relating to my profession. I have faults, Kate, plenty of them, but I believe I'm entitled to that much."

She stood—with difficulty, he observed—reached out to him, and immediately let her arm fall to her side. "I . . . I do, but—"

"I can't compromise on this. If you can't tell me I did

the right thing when I lived up to my oath of office and arrested Jethro Raven, there isn't anything for you and me."

"Why can't you understand?"

"We're at loggerheads, Kate. That's the same question I'm asking you." A new kind of loneliness ate at him when she squeezed her eyes shut and shook her head, yet released no tears. "God knows I don't want to leave you right now. But I can't stay."

He sympathized with her love for her father—because he'd loved his own beyond words—but that love shouldn't blind her to what was right. He let himself out.

He turned on the red flashing light atop the Buick so that drivers would do what they usually did when they saw a policeman—drive carefully—because he could hardly focus on anything. He'd thought they'd be celebrating by then, but no. She'd tried to come to terms with her dilemma, and he knew it, but she hadn't been able to accept that her father could have committed a crime, intentionally or not.

He parked in his garage and entered his house by the side door, and for all its elegance, its void cried out to him. No loving woman greeted him to wrap him in the warmth of her smile and let her lingering kiss tell him how much she wanted and needed him. He didn't hear the laughter and playful patter of his children. There was no music to welcome him home, darkness where there should be strong, glowing light. He made his way up the stairs without bothering to turn on a single lamp. The less emptiness he saw, the better.

He walked into his bedroom, saw the red light flashing on his answering machine, pushed the button, and sat down to listen.

"Luke, this is Cowan. Do you know a black Cadillac tailed you from Ms. Middleton's place straight to your house? I wonder what would have happened if your squad light hadn't been flashing."

"You're sure of this?"

"No doubt about it. He pulled off about two car lengths behind you and tailed you home. I was right behind him."

He slapped his forehead. "Shows you how tired I am. Imagine not looking in my rearview mirror. Did you get his license plate number?"

"Yeah, and I checked it out, but it's a fake. I didn't see his face, but he's tall, judging from the way he sat behind the wheel. That's all I got. I put a tail on him, but if he's clever he'll shake it. All for now."

"Good job, buddy. That guy's getting antsy."

Imagine missing something that important. He'd been right at the outset. He shouldn't have let her get inside of him, possess him so completely that he couldn't protect her, or, for that matter, himself. For that's what had happened. She'd given him such a wallop to the gut that he had a fogged brain, but it wouldn't happen again. From now on, he'd make sure his head was screwed on right.

He showered and got ready for bed. What was that she'd said? *Good Lord! Right before his eyes!* How could he have missed it? The man who gave Raven that package of cocaine thought Raven had revealed his identity to Kate, and information about his drug dealings. And he'd stepped up his harassment since her trip to Cumberland. That was it, and the threats Raven mentioned to Kate confirmed it. Now, he had a motive, and that was all he'd needed.

But he wanted to know for whom that package had been intended. Raven's lawyer hadn't called him to the witness stand, so the question hadn't been asked. He had traced the handlers through his underground source and broken up the ring, but the bosses had escaped.

Ten-fifteen. He called Rude Hopper. "Rude, this is

Luke. Remember that cocaine case that surfaced right after you brought your boy to me?''

"Raven?''

"He's the one. I need to know where that stuff was headed. I'm not interested in how you find out or who tells you. Got it?''

"Right. Rent a car and come over here about six tomorrow. Wear a wig, a pair of clear glasses, and some beat-up jeans. We're risking a lot on this one, brother. And, Luke, I don't want to know a thing. That way, I can't tell a thing.''

"You have my word on it. See you at six.''

Kate wandered from room to room. Finally she rested her hands and forearms against the wall of her foyer and let it take her weight as she pressed her head against it. Her father hadn't shown any bitterness; indeed, he'd seemed at peace. The thought lightened her spirits, and she sat down and wrote him. This time, she put her new postal box address on the envelope in the hope of getting an answer.

Her phone rang the next morning as she prepared to leave home. "Hello.''

"Hello, Ms. Middleton. This is Officer Cowan. I'm out front, but wait for me before you come out. I'll ring your bell.''

Now what? "Okay, but . . . well, all right.'' She hung up and looked down at Randy. "You'll have to skip your French class today.''

His eyes brightened, and a grin bloomed on his face. "Oh, man!''

"You're going to the store with me.'' That took care of his grin.

The doorbell rang, and she took her son's hand, looked through the peephole, and stepped out to join Cowan. "Any problem?'' she asked him.

His blank expression provided the answer. "Walk directly behind me. Both of you."

She put Randy between herself and the detective and followed him to his unmarked car.

Cowan pulled away from the curb, and cold tentacles of fear coursed through her body when she glanced at the rearview mirror and saw a black Cadillac pull away right behind them.

"You interested in a black Cadillac?" she whispered to the detective.

He speeded up and headed in the opposite direction of her store. "I sure am," was all he said. He pulled up in front of the Second Precinct and parked. "We'll wait here a bit."

Cowan answered his cell phone, and she heard that deep sonorous voice and relaxed. "Hickson. Everything under control?" Cowan explained his position. "All right, we'll scout the area. Then you change cars and take them to the store. Good job."

Business was slow, and her nerves rioted each time she heard the store's buzzer.

"What's wrong with you, Kate? Honey, you act like you have to go out and meet a wildcat, I do declare. Girl, you better relax, take a vacation or something. So jittery."

"You're imagining things," Kate told Jessye.

Her cousin rolled her eyes toward the sky. "I suppose I was born this morning. Well, I do declare. Look who's at the door." She raced to open it.

"Luke, honey, you're just what a girl needs to raise her spirits. One little glimpse of you is worth my food and air."

The hussy, Kate thought. Making such a play for Luke with her less than two yards away. But she needn't have concerned herself.

"Where's Kate?" he asked.

"Somewhere around."

He sat on the sofa that faced the cash register. "Would you please ask her to come here?"

Kate rounded the row of bookcases. "You want to see me?"

He patted the space beside him in invitation. "Yes, I do. Would you sit down, please? Both of you."

It didn't surprise Kate that Jessye sat beside Luke as closely as she could without sitting on him.

He turned toward her. "Jessye, I've tried to do this in ways that wouldn't embarrass either of us, but I see you need it straight. Jessye, Kate is the only woman who interests me. I'm in love with her, and have been since I first saw her. And the longer I know her, the more she means to me. There's no chance that anyone else will get my attention, not for years to come, and maybe never. Those are the facts."

"I . . . I thought things had cooled down between you two."

He braced a hand on each knee, giving the impression that he was about to stand. "We disagree about something important, but that's irrelevant to the way we feel about each other. Have I made myself clear? It's not my intention to hurt you, but I'm sure you want to hear it the way it is."

Kate reached for Jessye's hand. "I tried to warn you, because I didn't want you to be hurt."

Jessye shrugged. "I knew it all the time, but I couldn't help trying. It . . . It got to me. I'm going home next month in time for school opening. My fifth grade kids will be waiting for me." She looked at Luke, then lowered her lashes. "For the last seven weeks, I hardly remembered that old Ed, that walking disappointment, ever existed, and I can thank you for that."

"Jessye, what about Axel? He loves you," Kate reminded her, hoping to relieve the bitterness she detected in her cousin's voice and demeanor.

Jessye looked into the distance. "He's a nice guy. If I'm lucky, I'll miss him. But right now, I don't see us being more than friends."

Kate squeezed her cousin's hand. "I'm sorry, Jessye. I really am."

Jessye got up, effectively closing the conversation. "Don't cry for me, Kate, because I haven't been all that nice to you. I'm going home, and if nothing else I'll get to eat plenty of good old butter beans and okra." She winked at Luke. "You're the best, honey."

Luke took Kate's hand and walked to the door of her office, but—realizing that Randy was in there—she didn't open the door. "Marcus and his family will be at my place in Biddle for about ten days. Do you want Randy to stay out there with them? They'd all be at my house."

She didn't hesitate. "That would be wonderful."

"All right. Marcus will pick him up here tomorrow afternoon. Okay?" She nodded. "See you."

She stared at him, unable to believe he'd leave cold, with not so much as a smile. "Uh . . . okay."

She turned her back to him and let him go. After his strong remarks to Jessye about his love for her—and right in her presence, too—he'd had the guts to walk off from her without so much as a peck on the forehead. If he'd been sending her a message she got it, and *how*.

"I'd like to stop by the post office on my way home," she told Cowan that evening as they left her store.

"Sure. I'll go in with you. Never can tell."

She took the letter from her box, looked at it, and stuck it in the outer pocket of her purse out of Cowan's sight—the first letter she'd received from her father in six years.

"If you're going to Biddle tomorrow, let me know what time."

She must have gaped at him, because his fair skin flushed red with embarrassment. "You can't do that," she said. "You won't get home until midnight."

He shrugged both shoulders. "It's my job, and I'm glad to do it."

She thought for a minute. It didn't seem right that he should spend so much time on the job because of her. "Tell you what. I'll close at three o'clock, and you can be back home by nine."

Cowan seldom smiled, but when he did it was worth framing. "That works for me," he said, his smile enveloping his whole visage. "Be there at three."

She closed her apartment door, sat down at once, and opened the precious letter. Her father had answered by return mail, and she wondered whether he was hungry for news.

Dear Katie,

I was happy to hear from you so soon after your visit, but your letter disturbed me. How can you hold anything against the man who arrested me? He did his job, and if I don't blame him for it, how can you? What would you have done if you'd been in his place? Ignored what you found? My daughter, maybe you're just looking for an excuse to break up with him. If you are, don't let him believe you don't want him because he's an honest cop. I found him to be a gentleman. Thank you for that visit. It's still with me.

Love, Papa

She reread the letter, folded it, and put it away with his picture. She knew she wasn't using her father's tragedy as an excuse to break with Luke; she wanted and needed him too much. But from childhood she'd been taught the importance of family loyalty and support, and she couldn't bring herself to take a position against her father. And thinking about it, she realized that probably accounted for her tolerance of Jessye's occasional meanness.

She packed a bag for the weekend, wondering if she'd see him and how they would behave with each other if she did. One thing was certain; she wasn't taking that trip in Cowan's car when she had a perfectly good one of her own. If he insisted on tailing her, that was between him and the police department.

To her amazement, Cowan didn't contest her right to drive her own car.

Shortly after noon that day, Luke got in his car and headed for Biddle. Rude had shaken him up the previous evening with accounts of what he'd discovered about the Raven case. Jethro's lawyer was an employee of the cocaine ring, which accounted for the man's lackadaisical performance at the trial. Raven hadn't stood a chance because his lawyer wanted him to be convicted. But he'd have another day in court as soon as Luke arrested Miles Atkins—or Nero Peale, or the same guy by any of his other aliases. At three o'clock he brought the Buick to a stop in front of his house in Biddle, and a little of the emptiness that had plagued him in recent days eased away when Amy and Marc ran out to meet him and get their hugs.

"Uncle Luke, my daddy took Marc and Randy and me surfing on his back. We had so much fun. Can we go surfing on your back?" Amy asked.

Was he supposed to believe that? "If he shows me how he does it with the three of you at once, I might."

Each of them took one of his hands and walked with him into the house. He couldn't understand it. Where was the peace, the carefree mood that usually settled over him as soon as he turned the nose of that Buick toward Biddle?

"Where's your daddy?" he asked Amy.

"He's cooking dinner. We're having something good, and Lady's making apple turnovers and ginger snacks."

"You mean ginger*snaps*." His half smile was as much as he could manage. If you had a secret, you wouldn't let Amy know about it.

He hugged Amanda and Todd. Then he saw Randy standing afar, watching him, and he walked over and hugged the boy. The child's fierce response took him aback; the boy needed a father's love. He walked into the kitchen, where Marcus assembled shish kebobs.

"I didn't expect you so early. What's up?"

"I don't know. Something. My nerves don't stampede like this for no reason."

"You got a handle on it?"

"From some chilling news I got last evening, I suspect this business with whoever's pursuing Kate is about to come to a head. Would you believe it's tied to that Jethro Raven drug bust?"

Marcus stopped cubing meat. "What's the connection?"

"Raven is Kate's father."

Marcus blew out a long sharp whistle. "And somebody thinks she knows something."

Luke sat on the stepstool beneath the window, and stretched his legs. "In a nutshell. It's clear." He answered his cell phone. "What? Where are you?"

"At the intersection of Highway One Sixty-eight and the exit to Route Thirty four. Baker's with me."

"I'll meet you coming north on One Sixty-eight," he told Cowan, "leaving now. This time, we'll get him. But be sure to get between him and Kate. Watch for me."

"One of my officers just spotted my man tailing Kate here," he said to Marcus. "Later."

He felt in his back for his revolver, stopped, and turned around to look at his brother.

"What is it? What's the matter, Luke?"

"I've got to get to her in time. I can't let anything happen to that woman. She trusts me, and I love her. I can't let him get to her."

Marcus interrupted him. "And he won't, because you're the best in the business."

Luke whirled around. "Thanks, brother. I'd better get

my megaphone and that sub out of my trunk." The two of them raced out to the car and put the megaphone and submachine gun on the front seat.

He told himself to slow down, that if the man had followed Kate three-fourths of the way to Biddle he wouldn't give up until he caught her. As he approached the exit to Leeds, he saw Kate slow down to turn off at the exit and flash the turn signals of her red Taurus. He signaled Cowan. Baker flashed his headlights, and Luke flashed his in return. Then he phoned Kate.

"Kate, this is Luke. Pull over right now, stop, and lie down on the seat. *Now!*"

She didn't question him, thank God. The black Cadillac turned in three car lengths behind her, but Cowan sped up and darted in between the two cars. Baker stopped behind the suspect. When the hunted man attempted to back up, Baker blocked his way and turned on his red light. Luke pulled up behind Baker.

"You're under arrest, Atkins," Luke said, using his megaphone, "and if you make one false move, you'll have a long rest somewhere." Atkins backed up to ram the front of Baker's car, but Luke anticipated the move, swung out, and shot the man's rear tires. Cowan shot the front ones.

"Get out with your hands over your head. And you got just one minute. One—"

The driver's door opened, and Luke ducked seconds before a round of bullets whizzed by him. Cowan put a neat hole in the man's shoulder. They tied up the wound, handcuffed Atkins, and Cowan and Blake headed back to Portsmouth with their prisoner.

Luke locked the Cadillac and phoned the local sheriff. Then he looked up at the red-streaked horizon, breathed a word of thanks that he'd been there when she needed him, and took slow deliberate steps to Kate's car.

"It's over, sweetheart. He's in custody." He opened the car door, slid in, and wrapped her in his arms. He wondered if she could hear his heart pounding away in his chest, and if she could feel his joy that she was safe, that he'd protected her. He squeezed her to him, and brushed her forehead with his lips. Lord, how he loved her!

"You feel up to driving?"

"I guess so. I didn't know anybody was following me except Officer Cowan. That was scary, but I'm okay."

He ran his hands over her face and her hair, cradling her as if she were an infant. "If you're sure. If not, Marcus and I can come back for it."

She smiled, reached up and kissed his cheek. "I'm sure."

"Then let's go. I'll tell you all about it after supper."

At supper with Marcus's family, Randy and Luke, Kate managed to chew and swallow her food, but she didn't taste it. She talked with little interest in the conversation, though she did her best to put up a good front. Her thoughts didn't linger on the afternoon's events, dangerous though they had been, but on what remained of the night. In spite of the cool evening breeze, moisture accumulated at her temples, and, for the first time in years, she had to control an urge to bite her fingernails.

At last, Luke came over to her, reached down, and took her hand, and she stood, surprised that her knees didn't knock.

"I've read to the children and put them to bed. All of them. Let's go over to your place."

"Shouldn't I say good night to Amanda and Marcus?"

He pointed to the dimly lit corner, where the two sat wrapped in each other's arms. "Do you think they'd hear you?"

Don't stall, girl, her mind warned her. *This is probably your last chance.* She squeezed his fingers. "Let's go."

"Would you like something to drink?" she asked after they entered her house.

He shook his head. "The man we got this evening was the one who gave your father that package of cocaine. He was after you, because he thought you knew something. When the men he hired failed to do more than annoy you, he gave himself the task of finishing it. He'll give us the name of his partner because he won't go to jail for fifty years while the other man enjoys his freedom. So you're safe now."

"I can't thank you and your men enough. You know that."

"It isn't necessary. You saw what happened today. Tell me what you feel."

She'd been over and over it, and the only thing that concerned or distressed her was his being endangered. "Who fired those shots?"

His frown suggested that he might not like the question. "Cowan fired the last one, and the other six came from Atkins."

"And he was shooting at you?"

"Yes."

"Every time you leave me, I'll be scared for you."

He took both of her hands in his. "Is that the only thing about my job that bothers you?" She looked him in the eye. "All I can think of right now."

"What about your father's arrest and conviction?"

She'd known that was coming and had prepared herself, thanks to her father's letter. "You had no choice but to do your duty, and you did the right thing, just as you did this afternoon. My father respects your integrity, and so do I. I've been wrong in this, Luke. Terribly wrong. I wish I could undo—"

He was standing over her now, his hands on her shoulders, staring into her eyes. "I don't need to hear any more. Just put your arms around me. Oh, Kate. Kate!"

He lifted her to him, then held her away as if to be certain. "Are you sure you have no reservations. None at all?"

She shook her head. "Not one." Tremors laced her speech, and he held her closer, cradling her to him. "Sh."

The feel of his lips brushing hers softly, skimming her skin as though she was precious to touch, filled her with hope. She could hear her heart singing and feel the rhythmic beat of its music. His hands brushed her bare arms, and he folded her to him, pressing light kisses on her eyelids, cheeks, ears, and neck, telling her how he adored her in ways that words could not.

When he held her away from him and gazed into her eyes, she didn't see hot desire, but adoration, a sweetness that exposed a vulnerability she'd never seen in him and dragged a catch from her throat—an open wordless declaration of love. She reached up, placed her hands at his nape, and urged him to kiss her. Then his face bloomed in a smile, a sweet and wicked thing that excited and thrilled her, for she knew its promise.

She thought she would buckle beneath his gentle and tender caresses, that she couldn't bear the sweetness with which he loved her.

"Luke, kiss me."

His lips settled on hers, almost in reverence, but she flicked her tongue against them and his kiss began to heat her mouth, to burn her with the fire of his rising desire. Her body rippled in response to his need, a need that had suddenly flared in a blatant demand. She parted her lips for his tongue, and shivers coursed through her as he dipped into the honey that was for him alone. She could feel the tension building in him, and sucked in her breath as the heat of his body swirled around her like the rising wind of a coming storm. She pressed herself to his hard frame and rejoiced in the touch of his arousal against her belly. Jolts of electricity whistled through her veins, and her hips began their rocking plea for the feel of him inside her. Dizzy now with lust for the powerful aphrodisiac in her arms, she undulated wildly against him. When she tried to wrap her legs around him, he gripped her and pulled her up to fit him. The air snapped and crackled like unharnessed electricity, and she moaned his name in frustration.

"Luke. Love, I need you."

As if he'd been awaiting that cue, he lifted her into his arms, found his way to her bedroom, and placed her on her bed. She let him remove her clothing, besotted, drunk on his tenderness and passion. She gazed at him in his glorious nudity, licked her lips in anticipation, and opened her arms. But he needed more.

"Tell me that you accept who I am, and what I do," he said, and the tremors in his voice let her know what her answer meant to him.

She sat up. "I believe in you, and I wouldn't change you or anything about you."

She lay back on the bed, opened her arms, and he moved into them and buried his face in the curve of her neck. The feel of his skin electrified her whole body like a barrage of fireworks. She shifted beneath him, and he rimmed her lips with his tongue. She sucked it into her mouth and feasted on him until he withdrew it and then darted it in and out, promising and teasing. She spread her legs and reached for him, but he held her hands above her head and feasted on her breasts, sucking and loving until she moaned. "Luke, please. I'm aching. I need you."

But he charted his own course, dipping his tongue in the hollow of her neck, trailing his lips over her belly and thighs until he reached the ultimate, the center of her. There, he kissed her quickly, moved up her body and tortured her breasts, arms, neck, and ears with searing kisses.

Out of control now, she rocked beneath him until, exasperated, she found him, wrapped her fingers tight around him and brought him to her. But he moved away, slipped on a condom and took her mouth in drugging kiss. Then she raised her body and gloried in her womanhood as he capitulated and drove home. She knew him now and raised herself to his powerful marksmanship, meeting his strokes and riding his rhythm.

"Do you feel what I'm doing to you?"

"Yes. Oh, yes. *Yes!*"

She was going to die. That earthquake inside of her wouldn't stop trembling, and wouldn't let her burst wide open.

He sucked on her left breast and stroked the nub of her passion, filling her until cyclonic waves plowed through her, and she exploded all around him, spent. He kissed her to smother her keening cry and collapsed in her arms as he joined her flight to ecstasy.

Luke stretched out on his back with his arm tight around Kate. She was so quiet. He turned on his left side and looked at her. "Planning to put me out?"

Relief spread over him when she stretched leisurely as she always did when she was well sated, reached down, and pinched his buttock. "Try getting out of that door, and you'll discover how crafty I can be."

"What about . . . You once told me you wanted us to be together forever. Did you mean that?"

She sat up and leaned over him. "I meant it."

"That means you'll marry me?"

"Not necessarily."

He sat up and eased her down in the bed. "I'm serious, Kate. Will you marry me?" He gazed down at eyes glistening with love and at arms raised to him.

"I was hoping *I* wouldn't have to ask *you*. Of course I will," she said.

He lowered himself into her arms, and the touch of her sweet lips and warm welcoming body sent showers of joy zinging through him. "I love you, Kate. I love you so much."

"You're my heart, Luke. I've loved you almost from the first." She frowned, and seemed to draw into herself.

"What is it? If you have any reservations, any questions, tell me now."

"You don't mind that . . . that your father-in-law will be a prisoner?"

He gazed into the face of the woman whose love gave him the peace he'd longed for. "Maybe not for long. From what I discovered a few days ago, he should get a new trial, with a new lawyer that you and I will chose."

"You think there's a chance?"

"I know there is."

Her face bloomed into the smile he loved. "Then maybe he can finally see his grandson."

"A man has the right to kiss his woman's nose," Luke said, so he did just that. "I wish I knew how to reach Lucy Watkins Monroe."

"Why? What do you want with her?"

"She told me the man would be driving when I caught him. I want to congratulate her. What do you say we take Randy to visit his grandparents in Hawaii and go on to Tahiti for our honeymoon?"

"Wherever you go, love."

He cradled her to him. "And whatever you do, I'll be there for you."

Dear Reader,

I hope you enjoyed Luke and Kate's story. After publication of *BEYOND DESIRE,* the story of Amanda and Marcus, hundreds of you wrote asking me to write the story of Luke, Marcus Hickson's brother. I had decided that my next Arabesque book would be *Scarlet Woman,* which is now due out in June of 2001. However, my editor agreed with the readers that it would be a good idea to write about Luke while many of you still remembered him. I'm glad for that decision, because I fell completely in love with Luke Hickson and enjoyed writing about him. I hope the story gave you a few hours of enjoyment.

My thanks to those of you who purchased and read *SWEPT AWAY, FOOLS RUSH IN* and *AGAINST THE WIND.* Your overwhelming response to THESE BOOKS has been most gratifying. I appreciate your support. If your local bookstore doesn't carry my books and other BET/Arabesque titles, ask the manager to order them.

If you enjoyed *SECRET DESIRE,* you may want to read others of my titles. You'll find them on my web page and in the front of this book. Also, be sure to read the note "About The Author." I hope to meet more of you on my tours for *SECRET DESIRE,* so please check my web page to find out where I'll be. And don't forget to write or e-mail me. I promise to answer you within three weeks. Web page: http://www.infokart.com/gwynneforster; e-mail—*GwynneF@aol.com.* If you send a letter to me at P.O. Box 45, New York, NY 10044 and would like an answer please enclose a self-addressed and stamped legal size envelope.

Fond regards,
Gwynne Forster

ABOUT THE AUTHOR

Gwynne Forster is a best-selling and award-winning author of ten romance novels and three novellas. *Romantic Times* has nominated her first interracial romance, *AGAINST THE WIND,* published in November 1999, for its award of Best Multicultural Romance of 1999, and has nominated Gwynne for a Lifetime Achievement award. The Romance In Color internet site gave *AGAINST THE WIND* its Award Of Excellence and named Gwynne *1999 Author Of The Year.* Her January 1999 book, *BEYOND DESIRE,* is a Doubleday Book Club, a Literary Guild and a Black Expressions club section.

Gwynne holds bachelors' and masters' degrees in sociology and a master's degree in economics/demography. As a demographer, she is widely published. She is formerly chief of (nonmedical) research in fertility and family planning in the Population Division of the United Nations in New York and served for four years as chairperson of the International Programme Committee of the International Planned Parenthood Federation (London, England), positions that took her to sixty-three developed and developing countries. Gwynne sings on her church choir, loves to entertain, is a gourmet cook and avid gardener. She lives with her husband in New York City.

Gwynne's previous books include *SEALED WITH A KISS* (October 1995), *AGAINST ALL ODDS* (September 1996), *ECSTASY* (July 1997), *OBSESSION* (April 1998), *NAKED SOUL* (July 1998, paperback–September 1999), *FOOLS*

RUSH IN (October 1999), *AGAINST THE WIND* (November 1999) and *SWEPT AWAY* (April 2000). Her first novella, *Christopher's Gifts,* is included in the anthology, *SILVER BELLS* (December 1996); her Valentines Day 1997 novella, *A Perfect Match,* is in the anthology, *I DO,* and *Love For A Lifetime,* her story of two passionate, battling attorneys is in the BET/Arabesque anthology, *WEDDING BELLS* (June 1999).

Critics for *Affaire de Coeur* magazine judged *ECSTASY* best contemporary ethnic romance of 1997, and the following year awarded *NAKED SOUL* best contemporary ethnic romance of 1998.

She is represented by the James B. Finn Literary Agency, Inc., P.O. Box 28227A, St. Louis, Missouri 63132. Reach Gwynne at P.O. Box 45, New York, NY 10044; E-mail: GwynneF@aol.com; Web page: http://www.infokart.com/gwynneforster.

BOOK YOUR PLACE ON OUR WEBSITE AND MAKE THE ARABESQUE ROMANCE CONNECTION!

We've created a customized website just for our very special Arabesque readers, where you can get the inside scoop on everything that's going on with Arabesque romance novels.

When you come online, you'll have the exciting opportunity to:

- View covers of upcoming books

- Learn about our future publishing schedule (listed by publication month and author)

- Find out when your favorite authors will be visiting a city near you

- Search for and order backlist books

- Check out author bios and background information

- Send e-mail to your favorite authors

- Join us in weekly chats with authors, readers and other guests

- Get writing guidelines

- AND MUCH MORE!

Visit our website at
http://www.arabesquebooks.com